To Hear A Nightingale

To Hear A Nightingale

The Life and Times of a Village Blacksmith's Family

Ivor M. Cave

The Pentland Press Limited
Edinburgh • Cambridge • Durham • USA

First published in 1996 by
The Pentland Press Ltd.
1 Hutton Close
South Church
Bishop Auckland
Durham

British Library Cataloguing in Publication Data.
A Catalogue record for this book is available
from the British Library.

ISBN 1 85821 428 9

Typeset by CBS, Felixstowe, Suffolk
Printed and bound by Antony Rowe Ltd., Chippenham

Dedicated to my wife Joan

Previously published
by the same author

Under The Cherry Trees

I have a great longing for the sound of distant steam trains on frosty mornings, for parsons who ride to church on horseback and the sight and scent of stooks of corn standing in shorn fields on long summer evenings. For dark hazel thickets where nightingales sing on warm June nights and long gone friends who walked with me part of the way.

In the writing of this story the Author draws quite a lot on his own boyhood. It is a nostalgic journey into the past and tells the story of the lives and times of two generations of a blacksmith's family. It covers the period that starts just before the outbreak of the First World War and draws to its end in the 1960s. During this time many characters appear, some to be lost in the telling whilst others like Tommy and Phyllis, who meet the son of the second generation in their schooldays, live on only for their lives to end in tragedy. It is the story of a village and how two wars affect it and its inhabitants. The sons of both generations go to war each in their own period in time but between there is a love interest which involves the lifelong friend Phyllis and an ATS girl called Mary who the reader will learn has a startling connection with the blacksmith's family. All in all it has its moments of happiness and its moments of sadness, the ending being far from predictable. The reader should remember that very rarely is anything as straightforward as it seems at first.

CONTENTS

PART I

Chapter I

With arms resting on the top rail the old man stood leaning against the gate gazing at the cluster of cottages that spread themselves below. The sun, which for most of the day had beat down from a cloudless sky was now beginning to lose its power, the horizon away to the west being already tinged with the purple of the coming night, and in the long grasses of the hillside nodding harebells vied with purple and white clover and wild pansies, the movements of their flowered heads by the soft breeze soundless in the vast silence; then, almost as if challenging him a curlew called, a plaintive haunting sound that just at that moment fitted his mood. Each tree, each undulating stretch of the hillside was etched on his memory. Below was the hazel thicket from which on many a soft night the nightingale had entranced with its song and where in the secrecy of it he had courted his wife Nancy; but that was long ago, just precious memories that were best recalled on long winter evenings when, with the shadows playing tricks, it was easier to journey back over the years. Pulling his coat about him he started back down the hill towards the village passing as he went the lane leading down to the deserted railway station; halting, he stood pondering for a moment, then, having made up his mind, turned and fought his way down the overgrown path.

With the long shadows beginning to creep he stood surveying the desolation and neglect about him. The breeze which had sprung up at the setting of the sun strained its way through the brambles that had invaded the now derelict buildings causing the sagging door of the old ticket office to swing noisily on its rusting hinges, a sound that made him straighten up and tense himself almost as if he expected someone to appear. From beyond the velvet shadows nostalgic sounds lay waiting, sounds that reminded him of the times when in the light cast by flickering oil lamps he had stood with others on that very platform. With head turned to the wind and ears straining he imagined he heard again the hiss of steam from under stationary carriages, the slam of

3

doors and the laughter and conversation as passengers alighted or settled themselves in the warm, dimly-lit carriages. Then stepping forward to the edge of the crumbling platform, he stood for a while seeing where once the shining rails had stretched away into the distance and the weed-strewn plot where the signal box had once stood. Now only an overgrown track remained, the haunt of fox and badger where elder and bramble linked hands to form a canopy that hid the nettled banks below. Taking one last look around he retraced his steps out into the old station yard, now littered with fragments of broken brick and the rubbish of time, where rotting and discarded the remains of the once immaculate white fencing lay amongst the tall wild grasses. Slowly and with laboured steps he made his way back to his cottage at the top of Callow Lane. The lane was not now as he remembered it as a lad, the hedges and orchards that once bordered it having long since gone to be replaced by new Cotswold stone houses that stood waiting to be mellowed by time. Closing the gate behind him he shambled up to the door of his cottage and lifting the latch, entered; then, after carefully hanging up his walking stick on the stand in the passageway he made his way into the parlour where, in the half darkness he sat in his rocking chair listening to the creak of the old timbers in the ceiling above and the steady tick of the grandfather clock in the corner.

They were all gone now, Nancy his wife, his father and mother and sisters Tessa and Beckey, and as he sat thinking about them he remembered the Christmas times when the family had gathered at Forge Cottage, where under the soft light of oil lamps, Nancy had played the piano for Mrs Beasley, who each year had sung the same old songs. He remembered too the mornings when as a child he had sat in front of the fire opening his presents while his father, pipe in hand, had sat in the same old rocking chair, nodding approvingly as each gift was unwrapped; but most of all his thoughts were of his wife Nancy, now at rest in the churchyard at the top end of the village, seeing her as she used to be, gentle and kind with smiling eyes and golden brown hair. Suddenly he thought he heard a voice from beyond the darkness. Raising himself up, he called out 'Nancy my love where are you?' But there was no answer, so lowering himself back into the chair, he sat for a while with eyes closed and hands clasped on his lap. Slowly the light faded and the shadows merged themselves into total darkness as the soul of John Mumford, blacksmith, started out on its long journey.

* * *

4

Being now in the autumn of my life it becomes expedient that I waste no time before putting pen to paper in case the memory of the happenings that I wish to tell you about fade beyond recall. My story has its beginnings in the little village of Lavington set under the Cotswold hills where I was born and where for the greater part of my life I lived with my parents and two sisters Tessa and Beckey. At birth I was christened John, such being the way of things in our family, the name having been given to the eldest son for generations, a good honest name as my father, a devout churchgoing man was for ever telling me. We lived at Forge Cottage which adjoined the blacksmith's shop at the bottom of Callow Lane, a warm creeper-clad red-brick building where Mother fed and protected us and gave us a good christian upbringing. Being the village blacksmith Father occupied an important place in the life of the community having almost the same status as Doctor Hemmings, Parson Collins, and Constable Hodges our local upholder of the law, who when out of earshot was always referred to as 'Bodger'. Just how he acquired the nickname no one ever knew or for that matter dared to ask. Lavington at that time was a small straggling village owned and watched over by Sir Howard Armstrong, our member of Parliament, who lived in the big house across the park. His estate consisted mainly of tenant-occupied three- or four-horse farms, the whole being administered by Mr Bowman who lived down at the mill but who had his office in the village next to Mr Lewis's shop at the top of Two Hedges Lane. We boasted a village hall, a butcher's shop which was owned by Harry Strait, affectionately known as 'Pincher', and last but by no means least a school, to which from the age of five I had daily wended my way to be introduced to the mysteries of the three R's – reading, writing and arithmetic. Looking back over the years I remember it as a memorable period in my life in which there never seemed to be any rainy days, but memories are like that, however on reaching the age of thirteen I said goodbye to school and entered into a new world where once suitably fitted out with a worsted suit with long trousers and a flat cap, and able to read, write, add and subtract, I was put to work alongside my father in the smithy. On reflection I perhaps could have started this story further back in my life and subjected readers to incidents, both pleasurable and painful, from my early youth, but perhaps such revelations are best left to another time. I was a strong lad, middling in size for my age and inclined to be a bit of a dreamer, however my reports on leaving school did speak of a certain amount of promise if only I had paid more attention to my studies, this assessment giving a great deal of pleasure and satisfaction to my parents who I learned later had fostered secret ambitions to see me enrolled at the grammar school in nearby Evesham. So, having set the scene, perhaps you will accompany me on a nostalgic trip into the past.

The year was 1914 and summer was well in, a time of haymaking, leisurely walks along honeysuckle-scented lanes and teas on vicarage lawns where with delicately-cut sandwiches and fizzy lemonade we sought out those secluded corners in which young lovers courted and kissed in the seemingly eternal sunshine. A time also for hand in hand romances when we wandered through fields waist high in waving grasses and proud moon daisies, those misty heady days of our youth spent in a soft undemanding world, which although we did not know it at the time was soon to be shattered by events taking place in faraway Europe. So this is where I shall start my story, for in all truth I cannot think of a better one and as the tale unfolds you will meet the people who by reason of their love and affection coloured and guided my life.

The village was sleeping peacefully in the warm sunshine that caressed the drystone walls that bordered its street and lanes, walls from whose lichen-encrusted chinks and crevices tufts of alyssum, arabis, and lampranthus reached out over the dusty sidewalks. From the gardens on either side, where flower beds edged with sage, lavender and myssop were heavy with flocks and sweet williams, the scent of white nevada roses set against warm brick walls drifted on the still air, while in the high elms beyond the churchyard noisy black rooks, busy doing nothing in particular, clamoured and clung precariously to the edges of discarded nests, their strident protests the only sound to break the silence, a silence that would soon be shattered by the laughter and chatter of children who, released from school, would come charging up the lane to spill out into the village street before making their separate ways to farms and cottages. In the cool interior of Bert Grinnel's milking shed the restless cows fidgeted and complained, eager to be relieved of their heavy load and be off back to their pastures in Two Farthing Acres down Nutmeadow. However nothing would happen until the church clock across the way struck the hour of four when, prompt to the minute, Joe Taylor would close the gate to his cottage and start on his leisurely way up to the farm to attend to the milking. From under the ivy-clad archway of Walton House, Doctor Hemmings emerged in his pony and trap and started off at a steady trot down to Columbine Lane to visit widow Whitty Salis where, under the cool thatch of her cottage, he would spend half an hour or so exchanging all the latest gossip, a weekly ritual that he had faithfully observed since the death of her husband. Down at the railway station Alby Stringer, the station master, sat on the long platform seat mopping his brow and complaining to his two porters Nathan Powell and Herbert Tanner who, standing with their backs to the ticket office, listened in silence. Suddenly almost as if voicing his thoughts Alby said, 'What's make of all this talk of war then, Nathan? I reckon as how some of us 'ul have to go if they Germans start anything.' Here he paused as if to collect his thoughts before pursuing the matter further, 'I suppose some of us 'ul have to go', he repeated, 'not that it 'ud worry I all that much, a few months away from the misses 'ud be more than welcome.' Another long pause then after mopping his forehead with his handkerchief he continued, 'still I don't reckon as it 'ul last all that long if it do come.' Nathan shifted his weight from one foot to the other and drew deeply on the cigarette that dangled from between his lips. 'They yunt going to get I,' he said, after which he took another deep draw before flicking the ash off the end and resuming his leaning position against the wall. Meanwhile Herbert, the youngest of the trio, stood for a moment undecided, until suddenly without any prompting he added, 'Reckon I'll go along with Mr Stringer. He 'ul need somebody to look after him with all they loose women about,' a statement that caused a faint smile of anticipation to flit across Alby's face. Suddenly all three were galvanized into action by the strident ringing of a bell in the ticket office. Rising to his feet, Alby dusted himself down. 'Three-forty's due,' he said, 'Bloody war can wait.'

At the bottom of Callow Lane, hard by the pond that bordered it, Charlie Wilmore stood leaning on the gate leading into Long Meadow, watching the horse-drawn mower lay the swathes of long grass, the clatter and rattle of the machinery providing a background for his thoughts. Away in the distance the broad flank of Bredon Hill brooded over the sleepy villages that nestled at its foot while ahead of him the outline of the Cotswold Hills raised itself out of the blue haze. Born and bred in Lavington, he had courted and won a girl from over the hill in Alderton and they had been married in the same little church to which his mother had carried him to be christened and where, each Sunday since the age of ten, he had sung in the choir. He thought of his boyhood schooldays and of the later years when he had courted his wife Cathleen, of their walking out days when seeking to impress her he had taken her bunches of flowers gathered from his parents' garden. Now married and with a family of his own, his life was complete, however, little did he know that events would soon turn his little world upside down. Silhouetted against the glow from the forge, Father was busy fashioning shoes for the young mare Charlie had brought down from the Hall stables. Gently holding her bridle I stroked her glossy neck, all the time whispering reassuringly into her twitching ears, a trick taught me by my grandfather many years before. Understandably the mare was restless, this being only the second time she had been shod, and I knew that at her tender age she would have been hard to control if she had chosen to object. With eyes smarting from the acrid yellow smoke that filled the smithy each time a hot shoe was placed, I watched as my father hammered and secured the shoes on the mare's hooves, a job that before long I should have to undertake seeing that I was now nearing the end of the apprenticeship which he had insisted on. However I was in no hurry to prove myself being quite content for the moment to leave things as they were. Engrossed in what we were doing we failed to see Charlie who, tired of his musings down by Long Meadow gate, was leaning against the arched brick doorway, hands thrust deep into the pockets of his riding breeches and cap pushed to the back of his head. Grasping the long tongs Father thrust the last shoe into the glowing embers of the forge and slowly pumped the bellows, then turning he said, 'What's reckon to all this talk of war then, Charlie? Paper be full of it,' after which he went on working. 'I don't rightly know what to make of it,' Charlie replied, 'some says one thing while some says t'uther; Doctor Hemmings reckons it be bound to happen afore long but I reckon he would say that seeing as how he is on the reserve.' For a while no more was said on the subject, the only sounds to break the silence being the spitting of the hot coals on the forge and the metallic clip of the mare's freshly-shod hooves as she fidgeted restlessly on the cobbled floor. Then Charlie spoke again, 'Reckon I'll go, George. Master Grahame 'ul be going. I heard Sir Howard on about it up at the stables.' Pausing, he turned to me, 'What about thee, John? Can't see thee staying behind. Several of the lads in the village be already talking of volunteering.' Luckily before I could answer, even if at that moment I had one to give, Father spoke up, 'leave the lad be, Charlie, he 'ul make up his own mind when the time comes if it do,' and so saying he turned and pumped the bellows causing the forge to spring to life and send showers of glittering red sparks leaping upwards into the rafters.

That evening, sitting in the parlour, I gave a great deal of thought to what Charlie had said. In her chair at the fireside Mother was busy with a pile of darning that lay heaped on the floor at her feet while Father sitting opposite her, obviously deep in thought, slowly and deliberately filled his pipe from the stone tobacco jar that stood on the table beside him. Putting down her darning Mother gazed over the top of her steel-rimmed spectacles and fixed him with a penetrating stare. 'And what will you do, George Mumford, if this war do come?' she asked. 'Mr Lewis at the shop do say that it only be a matter of time afore something happens.' Deliberating for a moment, Father took a spill from the container standing in the hearth, offered it to the fire and when it was well alight applied it to the bowl of his pipe. 'Well, lass,' he said between puffs, 'part of me says I ought to go while t'uther part says stay put and wait and see what happens, but whichever way it goes I reckon it 'ul need a lot of thought.' For a while no more was said. I was glad that Tessa and Beckey weren't there, seeing no reason for them to be worried. Then, taking up her darning, Mother gave a deep sigh and rested the skein of wool on her lap. 'When the time comes you'll have to do what you do think be right and proper,' she said and with that she started on her darning leaving Father to have the last word as usual. 'Aye lass, reckon that's best,' he said.

Up at the Hall members of the staff were going about their business as usual. In his study Sir Howard, hands clasped behind his back, stood looking out of the window seeing the broad expanse of parkland with its stands of oak, beech and elm that stretched away until it met the solid stone cottages of the village. Hard by the bottom lodge gates the grey weather-beaten tower of the church watched over the ancient churchyard where ivy-covered tombs and leaning headstones stood, lasting memorials to the generations of families who for nigh on four hundred years had served the Armstrongs faithfully. Each Sunday he and Lady Armstrong walked across the park to attend morning service, a special hour that they shared with their other family, and thinking about it made him realize that now more than ever a greater responsibility would rest on his shoulders in the dark days ahead. Still deep in thought he half turned at the sound of footsteps in the passageway outside. Quietly Lady Armstrong entered the room, closing the door behind her, before crossing over to join her husband at the window where, putting an arm through his, she stood with him in silence. Their only son Grahame had recently celebrated his twenty-first birthday and having now completed his education was at home, a fine capable young man who, in spite of his tender years, had already taken upon his shoulders much of the responsibility of the running of the estate. Captain of the village cricket team and bell-ringer when needed, he was well liked and respected, however there was one thing that now worried his parents and that was that they knew that in the event of war he would be one of the first to volunteer, his sense of duty overriding all other considerations. Turning to his wife Sir Howard put an arm around her. 'I have the feeling, my dear,' he said, 'that there are dark days ahead, but never fear, we shall cope as we have always done.' Turning her head she buried her face on his shoulder and the tears came, and he held her until there were no more to shed.

June, the month of haymaking and long warm evenings, came and went and in the early days of July the village forgot the threat of war for a while and busied itself preparing for the annual cricket match against neighbouring Kempston-under-Bredon, an event which had been faithfully observed for the best part of fifty years. Old men boasted of the days when in their youth they had taken part, recalling incidents both humorous and otherwise, incidents which over the long years of telling had taken their rightful place in the folklore of the village. Weeks before the game it was the main topic of conversation down at the Drovers Arms, where tactics were discussed over full glasses and tankards, sides taken and theories tested so much so that at times lifelong friendships were stretched almost to breaking point. However, come closing time, all would be forgiven and forgotten.

Sitting on the hard seat of the high-backed settle in the corner of the taproom I listened to the heated arguments that were drifting backwards and forwards, conversations that had been fuelled to a great extent by the many rumours that had been circulating for the past few weeks, rumours that for reasons best known to themselves had been started by the villagers of Kempston-under-Bredon. Smart in his white apron, Jack Harris the landlord, large white enamelled jug in hand and sleeves rolled up, journeyed to and from the tapped barrels that stood on trestles behind the bar counter, stopping now and then to contribute to one or other of the many arguments taking place. Tomorrow was the big day and although not chosen to play I had been elected to serve in the capacity of official scorer, an office which although not quite so important as playing did at least give me some sort of official standing in the proceedings.

From his favourite chair in the open fireplace old Zetter Parsons was holding forth to two young things who were holidaying in the district and who, with elbows resting on the table and chins cupped in hands, were hanging on to his every word. 'When I were a lad,' said Zetter, 'I remember one game us played agen Upper Thruxbury, a village t'uther side of Bredon.' Here he paused to bang his empty glass on the table at the same time wiping his beard with the back of his hand, a signal to Jack Harris who just at that moment happened to be passing. At a nod of assent from the two young ladies Zetter's glass was replenished.

'Now where were I?' Zetter continued, 'Ah yes, t'were like this, Harry Pugh were fielding on the boundary and in the next field were two hosses, one Black 'un and one White 'un. That same night after the match Harry were sitting where you be now, telling Percy Slatter from Home Farm, the owner of the hosses, a most remarkable tale. He reckoned that during the game one of they hosses leaned over the hedge and called out "excuse I, but that bowler at the church end ain't ever going to take any wickets, length be all wrong and he be trying to bowl too fast; have a word with captain and get him to put Eric Nurden on with his spinners." Well, message were duly delivered and Eric were put on to bowl; he took seven wickets for forty runs and won us the game. Strange to relate Percy didn't seem at all surprised at Harry's story. "Them two hosses of mine," he said at last, "which one were it, the Black 'un or the White 'un?" "Twer the White 'un," Harry replied. "Just as well," said Percy, "Black 'un don't know a thing about cricket."'

During the silence that followed Zetter raised his glass and drank deeply, then putting his glass down with a bang he continued, 'Harry were the only batsman to hit a cricket ball from our ground all the way to Winchcombe and that be nigh on six miles.' The two young things, still struggling to take in the tale about the two horses, continued to gaze open-mouthed at Zetter who, seeing that he still had a captive audience, continued with his story.

'Harry middled a ball, a real bouncer, and giving it all he had got he watched as it cleared the boundary hedge to finish up in an empty wagon of a passing goods train on its way to Cheltenham. On seeing what had happened Twitcher Morris, one of the umpires, raced over to where his old bike were resting agen the wall of the changing shed and pedalled furiously down to the station where he got Alby Stringer to ring the station master at Winchcombe. Train were stopped and the ball recovered to be delivered back to the ground by the afternoon postie. On arrival Twitcher instructed one of the visiting team's fielders to recover the ball from the carrier in front of postie's bike, at the same time declaring that Harry were out, seeing as how the ball hadn't touched the ground from the time it left his bat until it was returned to the cricket field.'

Now most of us had heard these tales of Zetter's many times before but for all that we never ceased to marvel at the ease with which he managed to get free beer from those of our visitors gullible enough to believe them.

In the small parlour next to the taproom my mother and father were deep in conversation with Mike Beasley and his wife. Now the Beasleys had a daughter named Nancy and although as yet I had not formed any serious attachment in the matter of female company I had to admit that at times Nancy had attracted more than a fair share of my interest. She was a winsome young thing of about my own age who at the time was working in the kitchens up at the Hall, and looking back I remember thinking how strange it was that of a sudden we are apt to see people who we have known all our lives in an entirely different light, particularly if the subject of our interest happens to be female. However, in spite of this or perhaps because of it, events were already shaping that would eventually bring us together. Back in the taproom under the mellow light cast by the oil lamps suspended from the rafters the arguments went on until at last with 'Time' called we all made our way out into the night, where talk continued in the semi-darkness of the pub yard.

Saturday dawned bright and clear. Anxious faces peering from half-drawn curtains scanned the sky for any sign of rain but all was set fair. Up at the cricket ground Alex Hawkins' old horse Kitchener, leather shod and hitched to the mower, was making a last few circuits round the outfield, while on the centre square Nacky Pitt and Shenna Lawson trundled the medium roller up and down the wicket, all these activities being carefully supervised by a small gathering of early risers who watched and commented with professional eyes. Sight-screens, freshly painted, were rolled into position and around the ground wooden forms and bales of straw were being placed in readiness to accommodate the spectators who, come eleven of the clock, would be arriving for the game. At the far end of the field, hard against the fence bordering the fish pond, the wooden hut which did service as a changing-room was being swept out and made ready. By its side were stacked the metal number plates, white numbers on a black background, so as to be ready when scores were needed to be broadcast from the scoreboard fixed to the side of the hut, while in its pre-ordained place, a box stood ready to accommodate any small boy who, eager to be involved in things, failed to stretch the required inches when attempting to hang the number plates on the nails provided.

Down at the railway station Len Hubbard and his horse and wagon awaited the arrival of the train bearing the visiting team and its supporters from Kempston. Pacing up and down the platform he was all too aware of the importance of the duty he was annually called upon to perform, being mindful of the fact that the contest would begin the moment the visitors stepped out of the train. At last he caught the first sounds of it as it started up the long incline from Stebbington, round the bend by the signal box it came, puffing and hissing, until with a screech of brakes it finally came to a halt at the platform. Hardly had it done so than doors were flung open and out poured the visitors led by their team captain Tiny Larner, a veritable mountain of a man who had the reputation of being the fastest bowler in the county, a claim amply borne out by the many Lavington batsmen who had had to face him in the past. Normally he was an amenable sort of chap, well liked by both friend and foe, however once on the field of play it was as well to be on one's guard as Tiny 'took no prisoners' as the saying went. After exchanging the usual pleasantries intermingled with a good deal of good-natured banter, the Kempston lads and their captain and gear were loaded onto Len's wagon and on the command 'walk on' the old mare took the strain and started at a leisurely pace up the lane towards the village, where tradition demanded that the first stop be at the Drovers Arms. Tumbling off the wagon with their tongues hanging out they quickly made their way to the back door of the taproom where once inside they got to work on the pints of strong ale that Jack Harris had laid out ready for them. With horse and wagon parked out of sight safe from the prying eyes of Constable Hodges, Len joined the visitors who by then were on their third pint. With practised cunning he carried out his instructions to the letter making sure that each of the Kempston players got as many pints as possible inside them before continuing their journey up to the cricket field, then at last with thirsts quenched they clambered back aboard the wagon and set off in noisy triumphal procession down the flag-bedecked village street.

Meanwhile up at the field, families in holiday mood spread their blankets in chosen spots under the trees that bordered the ground, leaving the youngsters to chase about in the park where no doubt they would play quite happily until hunger and the sight of chequered tablecloths at lunchtime brought them to heel. At the entrance to the ground Mr Capaldi's ice cream cart, which had trotted all the way from Evesham, stood surrounded by a small crowd of youngster who, with pence clutched tightly in hot little hands, jostled impatiently as they waited for the shutters to be raised and halfpenny cornets dispensed.

With fifteen minutes to go before the start of the game a sudden hush fell over the ground as the two captains started on their walk to the centre of the pitch to examine the wicket and toss the coin, Tiny Larner, his large frame resplendent in white shirt and cream flannels, the latter secured by a brightly-coloured webbing belt with a clasp in the form of a snake's head, and Master Grahame, the Lavington captain, resplendent in Varsity blazer and club cap. Up went the coin and down went the two heads in order to observe it as it lay on the grass at their feet. Suddenly a gasp of relief went up as it became clear that Lavington had won the toss and elected to put the visitors in to bat, a decision no doubt influenced by the fact that hopefully the effects of the journey and subsequent lubrication down at the Drovers Arms had not yet worn off.

At last the game got under way and out on the pitch Master Grahame and his opening bowler stood deep in conversation as they planned and placed the field. Meanwhile the two Kempston opening batsmen had started to make their way to the wicket where with much adjustment to pads and swivelling of caps to just the right angle they surveyed the field placings with a critical eye. Already at their stations the two umpires, smartly turned out in white coats and brown derbies, stood ready, all too mindful of the awful responsibility that rested on their shoulders, while behind the wicket Parson Collins, ageing panama hat rammed firmly on his head, crouched with gloved hands extended and knees bent. Then of a sudden the game was afoot as Gadget Sharp, Lavington's opening bowler, shouted 'Play' and began his run to the wicket. It was a wicked ball which, pitched short on the hard ground, rose to shoulder height causing the batsman to duck and Parson Collins to dive sideways. Away it went almost avoiding the efforts of Nathan Powell at third man who after making a desperate dive to his left managed to stop the ball before it reached the boundary. Lying at full length he held it aloft in triumph causing a cheer to go up from the Lavington supporters but infuriating the batsman

14

who, feeling that he had lost face, glowered at the umpire and shook his fist at Gadget who by then was already facing up for his next delivery.

And so the game progressed, until at twelve-thirty a halt was called for lunch and the players having left the field gathered round the trestle-tables that had been set up close to the changing shed. With flushed faces the busy wives and other helpers made their way amongst them bearing plates of cheese and pickle sandwiches and generous helpings of home-cured ham kindly donated by Pincher Stait, the butcher, all the time secretly enjoying the good-natured banter and bottom-slapping that was all part and parcel of the occasion. At the rear of the shed Eli Small was busy supervising the supply of liquid refreshment being drawn from the tapped barrels mounted on the tailboard of Len Hubbard's wagon while the sun, now at its height, beat down on the spectators lining the ground causing jackets and fashions to be discarded and ties and collars removed. Chatter and laughter from the womenfolk drifted across the ground as hampers were opened and their contents arrayed on chequered tablecloths laid out on the green turf, while the menfolk, content on the day, sat with their backs propped against the elm trunks puffing away at cigarettes and pipes, sending wisps of blue smoke spiralling upwards to be lost in the leafy branches above. Out in the park the more knowledgeable strolled about in two's and three's discussing the game and its possible outcome, having to dodge and sidestep the youngsters who, full of good things, were working off their excess energy as they chased each other in and out between the trees. Off to one side and well out of earshot Master Grahame, Parson Collins and Doctor Hemmings stood deep in conversation, no doubt formulating tactics for the next stage of the game. With the visitors score at sixty for five wickets things look promising, however, previous encounters had taught them that on this of all days nothing must be left to chance.

At two of the clock Parson Collins, brass bell in hand, wandered amongst the players calling out 'time to go lads, let's be at it', whereupon the Lavington players took the field closely followed by the two Kempston batsmen, who after much hitching of pads and trousers pronounced themselves ready. A cheer went up as the ball was tossed to Harry Gibbons, one of the estate gamekeepers, a lad of some twenty summers, who was larger than life in both width and height. Famous for his speed of delivery he was also well-known for the psychological effect he had on opposing batsmen when, with sleeves rolled up and a look of grim determination on his face, he paced out his run,

15

an operation that took him almost to the boundary line. The Kempston man who was to face Harry's opening over took up his stance at the wicket, bat and pads square as he viewed the far end of the field where Harry was scuffing the ground and swinging his arms in a most menacing fashion. Suddenly he was on his way thundering towards the wicket. With eyes half shut and a hopeful expression on his face the batsman waited as, pitched short, the ball rose to head height as it sped over him on its way to the boundary where it finished up with a resounding smack against the sight-screen.

The game went on until at three-thirty with the last man in the score stood at 120. Harry Gibbons now well into his stride came thundering down and the batsman not being quite sure where the ball was, struck out blindly. Away on the boundary Herbert Tanner, mouth open wide and arms outstretched in readiness swayed backwards and forwards as he followed the progress of the little red blob that was now almost within his grasp. Behind the wicket Stodger Millet the umpire closed his eyes in prayer muttering to himself, 'He'll miss the bloody thing, he'll miss it.' But he need not have worried for with one supreme effort Herbert caught and clasped the ball to his chest before collapsing to his knees, a smile of utter triumph on his face. So that was that, Kempston were all out for 120. The batsman who had hit the catch groaned and threw his cap to the ground in disgust leaving Herbert to be carried off shoulder high and deposited at the rear of the changing shed, where Eli Small was already busy satisfying the thirsts of both friend and foe. Wearing a grin as broad as Bredon Hill and with a full glass in his hand Herbert accepted the congratulations of his team-mates, at the same time knowing only too well that if he had dropped the catch he would in all probability have finished up in the fish pond.

With thirsts eventually satisfied and order restored Tiny Larner, the Kempston captain, finally managed to get his men away from Eli's barrels and onto the field to prepare to deal with the Lavington team, whose opening pair Master Grahame and Doctor Hemmings were already making their way towards the wicket, putting on their gloves and talking in low tones as they walked. Taking his stance the good Doctor indicated that he was ready to take his guard from the umpire, then, this being done, he surveyed the field with a practised eye at the same time adjusting cap and pads and flattening out imaginary bumps on the pitch in front of him with the toe of his bat. At the opposite end Tiny Larner, having already marked the extremity of his

16

run, paced backwards and forwards all the time rubbing the seam of the ball on his thighs, then on the shout of 'Play' he raced towards the wicket, releasing the ball at the very last minute to send it speeding down. The delivery, pitched short, and on the offside, broke inwards completely deceiving the doctor who turned in amazement to find his stumps spreadeagled. For a moment there was a stunned silence broken only by the sound of Tiny jumping up and down and shouting 'Howzatt', then just as the Doctor was about to turn and make his way back to the changing shed the voice of Stodger Millet, the umpire, rang out loud and clear, 'No Ball!' Tiny couldn't believe his ears and rushing up to Stodger he demanded to know, 'if he were blind or summat'. However Stodger remained adamant as, unaffected by the outburst, he stood eyes raised heavenwards as if seeking divine intervention.

At half past four, with Lavington's score at seventy five for the loss of five wickets, a break for tea was called, willing helpers having already fetched the large tea urn and cakes and sandwiches from the dairy across the way. With trestle-tables set and well-laden the ladies, as always eager and ready, threaded their way amongst the players filling up proffered cups and stopping now and then to accept the well-earned compliments and thanks showered on them, sisters Tessa and Beckey, and Nancy Beasley, playing their part in things. All round the ground the lunchtime activities were being repeated causing the now hungry and dishevelled children to cease their romping in the park and rejoin their parents where, sitting cross-legged with a sandwich in one hand and sticky bun in the other, they listened to the conversation that drifted between their elders. The Kempston players seemingly well pleased with the state of play lazed around confident that the game was already won. With fifteen overs to go Kempston put on a spin bowler who took four more wickets for the addition of only forty runs. The situation was now beginning to look desperate. With only three balls left to play and six runs needed for victory Fred Newman, the village carpenter and handyman, braced himself to face the bowling. All round the ground there was a deathly hush as away on the boundary line Tiny Larner, who had been put on for the last over, paced and scuffed like an angry bull. The fielders, eyes firmly fixed on the batsman, tensed themselves, while clustered round the wicket the slips, with arms outstretched and hands cupped, waited in anticipation. The first delivery flashed by on the leg side and Fred made no attempt to hit it. The second pitched short and went over his head to be neatly taken by the wicket-keeper.

For the last ball of the game, even the birds in the trees around became silent as Fred with teeth clenched and hands sweating braced himself. Down thundered Tiny and the last and only time Fred saw the ball was when it left the bowler's hand. Closing his eyes he struck out blindly, the bat taking the ball squarely in its middle almost wrenching it out of his hand. For a brief moment the world seemed to stand still then a mighty cheer went up as the ball cleared the boundary to land in the park beyond. Stodger Millett with both arms raised to signal a six danced up and down and jubilant supporters rushing onto the field proceeded to carry Fred off shoulder high leaving the Kempston players to follow dejectedly, heads hung down. Gathered round the tailboard of Len's wagon they proceeded to drown their sorrows with the remainder of Eli's beer and cider, and so ended a memorable encounter which, although at the time we did not know it, would not be repeated for many a day.

With stumps drawn and the last of the liquid refreshment disposed of, the visitors loaded themselves and their gear onto the wagon for the return journey to the station. With cricket bats and other items safely stored away in the guards van they boarded the train, then as it pulled away hands were shaken and promises made to meet again the following year. Leaning out of the carriage window Tiny Larner took the extended hand of Doctor Hemmings. 'See you again next year, sir,' he said. The Doctor nodded then stayed to watch until the last of the carriages disappeared round the bend by the signal box. With a heavy heart he turned and made his way to the station exit, sure in the knowledge that it would be a long time before they would all meet again, and it was with this thought in mind that he stood for a moment at the top of the lane listening to the sound of the train as it disappeared into the distance.

That night down at the Drovers Arms victory was toasted with full tankards and glasses and the highlights of the game relived over and over again, all accompanied by a good deal of good-natured banter. Fred Newman, the hero of the day, well in his cups, demonstrated again and again the master stroke that had given Lavington victory, an exhibition that, encouraged by the continual refilling of the glass at his elbow, eventually caused him to collapse to the floor from where, when the occasion demanded, he was rescued and lifted back into his seat. Sitting in the corner of the taproom, I joined in the celebrations, feeling a sudden warmth towards these people with whom I was privileged to share my life: Alice, my mother, hair now flecked with grey,

18

was still an attractive woman, Father, short in stature but larger than life in personality, and my two sisters Tessa and Beckey. Tessa was a year younger than me, a quiet thoughtful girl who wore her hair in plaits, being in both looks and temperament the image of her mother. Since leaving school she had worked at the village stores assisting Mr Lewis, helping in the shop and with domestic duties, Mrs Lewis being an invalid and confined to her bed. Beckey, a year her junior, was the tomboy of the family; wayward and capricious, she had a habit of running at life as if wanting to meet it head on. A little on the wild side she seemed not to favour either parent, although it had to be admitted that she knew how to get her own way as one look from those grey eyes that looked out from under a fringe of tawny-coloured hair was enough to melt even the hardest of hearts, as Father knew only too well. Mother had secured a position for her with Doctor and Mrs Hemmings as a daily help, a temporary arrangement as Beckey had made it quite clear right from the start that she had other ideas. However, in spite of our differences, and there were many, we were a close-knit family privileged to live in a home that was full of love and happiness. Looking over to where my parents were sitting I saw that Father was engrossed in a newspaper that lay open in front of him. I had no need to see the headlines as I had a fair idea what they were and it was then that a cold chill swept over me as I fell to wondering what would happen to us all if our worst fears were realized and there was to be a war. However I knew that there was very little that I, or for that matter anyone else, could do to alter the course of history.

Long after 'shut tap' we gathered in small groups outside reluctant to end what after all had been a memorable day until at last having regard for the lateness of the hour we began to disperse, inebriated elders leaning on old friends and others reliant on understanding wives who, taking charge, guided their husbands homewards. At last all was quiet and standing alone in the darkness I suddenly became aware of footsteps approaching. With eyes and ears straining I tried to identify the voices that were rapidly getting closer, then two figures came into the circle of light cast by the single oil lamp above the front entrance to the Drovers and I saw that it was Nancy Beasley and her friend Biddy Evans. Stepping out from the shadows I confronted them, my sudden appearance causing them to cry out in alarm, however I quickly reassured them and asked if I might walk them home, a suggestion to which they readily agreed, and so the three of us set off up the village street to the cottage where Biddy lived with her parents. On reaching the gate I left Nancy to say her goodbyes after which she joined me and for the first time I found myself alone with her. For some reason which at the time I failed to understand her nearness aroused feelings that I hadn't experienced before; there was a faint suggestion of perfume about her and the way she carried herself reminded me of a young fawn, light of step and timid. Glancing sideways at her I could just make out the tresses of long golden brown hair that hung about her shoulders, free from the restraint of the plain bonnet that she carried lightly in one hand, and the feeling of intimacy it aroused made me want to touch her. How strange I thought that I had never felt the same way about other girls of the village with whom I had had meaningless affairs in the past. Standing at the gate of her cottage we talked for a while. I wanted to hold her but there was something about Nancy that bade me proceed with caution. Then shyly she said goodnight and started up the path. Glancing over her shoulder I glimpsed the movement of a curtain in an upstairs window. Panicking, I called her name upon which she turned to face me, eyes bright and a faint smile lingering on her lips. 'Could I walk you out sometime?' I stammered. For a moment she didn't answer, then, 'We'll see, John Mumford, we'll see,' and with that she turned and entered the cottage leaving me standing alone like a love-sick swain. Over the years I have come to the conclusion that there are times when the gods in their wisdom say, 'this is where you change direction,' and standing there on that night all those years ago I was certain that that was one such occasion.

For the next few weeks Nancy was never far from my thoughts, her duties up at the Hall kept her busy during the day and although she didn't 'live in' I made no attempt to seek her out thinking it better to let things work out in their own way. However the fact that there was something special on my mind was painfully obvious to my parents who behind my back exchanged knowing glances. As for Tessa and Beckey, they took to dropping sly hints in my presence, neither of them being in any way discreet in such matters.

One Saturday morning when on my way home from the village stores, quite by chance I came face to face with Nancy, a meeting that if I were truthful I was not prepared for as must have been obvious from the way I confronted her, head lowered and shifting from one foot to the other. However at last I managed to ask if she were free that afternoon and might I walk her out.

20

Much to my surprise she didn't seem at all put out at my request and I had the feeling that she had been expecting it as, looking straight at me, she replied, 'What's up with thee, John Mumford, frightened to ask me out were you? Of course I'll meet you. Can't understand what took you so long in the asking.' Cap in hand and completely taken aback I managed to blurt out, 'Good, see you at half past two by the church gate,' and with that I turned and walked briskly down Callow Lane, my feet hardly seeming to touch the ground.

That afternoon, with dinner over, it was out into the wash-house with jug of hot water, soap and towel, after which I crept upstairs to change into clean shirt and Sunday best. Down in the parlour the family watched my goings on without comment although it was plain to see that there were questions that they were dying to ask. Behind my back Beckey and Mother exchanged knowing glances as if they were privy to my secret and Tessa, not to be outdone, stood fingering her plaits and making kissing noises. Needless to say I was mightily glad when, scrubbed and freshly clad, I made my way up the lane to the church. How strange it is that one's first serious date becomes so indelibly etched on the memory: the butterflies in the stomach, the desperate need to impress and say all the right things, but like a fly in a spider's web eventually to stop struggling and accept the inevitable. She was waiting for me at the church, a picture of loveliness as she stood under the roof of the lych gate, her long white dress reaching down to her neat button-up boots and a ribboned bonnet from under which strands of golden brown hair peeped out invitingly. Turning to face me she watched as I approached, eyes smiling and lips slightly parted to show the evenness of her white teeth, a deliberate and challenging look, and it was in those first few moments that I realized that I was now falling in love with her, a turn of events which I was sure she was already aware of. Walking side by side through the park I found myself floundering in deep waters as I struggled to say all the things that I knew were expected of me. It was just as if I were seeing her for the first time, a far different Nancy to the one I had known since schooldays. Talking of nothing in particular we sometimes touched and I still remember the feeling of intimacy that I felt, however not being the impulsive sort I hesitated, realizing that it would not be proper to try to take advantage of her at this early stage in our relationship. Halfway up Oak Hill we stopped to catch our breath and rest awhile in the long grass where, with bonnet discarded and hair blowing about her shoulders, Nancy sat with her hands clasped around her knees staring into the far distance

21

while I, lying full length beside her, head resting on folded arms, watched as wisps of her hair, stirred by the breeze, parted to show the paleness of her slim arched neck. Unable to restrain myself I called her name upon which she turned and bent over me. Reaching up I put my arms around her and drawing her close kissed her as I had never kissed anyone before. 'Oh John, my dear,' she whispered. 'Oh John, what took you so long?' And so we lay wrapped in each others arms, two young people who, although they didn't realize it, had taken the first tentative steps along the road of love and companionship. In those first precious moments the world and all its troubles seemed far away, nothing mattered any more and as I held her I could feel the warmth of her. It was then that the urge came to take her, however, I realized that this was not the moment, so summoning up what little self-control I had left I rose and intimated that it was time for us to leave.

The weeks passed and Nancy and I entered into that trial period known at the time as walking out, and parents and friends came to accept that there was an understanding between us. And so with the days of high summer beginning to wain, Bank Holiday Monday arrived, the time of the traditional outing to the seaside at Weston-Super-Mare, a day when all the villagers that could be spared from farms and other duties got together to relax and enjoy themselves. The morning of August the third dawned bright and clear giving promise of a fine day ahead, under thatch and slate families were busy with preparations. Hampers were packed by harassed wives doing their best to cope with half-washed children who would insist on getting underfoot.

Then at eight of the clock the exodus began as, all down the village street, cottage doors were locked, and families made their way down to the village stores where, once assembled, they moved off in one long laughing procession down to the station to board the train which, especially chartered for the day, was waiting with steam up. Excited children clutching buckets and spades, and scrubbed and polished to near perfection, chased ahead of their parents, the girls in white cotton frocks with frilly lace collars and cuffs and gay print dresses, the lads in belted Norfolk jackets, knickerbockers and black lace-up boots, not forgetting the very young who tagged along in their sailor suits and round straw sailor hats. Mr Stait, the butcher, pink of face and smartly turned out in faded striped blazer, cream flannels and straw boater beamed on everyone as he escorted the smiling Mrs Stait, while Constable Hodges, on special duty for the day, stood at the top of the lane feet apart and thumbs hooked under the flaps of his tunic breast pockets as he exchanged banter and issued warnings to one and all to behave themselves, not that anyone took a great deal of notice of him, however. Nacky Pitt and Shenna Lawson, hair plastered down and parted in the middle and with shining boots and stiff white collars, lounged about in the station yard eyeing the village maidens who, decked out in ribboned finery and with saucy straw boaters pinned and perched at just the right angle, peered from under parasols with downcast eyes as with provocative shrugs of their shoulders they issued a silent challenge to the lads to pursue them if they dare. Nancy and I – for now I had become her constant escort – walked hand in hand behind our parents who, loaded with hampers and coats and other sundry bits and pieces, were making their way down the lane. From the banks on either side foxgloves, their feet encased in common mallow and field mint, raised their trumpet-like heads above the tall grasses and in the hedgerows honeysuckle cascaded down, its scent lingering on the warm morning air. In the fields that bordered the lane young calves, tails up, pranced and chased to gaps in the hedge where puffing and snorting they viewed the procession below, no doubt wondering what all the noise was about, while down in the station yard the children, still brimming over with energy, chased each other dodging agitated parents eager to keep their broods intact. Wives and mothers wearing lavishly adorned picture hats and neat bonnets and with freshly laundered and starched dresses chatted amongst themselves, leaving their menfolk, elegant but uncomfortable in bowler hats and Sunday go-to-church best, their waistcoats hung with thick silver or gold watch-chains, to guard hampers and wicker baskets.

After a great deal of puffing and complaining the train drew out of the siding where it had been waiting and with a last protesting screech of brakes came to a halt at the platform whereupon there ensued a mad scramble as carriage doors were flung open and a tide of eager children, bent on evading the clutches of their parents and make their own arrangements, made a grab for seats by the window, a game of musical chairs, which after much pulling of hair and kicking of shins left the weaker ones to sit primly between parents. At the back of the crowd, pressed hard against the ticket office door Parson and Mrs Collins, self-appointed stewards for the day, endeavoured to create some sort of order, however, after several futile attempts to do so, they finally gave up and joined in the rush for empty carriages. In the cab of the engine

23

Sid Hawkins, the driver, leaned out, oily rag in hand, as he waited for the guard to signal with flag and whistle, while on the platform the two porters, Nathan and Herbert, raced up and down the length of the train checking and securing doors and pushing back to safety youngsters who in their excitement were leaning too far out of the windows. At last all was ready and with a 'Right away, Mr Marshall' and a 'thank you, Mr Stringer' from the guard the train, with much puffing and spinning of wheels, moved off leaving the station staff to mop their brows and relax, safe in the knowledge that come the end of the day the whole noisy episode would be repeated.

Sitting in the compartment we were sharing with our parents Nancy and I watched the smoke from the engine go rolling across the countryside, where in nearby fields grazing cattle raised their heads to peer at us through the gritty, black-grey clouds that enveloped them. In one of Percy Slatter's meadows a mare, followed by her foal, galloped ahead of us until they reached the far end where with eyes wide and ears pricked they stood watching us pass, and in an adjoining pasture Harry Pugh, busy feeding his pigs, paused for a moment to take off his cap and wave us on our way. Slowly the train gathered speed causing the telegraph poles to either side to flash past in monotonous procession, the wires strung between them dipping and rising in rhythm. Swayed by the rolling of the carriage I pressed closer to Nancy and put my arm around her hearing her sigh contentedly as, with eyes closed, she rested her head on my shoulder. At Pipers Crossing, Harry Stevens, lolling on the seat of his wagon, pipe clenched between his teeth, chatted to Mrs Underwood, the crossing lady, who waited to open the gate after we had passed, the engine driver giving her a short blast on his whistle. Soon we were out of familiar countryside and heading for the sea and during a lull in the conversation I looked over at Mother who was sitting opposite, smartly turned out in her best costume and a hat adorned with artificial fruit and flowers that Father had bought her on their last visit to Cheltenham. She still looked young, the passing years had been kind to her and as I watched I couldn't help but wonder if perhaps she was thinking back to her own courting days when in the first flush of youth she and Father had taken the same train trip, and if she was remembering other times when they had roamed the woods above the village and listened to the nightingale as it sang in the thicket on the slopes of Oak Hill. In the next compartment Tessa and Beckey, in the company of other maidens of the village, sat primly with hands folded on laps determined to look their best on arrival, being sure in the knowledge that the eager young lads would be first out on the platform to catch sight of a well-turned ankle and choose their partners for the day.

As the train neared its destination young faces were pressed against carriage windows to catch the first sight of the sea and parents, stiff from sitting, rose and proceeded to adjust and smooth their attire before retrieving coats and other items from the luggage racks above the seats. Slowly and with obvious relief the train came to a halt at the platform, mothers gathered their children about them, fussing and scolding like hens with broods of chicks, leaving their menfolk to collect hampers and baskets from the guards van. Then in family groups the procession of chatting parents and excited children left the precincts of the station and headed for the beach, passing as they went the waiting cabbies on the cab rank, whose horses viewed the commotion with eyes wide and ears twitching. With the sun shining down from a cloudless blue sky and seemingly without a care in the world they made their way down onto the sands to choose their spots before settling down in rented deckchairs.

Tessa and Beckey and several other village maidens made for the seafront where they paraded up and down to admire and be admired. Then, after a while, they stood listening to the band on the bandstand at the end of the promenade, having very little interest in the music, being more concerned with the young men who, lounging against the sea wall, were casting admiring glances in their direction. Stodger Millett, neatly turned out in striped blazer, flannels and straw boater, with side-whiskers and moustache carefully trimmed, trudged up and down the sands making sure that everyone was comfortably settled, occasionally ducking behind the sea wall to take a swig from his hip flask which had been carefully primed before leaving Lavington. On the beach, almost at the water's edge, a string of weary donkeys, heads hung down, trudged backwards and forwards carrying corpulent men and women who, flouting dignity, sat like sacks of corn on the animals' backs, the men with trousers rolled up and knotted handkerchiefs on their heads reliving their long-lost youth much to the embarrassment of their better halves, some of whom watched from a discreet distance. Children, busy building sandcastles, kept up a constant demand for ice cream and lemonade, pestering sleepy parents who themselves were forced to keep a watchful eye on the more venturesome of their brood, who in sheer bravado or relief in their newly-

25

found freedom, plunged fully-clothed into the water from where they were eventually rescued and hung out to dry. Tessa and Beckey, by now having found escorts, promenaded through the town shyly protesting when an arm was placed around a waist but secretly enjoying it, refreshments being taken in one or other of the many tearooms where, in secluded corners, half-hidden by ancient aspidistra plants, hands were held under tables bringing flushes of pleasure and half-hearted protests from young ladies clinging precariously to their newly-found adulthood. Happy in our own company Nancy and I explored the town, taking tea in a quaint little tea shop run by two dear old ladies who, in lavender and lace, fussed over us almost as if we were their own, after which we made our way down to the park. Sitting on a secluded seat, we listened to the band and kissed, and it was then that I felt the need of her and drawing her close I felt her tremble.

And so the day wore on until at last regretfully it was time for us to make our way back to the station for the journey home. Children, dog-tired and half-asleep, clung to the skirts of their mothers while fathers, worn out and with jackets and ties discarded, shouldered the very young ones whose little legs had long since given out, leaving older brothers and sisters to make their own way in the company of their chosen partners. Safely aboard the train the tired youngsters rested their tousled heads on the laps of their equally tired parents as they dreamed of donkey rides, ice cream and sandcastles, leaving the young maidens weary and ruffled but blissfully happy to sit with closed eyes, thinking of the young lads who had been their sweethearts for the day and with whom they had made tentative arrangements for future assignations. With the sun sinking over the horizon and twilight threatening, the landscape slipped by in a purple haze and in the dimly-lit carriages blinds were lowered and silence prevailed as the occupants relaxed and enjoyed their own special memories of the day. Then in the soft velvet darkness the train pulled in to Lavington station where under the light cast by the hanging oil lamps Alby and his two porters went up and down the line of carriages opening doors and assisting the weary travellers out onto the platform. Outside in the station yard a few traps waited to convey those who lived in the more isolated farms and cottages, muted good nights drifted between those making their way up Two Hedges Lane, until at last all was quiet leaving the station to sleep until the arrival of the milk train in the morning.

26

Chapter II

Tuesday August the Fourth, a day that for many reasons would be long remembered. Out in the steam-filled wash-house in the yard Mother bent to her task with sleeves rolled up and wisps of damp hair across her forehead. Mechanically she stirred the tangle of soiled linen that bubbled and protested in the soapy depths of the lead-lined copper then, pausing for a moment, she wiped her forehead with the back of her hand and rested against the wall thinking all the while of the headlines she had seen that morning in the paper, headlines that told of general mobilization and the threat of war which, if it were to happen, she knew would only bring tears and misery. Turning the thought over and over in her mind she at last came to the conclusion that there was little sense in worrying as events would take their course however much she fretted. So with one last long deep sigh she grasped the bamboo copper-stick and reaching over began to stir the clothes vigorously, and the day passed leaving most of her questions unanswered, that is until that same evening, with the Germans having ignored all ultimatums, at 11 p.m. a state of war was declared.

The next day speculation and rumour were rife. Outside the village stores a small group of villagers had gathered to discuss the momentous news brought in by the early postman from Evesham, and Yanto Jones, all excited and patriotic, marched up and down with walking stick at the slope, declaring to one and all what he would do if only he were younger. Mr Lewis, in clean white apron, stood on the steps of the stores declaring that his compatriots from the Welsh valleys would soon sort the Kaiser out, and all that was needed to complete the picture was for the Alderton Band to come marching up the street, when for certain they would all have fallen in behind and marched all the way to Germany. Down at the smithy it was work as usual; there were horses to be shod, lengths of chain to be fashioned and a hundred and one other small jobs to be seen to, thus for the time being at any rate work helped to keep our minds off the devastating news. Sitting taking our usual morning break I watched Father as he stirred the contents of the large china mug that rested on the brickwork of the forge, a ritual he carried out each working day promptly on the stroke of ten and again at three in the afternoon. The old mug had belonged to his grandfather and when not in use occupied an honoured place on a shelf above the workbench, where it had stood for many a long year. For a while we sat in silence, a silence broken only by the spit and crackle of the coals on the forge and the occasional rush of wings as some stray bird, seeking warmth and sanctuary, flew in to perch on the rafters above our heads. Then Father spoke. 'I ain't going to volunteer, lad,' he said, 'I've given it a deal of thought and I reckon that unless I be conscripted things 'ud be better served if I stayed put and looked after things here.' Pausing, he waited to see what effect his decision had had on me. Searching my mind for a suitable reply I deliberately took my time finishing off the mug of tea I was holding until at last, realizing that some sort of reply was called for, I offered, 'I reckon that's best, Father. I know Mother 'ul be pleased,' a reply which he failed to hear as he turned and rinsed out his mug in the bucket of warm water that had a permanent place by the side of the forge, after which he wiped it out with his handkerchief before returning it to its place on the shelf.

During the next few weeks there was talk of several of the village lads volunteering. To them it must have seemed like a great adventure, a chance to get out of the village and see a little of the world especially as rumour had it that it would all be over by Christmas. In the world outside events were beginning to take shape as reservists were called to the colours and Army representatives toured the countryside commandeering horses, in spite of the protests of the farmers who pleaded that they needed them for harvesting and other essential work. Sir Howard had three of his best hunters taken, however Master Grahame managed to retain two of his mounts pleading that he needed them for his military service. Night and day trains passed through our station loaded with troops and supplies for the expeditionary force that would soon be leaving for France. Doctor Hemmings had received his papers ordering him to report to the nearest RAMC Depot, Master Grahame had volunteered and Charlie Wilmore had agreed to go with him as his groom and batman. Under the supervision of Lady Armstrong the village hall was commandeered for use as a military hospital ready to play its part in caring for the casualties that before long would be returning from the battlefields of

France and Belgium. Mother, in a fit of patriotism, together with several other ladies of the village, had volunteered their services and soon were busy attending first aid lectures organized by an elderly Matron on loan from the cottage hospital in Whinchcombe. In due course beds, blankets and a hundred and one items necessary for the transformation were delivered from a central stores in Gloucester, the sight of which caused near panic, however the good ladies soon got things sorted out and in a very short time things were more or less organized. The stalwarts of the Women's Institute, gathering up their skirts, met in urgent conclave in the study at the parsonage where, aided and abetted by cups of tea and digestive biscuits, they planned and discussed jam-making and bandage-rolling. And so one way or another our little community got itself ready to do its bit for the war effort.

On 20 August the Germans entered Brussels and the opposing armies made their first contact north of Mons, closely followed by the first battle of Ypres. Casualty lists began to appear in the daily papers, propaganda lengthened its stride and soon cartoons showing German soldiers with babies transfixed on their bayonets, and terrified nuns being ravished on the altars of churches, occupied prime space, all designed to fuel the fires of patriotism that were sweeping the country and bring the realities of war nearer. In spite of his earlier protestations Nathan Powell had volunteered and was training somewhere up in Yorkshire, Nacky Pitt and Shenna Lawson, the inseparables, had also decided to go and were awaiting their reporting instructions, and much to our surprise Nancy's brother Ted had volunteered and had been accepted for the Royal Navy. Tessa and Beckey had volunteered their services as part-time helpers at the village hall and had been accepted. As for me, I had to admit that all the activity had left me harbouring a feeling of guilt seeing that for the moment I didn't seem to be contributing anything useful.

Christmas came but in view of the war news it was not greeted with the usual enthusiasm. At Forge Cottage we decorated with holly, mistletoe and paper chains trying hard to foster the true spirit of Yuletide but on all our minds was the thought that somewhere across the channel young men were laying down their lives in a strange country for a cause which few of them really understood. On Christmas Eve, with preparations more or less in hand, Nancy and I took a walk up the village as far as the church where, standing under the lych-gate, we courted and kissed remembering our first meeting there on that summer's day. Up in the dark tower the silent bells awaited the morrow when once again they would ring out their message of hope, then suddenly out of the darkness we saw a bobbing light making its way towards us and as it drew nearer a voice called out wishing us a Merry Christmas. Recognizing the shambling gait of its owner we replied in like fashion realizing that it was only old Zetter Parsons who, lantern in hand, was making his way down to the Drovers Arms.

The first Christmas Day of the war dawned crisp and clear. In the early morning we looked out of windows laced with frost where spiders' webs swung gently showing off their jewelled beauty and where, in candlelit bedrooms of the thatched and slated cottages of the village and under the eaves of ancient farmhouses excited children, mercifully unaware of the tragedy being enacted in the world outside, were busy unwrapping their presents. Parents roused early from their beds knelt to rake out the ashes of yesterday's fires and make ready to face the busy day ahead. Meanwhile at home Mother, always the first to rise, was rekindling the fire in the kitchen range, ready to get the old black kettle into its best singing mood leaving Father, who had already disposed of the ashes and relayed the fire in the parlour, to go across to the smithy to make sure all was well there. At last with all the chores attended to we sat around the breakfast table exchanging presents and expressing our delight as we unwrapped handkerchiefs and sundry items of toilet needs which Mother and the two girls had so carefully wrapped in festive paper. Then, with breakfast over, Tessa and Beckey, suitably wrapped against the cold and with hands warm in rabbit's fur muffs, made their way up the village street calling on friends and neighbours to exchange Christmas greetings, being well supplied with tots of home-made wine and mince pies on the way.

Later, with the bells ringing out across the silent countryside we all went to church to give thanks to the good Lord for the birth of his Son, to pray for victory and ask for the strength and courage to face whatever lay ahead in the coming months. Sitting in the hard wooden pew with Nancy by my side, I looked around at the sea of solemn faces that were gathered there and up at the choir stalls where young lads, scrubbed and angelic in their white surplices, fidgeted and nudged each other seemingly quite unaffected by the solemnity of the occasion, being more concerned with thoughts of the presents they had unwrapped earlier that morning. But who could blame them? War had not

30

affected them yet. Only half listening to the sermon I let my mind wander back over the last few months realizing as I did so that great changes were taking place. With very little warning I had entered a cold grey world leaving those happy carefree sunshine-filled days behind. However there was one consolation – I now had my dear Nancy to share this new world with me.

With the sermon concluded Parson Collins stepped down from the pulpit and, standing on the altar steps, raised his hand. 'The blessing of God Almighty, Father, Son, and Holy Ghost be among you and remain with you always.' Although I had heard that blessing many times before, just at that moment it seemed to have a special significance. And so the service ended and trying not to show undue haste we made our way out into the churchyard where, standing rubbing our hands together and stamping our feet to restore lost circulation, we wished friends and neighbours the compliments of the season before making our separate ways home, perhaps for the last time, as families observed a traditional Christmas.

Later, seated round the table in the parlour, we awaited the arrival of the plump goose that had been cooking away in the oven of the kitchen range since early morning. Each time Mother had need to inspect its progress the smell of it had drifted around the house to mingle with the scent of pink and white hyacinths, apples and oranges all of which added to that special aroma the memory of which stays with us long after our childhood has drifted away into the mists of time. Nancy and her parents had joined us for the day and although they appeared to enter into the spirit of things, I sensed that deep down they were missing their son Ted who had already left to do his training in Portsmouth. With dinner over Mr Beasley, Father and me made ourselves comfortable in chairs round the fire all ready for a quiet snooze, leaving the womenfolk, faces flushed with too much home-made wine, to busy themselves with the washing up, their tongues clacking nineteen to the dozen as they dodged and ducked in the confines of our small kitchen. Then, with all the clearing up seen to and the remnants of the goose safely stored away in the larder where it would stay ready to contribute its remains to sandwiches and broth, we all sat round the table playing cards, in between times making frequent trips to the welsh dresser on which was arrayed a display of biscuits, fruits and nuts. With daylight fading and only the flickering light from the wax candles on the Christmas tree to illuminate things, Mother lit the two brass-stemmed oil lamps and placed one at each end of the table, the light

31

from their tall glass chimneys and rose-coloured bowls casting a mellow glow into the dark corners. And so we sat and talked late into the night until at last it was time for Mr and Mrs Beasley to take their leave of us and me to escort Nancy home.

The next day, Boxing Day, Nancy and I walked over the hills to Alderton to pay a visit to her grandparents. It was a cold raw day and from a powder blue sky a weak sun glinted on the frost-covered trees and bushes as, hand in hand, we made our way through the woods, our breath vapourizing in the cold air. A cock pheasant, resplendent in winter plumage, crossed our path hesitating just long enough to cast an inquisitive eye in our direction before scampering off into the undergrowth, and close by a solitary blackbird, startled by our presence, sent out its nervous scolding chatter to warn others of our passing. On each side of the pathway jewelled cobwebs hung from the frost-laden branches from the tips of which tiny drops of moisture hung glistening like pearls, while in the trees above birds marked our progress sending small clouds of shimmering powder earthwards as they flew from branch to branch. Bright of eye, light of step and with hair glinting in the dappled sunshine Nancy walked by my side occasionally to run ahead as if to leave me, then she would stop and wait for me to catch up and take her in my arms, treasured moments to be remembered for ever. On the descent into Alderton we met up with Fred Waddon, one of the estate gamekeepers, who kept us talking for a while and it was most noticeable that whenever the subject of the war came into the conversation Nancy withdrew into herself almost as if she was afraid of facing the reality of it although as it happened, future events were to prove that this was not so. After enjoying a brief visit to her grandparents, who lived in a cottage near the church, we started back through the woods, eventually arriving at Ryes Furrough where we rested for a while marvelling at the scene that stretched away below us. In the distance smoke from village chimneys drifted lazily in the still air and somewhere unseen amongst the frost-laden trees in the park a dog was barking, a still, white shimmering world that stood out clear against the dark outline of the Cotswold Hills. It was almost as if the land was resting before entering the coming new year and all its attendant problems. Briskly we made our way back to the village stopping only to exchange a few words with George Nurden at the dairy before reaching the Beasley cottage where we joined my parents and Tessa and Beckey to spend the remainder of Boxing Day. Gathered round a roaring log fire we roasted chestnuts and drank each others health in elderberry wine, sloe gin and cider, played endless games of charades, snakes and ladders, and ludo until at last, drowsy and sleepy, we sat in silence to take in the unforgettable aroma of slow-burning apple logs and watch the flames curl their way up the dark chimney.

And so the first Christmas of the war passed into history and soon it was New Year. With the news from France getting grimmer by the day we entered into 1915 apprehensive but hopeful. Master Grahame, Charlie Wilmore, Nacky Pitt and Shenna Lawson were away training with their respective regiments; Nathan Powell was due home on leave, his last before leaving for France; and Doctor Hemmings was already across the channel serving in a field hospital somewhere in Belgium.

A week after Christmas, amidst scenes of feverish activity, the hospital staff from the village hall gathered at the railway station to receive the first casualties that were arriving in carriages attached to the London train. Supervised by two nurses from Queen Alexandra's Imperial Nursing Service, the ladies were eager to put into practice all they had learned during their weeks of training. As the train came to a halt they made their way to the rear carriages where they assisted the walking wounded out onto the platform and helped with the unloading of the stretcher cases. Meanwhile those who were able made their way out into the station yard where they were accommodated in traps and other conveyances which had been commandeered for the occasion, leaving the stretcher cases to be dealt with by the crews of the two motor ambulances on loan from Cheltenham. Down at the village hall everything was ready to receive them and before long, cleaned up and fed, the new arrivals settled in, and so it was that at the end of the first week the ladies were going about their business like veterans. It was amazing how quickly they learned to cope. The hours were long, but encouraged by the example set by Lady Armstrong, they survived, and at the end of their long periods of duty they staggered home to sleep and gather strength for the next day, happy in the knowledge of a job well done. Nancy helped for two or three evenings a week and although she only had one free day, usually a Saturday or Sunday, we still managed to get a bit of courting in.

When the day came for the departure of Master Grahame, Charlie Wilmore, Nacky Pitt and Shenna Lawson for France the village turned out in force to see them on their way. At the far end of the platform the Alderton Brass Band, brave in their blue tunics, blew lustily adding to what, but for the underlying reason for the occasion, might well have been a festive affair. Union Jacks and bunting hung from the roof above the platform and Constable Hodges, always available at such times, walked up and down assuming an exaggerated air of authority, put on specially for Sir Howard and Lady Armstrong who had come to see their son off. In the porters' room Eli Small, Stodger Millett, Twitcher Morris and Jack Harris, well fortified with cider drawn from the tapped barrel standing on a table in the corner, leaned their backs against the wall as they toasted the departing lads, no doubt thinking back to the time not so long ago when they had watched others from the village depart to fight the Boers in the dust and heat of Africa, none of whom had returned. Out on the platform, surrounded by the cheering villagers who had come to see them off, Master Grahame resplendent in his officer's uniform, accompanied by Charlie Wilmore in riding breeches and puttees, shook the proffered hands and accepted the good wishes and hopes for a speedy return. Nacky Pitt and Shenna Lawson, rifles slung and proud in their new uniforms, paraded up and down making the most of their moment of glory while Charlie's wife, flushed and agitated, fussed around arranging her husband's kit, leaving their two children sitting on the long platform seat, wide-eyed and mystified by all the goings on. Sir Howard and Lady Armstrong, mingling with the crowds that clustered round the open carriage windows, shook hands and offered best wishes, the young faces that leaned out making the most of that brief moment when they were the centre of attention. Slowly Sir Howard and his lady made their way down to where Master Grahame had installed himself in a first-class carriage. With stiff upper lip they shook hands formally, considering it unseeming that they should show any emotion in public; no doubt in the privacy of their home it would be different. When the time came for the train to leave, mothers held on to hands until the last minute, fathers put on a brave face shouting advice most of which was lost in the cheering of the crowd and the music from the band, and so, still waving and cheering, they watched until the last carriage disappeared round the bend by the signal box where Arthur Rawlins, the signalman, leaning as far out of the window as he dared, waved his cap and cheered the departing heroes on their way. Back on the platform the band, now sad of face, packed up their instruments and music stands and boarded Len Hubbard's wagon for the return journey to Alderton leaving the villagers to make their own way home in silence, knowing that there would be a good many departures before things got back to normal. And so the days passed, news from across the channel being avidly read and discussed especially by the regulars down at the Drovers Arms who, having set themselves up as armchair generals, planned and re-planned the strategy of the whole Western Front.

One fine Saturday morning, it being Nancy's day off, we decided to take a trip into Evesham and not wishing to go by train, we borrowed Percy Slatter's pony and trap. It was a beautiful April morning and as we set off down Nutmeadow even Smoky the pony seemed to share our happiness, tossing its mane and flicking its tail seemingly in time with the crunch and rattle of the trap wheels and the clip-clop of its hooves on the roadway. With cheeks flushed Nancy took the reins as we turned into Sedgberrow Road and sitting beside her, watching, I treasured every movement, every smile as the wind blew her hair around her shoulders.

Along the way we stopped off at Little Cheltenham to call on Mrs Kirkaldy and her daughter Dora, friends of my mother's, staying just long enough to take tea and bring them up to date with all the village gossip. Then it was off again at a steady trot towards Evesham where after stabling Smoky and the trap at the Red Lion in Port Street we made our way over the river bridge and up Bridge Street, a slow journey seeing that Nancy, as seems the way with all women, insisted on examining at great length the contents of every shop window that we passed. All down the middle of the High Street, drays and dray horses, spring carts, traps and day carts were parked, some of the horses being tethered to handy railings where they snuffled and snorted into their feed bags while others not quite so fortunate stood gazing impassively into space, apparently oblivious of the noise and bustle taking place around them. In Avon Street long queues of drays loaded with full chips and pot hampers waited their turn to get into the market to unload, their drivers, with nothing better to do at the moment, gathering in groups to chat and smoke. Dragged into the Bon Marche and several other stores I willingly suffered in the course of true love, but I must admit that I was greatly relieved when, shopping done, we made our way to a little tea shop in Winchcombe Street kept by an elderly spinster who claimed to be a relative of Nancy's on her mother's side. Seated in a quiet corner we drank tea and watched the customers come and

35

go, Nancy commenting on dress and fashion, much of which I am afraid fell on deaf ears, then a lad in khaki came in escorting a young lady and they sat themselves down at a table next to ours. He looked very smart in his uniform and his companion was obviously proud of him judging by the way she kept looking at him and holding his hand. Looking at them I began to feel guilty and glancing at Nancy I saw that she was watching me almost as if she knew what was going through my mind. So reaching over I took her hand in mine and squeezed it to reassure her, but she just smiled and put her finger to her lips as if to say that no explanation was necessary. Looking back I am sure that it was at that moment that I made up my mind on a course of action which would, in the not too distant future, have a great effect on both our lives.

Leaving the tea shop we started to make our way back to Port Street and the Red Lion, passing on our way an organ grinder at the top of Bridge Street who was churning out his music. Lingering for a while, we stood listening and watching while a few of the more venturesome ladies danced in the roadway, some of them raising their skirts in high delight, not being at all shy in showing a neat ankle in the process. Being in no great hurry we took the long way round through Bell Tower Gardens and down onto the river front where we sat for a while watching the rowing boats and punts on the water. Such was the tranquility of the scene that it was hard to believe that it was wartime, however, realizing that we had the pony to harness up and the return journey to make, we rose and crossing the river bridge made for the Red Lion.

On the journey home Nancy was very quiet and having a fair idea what was on her mind I let it bide, reasoning that she would tell me in her own good time. Once or twice she sighed deeply and when I pressed her hand to reassure her she quickly looked away. Somehow the magic of the day had gone and in a way I was relieved when we reached the bottom of Nutmeadow.

Back in the village we returned Smoky and the trap to Percy thanking him for their use after which we made our way through the churchyard to Nancy's parents' cottage where her mother was waiting to hear how our day had gone. Sitting at the table not wishing to be drawn into the conversation taking place between mother and daughter, I thought back over the day's happenings and the incident in the tea shop, then, reaching into her handbag, Mrs Beasley took out a photograph of her son Ted and handed it to me. It showed him in his uniform and as I sat looking at it I wondered if there had been a reason for her showing it to me, however I hadn't long to wait, for suddenly she asked the question I had been dreading. 'Have you made your mind up about joining up, John?' she asked. Caught unawares I hesitated before replying, not being quite sure what to say. Luckily at that moment Nancy rose from her chair and with handkerchief pressed to her face dashed out into the kitchen followed by Mrs Beasley, and this gave me the opportunity to take my leave, realizing that just at the moment I shouldn't be wanted. On reaching home I learned that three more local lads had volunteered for the Army: Walter Richards from Leyfield Cottages, Harry Stevens from Little Didcot and gamekeeper Harry Gibbons, the cricket team's fearsome bowler, news which under the circumstances didn't help. Although at the time I didn't realize it, my mind was already made up to follow them.

At the village hall patients came and went, some not staying long enough for us to get to know them, while others more fortunate, their war over, were discharged and sent back to their homes to take up what was left of their lives. In the hall of the village school we were treated to the occasional film show put on by Mr Samuel Davis, a travelling entertainer who hailed from the other side of Gloucester. Sitting in the dark we watched the flickering antics of Charlie Chaplin and others, always finishing up with a short newsreel of our troops in France which Mr Davis informed us he was obliged to show in the interests of morale.

In late April the village suffered its first casualty, Nathan Powell, who had been killed in the Second Battle of Ypres. His had been a short war and his loss affected the whole community. On the Sunday following the news of his death a special service was held in the church where, sober-suited, we knelt and prayed for the soul of a young man who had given his life for his country, knowing that never again would we see him down at the railway station or meet him for conversation in the village street. At the back of the church Lady Armstrong and members of the Hall staff who had come to pay their respects sat stern-faced and dignified, while down in the front pew Mr and Mrs Powell comforted each other, two grief-stricken people who as yet had not quite come to terms with the loss of their son. On the plain whitewashed wall opposite to where Nancy and I were sitting, the spring sunshine, straining its way through the branches of a willow tree in the churchyard, threw dappled patterns that danced on the bare walls, and as I watched them I thought of the other young lads who had left so cheerfully that morning down at the station, lads who, swept away on a tide of patriotism, had been blissfully unaware of the dangers and horrors that lay ahead. Hiding his feelings Parson Collins stumbled through the service. It was an emotional occasion particularly during the singing of the hymn 'Abide with me, fast falls the eventide'. I knew that Nancy was crying and I must admit that I felt a sense of relief when at last we were able to make our way out into the spring sunshine. No doubt there would be others who in the future would be called upon to make the supreme sacrifice, but somehow Nathan's death being the first affected us all deeply.

Spring was now well in bringing new life and new hope. At the edges of the pond hard by the smithy dog mercury, marsh marigolds, and celandines confirmed it, and Master Robin having found a mate had set up home on the high shelf above the forge where he was wont to sit puffing out his chest and singing fit to bust. In the smithy Father and I were kept busy although, due to the number of horses that had been taken by the Army, there was not a great deal of shoeing to be done. However there was plenty of other work, repairs to ploughshares and new parts for carts and wagons taking up a great deal of our time. On several of the farms around women had replaced the young men away at the front. They were mostly city girls who at first seemed ill at ease not being used to our country ways, however after a while they seemed to settle down and soon became an accepted part of our little community.

Late one afternoon in June, in the magic stillness that only an evening in early summer can capture, Nancy and I went walking over the hills above the village, the woods to either side being quiet and still. Hand in hand, we made our way along the soft bridle paths, heedless of the direction we were taking, until with the sun just beginning to drop behind the woods above the village we found ourselves on the sloping sides of Oak Hill. For most of the time we had walked in silence, almost as if each of us knew that this was to be a special night. Suddenly I began to have doubts as to whether I should be able to cope with the situation and glancing at Nancy I could see that she too was troubled. Reaching the stile that gave access to the hazel thicket we hesitated, both knowing that if we stepped over that stile there would be no going back, then, almost as if she were pleading for me to do so, I took her in my arms, feeling her tremble. Looking up at me with eyes misty and half closed she whispered, 'Oh yes, John my darling, Oh yes,' and after that there was no need for words. Climbing the stile we fought our way down an overgrown path, the bushes closing behind us as we went until at last we came upon a secluded dell overhung with hazel and there, in the still of that June evening, she gave herself to me.

Long after it was over we lay wrapped in each others arms listening to a nightingale as it trilled its song, the clear vibrant notes piercing the stillness around us. With trembling hands Nancy pulled me towards her and as I ran my fingers through the tresses of her hair that hung about her bare shoulders, she sighed. The storm had passed and for a while we were in another world as mindless of the passing of time we lay listening to the haunting song that rose and fell on the still night air, a magical moment that both of us were to remember for the rest of our lives.

Soon the time came for us to go and dressing we made ready to start for home. There was a new feeling of intimacy between us now, a closeness that hadn't been there before. Now that the desires and frustrations of the past were gone we were at peace with one another, as with my arm around her waist we walked back through the darkening woods. In a far off thicket a vixen called to her mate, an urgent call that set the nerves tingling and in the branches of a nearby oak tree a screech owl proclaimed to the world that he was on the hunt, a mysterious silent world in which as far as they were concerned we were two uninvited travellers. Standing at the cottage gate Nancy reached up and kissed me full on the lips. 'No regrets, my love,' she whispered, 'no regrets,' and with that she turned and ran up the pathway pausing only to wave before closing the door behind her.

That night I lay in my bed too restless to sleep as I dwelt on the momentous happenings of the past few hours. Outside the window of my bedroom the moon shed fitful shadows in the courtyard below and in the unused chimney bats chirped to each other as they readied themselves before venturing out into the night. There was no going back now, I thought, I was committed. However once I had come to terms with this I felt a lot happier; also, it helped to erase any feelings of guilt I may have been harbouring.

Soon it was high summer, a busy time on the land when, in the evenings and at other times when I could be spared, I helped with the haymaking and harvesting. Much to our surprise and delight Tessa had taken up with a young soldier who had been sent to our hospital after being wounded in France. His name was Arthur, a quiet likeable lad who before the war had worked with his father on a smallholding in the village of Bengworth just outside Evesham. She seemed quite fond of him and after a great deal of persuasion from Mother she brought him home to Sunday tea. He said very little about his experiences in France and we didn't press him on the matter. For us it was sufficient that our Tessa was happy having at last found someone upon whom she could lavish the loving care and affection that was in her nature. Beckey on the other hand was a different kettle of fish. Flirting with anyone who took her fancy, she changed her escorts as the whim took her. Each one she brought home we all hoped would be the chosen one but it was not to be. Like a pretty butterfly she flitted from one to the other, never staying long enough to settle.

On my twentieth birthday I made up my mind to ask Nancy to become my wife, reasoning that in the event of my being called into the Army we should at least have each other for a while and I must admit that my proposal when it came didn't exactly sweep Nancy off her feet. There was no going down on one knee while my intended stood blushing with lowered eyes, no hesitant sighs of disbelief, however in spite of the lack of traditional courtesy she accepted me as I knew she would. That evening we went down to obtain her parents' consent and blessing, both of which were freely given, then it was on down to Forge Cottage, where on imparting our momentous news we were calmly informed that they had all seen it coming for quite some time. Tessa and Beckey hugged and kissed Nancy, Mother had a little weep all to herself in the kitchen and Father, unflappable as ever, insisted that we celebrate with a bottle of his infamous elderberry wine.

The decision having been taken there was a great deal to be done and Beckey and Tessa were soon busy arranging and fashioning their bridesmaids' dresses, having quite rightly assumed that they would be called upon to perform that very important role. Meanwhile Mother fussed and worried while Father, keeping well out of the way, took the whole thing in his stride, however I knew he was pleased as I had long since come to realize that he had a soft spot for my Nancy. As soon as the news spread through the village we were congratulated by both friends and neighbours. As for me, I was rushed off to Cheltenham to be fitted out with a new suit, a journey taken under extreme duress as I had argued that the one I already had was quite fitted for the occasion, but the womenfolk would have none of it so at last, being greatly outnumbered in the matter, I finally gave in. Nancy's brother Ted, who I had wanted for my best man, had applied for special leave and this had been granted, subject of course to service commitments, and her father, who was to give her away, suffered the same fate as myself being rushed off to Cheltenham to be fitted out with a new suit. There seemed a hundred and one things to be seen to and arranged and time was short seeing that we had decided to get married in the August. In due course we went up to see Parson Collins at the parsonage to arrange for the bans to be called, and as was to be expected he gave Nancy and I a long talk on the sanctity of marriage and its commitments.

Then at long last the great day arrived the morning of which I feel I cannot let pass without comment. The cottage was in an uproar. In addition to the members of our two families there was a host of relations and a couple of our near neighbours who had come in to lend a hand. Bodies were everywhere and Mother, trying to do two jobs at once as usual, finally collapsed into a chair from sheer exhaustion and had to be revived with a stiff brandy. Aunty Maud, her sister from Sapperton, sat in a corner of the parlour relating to anyone who cared to listen to details of her operation, while Father's collie bitch Moss, not wanting to be left out of things, charged about getting under everyone's feet, seemingly not being able to come to terms with all the fuss and commotion that was disturbing her normal routine. Having sought sanctuary upstairs in my bedroom I struggled to come to terms with my recently purchased finery, shirt, jacket, and trousers feeling stiff and unfamiliar. Oh, how I would have loved to resort to my well-worn and comfortable Sunday best, however, I had long since realized that it was useless to protest in the face of such overwhelming female opposition. Father came up to give me a hand all the while giving me the sort of good advice which I suppose all well-meaning parents feel duty-bound to give on such occasions.

'John, my lad,' he said, 'there are some things that it is well that you should understand about women. They will cry for no reason at all and when you ask them why they are crying they won't be able to tell you. They will blame you for things they themselves have done and carry on at you for not doing things that you didn't even know they wanted done, but be patient with them, lad, and at the end of the day just take them in your arms and hug them; that's all they want.'

It was a long speech for Father to have made, and knowing the effort that it must have cost him to make it made me appreciate it all the more. Much later

41

in my life I was to learn this was expected of a lad's father when, with well-meaning fumbling and stuttering speech they tried to instruct their offspring in the facts of life, little realizing that their sons were as well if not better versed than themselves in such matters. At the last minute Mother announced that she couldn't find her cherished silver fox stole whereupon a frantic search ensued, the missing article being eventually rescued from the bottom of the garden where Moss was in the process of burying it. At last with peace restored and accompanied by the sound of the church bells, Ted and I walked to the church taking the short cut through Grinnels Orchard, leaving Father, Mother, Tessa and Beckey to follow the long way round on Len Hubbard's farm cart. Up in the belfry Ted Walker and his team of ringers were putting their backs into it being well fortified with liberal horns of cider from the jars which they had smuggled in before the arrival of Parson Collins, the ringing tending to lose its rhythm as the jars became emptier. Luckily, however, no one seemed to notice. The church was already full as Ted and I made our way down the aisle to the front pew, where kneeling, we bowed our heads in prayer before taking our seats to await the arrival of the bride, who was being driven to the church by her father in Percy Slatter's dog cart. Taking advantage of the lull in the proceedings I took time to have a look around. In the pew behind my mother and father sat proudly accepting the nods and smiles of congratulation from fellow villagers, while across the aisle Nancy's parents and their friends and relations gossiped amongst themselves, obviously well pleased with things. Down in his usual place by the door Zetter Parsons, all dolled up and grinning fit to bust, sat staring straight in front of him completely oblivious of the fact that he had forgotten to remove his bowler hat when entering the church. Fortunately this omission was soon put to rights by Alby Watnot, one of the church wardens, who with maximum discretion tapped Zetter on the head with his prayer book as he was passing.

On the subject of hats I have to admit that never had I seen such a variety as worn by the ladies that day. There were large-brimmed picture hats, close-fitting bonnets, straw hats with ribbons and others that sported a veritable profusion of artificial fruits and flowers, some even being topped with drooping pheasant's tail feathers which had a habit of brushing across the faces of the unfortunates sitting behind each time the wearer turned her head in conversation.

Suddenly I was brought back to earth by the shuffling of feet and the turning of heads as the organist struck up the wedding march. Rising, Ted and I joined Parson Collins at the altar steps where, not daring to look round, I waited as Nancy, on her father's arm, followed by Tessa and Beckey in their bridesmaids' finery, started their slow walk down the aisle. At last she was standing by my side radiant and beautiful in her wedding dress, so radiant that I could hardly bring myself to dwell on her in case she should see the tears of pride that were already beginning to moisten my eyes.

Of the service itself I remember very little, everything seeming so unreal, however apparently I managed to say all the right things in the right places, the placing of the ring on Nancy's finger and hearing Parson Collins say, 'I now pronounce you man and wife' finally bringing me back to reality. Afterwards, walking back down the aisle with my wife on my arm, I nodded and smiled at the sea of faces that beamed at us from either side, an ordeal that I wouldn't want to go through too often. Then it was out into the sunshine where Mr Pugh the photographer was waiting, a pompous little man who had been brought over specially from Evesham, and who with a great deal of fussing and tutting arranged and re-arranged us into groups, in between making innumerable trips back to his tripod-mounted camera, where he disappeared under the black cloth draped over the rear of it. How strange that after the passing of the years I can still see it all so clearly Nancy flushed with the excitement of it all, parents kissing and congratulating each other and Parson Collins, prayer book clutched to his chest, beaming as he elbowed his way into every photograph. It was indeed a day to remember.

With the church formalities over we made our way on foot down the village street towards the school where the reception was to be held, on our way calling in at the village hall where we received the good wishes of both staff and patients and where, much to our surprise Matron, human for once, presented us with a canteen of cutlery, a wedding present to which they had all contributed. Then it was on down to the school where another surprise awaited us. In the large hall all the usual school furniture had been removed and stored away and in its place were a double row of trestle-tables covered with snow-white tablecloths and laden with a variety of good things, the final touch being the floral arrangements set at intervals and obviously brought down from the Hall gardens, all of which we learned later had been at the instigation of Lady Armstrong, a kindly gesture for which we were most grateful.

43

Seated at the head of the table with my wife by my side I listened to the speeches of congratulations from relatives and any others who managed to rise to their feet and get a word in edgeways. Ted the best man had his say, paying glowing tributes to the two bridesmaids who giggled and blushed most becomingly, after which he added a few well-rehearsed tales about me when I was a boy, tales which I had forgotten or more likely were figments of his vivid imagination. Then came my turn. Rising I stood awkwardly shifting from one foot to the other, not being quite sure where to start or what to say, but somehow I managed to thank them all for coming and for the presents they had given us, my most sincere and heartfelt thanks going to Mr and Mrs Beasley for the gift of their daughter Nancy. Turning to Lady Armstrong I thanked her most warmly on behalf of us all for the part she had played in the arrangements, the expressed sentiments being received with sustained handclapping followed by 'For she's a jolly good fellow', a gesture that was greatly appreciated by her Ladyship judging by the smile on her face.

With the meal over tables were cleared and stacked against the walls, chairs being placed around the room to accommodate any of the older people who wished to take the weight off their feet. Glasses and tankards were replenished from the barrels brought in from the Drovers Arms and from the plentiful supply of bottles of home-made wine donated by friends, after which Nancy slipped away to change into something more comfortable, Lady Armstrong taking her leave of us at the same time. I escorted her to the door and after I had thanked her again she shook my hand and wished both Nancy and I well. Back in the hall Miss Amy Leadbetter, a spinster of the parish, was getting herself ready at the piano to provide an assortment of tunes to which we danced and jigged with great enthusiasm, and Zetter Parsons, by then not quite sure whose wedding he was at, insisted on playing the spoons, an act which he performed better drunk than sober. Harry Pugh, whose voice was well past its prime, entertained us with 'The Road to Mandalay' while Constable Hodges, not to be outdone, charmed us with a colourful but tearful rendition of a monologue entitled 'My faithful friend', an offering that caused the more maudlin of the guests to gaze sorrowfully into their beer mugs. However by far and away the best entertainment of the day was provided by Stodger Millett who to the dismay of the ladies had brought along his performing ferret. Unfortunately, however, it appeared that it was one of the animal's off-days as at first no amount of coaxing or threatening would induce the animal to leave the warmth and safety of Stodger's pocket to do its stuff, that is, until someone had the bright idea of giving it a sip of malt whisky which seemed to do the trick. Out on the floor it jumped, causing the ladies to emit piercing screams and run for cover with their skirts held high. Under tables and chairs it went evading all attempts at capture, while Stodger, with jacket discarded and sleeves rolled up and sweat pouring down his face, cursed and chased it in and out of the stacked furniture until at last, having left its cover, it was pounced on and placed in an empty cardboard box and locked away in a broom cupboard, the only casualties being two old ladies who had to be revived with tots of brandy. It was late evening before our guests finally began to depart and standing in the doorway Nancy and I thanked each one as they left for a truly memorable day, then, leaving friends and parents to clear up we quietly slipped away to Forge Cottage where we were to spend the night and for that matter live.

Lying beside Nancy in the room that had been mine since boyhood I realized the responsibility that now rested on my shoulders. From now on I had her to consider knowing that she would look to me to provide, love, and protect her. Half asleep she stirred and sighed almost as if she were reading my thoughts. Leaning over I took her in my arms, feeling her warm and supple against me, then trembling, we made love. This time there was no nightingale but it didn't seem to matter. Wrapped in each other's arms we lay through the long night and early next morning, with the sunlight streaming through the window, I went over and drew the curtains and stood looking down at the yard below. The warm red brick of the smithy was already aglow as the morning sun touched it and somewhere from the cool depths of Grinnels Orchard an early blackbird was in full song, its clear notes rising and falling above the chirpings of other early risers. In a strange way I felt in tune with it. This was also the beginning of a new day for me, the beginning of a new life. For a while longer I stood watching the morning breeze rustle the leaves of the bough of mountain ash nailed above the doorway of the smithy, then silently thanking that unknown blackbird who had welcomed the day with me I crossed over to the bedside where kneeling I gently fingered the loose strands of hair that lay across her face. Sensing my presence she stirred and opened her eyes. I shall always remember the picture of her as she lay with her golden brown hair lying in disarray on the snow-white pillow. Taking her in my arms I held her and just at that moment the tears came and I wept like a child. To this day I

45

don't know why, but I have a feeling that Nancy understood.

Meanwhile downstairs in the kitchen we could hear the rest of the family busy preparing breakfast, so using the water from the jug and basin on the washstand we made ourselves presentable, after which we dressed and went down to join them. There was a look of tenderness on Mother's face as she came over to where Nancy and I were standing in the doorway at the foot of the stairs. 'Welcome to the family, my dear,' she said, and it was with those few heartfelt words we started out on the first day of our lives together, the first day of a journey which we both hoped would be up a long, long road.

Chapter III

With harvesting done the year drew to its close and in the smithy we were kept working six days a week being mightily glad of Sunday rest. Nancy for the time being kept her job up at the Hall and Beckey, still searching, played the field and remained footloose and fancy-free much to the disappointment of Mother who longed to see her settled down with a good husband. As for myself, I was getting restless knowing that it was only a question of time before one way or another I should have to make up my mind as to which direction my sense of duty would take me. Talking it over with Nancy I tried to explain that there was a part of me that felt I ought to volunteer yet on the other hand I realized that she needed me at home. There were tears of course, but that was only to be expected, however, once she realized that in spite of any arguments to the contrary I had made up my mind to go, she seemed to come to terms with it. Mother she received the news in silence, expressing no surprise, almost as if she had been expecting it. Father took me aside and we discussed the matter during which he pointed out the for's and against's, adding that whatever happened the family would be behind me and that I had no need to worry about Nancy as she would be well looked after. In a selfish sort of way it was a great relief to have the matter out in the open. It helped ease the feeling of guilt I had been harbouring for some time so, having made my decision, I realized that the sooner I moved in the matter the better it would be for all concerned.

Taking the day off I travelled to Cheltenham and after being misdirected several times I eventually found the recruiting office where after joining the long queue of other hopefuls in the street outside I waited, finally to be interviewed by a sergeant and an elderly major who, judging by the row of medals on his chest, had already done his bit for King and Country. The outcome, for want of a better word, was that I was taken on for the duration of hostilities, choosing my county regiment, the Gloucesters, at the same time expressing a preference for anything to do with horses. So for the time being that was that.

Two weeks later I received orders to return to Cheltenham for a medical examination. Why they didn't give us one in the first place I failed to understand, however when I came to know the Army better I realized that they were never expected to do the obvious. The medical examination was an unforgettable experience. Standing in rows bared to the waist we dropped our trousers, not daring to look each other in the face as we awaited the arrival of the Medical Officer, who, with an air of 'let's get it over as quickly as possible' passed down the line prodding and poking, chests were tapped and eyes and ears given a cursory examination. Then, seemingly satisfied, he disappeared into an inner office leaving us to get dressed. During the long walk back to the station, and afterwards sitting in the carriage on the return journey, I fell to wondering if I had made the right decision. Perhaps if I had waited I might, in view of my trade, have been exempt, however I knew that I wouldn't have wanted it that way.

The next few weeks seemed to drag and so it was with a feeling of relief that I opened the official envelope that arrived by the morning post to learn that I was to report to Horfield Barracks, Bristol. On the morning of my departure I woke with a sick feeling in my stomach. This was the day that secretly I had been dreading, however, knowing that there was little I could do about it, I tried not to show my feelings for the sake of the family. Nancy came with me to the station. Surprisingly there were no tears, and standing on the platform we just held hands, finding ourselves at a loss for words. As the train pulled away I leaned out of the carriage window to wave to the forlorn figure standing dabbing her eyes, wondering how she would cope in my absence. Sitting watching the countryside slip by I was already feeling homesick, however, determined to put a brave face on things, I opened the window and let the cold air sting my face and before long we were at Pipers Crossing where the train stopped to deliver the two daily churns of fresh water and take aboard the empties. Mrs Underwood, the crossing lady, obviously having heard of my departure, came over to wish me luck at the same time enquiring if I would like a rabbit's foot to take with me, an offer I declined, thinking that perhaps it was a little too early in my Army career to need luck. In the early evening I arrived at Bristol and seeing no other means of transport available,

48

made my way on foot to Horfield Barracks, my first impression of which was one of extreme foreboding as, clutching my battered suitcase, I walked over to join other new arrivals who were waiting in small groups outside the guardroom. Standing and chatting amongst ourselves we were abruptly brought to order by a fearsome-looking Sergeant sporting a waxed moustache who, after taking a roll-call, marched us away to a collection of drab-looking brick buildings where he left us.

I have no wish, neither does it seem necessary, to dwell at any great length on my first few weeks in the Army. There were times when I was so homesick that I could have cheerfully walked out and caught the next train back to Lavington, however, once I got over the initial shock, I came to the conclusion that it was just a case of settling down and making the best of things. There were days of interminable drilling on the barrack square and training exercises in the surrounding countryside where, with rifle and bayonet at the ready, the main idea seemed to be to get us flopping down in the wettest, muddiest ground they could find. In off duty hours, of which there weren't many, I wrote long letters to Nancy, hers in reply going a long way to preserve my sanity. Missing her as I did I often lay in my uncomfortable bed at night aching for her and wondering if she too was thinking of me.

Amongst the batch of new intakes was a lad from Hereford called Charlie Bowers. He was about my age and for some inexplicable reason we struck up a friendship. It would be hard to describe Charlie. He was one of those enviable characters who appeared to go through life never taking anything too seriously, his wonderful attitude to things enabling him to see the funny side of most situations. His charm, however, was something else – a weapon he often used to good effect on the ladies. In civilian life he had been a carter and so naturally he shared my love of horses. In fact we soon found that we had a lot in common, the only big difference being the fact that he was as yet unmarried, something which surprised me knowing how fond he was of the ladies. As far as his home life went he said very little and I didn't press him on the matter, feeling that if there was anything that he wanted me to know he would tell me in his own good time. However I was glad that I had found someone like him, a mate with whom I could share things when the going got rough as it often did, and as time passed our relationship blossomed so that we became more like brothers than just friends, one of those things that in thinking back was probably brought about by the unusual circumstances in which we had chosen

49

to live and which we both shared.

Christmas 1915 and much to our surprise we were given seven days leave. Feeling strange and not too comfortable in my uniform I travelled home to Lavington eager for Nancy and, if only for a short while, to sleep between sheets instead of army blankets, and perhaps recapture some of the life I had left behind seemingly years before. It was Christmas Eve and as the train drew into the station the first person I saw was Nancy standing on the platform eagerly scanning the descending passengers. Suddenly she saw me and with outstretched arms ran the few yards between us, ignoring the knowing smiles and nods of some of my late fellow-travellers who by then were making their way to the exit. God, it was good to hold her again after all those long days and nights that we had been apart. Kissing away the tears that were running down her cheeks I tried to remember all the intimate things that I had wanted to say and which I had rehearsed on the journey, but try as I might, nothing came, however, just at that moment it didn't seem to matter. Then the voice of Alby Stringer brought us both back to earth. 'Ain't you two love birds got a home to go to?' all the time shaking my hand. 'How long hast got then, lad?' he asked, and when I told him seven days he added, 'then get thee off home and make the most of it.' So bidding him goodnight and wishing him a Merry Christmas we left the station and started up Two Hedges Lane towards the village, each trying to talk at the same time, there being so much to say. Standing at the door of Forge Cottage with one arm around her waist, I lifted the latch and quietly pushed open the door, and as I did so a shaft of golden lamplight lit our faces. The homely smell of burning logs and the lingering aroma of Father's tobacco came drifting out to meet us, and as we stood there I could hear the regular slow tick of the grandfather clock and the subdued hum of voices from the kitchen. Then Tessa followed by Beckey came into the passageway and we were hugged and kissed until at last I was forced to seek sanctuary in the parlour where Mother was busy tending the fire. Creeping up behind her I grabbed her round the waist whereupon she turned and flung her arms around me, at the same time trying to wipe away the tears with the hem of her apron. 'Welcome home, John.' She said nothing more but it was enough to let me know how much I had been missed. As for Father he just shook my hand before returning to his rocking chair. Looking about me I could see that the Christmas decorations were already up and the tree with its waxed candles and glitter was in its usual place in a corner by the window. Taking a sprig of mistletoe from a branch behind a picture, I captured Nancy in the kitchen where she had gone to help prepare supper. It was a long and passionate kiss that brought a rush of colour to her cheeks and loud ooh's and aah's from Tessa and Beckey. Then there was a special kiss for Mother, after which I chased the two girls into the parlour, their noisy protestations unconvincing as I was sure that they had had to run the gauntlet many times before.

With supper over we all gathered around the fire to talk and watch the ever-changing patterns and pictures in the glowing embers, the family naturally wanting to know all about my life in the Army and my friendship with Charlie, expressing the wish that they hoped to meet him one day. And so we sat late into the night, Mother turned down the wicks of the two oil lamps leaving the parlour to the mercy of the flickering flames that were leaping their way up the dark chimney, then just before midnight Nancy and I quietly left and made our way up to our bedroom.

Christmas morning and rising early, a habit I had been forced to develop during my short stay in the Army, I washed and shaved in the brick wash-house in the yard. Later, leaning against the wall at the bottom of the garden, I looked out over the fields towards Broadway, seeing an unchanging scene that because of its beauty and serenity is for ever etched upon my memory – the flat stretch of Long Meadow reaching down to the Evesham Road, the rise and fall of the land towards Aston Summerville and the Cotswold escarpment, a barrier where the soft undulating folds of the vale of Evesham come to a halt like a tide straining against the cliffs. Suddenly I became aware of someone standing behind me and turning, I saw that it was Mother who, unknown to me, had been watching from the kitchen window. 'Everything all right, John?' she asked. 'Yes,' I replied, 'everything is all right.' Then putting my arm around her I walked her back to the house knowing that in her love for me she would certainly have known what my thoughts were all about. Upstairs in our bedroom Nancy was bending over the washstand rinsing her face. Towel in hand she turned to face me as I entered. 'I love you, Nancy Mumford, more than you will ever know,' I said. Dropping the towel she came over to me. 'I love you too, John Mumford,' she said.

With breakfast over we all went to church calling in on the way to collect Nancy's parents. Passing the butcher's shop we stopped to exchange a word

51

with Mr Stait who shook my hand and wished me well, adding for good measure that he thought I looked a rare sight in my uniform and that my legs had taken most kindly to puttees, observations which Nancy took kindly judging by the way she clung to my arm. Settled in our favourite pew I looked around at the assembled congregation. Old Zetter Parsons was there in his seat by the door, an arrangement that enabled him to sneak out just before the sermon so as to be first down at the Drovers Arms. In the front pews Charlie Wilmore and his wife and children sat looking impassively into space while across the aisle Nacky Pitt and Shenna Lawson, also home on leave, mouthed their congratulations, indicating by various signs that they would meet me at the Drovers after the service, and I could do no more than nod my agreement. Before beginning his sermon Parson Collins, leaning over the pulpit edge, welcomed each serviceman by name, having a few words to say about each, a most embarrassing moment; at least it was for me. There in the semi-darkness, a darkness that was relieved only by the shafts of weak sunlight that were piercing the leaded windows, I fell to wondering just how many of us would be together in a year's time, Nathan Powell now lying in an unmarked grave far from the peace and quiet of his native village, having already paid the price. But pulling myself together I knew that no good would come of dwelling on what might or might not happen; whatever was meant to be would come about anyway so perhaps it was better to leave the future to look after itself.

After the service I walked Nancy home before joining Nacky and Shenna down at the Drovers Arms. But having been given strict instructions to be back in good time for Christmas dinner, and at the same time not wanting to appear unsociable, I stayed just long enough to share a couple of drinks with them before making my excuses and leaving. Luckily I managed to reach home in time to be present at the traditional carving of the goose as it sat on Mother's large willow-pattern meatplate, legs trussed and surrounded by roast potatoes and plump brown sausages. Sitting at the head of the table as was his privilege Father sharpened the carving knife on the steel before commencing to slice off portions of breast and fork them onto the proffered plates, where they were immediately surrounded by generous helpings of Brussels sprouts, roast potatoes, stuffing and gravy, the latter being one of Mother's specialities. Setting to with a will we began to do justice to it and for a while all that could be heard was the busy use of knife and fork and the occasional grunt of satisfaction.

With the main meal disposed of it was time for the Christmas pudding, an extra large one, made in an oversized basin which each year was borrowed from Mrs Lyes in the village. Placing it on the table Father poured a liberal dose of brandy over it, then taking and striking a match he set light to it, the blue flames hovering on the top and over the sides until, with a last flicker, they burnt out, after which Mother, by then flushed with success, went about the business of dishing out large helpings at the same time warning us to watch out for the silver threepenny bits she had put in at the mixing. And so, full to the brim and by this time devoid of all energy, we left the womenfolk to clear away and wash the dishes while we mere males dozed in the chairs by the fire.

The next day being Boxing Day we all went down to spend time with Nancy's parents and do justice to two fat hens that had been specially kept for the occasion, followed by more Christmas pudding and mince pies. Tessa and Albert, having arranged to spend a few days with his parents in Evesham, left after dinner and Father, Nancy and I walked with them down to the station to catch their train, glad of the fresh air and exercise, after which, back at the cottage, we relaxed to play cards and drink far too much home-made wine than was good for us, finishing up grouped around the fire each of us half asleep. At the end of the day, jolly but fairly steady on our feet, we lit the hurricane lamps and started for home passing as we went other cottages from behind whose drawn curtains the sounds of carols could be heard, and pausing for a moment to listen, I couldn't help but feel that the words 'Peace on earth and mercy mild' had very little meaning just at that moment.

All too soon my leave came to an end and once again I was back on the station platform saying goodbye to Nancy knowing this time that my next leave would no doubt be my last before leaving for France. We didn't speak of it but I was sure that she was thinking the same as me, however, as neither of us had the courage to put our thoughts into words the matter wasn't mentioned, which was perhaps just as well. Back in barracks I settled down to the usual routine of Army life, Charlie and his sense of humour helping me to cope with the feeling of homesickness that had bedevilled me since my return. Then, much to everyone's surprise orders came informing us that we were to be ready to move out at a moment's notice.

Two days later just as daylight was breaking we paraded on the barrack square in full marching order, stores and heavier equipment having already been loaded on a convoy of Albion lorries which had arrived on loan from Aldershot. After being briefly inspected we were marched down to the railway station where a special train was waiting in the sidings, and after travelling for most of the day and being shunted into innumerable sidings to allow the passage of other troop trains, we eventually arrived at Brockington in the New Forest where, detraining, we formed up in the street outside watched as I remember by a solitary policeman whose reason for being there escapes me. After a long and uncomfortable march through unfamiliar countryside we arrived at a canvas encampment set on a desolate heathland.

Chapter IV

It was now the spring of 1916 and for the next few weeks we carried out training exercises, spent hours on the rifle range perfecting the art of killing, had medical check-ups and generally got ourselves into a state of readiness. By this time our numbers had been swelled by the arrival of three batteries of the Royal Artillery and a battalion of the Hampshires, and no sooner had they got settled in than orders were posted that there was to be a big parade involving the whole camp.

When the day arrived it turned out to be a wet and miserable one as, led by the regimental band of the Hampshires, we were marched to a large recreation ground some three to four miles from the camp where in parade order we waited for over an hour in the pouring rain. With groundsheets draped around our shoulders we stood at ease while the rain dripped down between our tunic collars and necks to eventually find its way down to our middles. My boots, on which I had lavished hours of spit and polish, were sodden and covered with mud, and standing there watching the puddles form at my feet I wished myself anywhere but on that miserable recreation ground. All along the ranks soldiers, muttering under their breath, shifted from one foot to the other as the rain continued to come down like stair-rods, and it was only the fact that Charlie, who was standing next to me, kept cracking jokes that kept me going. At last it must have dawned on the officer in charge that something had gone drastically wrong for suddenly we were called to attention and marched back to the camp where, after being dismissed, we went back to our bell tents and hung up our sodden equipment on the hooks that were screwed into the centre pole. Later, sitting on the bare floorboards, wet and miserable, I could only assume that the general who was supposed to have inspected the parade had decided that it was too wet to venture out. Settling down we made the best of what could only be called a bad job, however, there was one ray of sunshine in the offing as shortly after our disastrous parade came the

55

news that we were to be given seven days leave before proceeding overseas, which meant only one thing – France.

As the train rounded the bend at the top of Stebbington incline, eager and excited, I leaned out of the carriage window to get a first glimpse of the familiar sight of the signal box at the approach to Lavington Station. With a squeal of brakes and a juddering protest the carriages came to rest at the platform, but even before they had done so I had half opened the door to eagerly scan the small groups of people who were waiting. Then I saw what I had been looking for and, jumping out of the carriage, I ran towards her, eventually holding her so tight that she had to beg me to let her go in order that she might catch her breath. The scent of her, the warmth of her against me, made me forget all else until a tap on the shoulder brought me back to earth and turning, I saw Herbert Tanner holding my rifle and equipment which in my haste I had left in the carriage. Poor old Herbert, in a way I was envious of him as, having failed his medical for the Army, he would be spending the rest of the war looking after Alby Stringer, the station master.

By then the crowds had gone, so taking Nancy by the arm we left the station and walked up the lane towards the main road. Now she was by my side my longing and need of her became almost too much to bear and somehow I felt that she was feeling the same. Reaching the top of the lane we stopped, and drawing her to me, I kissed her, the passion behind it seeming to stir her for without my having to put my thoughts into words she looked up at me and said, 'To hear a nightingale, my love, to hear a nightingale'. Crossing over the main road we made our way up the footpath leading to Taylor's barn, an old red-brick building that stood on the edge of a small wood. It was a place that we had both known since childhood, a secret world where in the past we had played out our fantasies and where each summer the sweet-smelling hay was lodged. Opening the creaking door we entered, the smell of stacked hay and oiled and greased farm implements greeting us from the depths beyond the faint light coming from the half-open door. In the silence we could hear the wind softly moaning as it made its way through loose tiles on the roofing, an eerie sound that caused Nancy to cling even tighter to me. Laying down my rifle and kit, I took her by the hand and led her towards the rear of the barn to a spot where a quantity of hay had fallen down from the loft above, where after reaching for the ladder we climbed into the haymow. She was trembling and I squeezed her hand to reassure her. Slowly we took off our clothes until at last we stood naked and unashamed. Taking her by the shoulders I gently lowered her into the bed of sweet-smelling hay where for a while we just lay locked in each others arms until at last the need for each other became too hard too bear. Feverishly and wildly we made love, all my longing and need of her, all my pent-up emotions were released as uninhibited she gave herself to me, and long after it was over and the fires quenched we lay with our two bodies entwined, heedless of the cold and darkness.

Just how long we lay there was of no importance. Time didn't seem to matter, however, forced to face reality, we at last rose, dressed and left the barn closing the door behind us before making our way back to the main road eventually to arrive at Forge Cottage, where we were received with open arms, even though at the back of their minds they must have realized that this would be my last leave before going overseas.

With so little time to spare, Nancy and I spent most of it walking the countryside and on my last day we took a nostalgic walk up Oak Hill where, content in each other's company, we sat enjoying the silence and solitude. Overhead a hawk hung motionless as it sought its prey below in the long grass of the hillside, no sound coming from its wings as it hovered, then, as we watched it suddenly dived earthwards and disappeared from our view. At the edge of the thicket a rabbit, full of curiosity, and looking as if it had overslept, poked an inquisitive nose out of its burrow, then, not even bothering to glance in our direction it scampered off down the hill in search of its breakfast. All around us the earth was alive with the freshness of spring. In the hazel thicket where on that June night so long ago Nancy had given herself to me for the first time, early bluebells had made a carpet on which the dappled sunshine danced and, in the trees above, birds busy with courting and nesting flew in and out of the branches, the joy of their being alive plain to see in their chirping and singing. Watching Nancy I could almost guess what was going through her mind. 'Do you remember the night we came here and listened to the nightingale?' I asked. Looking up at me, she smiled.

'So much seems to have happened since then,' I continued. 'There is one thing I want you to know and always be sure of. I love you now more than I ever did, if that be possible, but there will be times in the months ahead when you will have need of me and I shall be too far away. That's when you must cling to the memory of the good times we shared and this will give you the strength to carry on until I come home again.'

With eyes now moist with tears she raised her face to me and drawing her close I held her. The hawk had long since found other places to hover and seek his prey and the rabbit found other things to do. I knew she was crying; I could feel the wetness of her tears against my cheek.

Early the next morning I left leaving Nancy to sleep as I felt it better that way. Father walked with me to the top of the lane where, halting, he took my hand. 'Take care, lad, and may God watch over you and keep you safe.' Then, turning, he made his way back to the cottage where I knew Mother would have need of him. Once aboard the train and settled in an empty compartment I sat going over the happenings of the last seven days and giving thought to what might lie ahead. The countryside flashed by and at stations where we stopped people got into the carriage and others left, but I hardly noticed them.

And so after what turned out to be a long and tedious journey, I arrived back at camp in the early evening where after reporting in at the guardroom I made my way to the tent which I shared with Charlie and four others, only to find it empty, however, just as I was about to give up he appeared apparently having arrived back earlier. Fancying a mug of tea we made our way round to the back of the cookhouse where after sweet-talking the cook on duty we managed to scrounge a mug each, then it was back to the tent to share the sandwiches which Nancy had packed for me and talk. There was one thing that still puzzled me about Charlie and that was he rarely said anything about his parents or home life, the only thing he did disclose quite early in our friendship being the fact that he was single, however, having the feeling that there were certain things which he didn't want to discuss, I respected his privacy knowing that if there was anything he wanted me to know he would tell me in his own time.

That evening, having little else to do, we set off to walk to the 'Highwayman', a pub some two miles from camp, only to find on arrival that owing to a minor disturbance a few nights earlier it had been placed out of bounds. Now for reasons best known to himself this didn't seem to worry Charlie. Making his way to the rear of the building he knocked sharply on the back door which opened after a few moments and a female voice demanded to know who it was, a question that Charlie answered in a quiet whisper. However it seemed to do the trick for, opening the door wide, the landlady, for by now I had assumed that it was she, gave a furtive look around before ushering us inside and upstairs to her living quarters. Studying her in the lamplight my first impressions of her, I had to admit, were more favourable. She was an attractive woman who I judged was a little older than Charlie and watching them I had the impression that this wasn't Charlie's first visit. For a while the three of us sat talking and I learned that her husband was away in France in the Army and that she had been left to manage the pub. Other than that she said very little about her private life. After about an hour Charlie and she rose and, making their excuses, left the room and disappeared up a dark passageway leading to the bedroom, leaving me to draw my own conclusions. Lucky Charlie, I thought, but that is as far as it went. Later when making our way back to camp I tackled him on the subject of the landlady but got nothing out of him other than an admission that he had visited her before, presumably doing so when I was occupied with one or other of the many details we had to carry out.

Three days later we were rudely jolted out of our complacency by the news that once more we were on the move. Stores were packed and early one morning we were marched down to the railway station and after a short and uneventful journey found ourselves on the docks at Southampton where after detraining we formed up for roll-call, and were then left to our own devices. I managed to scribble a hastily-pencilled letter to Nancy, being lucky enough to chance on a friendly docker who promised to post it for me, after which Charlie and I managed to locate a Salvation Army canteen where, keeping a weather eye open for any prowling NCOs or officers we managed to down a couple of cups of tea and a few cakes. All around was a hive of activity. Agitated sergeants dashed about clutching sheaves of official-looking documents, dodging in and out of busy stevedores who, seemingly unaffected by their presence, swung stores and equipment into the holds of the waiting ships. Terrified horses, ears flat, nostrils flared and with the whites of their eyes showing were swung aboard in nets by the steam cranes. Twisting and turning they swung to and fro, being unused to not feeling the ground beneath their feet.

Late in the afternoon we were rounded up, checked, and put aboard the steamship *Pride of Dorset* which was moored alongside, and which we learned was bound for Le Havre. Once aboard and in the absence of any other more suitable accommodation we made ourselves as comfortable as possible on the open deck. Luckily however we hadn't long to wait as in the late evening the ship got under way and edged its way out past the boom at the harbour entrance into the dark waters of the channel. Orders had been issued that no lights were to be shown and in the darkness NCOs, still endeavouring to create some sort of order out of near chaos, stumbled over prone bodies. Charlie, however, true to form, had found refuge in one of the lifeboats that swung in its davits above where we lay where he was able to smoke and get an hour or so's kip. Huddled together for warmth with only our greatcoats for protection the rest of us spent a miserable night cursing and protesting each time one or other of our comrades was forced to make the perilous journey down to the ship's latrines. Then, with the first streaks of dawn beginning to show, we steamed into Le Havre harbour where much to our relief a hot meal had been organized. So with this and a couple of mugs of hot sweet tea inside us things began to take on a new light and it wasn't long before we began to feel normal again.

Confined to the ship we spent most of the day watching the activity taking place on the docks below. It was all new to us and even the air felt and smelt different, all this making us realize that we were now in a foreign country separated by a channel of heaving grey water that even in daylight looked most formidable. We spent one more night aboard in harbour and early in the morning of the second day we left and steamed up the Seine, finally to dock at a small harbour whose name I have long since forgotten where stores were unloaded, and after a brief rest we were once again on the march, this time to a camp some miles away where once again we found ourselves under canvas. Confined to the camp area and more or less left to our own devices, we found that there was very little to do, however it gave me the opportunity to write to Nancy telling her as much as I felt would be allowed about our journey so far, and assuring her that I was fit and well and not to worry as I had Charlie to look after me, the more intimate parts of the letter being for Nancy's and the censuring officer's eyes only.

During the next few weeks we trained and attended lectures on this and that but mainly on the subject of personal hygiene, great emphasis being placed on the methods of dealing with lice and other not too friendly parasites that we were reliably informed would be waiting for us up at the front. Apart from this and a few irksome camp duties there was little to occupy our minds. Fortunately, however, there was a YMCA hut where we spent most of our free time drinking tea and attending the occasional concert put on by one or other of the various units in the camp.

In late May we were on the move again. Marching south we passed through fields knee-high in waving grasses where the air was heavy with the scent of may blossom and cow parsley, and where in the deserted orchards the last of the apple blossom hung, the sight and scent of it all bringing back memories of the fields and quiet country lanes back home. We rested up in deserted farms where in the weed-strewn yards wagons stood silently, shafts down and noisy clucking hens, with no one to attend them, wandered in and out of abandoned buildings from whose windows ragged white curtains blew like flags of surrender, their late occupants having gone to join the army of refugees that was making its way to safety.

In one of the villages through which we passed a deserted blacksmith's shop stood hard by the roadside, its forge cold and unused as it waited for the return of the smith, and seeing it conjured up a picture of my father in his cap and leather apron bending over the glowing coals, one hand pumping the bellows, the other holding the long-handled tongs with which he held and turned the white-hot shoes in the furnace. Somewhere out there amongst the columns of frightened people the smith was perhaps thinking about his forge, wondering if it would still be there when he returned.

Marching on we slept and ate where we could, all the time getting nearer and nearer to the front, the end of our long march coming at Bayencourt where, unknown to Charlie and I, we were to get our first taste of war. Resting by the roadside we listened to the rumble of our guns as they pounded the enemy lines and watched the limbers and supply wagons as they weaved their way in and out of the columns of marching troops and streams of refugees who, silent and lost, trudged wearily along the dusty road. What a heartbreaking sight they made as they trundled their few possessions along in old prams and ancient wheelbarrows, a few of the more fortunate having carts drawn by lean, dejected horses, carts that were piled high with items salvaged at the last moment and on top of which the old and very young perched precariously, their faces devoid of hope as they moved mechanically down the road followed by the older children and their parents. A small dog, lost in all the confusion, chased up and down searching and barking, no doubt as frightened and confused as its missing owner. Strung out in single file on either side of the road we were powerless to help. A field ambulance threaded its way through, honking its horn, but no one seemed to take any notice, while further along a

61

column of wounded Tommies passed, their faces grey with dust and grime, their eyes dull and unseeing, the bandages they wore dirty and caked with congealed blood. This was the grim reality of war and from then on each hour of each day was to be filled with new experiences. We saw our first German prisoners in their field grey uniforms, young lads with the faces of old men who, much like ourselves, had been drawn into the maelstrom of war. I couldn't help but feel sorry for them, no doubt they too had wives, mothers, and sweethearts back at home who worried and prayed for them. In the fields to either side our troops gathered around cook wagons from whose blackened chimneys smoke rose. Battle-weary and worn out from lack of sleep many of them slept on the bare earth seemingly oblivious of the noise and bustle going on around them.

Just before darkness fell a halt was called and we rested up in a collection of deserted farm buildings where our cook wagon, having caught up with us, soon had a hot meal going. All through the night we lay listening to the guns, then at first light a battery of eighteen-pounders opened up from woods behind and we could hear the whine of the shells as they passed over on their way to the enemy lines. Charlie, on the scrounge as usual, managed to get hold of a plump chicken which, when duly despatched, plucked and prepared was roasted over a fire lit in the shelter of one of the barns. It had seemed a shame to kill it, however I consoled myself with the fact that at least it had given its life for its country.

The following night we had our first taste of trench warfare, a patrol being needed to reconnoitre the enemy lines and if possible bring back a prisoner or two. Charlie and I were detailed to take part, so with greatcoats and large packs safely stored to await our return we set off at dusk for the front line some two miles away. I find it hard, if not nigh impossible, to describe my feelings as we made our way in single file through the darkness. In moments like that fear had a tendency to take over. My stomach, usually quiet, rumbled and gurgled most alarmingly so much so that I began to fear that it would give the enemy notice of our coming. Cautiously we groped our way forward and except for the occasional 'Are you all right, mate?' from Charlie who was following immediately behind me, we went in complete silence. At intervals star shells lit up the landscape throwing everything into relief, giving us a brief glimpse of the havoc and desolation through which we were passing. What had once been gentle countryside was now stark and devoid of greenery, the few remaining trees standing gaunt against the skyline, their gnarled and splintered branches pointing upwards like old withered fingers. The earth, churned and degraded almost beyond recognition, was pitted with water-filled shell holes and abandoned trenches in front of which strands of rusting barbed wire hung from twisted iron stakes. There was a smell about it all, a strange unfamiliar smell that spoke of death, cordite, and damp, soggy earth, a taste of hell long before it was due. Half running, half slithering and sliding we somehow managed to dodge the many obstacles in our path, the sound of small arms fire getting louder and louder as we went, until at last to everyone's relief we slid down into a trench where a faceless figure wrapped in a blanket challenged us out of the darkness, the first sign of life we had encountered so far.

On we went sometimes ankle deep in mud and water until thankfully we arrived at our rendezvous where we were met by an officer of the East Lancs Regiment who briefed our own officer on the proposed raid. Standing waiting on the firing step I leaned against the sandbags watching as dark shadows passed below, the occasional 'Good Luck' or 'Don't forget to duck' confirming that the mud-covered figures were indeed human and not figments of my imagination. Close by my side Charlie pulled his steel helmet lower over his eyes, muttering 'I couldn't half go a bloody pint mate,' a request that absurd as it was under the circumstances certainly helped to relieve the tension.

As luck would have it we hadn't long to wait and on the whispered word of command we climbed over the parapet and made our way through a gap in the wire out into no man's land, managing by some miracle to avoid falling into any of the many water-filled shell holes on the way. Then suddenly a flare went up directly overhead lighting up the whole area around. Slowly it drifted to earth and diving into a nearby shell hole we crouched and waited, heads down as the enemy machine-guns opened up, spraying the ground in front of us, making it obvious that our patrol had been spotted. This was our first experience of being under fire and it wasn't a pleasant one. Peering cautiously over the rim of the crater I watched as one of our lads who had been caught out in the open endeavoured to reach cover, but he was too late as a burst of fire caught him and spun him sideways. Staggering drunkenly he clutched vainly at the air before falling face down in the mud and for the first time I experienced a cold clammy feeling in the pit of my stomach. I didn't know the man but watching him die made me realize the frailty of

63

humanity and for a moment my courage began to waver, until a voice behind me said, 'Stay where you are, mate, he never had a chance, poor sod.' Crouching and running we started forward again, and after what seemed an eternity we came across a gap in the enemy wire through which we dived to find ourselves in what we took to be an abandoned trench, and it was at this point that I realized that Charlie and I were alone, the rest of the patrol having gone on ahead to reconnoitre another one that branched off to our right. Suddenly another flare went up and by its light I could just make out a figure in a field grey uniform coming towards me, rifle at the ready. For a split second I froze, being unable to move either arms or legs, then, raising its rifle the figure pointed it straight at me. Instinctively closing my eyes I waited for the end. What went through my mind during those few moments I have little or no recollection; from behind me came the crack of a rifle and the figure staggered a few paces before dropping to the ground. Pushing his way past me Charlie bent down and examined the now still body then, turning, he said, 'Jacko', he always called me that in moments of stress, 'Jacko, that was a bloody near thing,' and it was then, realizing just how near I had been to death, that I leaned against the side of the trench and was violently sick. Of one thing I was certain: Charlie had saved my life, a debt that although I did not know it at the time I was never going to be able to repay. We didn't take any prisoners and thankfully most of our patrol made its way safely back to our billets where after a hot drink we got our heads down and tried to snatch a few hours sleep.

The next day the mail caught up with us and in it were two letters for me, one from Nancy and one from Mother. Tessa had got herself engaged to her Albert and Beckey had volunteered for nursing service overseas and was due to leave anytime. Harry Stevens from Little Didcot, a lad with whom I had shared my schooldays had been killed in action and Dewie Taylor and Bill Meadows, two grooms from the stables, and Pete Garnett and Harry Fieldman, gardeners from the Hall, had been called to the colours. Doctor Hemmings, having been wounded, had been discharged and was now back in Lavington and the hospital in the village hall was still going strong while some of the girls who had come to work on the land were being accommodated up at the Hall. As always Nancy's letters were comforting and very special and reading them I thought that perhaps after all there was some reason for all this suffering. Hopefully when it was all over we could all go home and take up where we had left off, however there was always the chance that time and circumstances in their perverseness might prove otherwise.

Just as June was getting ready to welcome July we moved up into the area around Ovillers where, judging from the activity taking place, it was obvious that something big was in the offing. Day and night, ammunition wagons lumbered their way towards the front and columns of fresh troops poured into the Somme district. During the last few days of June our guns pounded the enemy lines day and night giving neither us nor the Germans any rest. In the closing days we moved into the forward trenches where we 'Stood To', not then realizing that in the next few days we were to play a very small part in a great Allied breakthrough which we had been led to believe would shorten the war.

On 1 July the shelling ceased leaving an uncanny silence. Standing on the fire-step of the trench I looked over the devastated landscape seeing where in the near distance a few splintered trees stood out drunkenly against the summer sky, and perched in one of them a lone bird was trilling and preening itself, the sound sweet and clear in the unnatural silence, reminding me of home and that night so long ago when Nancy and I had lain in the hazel thicket listening to the nightingale. This of all times in life was the time to give serious thought to religion and the hereafter. 'Lead kindly light amidst the encircling gloom', how well I remembered singing those words in the church back home. Suddenly I began to feel afraid of death and in something akin to panic I wiped away the sweat that was beginning to pour down my forehead. Then a hand gripped my shoulder and a voice said, 'Steady, Jacko.' Slowly the panic left me; good old Charlie, I thought. All down the line men were taking puffs from cigarettes shielded in cupped hands. Men from the terraced houses of the industrial north and from the fields and cottages of Devon and Somerset stood waiting shoulder to shoulder with other young lads from the hills and valleys of Wales, the Highlands and Lowlands of Scotland and the green pastures of Ireland, all tensed and fearful of what they would be called upon to face in the next few hours. Not far away an unknown soldier started singing in a nervous high-pitched voice, 'Take me back to dear old Blighty, put me on the train to anywhere,' until the rasping voice of a NCO ordered, 'Silence lad, you don't want to wake the bloody Germans, do you?' And so we stood fidgeting with our rifles and taking quick looks over the parapet where through the gaps in the barbed wire we could just make out the unfriendly stretch of no man's land over which we should soon be crossing. Up and down the line officers were giving out last minute instructions and offering words of encouragement to young soldiers some of whom were facing fire for the first time, then the whistle sounded and with bayonets fixed we scrambled over the parapet led by our Company Commander, Major Glover. No sooner had we cleared our own barbed wire when all hell was let loose as the enemy machine-guns opened up. The Major was killed before he had gone a few yards and the first two ranks of advancing men went down like corn before a sickle. Diving into a convenient shell hole Charlie and I crouched listening to the cries of the wounded as they struggled for cover, many of them only to drown in the muddy water before help could reach them. Climbing out we stumbled on dodging and weaving through the smoke. Then I saw a gap in the enemy's wire in front of me. Gasping for breath and praying, 'O God, let me live, let me live,' I flung myself into the comparative safety of the trench where I waited for Charlie to join me, but he never came. Climbing back over the parapet the first thing I saw was a limp body hanging on the barbed wire and it was at that moment that the horror of it struck me: it was Charlie.

Dropping my rifle I crawled towards him, hoping against hope that he was still alive, but when I reached him I realized that death must have been almost instantaneous. Then a voice beside me said, 'Hang on, mate, I'll give you a hand to get him back into the trench.' There wasn't time to thank him and afterwards he disappeared. Kneeling beside the limp body I held his hand, calling out his name and not wanting to admit that he was dead. Not minutes before he had been by my side laughing and cursing. Dear God, I thought, what a bloody waste it all was. At last, realizing that there was very little I could do I felt in his tunic pockets and took out the contents, a silver watch and chain and a small bundle of letters. Suddenly a hand was placed on my shoulder and a voice said, 'Leave his identity tag, lad, there's nowt more you can do for him now.' It was our Company Sergeant Major. Choking back the tears I managed to ask, 'Why did he have to die for God's sake?' 'Because he was here, lad, because he was here,' came the reply. Reluctantly I got to my feet knowing that there was little else I could do. Then a sudden coldness came over me; gone were any doubts I may have harboured about killing another human being and, crouching in the entrance of an abandoned dugout,

I fired into the yelling faces that were now charging down the trench towards me, my actions purely mechanical.

Thinking back I have no clear recollection of what happened, everything seemed to be obscured by a red mist, then quite suddenly it was all over. Others who had taken part in that brief skirmish pushed past me and for a while I just leaned against the side of the trench thankful to be alive, then gathering up what little courage I had left I climbed over the pile of still bodies and after a while managed to catch up with the rest of the platoon. Further along we came cross a young lad from one of the Highland regiments who had been wounded in the legs and shoulder, and stopping for a moment, I rendered what first aid I could, waiting until the stretcher bearers came and took him away. I hope he made it; he had suffered enough.

The rest of that eventful day now seems like a dream. Perhaps it is just as well that I cannot remember it in detail, my only concern at the time being one of survival. All along the sector our troops were beginning to fall back, casualties were heavy and men were still falling. What had started out as a professed well-planned operation had ended up a disastrous failure. No doubt the generals who had planned it all, safe behind the lines with their maps and polished boots, would one day be able to explain why, in spite of the loss of thousands of lives, we had finished up back where we had started from Reaching the comparative safety of our own trenches we sought refuge in damp candlelit dugouts where all through the night we crouched while the enemy mortars pounded our lines.

For three days and nights we held on in spite of the constant shelling and counter-attacks, then mercifully on the fourth day orders came for us to move out to the rear. On the way we passed our relief, youngsters fresh of face and as yet unblooded and looking at them I thought of Charlie hanging on that barbed wire. He too had been young and fresh of face. I hope they recovered his body and gave it a decent burial. On our way to the rear we passed six tanks making their rumbling way forward churning up everything in their path while overhead two of our aeroplanes dodged in between the puffs of anti-aircraft smoke, the drone of their engines rising and falling as they weaved and dived. Pity we didn't have them with us on that first attack, I thought. Tired, dirty and battle weary we somehow managed to keep going. I was already beginning to miss Charlie, miss his cheerful companionship; he had always been around when I needed him just like a brother and I vowed there and then that once the war was over and should I survive, I would seek out his parents and return the personal items I had taken from his body.

In the vicinity of Bayencourt, well away from the front line and its horrors we took over the billets of the troops who had relieved us and for the first time in months we revelled in the luxury of hot baths and a change of shirt and underwear. I even managed to scrounge a pair of boots from a passing supply wagon, the soles of mine having decided to part company with the uppers.

For the next two weeks we relaxed and enjoyed the comparative peace and quiet then just as we were getting used to our idle existence, orders came for us to move to the Armentières sector where, in an abandoned farm some three miles out of town, we settled down and made ourselves as comfortable as possible. With restrictions relaxed, day passes became available on a rota basis and when my turn came I joined up with two other lads from Three Company for the trip into town.

The short journey took us all of two hours mainly due to the fact that we kept losing our way, and not being able to speak the language with any degree of proficiency, we found it difficult to ask directions, however, we managed to make it and on arrival our first thoughts were naturally of food. To this end we chanced upon a small eating place in a back street, the owner of which was an enormous French lady. Seated at a real table with a clean white cloth covering it, we ordered, not being too fussy what she might put in front of us. Luckily, however, what we had was good although I doubt if any of us could have put a name to it. With hunger satisfied we set out to explore the town ending up at the cathedral which by some miracle had escaped the worse ravages of the war, most of its paintings and statues having been hidden behind piles of sandbags. Sitting in the nave with the sun's rays lighting up the stained glass above the altar I tried to push the memory of the horrors of the last few months out of my mind. Then through the silence I heard the sound of shuffling feet and turning, I saw an old lady dressed in black with a shawl draped over her head coming down the aisle muttering to herself as she walked. Reaching the altar rails she knelt and crossed herself before taking a seat in one of the front pews where with her head bowed in prayer she remained motionless. Watching her I couldn't help but wonder if she was praying for the soul of someone near and dear to her who had become a victim of the senseless war I was involved in. Back outside in the daylight I turned to take one last look at the massive building with its weather-beaten stonework, wondering if it would still be there in another thousand years when future generations, having learned the futility of war, would turn the pages of its long history and come to know and love it. Regretfully the time soon came for us to return to our billets so for the time being we had to turn our backs on Armentières.

I have no wish, neither is it seeming, that I recount or dwell in any detail on my experiences during the last year or so in France. However there are certain things which even after the passing of the years I cannot erase from my memory. Often in the quieter moments I see again the columns of wounded, some with bandaged eyes, being led by others trying to breathe with lungs burnt by gas, and the bloated corpses of dead animals lying by the roadside. I see again the hastily-dug graves of comrades who had been buried where they fell, their only markers being crude wooden crosses fashioned out of discarded ammunition boxes upon which hung steel helmets now no longer required by their late owners, all part of the desolation of a war which had left ruined villages and shattered cities, places that had once been home to people much like myself who after it was all over would hopefully return to rebuild their lives. But clearest of all I remember Charlie, one of the many young men who had given their lives so that we should have a tomorrow. There are times at night when I wake in a cold sweat seeing him hanging on the barbed wire and in my dreams I call out to him. He does not hear me but just looks with eyes full of sadness. Perhaps with the passing of the years the dream will fade leaving in its place happier memories of laughing comrades who cheerfully went off to war as boys but who died or survived as men.

Arras, Ypres, Maroeuil and the great German offensive happened and passed into history. I was wounded twice and spent three months in a military hospital in Belgium with several fragments of shell splinter in my side, and it was while I was there that a letter reached me from home giving me the news that Tessa's Albert had been killed. She had evidently taken the news badly as was only to be expected, however what was more serious was the fact that she had withdrawn into herself making it difficult for either Mother or Nancy to help. Beckey was somewhere in France nursing, and Father, fit and as well as ever, was keeping busy in the smithy.

One afternoon while I was sitting reading and not taking a lot of notice of what was going on around me one of the nurses came over and told me that

I had a visitor. Wondering just who it could be I looked around but couldn't see anyone that I immediately recognized. Then, happening to glance towards the entrance to the ward, I saw someone standing there who I knew I must know but for the life of me couldn't put a name to. There was something very familiar about the figure in the grey nurse's cloak that was standing there hesitating and suddenly it dawned on me, it was Beckey. After the initial shock of seeing her had worn off we sat and talked and talked, there was so much I wanted to know and catch up on. She told me that she was serving in a hospital in another sector and by sheer chance had been given the opportunity to accompany one of the senior doctors who was visiting to attend a meeting. Looking at her as she talked I could see that she had changed, not so much in her looks, but more in herself; she had grown up but that was only to be expected in view of her experiences since leaving Lavington. However she still had that mischievous twinkle in her eye and that same disarming smile behind which as I well knew she was often wont to hide her true feelings. When the time came for her to go she leaned over and kissed me. 'Take care of yourself, John,' she said, 'they are all waiting and praying for you back at home,' and with that she left leaving me near to tears, and that was the last I was to see of her for quite some time. That same night lying in the darkened ward I fell to wondering just where our youth had gone; we all seemed to have grown up far too fast; perhaps it was the momentous events into which we had been pitchforked. Anyhow, not finding a satisfactory answer I gave up worrying about it and eventually went to sleep.

Chapter V

On 11 November 1918 we were in billets in the vicinity of Mons. One morning, sitting out in the sun, which although not having a great deal of warmth in it was at least comforting, I was halfway through reading Nancy's latest letter which had arrived with the ration lorry, when my attention was drawn to an Army Transport Corps lorry that was careering down the road towards me, its driver pumping his horn and shouting something at the top of his voice. By this time several of the other lads had joined me, curious to find out what all the commotion was about. Braking hard, the lorry drew level and some moments after came to a juddering halt, upon which out jumped the driver. 'War's over, bloody war's over,' he shouted, 'Armistice has been signed and all fighting stops at eleven o'clock,' after which, having delivered his message, he jumped back into the cab of his lorry and drove off at a furious pace still shouting and honking his horn.

For a long while after he had gone we stood unable to believe that at last it was all over, but it was and for the next few days we found it hard to get used to the silence which in a way was unnerving, much like the silence before an attack. It took quite a while for us to get used to the idea that there would be no more killing, no more muddy trenches, no more trips up the line, but once we had, our thoughts naturally turned to home and loved ones, our only concern being that by some stroke of misfortune we might be detailed to be sent forward as occupational troops. However, as it turned out our fears were groundless.

Christmas came and went, a parcel from home containing a cake and one or two other good things arriving just in time for us to celebrate the New Year. Nancy's letters, full of hope, asked when I would be coming home, a question to which as yet I didn't have an answer. Tessa had at last come to terms with the loss of her Albert and was slowly getting back to her old self again; Nacky Pitt had fallen somewhere in France while his lifelong pal Shenna Lawson,

71

having been wounded, had been invalided out and was now back at work on the estate. Nancy's brother Ted had been home on leave before sailing out to the Middle East and Harry Gibbons, who had survived the war, was back home doing his old job of gamekeeping, Sir Howard having managed to get him an early release.

In February the news that we had been waiting for came: we learned that we were to be shipped home, and after several false starts we finally began the long journey back. Packed into empty wagons we wiled away the time playing cards and making plans for the future, finally arriving at Boulogne where, after waiting for over two hours in the pouring rain, we boarded the steamship *Paragon*. In spite of the cramped conditions most of us managed to snatch a few hours sleep. Luckily the crossing was fairly smooth but I must admit that I was glad to see the dockside at Folkstone, glad to have firm ground under my feet but gladder still to relax in the empty custom shed where we had been billeted and where, after the customary roll-call we were left to our own devices. Ladies from the Salvation Army and the various voluntary organisations passed amongst us with tea, buns, and cigarettes, writing paper and pencils being available to those who wished to scribble a hasty note home. Not being sure of just how long it would be before my eventual release I hesitated to write to Nancy and my parents, however as it turned out things moved much quicker than I had hoped for as shortly after our arrival we once again boarded the train and headed for Bristol and Horfield Barracks from where it had all started.

Our stay there fortunately was brief. In a way I think they were glad to see the back of us and after observing all the usual formalities such as medical check-ups, and the handing in of equipment, we were finally given our discharge papers and railway warrants to our homes. Waiting on the platform for the train to arrive, and with the last three years now behind me, I suddenly realized what a nightmare it had all been and standing well back, I watched as the crowds of homeward-bound servicemen stood in knots laughing and joking amongst themselves. But for some reason I was in no mood to join them; all I knew was that I was going home and that there would be no more war, that part of my life was over. Later, sitting in a corner of the carriage I watched as the countryside slipped by wondering how I would cope with the brave new world that they had told us was waiting at the end of the line, the old one having disappeared in that now faraway summer of 1914. Lulled by the movement of the train as it counted out the rail-joints, I watched the rain as it ran down in rivulets on the outside of the carriage window, following each drop as it weaved its erratic way down to the sill where it joined others, only to be blown off by the gusting wind. Changing trains for the last leg of the journey I bade goodbye to my late companions and left them to travel on to fulfill their own destinies. Fortunately by then the rain had stopped and the sun had swept away the dark clouds sending them scudding away over the Malvern Hills. Was it a lifetime, I asked myself, since Nancy and I had passed that way in those now far-off days when, young and in love and filled with plans for the future, we had made that trip to Weston-Super-Mare?

At Pipers Crossing, Mrs Underwood was waiting to swing the gates back after we had passed, the engine driver giving her the customary blast on the whistle, then the long climb from Stebbington. Lowering the window I leaned out and was just able to make out Oak Hill now tipped with the rays of the dying sun. I wondered if the nightingale still sang there in the hazel thicket but then why shouldn't it? After all, it hadn't been to war. Home Farm came into view with its solid dependable byres and barns. No doubt Percy Slatter still farmed there; perhaps Nancy and I might borrow his pony and trap again and take a trip into Evesham, I thought. On we rattled passing the two fields tight to the railway line where Harry Pugh always kept a few sheep and a couple of pigs; it all looked much the same, the hand of war had not touched it to ravage and rape as it had done in France and Belgium, no ruined homes, no acres of shell-pocked ground, and looking at it brought back the memory of the deserted smithy by the roadside making me wonder if the blacksmith had ever returned to light up his forge again. In the countryside around him nature would come to the rescue as time passed and soon the scars of war would be hidden under fresh green fields where poppies would grow, but what of those of us who had survived those years of hell, what of the scars we should have to bear?

Lowering the carriage window I leaned out, the rush of the cold air stinging my face and bringing tears to my eyes. There was no one waiting for me on the platform. Hesitating with one hand on the handle of the door, I waited until the other passengers had alighted and made their way out of the station, not at that moment wanting to meet anyone I knew. I wanted to be alone for a while to get my bearings before stepping back into the past. By then, what little sun there had been had long since disappeared behind the woods above the village, and in the gathering darkness I stood alone on the platform watching the flickering red lamp on the rear of the departing train until it passed out of sight round the bend by the road bridge. Borne on the wind that rattled its way through the bare branches of the trees came the familiar scent of log fires that were burning behind drawn curtains and latched doors and so absorbed was I with these thoughts that I failed to see Alby Stringer who was standing watching me from the doorway of the porters' room. 'Good God, if it ain't John Mumford,' he called, 'where the blazes hast thee come from lad? Welcome home,' all this accompanied by vigorous handshaking and back slapping. Luckily after a few more, 'well I'll be damned' he walked with me to the exit, his parting words being, 'It be all over now, lad. Thank God you'm safe. Now get thee home, that wife of thine 'ul be waiting.'

Walking up the lane I couldn't hurry, my legs just wouldn't let me. Taking in deep gulps of the crisp, cold air, I desperately wanted to catch the scent of honeysuckle, but alas it was only February and summer would be a long time in coming; I could wait. On reaching the church I stopped for a while to catch my breath. All down the village street fingers of light reached out from chinks in curtained windows and behind me I could hear the measured tick of the church clock as it marked the passing hours unaware of the distance in time and the miles that had separated us since the last time I stood there. Moving on down the street I passed the gate of Nancy's parents' cottage and pausing wondered if I should call on them, but on reflection I thought perhaps not. For some reason, just at that moment, I felt like a stranger. Pulling myself together I turned into Callow Lane, my steps becoming lighter and more urgent as I did so, then rounding the bend by the pond I could see the welcoming lights from the cottage windows, and as I drew nearer I could just make out the dark shadows that, unaware of my presence, moved backwards and forwards behind the drawn curtains. This was the moment I had visualized and waited for on many a dark, lonely night and standing by the door, I raised the knocker knowing that all the people that I held most dear were there on the other side.

Suddenly the door was thrown open and there silhouetted against the lamplight was Nancy. For a brief moment we just stood looking at each other, during which time I heard Mother's voice enquiring who it was, then the flood of our emotions broke. Flinging herself into my arms Nancy cried and laughed both at the same time, 'Oh John, Oh John, thank God you are home.

Why didn't you let us know you were coming?' I didn't answer but just stood there holding her and stroking her hair, all the things I had so desperately wanted to say were choked by tears. Then Mother came over and with an arm about each of them we went into the parlour where Father was sitting by the fireside. Rising he put both arms round me. 'Welcome home, son,' he said, nothing more. Tessa, who had been standing in the background came forward, eyes moist. Perhaps just as that moment she was feeling that it should have been her Albert coming through the door. Turning, I took her in my arms and she buried her face on my chest and sobbed until Mother came and gently led her out into the kitchen, closing the door behind her.

Late into the night we sat around the fire talking of the old days and the war. Nancy barely left my side and, kneeling by the chair in which I was sitting, she held my hand pressing it to her cheek, and looking down at her I realized just how much I loved her. Tessa having dried her tears came back and joined in the conversation although we were careful to avoid any reference to her Albert, however, as it turned out we need not have worried as Mother told me later that she had come to terms with his death and had gone back to work for Mr Lewis at the village shop. There had been several letters from Beckey and in her last one she had said that she hoped to be home soon. Master Grahame and Charlie Wilmore had been demobbed and were now back, Charlie having taken up his old job as groom at the stables. Nancy, much to her and her parents' delight, gave us the news that her brother would soon be home from the Middle East and so it seemed that before long our families would be together once again.

Sitting looking at Mother I could see that she had aged. There were a few more grey hairs, a few more worry lines but I suppose that was only to be expected. Father on the other hand seemed to have weathered the storm well, sitting in his rocking chair by the fireside, pipe in hand, he looked much the same as he did on that never to be forgotten day when he and I had said goodbye at the top of the lane when I left for France. And so we talked. Mother now well into her stride dashed from parlour to kitchen and kitchen to parlour with plates of sandwiches and pots of tea, all the time chattering away nineteen to the dozen, a way she had when attempting to hide her feelings. On the wide mantleshelf above the fireplace the same old ornaments looked down, and in the corner by the window the pendulum of the oak grandfather clock swung backwards and forwards in its glass-fronted case just as it had done since the days long ago when as a child I had sat watching it until at last, mesmerized by its rhythm, I would curl up on the hearthrug and go to sleep. Thinking about it all I realized that it was in the continuity of it all that my roots were buried, the village and its familiar faces and places, the smithy, the cottage with its low-beamed parlour and the faded pictures that hung from its papered walls in quiet sepia serenity. Oh yes, I had a lot to be thankful for.

When I thought the time was right I told them about Charlie and his death. I hadn't mentioned it in any of my letters, feeling that it was better left until I was able to give them the details in person. Sitting around me they listened in tense silence while I told them about the events of that fateful day. It was hard for me in the telling and the memory of that evening stays with me yet. There are still times when I see, oh so clearly, the drawn and intent faces of my loved ones as they sat in the lamplight listening to my story. Then with the telling done we all sat in silence, each occupied with their own thoughts until at last Mother rose to her feet and started for the kitchen. As she passed behind me she stopped and bending forward she kissed me lightly on the cheek; there was no need of words between us as I was certain that she knew just what it had cost me to relive those terrible moments.

Settling down into the old ways wasn't easy and there were times when I would pause, sometimes in the middle of shoeing a horse, to think back. I knew that Father was watching me but he never asked any questions. Nancy, bless her, was also very patient seeming to understand that it was best that I be left to find my own way back and for that I was grateful. The weeks passed and slowly I eased myself back into the real world, but there was one chore that had been on my mind for some time and that was the promise I had made to myself and Charlie that if I survived and returned safely I would seek out his parents and return the watch and letters I had taken from his body on the day he was killed. Alone in the bedroom I took them out of the drawer of the old dresser where they had lain since my return and realizing that I needed to have an address I took one out and read it, then, sifting through the rest I noticed one that was written in a different handwriting to the others. Taking the single-page letter from its envelope, I saw that it was signed 'all my love, Aimee', and on reading it I gathered that there had been some sort of understanding between her and Charlie, however, tired of waiting, she had found someone else and they had got married. Poor old Charlie, I could imagine how he must have felt the day he received that letter, his world must have collapsed. It was strange that he never once mentioned anything to me about having a girlfriend but no doubt he had his reasons.

Carefully putting them back into the drawer I sat for a while planning what I should do, the outcome being that one Saturday morning, after carefully wrapping up the watch and letters, I took a train for Hereford where on arrival I sought directions to Ryeland Street which was the address given in the letters. After about half an hour's walk I arrived at Number 29 and standing on the pavement I took stock of the house that had once been Charlie's home. Paint was beginning to peel from the door and window frames and the lace curtains that covered both upstairs and downstairs windows seemed to be signalling that the occupants wished to be left in peace.

For a moment I hesitated, uncertain what to do next, however having come thus far there was no point in giving up, so standing on the doorstep I grasped the knocker and let it drop with a thud. For a while nothing happened then through the frosted glass door panels I could just make out the blurred outline of an approaching figure. Suddenly the door opened and I was confronted by a woman who I immediately took to be Charlie's mother. She was small in stature and I guessed that she must have been in her late forties, although not being in any way an expert in the matter of judging women's ages I could have been wrong. Her face was a strong one and although etched with worry lines it was plain that in her day she must have been quite a beauty.

All this I took in at a glance, then feeling that some explanation for my visit was needed I managed to introduce myself and state the reason for my appearance at her front door. When I had finished she seemed to relax and holding out her hand said, 'Come in, I have been expecting you,' a statement which took me completely by surprise seeing that the only people I had told of my intentions were Nancy and my family. However, feeling that perhaps she could explain later, I followed her along a dark passage and eventually into what I took to be her front parlour. After seeing me seated and a few remarks about the weather she made her excuses and left, returning shortly afterwards with a tray upon which were two cups and saucers, a milk jug, and a brown china teapot wrapped in a green knitted tea cosy which she placed on a side table. Up until then little or nothing had been said about the reason for my visit. Sipping our tea we sat in nervous silence waiting for each other to start up the conversation; it was an awkward few minutes.

Just as I was beginning to feel decidedly uncomfortable she started to tell her story and as her tale unfolded I learned that Charlie's father had passed away less than a week after the news of his son's death had reached him. Apparently they had been very close and the shock had been too much for him. One morning in the early hours he had died quietly in his sleep and since then she had lived in the house alone. Her parents were still alive and lived up north in Newcastle upon Tyne but although they kept in touch by letter it was some time since she had seen them.

Then she told me about Aimee, the girl mentioned in the letter about which I wasn't supposed to know. It appeared that she had been a childhood sweetheart of Charlie's and it had been the wish of both families that one day they would marry as indeed they might have done had it not been for the war, and it had been on Charlie's insistence that they wait. The rest of course I knew; tired of waiting she had found someone else and they had married. What of course Charlie didn't know, and for that matter neither did I, was that she had given birth to a baby daughter, a child that was undoubtedly his. As luck would have it the husband accepted the situation and agreed to bring up the child as his and eventually they had moved away and as far as Mrs Bowers knew they were living in London. Listening to her I couldn't but wonder why she had never told her son; perhaps she had only learned about the child later by which time it was too late.

Whatever the reason was I didn't intend to make it my business to query it. Taking the bundles of letters and the watch from my pocket I handed them to her, then, carefully choosing my words, I began to tell about my friendship with Charlie and of his death during which she sat staring into space, her hands folded on her lap. I had expected tears but none came. With the loss of both her husband and her only son she had probably hardened herself against any show of emotion, a bit of her having died with each of them.

At last I came to the end of my story and for a while we just sat there each absorbed in our own thoughts, then rising from her chair she went over to an oak desk that stood in one corner of the room and opening one of its drawers took out an old shoebox, the lid of which was secured with blue ribbon. Without saying a word she came back and sat beside me and we spent the next hour on a nostalgic journey into the past. As each faded and creased photograph was taken out and handed to me she told me stories of summer holidays long ago when the three of them had picnicked on the sands, each photograph in a way being a page out of her life. Watching her as she relived those happier days, I could see that she was just another lonely woman who would spend the rest of her days wondering what might have been.

At last the time came for me to leave; she came with me to the gate. 'Thank you for coming,' she said as she shook my hand, 'and thank you for the friendship that you shared with my son.' Looking at her as I held her hand I wished with all my heart that I could have turned the clock back and restored things to what they had been, but the past was the past and however lonely her life would be from now on it had to be lived. Letting go of her hand I turned and walked briskly away, hoping that she wouldn't see the tears in my eyes. At the bottom of the street I stopped and looked back at the lonely figure in a flowered pinafore standing at the gate watching me, and although up until then I hadn't given it a thought, it was to be the last time I should see her.

It was a sad journey that I made back to Lavington, realizing as I did that this was the last chapter in a very sad story. Little did I know that fate has a habit of proving us wrong and as you will see the future was to hold the answers to what were as yet many unanswered questions. Nancy was waiting for me when I reached home eager to learn how I had got on and what Charlie's parents were like. Slowly and carefully I went over the events of the day leaving nothing out. There was no joy in the telling, in fact, it made us both feel sad, however, I drew great comfort from the fact that at least I had kept the promise I had made to myself and my friend in that muddy water-filled trench in France.

The weeks passed and life and events in the village settled themselves back into an almost familiar routine and there was even talk of a cricket match with Kempston-under-Bredon, however, there was one thing that was causing the family concern. Watching Father at work we could all see that he had lost a lot of his usual energy; frequently he would down tools and go outside and sit on the bench, something that was most unlike him, so after talking it over between ourselves we decided to get Doctor Hemmings to check him over. Being the stubborn man he was he took a lot of persuading but at last he gave in and after completing his examination the doctor told us that he was going to arrange for Father to see a specialist at Cheltenham Hospital and although we taxed him in the matter he wouldn't commit himself saying that he would rather leave things until he had the specialist's report.

In due course Father went into hospital. Needless to say we were all worried and it came as a great relief when, after three days, we went by train to collect him. Luckily before we left the hospital we managed to have a word with the specialist who told us that he had diagnosed a slight heart condition and that in view of the nature of Father's work it would be as well if he took things easier, or better still give up altogether, advice that came as a shock to us all. However, after a great deal of persuasion he finally agreed to hand over to me and although I had always known that one day it would happen I would rather it had been under different circumstances.

And so we entered into the new order of things, continuing to take our ritual morning and afternoon tea breaks. Sitting on the old bench seat by the forge Father, at the appointed time, would take out his watch from his waistcoat pocket, flip open the cover and give a pronounced grunt just to remind me that it was time to brew up, then taking the old mug down from the shelf above the workbench, he would place it handy before lighting up his pipe. There we both sat talking of this and that until feeling that we had wasted enough time he would take another look at his watch before rising and washing out his mug in the bucket of lukewarm water standing by the forge. In respect for his feelings I saw to it that he was involved in many of the smaller jobs which required the minimum of effort on his part, making sure that when anyone came for advice he did the talking. Thankfully the arrangement seemed to work and as the weeks passed we accepted our change of roles and were happy in the working of them.

Slowly the world eased itself back into some semblance of normality. In the village there was once again talk of resuming the annual cricket match with Kempston-under-Bredon, although sad to relate, Tiny Larner, their captain, who we had entertained in those halcyon days before the war had been killed in France just one week before the armistice was signed. Two more of the lads from our little community hadn't made it back, Walter Richards from Leyfield Cottage and Harry Fieldman, one of the gardeners from up at the Hall. Len Hubbard, back from serving as a special constable in Gloucester, was already talking of putting his old horse out to grass and getting himself, as he would say, one of them newfangled motor vans. As for the village hall, its services no longer required, it had resumed its original role in the community, a permanent record of its former occupants being enshrined for ever in the many sepia photographs that for years afterwards held pride of place on many a cottage mantleshelf.

The summer of 1919 came bringing promise of sultry days and long hot evenings. Often when work was finished Nancy and I would sit at the bottom of the garden watching the velvet shadows deepen over the hills above Broadway. Memories of the war and its horrors were already beginning to fade and in the outside world houses were once again becoming homes as returning servicemen took up the threads of life.

In the June the village held a belated victory celebration which took the form of a carnival procession of decorated wagons led by the Alderton Brass Band, followed by various sporting events held on the cricket ground; Nancy and I played our part by organizing the three-legged race, the egg and spoon race, and the sack race, all three events being greatly enjoyed by both children and their parents. Master Grahame and his fiancée, a charming, elegant lady who it was said he had met in London during the war, mingled with the crowds, passing the time of day with all and sundry. To us they seemed a well-matched couple and we were glad to receive them into our little community. At the far side of the ground a large marquee had been erected inside of which on trestle-tables were displayed a variety of fruits and vegetables and home-made produce all of which had previously been judged by Lady Armstrong and her committee, and awards given. Alongside was the beer tent outside of which Charlie Wilmore and his missis and kids stood in earnest conversation with Doctor Hemmings and his good lady, Charlie having acquired a dashing moustache of which he was very proud, judging by the way he kept stroking it with the back of his hand. Under an elm tree that bordered the ground Twitcher Morris and Stodger Millett sat watching over a prone Zetter Parsons who, having imbibed too freely, was lying in a state of blissful inebriation, one hand clutching a stone cider jar, his long white beard tucked into the top of his waistcoat. Leaving Charlie Wilmore to join the rest of his drinking companions inside the beer tent Doctor and Mrs Hemmings toured the ground stopping now and then to chat with one or other of the villagers, he leaning heavily on a stout walking stick to ease the strain on his leg, a legacy of his service to his country, but there he was one of the lucky ones.

For a brief moment, free from their journey into eternity, the ghosts of Nathan Powell, Walter Richards, Harry Stevens, Nacky Pitt, Harry Fieldman and Tiny Larner looked down. It was sad that they could not be there to meet and once more enjoy the company of old friends. No doubt as the years passed the memory of them would grow dimmer and dimmer until at last all that would remain would be names carved for posterity on the village war memorial. In spite of the talk there was no cricket that summer, the village as yet not having settled down to its peacetime routine.

Autumn came and the evenings began to draw in, the glossy green leaves along the lane having already begun to take on a golden hue as they hung waiting for the first chill winter winds to shake them from the vantage points from where they had watched the crisp days of spring and the long hot days of summer come and go. Tessa much to our surprise and delight announced that she intended to marry Arnold Lewis from the village shop, his wife having passed away the previous summer, and on the same day we received a letter from Beckey containing the good news that at last she was coming home. So it was that in spite of the partings and heartache of the past years it seemed that we should soon all be together again.

One evening in late September Beckey walked in unannounced, taking us all by surprise. Putting her battered suitcase down she stood in the doorway, arms reaching out to Mother who rushed to her and they clung to each other, both of them near to tears, while Father and I stood to one side, all too aware that it was a special moment that belonged to mother and daughter. Long after supper was over we just sat and talked and how the tongues did wag, there was so much to catch up on. The news of Tessa's forthcoming marriage took Beckey by surprise, although she agreed with us that in spite of the difference in ages she and Arnold would be good for one another. Then in the early hours of the new day, hardly able to keep our eyes open, Nancy and I made our excuses and went on up to bed leaving Father, Mother and Beckey to welcome in the small hours, happy in the knowledge that, if even for a short while, the family was once again gathered round its own fireside.

Early in December a belated Victory dance was arranged at the village hall, an event which families from the village and surrounding farmsteads attended. Inside the hall young girls, in best party frocks, some sporting the latest bobbed hairstyles, cast hungry eyes over the eligible young men, then with partners chosen, they waltzed and foxtrotted, some even attempting the new Charleston dance which was becoming all the rage. Beckey having found herself a beau in the shape of one of the Collins boys from Bank Farm was in a happy mood as she showed off her paces, while around the edge of the dance floor on seats provided, the older inhabitants sat scandalizing and watching. Stodger Millett, recently widowed, sat chatting to Eli Small, both of them now beginning to show their age while Twitcher Morris, free for a while from the clutches of his possessive wife Maggie, twirled around the floor with buxom Floss Reynolds, one of the land girls who after the war had decided to stay on in the village. Side by side in a quiet corner Nancy and I sat with our parents, neither of us being over proficient in the art of dancing. Good with a hammer and anvil I may have been but my footwork left a lot to be desired. Suddenly she stood up and taking me by the hand said, 'Come dear, I have something very important to tell you.' Full of curiosity as to what it might be I followed her outside where in the cool of the night we stood leaning against the wooden fence that enclosed the adjoining paddock. Taking her in my arms I demanded to know what it was that was so important that it necessitated me leaving the warmth of the hall to stand in the chilly night air. Looking up at me with eyes bright and shining she calmly announced, 'You are going to be a dad, my love.' It took a few moments for her news to sink in and when it had I hugged and kissed her until in sheer desperation she had to beg me to stop in order that she might catch her breath. 'Have you told your parents yet?' I managed to ask in between kisses. 'No, my love,' she replied, 'you are the first to know and that is as it should be. Oh John, I am so happy,'

Back inside the hall we sought out Nancy's parents and mine to break the good news to them, embraces and congratulations followed so much so that people started to wonder what all the excitement was about, then, climbing up on to the stage, Nancy's father motioned for the band to stop playing and called for order. Drawing himself up to his full height he began, 'Friends, I have some very important news for you. John's wife, our Nancy, has just told us that she is with child, our first grandchild.' Well, what with all the cheering and handclapping you would have thought that he had made an announcement of national importance. Nancy blushed becomingly whilst I, with head hung, shifted from one foot to the other, not being sure just how a prospective father should behave.

Aided and abetted by time the old clock in the parlour ticked away the hours and slowly the days and weeks passed. Nancy gave up her job at the Hall and stayed at home to help Mother who secretly loved having her, fussing and protecting her like a hen with one chick, but Nancy took it all in good part and never had I seen her so happy. There were of course the inevitable discussions about names, the list becoming longer and longer until at last we had to put an end to it by announcing that we had decided to wait until we saw whether it was a boy or a girl before making the final choice.

Christmas came and went and in the February Tessa married her Arnold, the ceremony taking place at the Register Office in Evesham. It was a quiet, informal affair with only members of the family present, but that was the way she and Arnold wanted it. Afterwards we returned home where Mother, with the help of Beckey and Nancy, had laid on a small reception. It all went off very well and Tessa looked the picture of happiness. There was to be no honeymoon and much as Nancy and I had done they spent their first night at Forge Cottage after which, on the following day, we all helped to move Tessa's few possessions to her new home at the shop. At first it seemed strange not having her at home and Mother took quite a while to get used to the idea, however as we pointed out, Tessa was only a short distance away up the village street.

Nancy's brother Ted, having finished his time in the Navy, had got himself a job in the new powerhouse that Sir Howard had had built adjacent to the cricket ground to provide lighting for the Hall, the church, the stables and the village hall, the rest of us being quite content to carry on with oil lamps as we had always done.

After much discussion and meetings in the village hall it was decided to have a war memorial erected at the top of the village where the road from Leyfield meets Nutmeadow and in due course the work was carried out. It was a simple pillar and cross of Cotswold stone mounted on a granite base on which were carved the names of those who had given their lives. It still stands there to this day in its carefully tended plot and many are the strangers who pause for a moment to read the names and pay silent tribute to those long ago heroes who had left the village with such high hopes, never to return. On the day of its dedication, a service was held, the church was packed and amongst the congregation were Sir Howard and Lady Armstrong, she still retaining that air of dignity that was so characteristic of her as she sat soberly dressed in black as fitted the occasion. As I looked around it was comforting to see so many of the old faces, sadly, however, some were missing and it was to these that we had come to pay our respects and remember.

The seat at the end of the pew hard by the South door was empty and it was strange not to see old Zetter sitting there, head bowed, eyes closed, as he waited for an opportunity to slip out and make his way down to the Drovers Arms, but he wasn't far away – just a few paces from the North door where a freshly-turned mound marked his last resting place. At the Drovers Arms his empty chair still stood in the inglenook. No one sits in it now and there are those that swear that at times they have seen it rocking gently backwards and forwards.

Down at the railway station Alby Stringer was still station master, ably assisted by Herbert Tanner, a new lad having been taken on to replace poor old Nathan Powell. All things considered the years had been kind to those of us who had survived the war, but in our complacency we failed to hear the words of warning that fate was whispering, and had we but known it some of the generation to whom we had bequeathed our hard-won peace would, in the not too distant future, be called upon to make the same sacrifice.

That summer the cricket team was reformed and I managed to get selected for the second eleven the only reason for this being that they were short-handed, however, it was a step up from being scorer. Luckily other villages were now seeking fixtures so we managed to arrange quite a few local games.

At home things were much the same although we had noticed of late that Beckey was getting restless. We didn't challenge her in the matter, knowing that even if we had she would have been unable to give us a reason. Since her return she had filled her time doing relief work in local hospitals but it was plain to see that this was not enough. No Mister Right had yet appeared on the scene and Mother was beginning to lose all hope of ever seeing her settled down, however, what we didn't know at that time was that she had applied for a nursing post in Canada, no doubt seeing it as a new and exciting challenge. The day the news of her acceptance came she calmly announced that she would be leaving about three weeks later, by which time all the formalities would have been completed. To say that we were all shaken by her news would be to put it mildly, although to be fair we had for some time suspected that something like it might happen, but Canada, that was something different. Luckily, however, Mother put on a brave face and although once again her family was being torn apart, realizing the inevitability of it she gradually came

85

to terms with the fact that her beloved Beckey would soon be far away across the sea in a strange land, the distance that soon would separate them being greatly magnified by the heartbreak of parting.

The night before her departure the family gathered in the parlour, Tessa and Arnold were there and so, perhaps for the last time for quite a while, the family was complete around its own fireside. The conversation, such as it was, centred around village gossip, none of us wanting to broach the subject of the coming day, this being mainly for Mother's sake as we could all see how hard she was taking it. That night she had very little sleep and we could hear her down in the parlour rocking backwards and forwards in Father's chair. Nancy wanted to go down to her but I persuaded her not to, explaining that she was best left alone to prepare herself for the coming morning when she would have to face the moment of parting.

We all arose early that morning and after loading Beckey's few suitcases on to Father's wheelbarrow, we went with her down to the station where, waiting for the train to arrive, we did our best to lighten the atmosphere, but I must admit with very little success. Alby Stringer came over to wish Beckey well as of course news of her departure for foreign parts had already gone the rounds of the village. There were so many things we all wanted to say but in the strained atmosphere that existed we forgot most of them, only remembering long after the train had gone. However there was one thing in which we were all in complete agreement: even if we had been able to persuade her to stay it wouldn't have worked out, she would have been like a caged animal and even her love for us all wouldn't have been enough to quell that restless spirit that was taking her away. With suitcase stored safely on the luggage rack Beckey leaned out of the carriage window and we each embraced her in turn. Slowly the train pulled out. 'I'll write, Mum, I'll write,' she said through her tears and then she was gone and we stood watching until the last carriage disappeared round the bend by the signal box, after which we left and made our way back to Forge Cottage. There was a strange silence everywhere and for a while there would be an empty place at the table, but we consoled ourselves with the fact that life has to go on. Time, they say, is a great healer.

As summer got into its stride we celebrated the wedding of Master Grahame and his fiancée Miss Ruby Wallace. Not before time, we all thought. It was a grand occasion, the village being hung with flags and bunting, the Alderton

Brass Band having been engaged to lead the procession of carriages from the Hall down to the church, the inside of which was filled with a great profusion of flowers, the breath of them filling the air with summer fragrance that drifted out to mingle with the quiet sounds of a summer's day and the hum of conversation from the arriving guests as they descended from their carriages. Every pew in the church was occupied, the whole neighbourhood, or so it seemed, having turned out to witness the proceedings. In the choir stalls many of the young lads that were had now moved to the back pews, their voices broken, and in their places were others who at the outbreak of war had been just babes in arms.

What an unforgettable sight it all made: the bride radiant in her wedding dress with its long white train, a train that had so carefully been carried into the church by the two little attendants; the bridegroom immaculately turned out in grey morning suit; and the best man, a friend of the bridegroom, resplendent in the uniform of Master Grahame's late regiment. Standing behind her, the bride's father, a very distinguished looking gentleman, was keeping an eye on the two young attendants who, duty done and slightly overawed by the occasion, were tending to fidget, not that anyone else took a great deal of notice being far too busy gawping at the fashions that the guests from London were wearing, Mother and Nancy of course were in their element, no doubt planning how soon they could get busy with needle and thread and watching it all made me think back to the day when Nancy and I had stood at the same altar and of all the things that had happened since. Proudly the newly-weds walked back down the aisle acknowledging the smiles and nods of the villagers, their adopted family, the responsibility for whom they would carry for the rest of their lives. Up in the belfry with cider jar handy and still in charge Ted Walker waited for the signal to tell him that the bride and groom had emerged through the North door, and when this had been given a merry peal was soon ringing out over the countryside.

After the usual photographs and exchanges of congratulations, which of course included kissing the bride, the bridal pair and visitors got back into their carriages for the short ride back to the Hall where the reception was to be held, leaving the rest of us to make our way down to the village hall where a separate 'do' had been laid on; and what a 'do' it turned out to be, never before had we seen such a spread or such a quantity or variety of liquid refreshments. Sitting down we set to with a will to do justice to it.

Time passed quickly and at six of the clock word arrived that the bride and groom were leaving the Hall for the station where they were to take the train for London. Leaving the festive table we all trooped down the lane and gathered in the station yard to await their arrival. It wasn't long before, with a clatter of hooves, a rumbling of carriage wheels and with all the grandness of a Lord Mayor's show the carriage bearing Master Grahame and his new bride swept into the yard and came to a halt outside the entrance to the platform. In the carriages that followed, Sir Howard and Lady Armstrong and their guests drew up behind the grooms dashing to hold horses heads and lower carriage steps, all this activity being accompanied by prolonged cheering from the assembled villagers. Inside the station, on the flower-bedecked platform, Alby Stringer in his best uniform and sporting a white carnation in his buttonhole dashed about dusting seats and organizing his two porters, while at the head of the train the gleaming engine waited, its front decked with a garland of flowers that someone had tied to the boiler door handle. Bemused and excited passengers welcoming this unusual break in their journey leaned out of their carriage windows to get a glimpse of the bride as she made her way to the reserved first-class carriage at the rear. With a short blast on its whistle and a 'Right away, Mr Hawkins' and a 'Thank you, Mr Stringer' the train slowly pulled out of the station to the accompaniment of music from the Alderton band and loud cheers and clouds of confetti from the onlookers. Chatting and laughing we all returned to the village hall to continue the celebrations leaving Alby and his staff to clear up in readiness for the London down train due within the hour. After a while Nancy decided that she wanted to leave, she was nearing her time and tired very easily, so leaving the rest to celebrate which they did well into the night, we made our way back to Forge Cottage.

In August Nancy's time came. One Sunday morning we were sitting together at the bottom of the garden enjoying the warm sunshine when she suddenly contracted with pain and instinctively I knew that the end of her waiting was near. Helping her up from her chair I walked her back into the house and upstairs to our bedroom. Mother, by then fully alerted, put on her bonnet and went to fetch Doctor Hemmings and warn Mrs Lyes, the midwife. Meanwhile I laid on a good supply of hot water and clean towels. Kneeling beside her I wiped away the beads of sweat from her forehead and comforted her the best

I knew how, however on the arrival of the doctor and the capable Mrs Lyes I was ordered downstairs and told to keep out of the way. Father came in from the forge to keep me company and the two of us sat in the parlour, one each side of the fireplace, wondering what to talk about or what to do. Then at midday the doctor left saying it would probably be some time before the birth; Mrs Lyes however stayed on and for this we were grateful. That night our child decided that it was time to make its entrance and sitting downstairs in the parlour, hands clenched, I listened to Nancy's cries as she strained with the birth, knowing that there was very little I could do to help, at the same time vowing that I would never let her go through it again. Suddenly it was all over and we heard the plaintive cry of the baby as it took its first breath. Rising to my feet I stood for a while listening, my feelings just at that moment being a mixture of elation and relief. Father got up from his chair and without saying a word went out into the kitchen returning soon after with a bottle of wine and two glasses which he set down on the table. 'Congratulations, lad,' he said, 'you can relax now, the worst be over. After you've supped your wine, best get down to Nancy's parents and give them the good news.' Not needing any encouragement, I downed my drink, grabbed my jacket which was hanging from a hook behind the door and set off up the lane like a scalded cat, arriving at the Beasley cottage breathless and completely out of puff and it was then that I realized that in my haste I had forgotten to enquire whether it was a boy or girl. No matter, the important thing was that it had arrived safely. Naturally Mr and Mrs Beasley were overjoyed and after making me drink a stiff brandy they came back with me to see if they could help in any way and of course to see their new grandchild.

Down in the parlour the three of us, that is Mr Beasley, Father and me, continued to toast the baby's health as we waited, then from the top of the stairs Mother's voice called out, 'John, you may come and see your son now.' Needing no second invitation I dashed up the stairs nearly colliding with Mrs Lyes who was on her way down with a bundle of sheets and towels. She never said a word but just smiled; no doubt it was not the first time that she had had to deal with a brand new father. Nancy sat propped up in bed and by her side all wrapped up so that only its little face was visible was our son; and what a face it was, all red and wrinkled like an apple that has been kept too long in the dark. Looking down at him I began to panic until Doctor Hemmings, seeing my concern, came over and assured me that he would look normal in a few hours time, and so greatly relieved I bent down and kissed Nancy lightly on the forehead. 'Thank you, my love, thank you,' I whispered. One by one the family came up to gather round and admire the new arrival; suddenly the little bundle started to cry with such vigour that I feared it might do itself an injury. 'Feeding time,' announced Mrs Lyes, and taking control she ushered us all out of the room while that delicate and most intimate moment between mother and child was attended to.

Down in the parlour we set to with a will to toast the baby's health with what remained of Father's parsnip wine, congratulating each other as if it were we that had gone through the ordeal of childbirth. Then just before midnight Mr and Mrs Beasley went home promising to return later, and slowly the household returned to something like normal. Lying on the horsehair couch under the window where I had decided to spend the night in order not to disturb Nancy, I found it difficult to sleep. The arrival of that little stranger into our lives was going to make a big difference; just how big only time would tell. Worn out by the excitement and activity of the past few hours I tossed and turned, the only sounds to be heard being the creak of floorboards and the steady tick of the grandfather clock in the corner.

Eventually however I must have dozed off for when I awoke the sunshine was streaming in through a chink in the drawn curtains. Rising I washed and shaved outside in the wash-house before creeping quietly up the stairs, taking great care lest Nancy be asleep. But I need not have worried. Tiptoeing over to the bedside I looked down at her and as I did so she opened her eyes and smiled. Bending down I put my arms around her at the same time uttering all those seemingly silly compliments that brand new fathers are apt to utter on such occasions. Then an unfamiliar sound attracted my attention and going over to the other side of the bed I soon discovered its source, for there, wrapped in a cocoon of shawls and flannel and lying in the bottom drawer of the chest of drawers, was our little son. Looking down at him I was relieved to see that he looked more human and that most of the wrinkles had gone, but there he was, a tiny replica of Nancy and me and just at that moment I couldn't help but wonder what sort of a world we had brought him into. Suddenly Nancy stirred and almost as if she was reading my thoughts reached up and took my hand. There was a faint lingering scent of carbolic and mother's milk about her but I took no heed of it. 'Well, my love,' she said, 'what do you think of our son? Did I make a good job of him?' The emotions that welled up inside

90

me just at that moment stifled any reply I might have wanted to make, so I just took her in my arms and held her.

When our child was a month old we decided that it was time that he be christened and to this end we made the necessary arrangements with Parson Collins. This naturally brought up the question of names and although the choice was mine and Nancy's we were eager to please both sides of the family if that were possible. In a way it was a hard and thankless job, however after a great deal of deliberation we settled for John Walter, John to follow the family tradition and Walter after Nancy's father.

And so it was that one Sunday afternoon we set off for the church, master John Walter in his best bib and tucker being carried in Mother's wicker clothes basket. Dressed in Sunday best the two families set out and what a brave sight we made as we made our way in procession through Grinnels Orchard. Parson Collins was waiting when we arrived and soon we were all gathered round the font where he reminded us that he had christened both Nancy and me, finishing up by reminding Ted and Arnold of their responsibilities as godparents. Master John, however, didn't take too kindly to being held by a stranger and having water, holy though it was, splashed on his forehead, and he proved it by the very effective use of a healthy pair of lungs.

With the christening over we all returned to Forge Cottage to enjoy the refreshments that Mother had laid ready. Master John was changed and fed after which he was laid down to sleep in his temporary crib in the drawer of the chest of drawers upstairs. When he had eaten and drunk his fill Parson Collins left us explaining that he had to get ready for the evening service and shortly afterwards Mr and Mrs Beasley and Ted took their leave of us, however just before he left, Nancy's father drew me to one side. 'John, my boy,' he said, 'today's happenings help in a small way to justify the suffering you endured during the war. All over the world new lives are taking the place of those of your comrades who laid down theirs in order that this special day be made possible and that your lad might have a future.' And with that he stepped out into the darkness leaving me feeling very humble.

All too soon the shortening days of summer began their slow journey into autumn and the countryside made itself ready to face the long dark days of winter. Swifts and swallows gathered on the roof of the smithy where they sat discussing their flight to warmer climes, and Jimbo our stray cat, who one day had appeared from nowhere and had been adopted by us, began to spend more of his time in his winter quarters close to the forge. Sir Howard and Lady Armstrong, now getting on in years, decided to hand over the estate to Master Grahame and retire to their London home where Sir Howard would be closer to his parliamentary duties, and so a new chapter in the long life of the village began. Before he left Sir Howard donated a new cricket pavilion to the village which was erected at the far end of the ground backing on to the fish pond. The old shed, which for so many years had been our pavilion was moved to a far corner under the fir trees where it was put into service as a work and storage shed.

To mark the occasion a friendly match was arranged with Kempston-under-Bredon, a match that took place one glorious Saturday afternoon in early September, the first day of what turned out to be a late Indian summer. Freshly painted and festooned with bunting and flags the pavilion stood shining and new and to one side, with their instruments at the ready, the Alderton Brass Band waited for the signal to strike up. Then with the crowd silent Sir Howard stepped forward, and with Lady Armstrong at his side cut the ceremonial tape adding a short speech in which he expressed the wish that the pavilion would stand and serve the village for many generations to come. The band taking their cue picked up their instruments and after much puffing and blowing and sorting themselves out into something like marching order set off to do two circuits of the field, followed by what seemed to be the entire youth of the village. Down at the station Len Hubbard was waiting to collect the visiting team and transport them up to the cricket ground, not this time with horse and wagon as he had done for so many years, but with his newly-acquired motor bus. This time there was no pre-game stop at the Drovers Arms, no Tiny Larner. There were new faces now, fresh youngsters no doubt eager to carry on in the footsteps of their fathers.

Not having been selected to play I reverted to my old job of scorer. There was a brand new scoreboard mounted on the side of the pavilion and the old metal number plates, resurrected and repainted, were stacked ready as always. Stodger Millett, now beginning to bend with age, and Doctor Hemmings, whose gammy leg had put paid to his playing days, stood resplendent in their white coats all ready to take on the responsibilities of umpires. On the long veranda seat of the pavilion Eli Small, Twitcher Morris and Mr Bowman, the retired estate manager, sat chatting over old times and getting themselves ready to voice their somewhat biased opinions as the game progressed. Under the trees in a far corner of the ground Nancy and Tessa sat doting over our young son who, lying in frilled splendour in his brand new perambulator we had bought in Evesham, watched with arms and legs threshing the movement of the leaves in the branches above. And so the scene was set to repeat the game played on that August afternoon just before the world had gone mad.

For some inexplicable reason there didn't seem to be the same magic about the occasion. Perhaps it was because of the missing faces or more likely the fact that we were all that much older. Whatever it was I just couldn't put a finger on it; perhaps I should have realized that times and people had changed. All of a sudden I began to feel old. The days of wandering through fields knee-high in waving grasses and moon daisies, those misty, heady days of my youth seemed no longer for me; a new generation would have need of them now. However looking over to where Nancy sat with our young son I appreciated the fact that in spite of it all there were compensations and for those I had to be grateful.

After the game we gathered at the Drovers Arms, not this time to celebrate victory but to toast the opposition, a sober-minded lot who like us were mindful of the ghosts that lingered in the dark corners of the taproom. Jack Harris, older and greyer, stood leaning against the counter talking to my father and in its place beside the fireplace old Zetter's chair stood dusty and unused as it had done ever since his passing.

Time passed and in towns and cities far beyond our village things were far from good. Ex-servicemen stood in the gutters selling matches, their medals pinned to their threadbare jackets, mute testimony to the service that they had rendered to their country in its hour of need, while up north in the mining and industrial areas they gathered on street corners in their working-class uniforms of cloth cap and muffler, their faces devoid of hope, as they queued for jobs in a land that they had been promised would be fit for heroes. Safe in our little community we watched our son grow from a wrinkled babe in arms into a sturdy young lad who had inherited his mother's good looks and soft ways, and each time I looked at him I could see my Nancy oh so clearly. There were times however when she would tease me in the matter of looks but

93

seeing the pretence hurt in my eyes she would put her arms around me and whisper the magic words, 'To hear a nightingale, my love, to hear a nightingale.' Naturally his grandparents spoiled him a little but that was only to be expected, Father in his retirement having taken the little fellow under his wing. The young grew up and the old got older as is the way of things leaving Nancy, Beckey, Tessa and me and all the other characters we have met along the way to continue to play their parts on a fresh stage, and it is from this point in my story that I feel that it would be better to leave the telling of the rest of it to my son.

PART II

PART II

Chapter VI

In taking up the story from my father I soon came to realize that memories are like scatterings of gossamer thistledown being blown about on the soft breeze of a summer's day, hard to capture and still harder to hold on to. Amongst my earliest memories are those of the old red-brick smithy with its creeper-covered walls, inside of which, on rusting nails, hung row upon row of horseshoes and the tools of my father's trade. Oft in quieter moments I can still conjure up a picture of him as he stood in his leather apron and cloth cap working in the glow of the forge, the beads of sweat running down his face, as with a box of tools at his feet he bent gripping the leg of a heavy dray horse between his thighs. I recall too his patience when one or other of his charges became restless and hear again the clatter of freshly-shod hooves on the cobbled floor, and savour the never-to be forgotten smell of the acrid smoke that filled the smithy each time a hot shoe was placed. There were times when Grandad Mumford would join him for tea breaks when, with cap removed and pipe lit and firmly clenched between his teeth, he would sit staring into the glowing embers of the forge. I remember long winter days when icicles hung outside my bedroom window shaped by cold winds that rustled the ivy branches on the cottage walls, where tiny blue tits came to peck between the brickwork and the noisy sparrows came to seek shelter. There were other things too, like the squeaks of protest from the pump out in the yard as Mother drew the water for washing and early morning tea-making, and the times when, snuggled in my warm bed, unwilling to put my feet out onto the cold boards, I would lie listening to the sound of a distant train as it negotiated the long climb from Stebbington, the sound of its whistle clear on the frosty air. How fortunate it is that in the autumn of our lives we are able to draw comfort from the past, recalling events and people we have met along the way, often a sight or sound helping to bring the memories of them flooding back. After all, no story really ends but survives as a link between the past and the future.

The people who shared my childhood are remembered with great love and affection – my mother and father to whose memory I am devoted, Grandma and Grandad Mumford, my father's parents, and Tessa and Beckey my two aunts about whom my father has already told you, not forgetting all the other unforgettable characters who walked with me along the way.

Of Aunty Beckey I knew very little other than that she had been a nurse in a war Father sometimes talked about, the only image I had of her being contained in the silver-framed sepia photograph that ever since I could remember had stood on the mantlepiece above the fireplace. Long before I was born she had left to live in Canada, however she had kept in touch and letters from her arrived fairly regularly.

Aunty Tessa, Beckey's sister, was married to Arnold Lewis who owned the village stores, she being his second wife, the first Mrs Lewis having died in the great influenza epidemic of 1918. I remember Tessa as a kindly, loving person with blue eyes and hair done up in a bun at the back of her head, an understanding person who seemed to know all that there was to know about birds nesting and tiddler fishing and who, having no children of her own, was apt to spoil me in the matter of sweets and candy sticks which she would conjure into a bag each time I found an excuse to visit the shop. Listening to my parents talking when perhaps I shouldn't have been I often heard them mention someone called Albert who had been killed fighting the Germans in the war, and at the time I couldn't understand why they sounded so sad when his name was mentioned. Much later I was to learn that he had been something very special in Aunty Tessa's life. Thinking about it all I came to the conclusion that the old steel helmet that hung by its frayed strap from the rafters of the garden shed had some connection with those long-departed people the family spoke of, but being too young to understand I didn't think too deeply on the matter.

In those early days there seemed so much to see and do, so much to have explained and understand. There were, however, moments to savour like on dark winter evenings when, washed and made ready for bed and clad in my long flannel nightshirt I would sit on Grandma Mumford's knee while she told me stories about the little folk who lived at the bottom of our garden, impressing on me that if I was ever lucky enough to see one on no account was I to touch it or attempt to pick it up as they were very shy people, and if scared might well move out and go to live in someone else's garden, an eventuality that worried me no end. All these childish fantasies together with an unshakable belief in fairies and Father Christmas coloured, and in a way influenced, my early days.

Alas, however, as the years passed, like so many others, I was forced to come to terms with the realities of life. How sad that our early dreams cannot stay with us a little longer before becoming submerged in the painful process of growing up. Much of my learning of things in those early days I owe to Grandad Mumford who right from the time I could walk took me under his wing and it was under his guidance that I started out on the great adventure of life in which I found so many exciting places to explore in the little world whose boundaries were marked by the cottage, the smithy and the walls of the garden which stretched down to the start of Long Meadow.

Within its confines stood the old brick privy, the abandoned pigsty which had a gooseberry bush growing out from its crumbling brickwork, and a variety of nondescript sheds each of which had their place in the order of things. One of the more indisputable facts of life seemed to be that most buildings, providing that they be partially or wholly derelict, are to any healthy, inquisitive youngster a source of mystery and challenge, more so if they be covered with ivy, have a dark and sinister look about them and are home to a multitude of insects. Such a building was the brick privy at the bottom of the garden next to the pigsty. Its creaking elm door, old and worn, had a diamond-shaped peep hole cut into it at head height, and years of sunshine and showers had creased and cracked its planking leaving gaps which when the wind blew from the right direction let in blasts of cold air. Its rusting hinges, not having felt the relief of oil for many a long year, complained alarmingly whenever the door was opened or shut and I remember my father telling me that it was as well to be in good voice when using its facilities as its rusty bolt was none too effective.

Having completed my potty training and graduated to the grown-up privy every visit to its dark interior, lit in winter by a solitary candle placed in an empty jam jar, was an adventure. It was what was locally known as a 'three holer', two large ones for adults and one smaller one for the small bottoms which could and often did slip down, jamming the unfortunate user up to their armpits and causing them to cling to the edges of the wooden top in which the holes were cut. Each hole had its own wooden lid which was raised and lowered as required, and so it was that more often than not, owing to my lack of inches, I was forced to sit with the lid resting against by back, a most uncomfortable arrangement seeing that with the job finished and trousers gripped firmly with both hands, it was a case of sliding off the seat in order to get my feet on the floor, the result being that the lid came down with an almighty bang, the noise of which caused me to dash out into the garden to complete my dressing. Although aware of its importance I never quite knew what to call it, such names as Closet, Little House and Throne Room being banded about by the grown-ups. However I did notice that in polite conversation it was always referred to as 'The Netty', but be that as it may, the time I spent in its fascinating interior was always put to good use. At most times of the year it abounded with flies which were a source of food for the many spiders, both large and small, that had their homes in the dark, cobwebbed corners, corners where tendrils of ivy, having found their way in under loose slates on the roof, had curled themselves around the rafters, the paleness of their foliage being in stark contrast with the whitewashed walls. On wet days having put off the call of nature until the very last minute and faced with a mad dash down the garden path, it was as well to take Grandma Mumford's umbrella along as the roof, not being over watertight had a habit of letting trickles of water drip down on the poor unfortunate sitting below.

There was, however, another absorbing pleasure it afforded which, when able to take advantage of it, passed away many a dreary half hour. In the absence of toilet paper, newsprint was cut up into squares and made up into a wad through which in one corner a hole was pierced to enable a length of bagging string to be threaded. Hung on a nail driven into the wall at a convenient height it served its purpose admirably, in addition providing a source of reading material. Unfortunately it did have its frustrating moments such as when, after being absorbed in some juicy article, the reader would search frantically through the squares of paper to try to find the remainder of the story only to discover that it had already been deposited down the dark hole over which he or she sat.

The periodical emptying of the privy was to say the least quite an occasion, old Bugler Pargitter, who carried out the task, having to be fortified with several glasses of Grandfather's home-made wine before he would commence operations, during which his old horse, seemingly impervious to the awful smell, stood dejectedly in the shafts, head down surveying the ground at its feet. Bugler was in his way quite a character; he had one pace which was a few notches above dead slow and his horse, who over the years had become used to it, moved at the same pace as its master. In his youth Bugler had been quite a good cricketer, as had his father before him, and when questioned on his prowess as a batsman he would reply that it were due to keeping a straight bat, a modest mind and drinking plenty of cider. There was quite a simple explanation as to why he was known as Bugler. Hung on the side of his cart was a battered old army bugle which he boasted had been brought back from the Boer War by his father. Thus, when taking a full load back to the tip in the woods above Glebe Farm he would blast away on it to warn folks of his coming.

He had only the one pal, a chap called Whistler Morgan, a tree-feller by trade and a teller of tales by inclination, the nickname Whistler having been given to him because of the noise his corduroy trousers made as they rubbed together as he walked. To the casual observer, they were an ill-assorted pair, but for all that there was an undeniable bond between them. Down at the Drovers Arms they had their own special chairs set in a far corner of the taproom well away from the fire, a necessary precaution seeing that they rarely changed their clothes other than to attend funerals or Sunday church.

It is a well-known and established fact that the young for some inexplicable reason love secret places, where they can hide away from prying eyes and the attention of interfering parents, while fantasizing in their play. In this respect I was lucky enough to have several buildings which ranged themselves around the perimeter of the back yard, the most presentable of these being known to the family as Grandad's Bolt-Hole, although its real use was as a garden shed. Inside it in addition to the usual collection of gardening tools, empty seed boxes and strings of onions hanging from the roof there was an old wicker chair and a rickety-topped table, both of which had seen better days, but were perfectly adequate for the use to which Grandad put them. At one end there was a wide shelf on which he kept a few bottles of assorted home-made wines and a small stone jar of cider all kept, as he would say, 'for medicinal purposes'. This was his hideaway, a place where, safe from Grandma's scolding and other distractions, he could smoke his Anstay's Black Shag Tobacco in peace, and when necessary 'wet his whistle' with the contents of the bottles on the shelf. When he was in residence there were very few who would dare to enter without his permission, however I was an exception and often sat with him while he recounted stories of his youth and others to compliment the ones Grandma told me about the little folk at the bottom of the garden. No one but

101

a child would believe that by fluttering its wings a butterfly could cause a storm on the other side of the world but that is what he told me, and the enchanting thing about it was that I believed him.

Now close to Grandad's Bolt-Hole was the cycle shed, so-called because of the assortment of cycle spare parts, long discarded, that littered its floor and shelf spaces, a veritable Aladdin's Cave where I spent many happy hours. There were two old bicycle frames, a collection of rusting wheels minus most of their spokes, a couple of old oil and wick cycle lamps and last but by no means least a battered tin trunk that was filled to overflowing with an assortment of odds and ends. However, in spite of its attractions, it came second in my affections to the old lapboard shed that leaned against one wall of the privy. This was my own secret hiding place, a private little world which with a little imagination I could turn into anything I wished depending on the demands of my play. After a great deal of coat-pulling from me and pressure from Mother, Father had carried out a few essential repairs to it which ensured that even on the wettest of days I was able to play in comparative comfort. It had only the one window, a small one that looked out over the fields towards Broadway, and Mother had fitted it up with a pair of her old curtains, Grandad's contribution to it being two squares of lino rescued from the loft above the wash-house which, when laid over the brick floor, rendered it reasonably damp-proof. Its furnishings were to say the least basic, consisting as they did of an old scrub-topped table which by reason of having lost one of its legs needed to be propped up on bricks, and a worm-eaten carpenter's chest in which I kept a seemingly useless collection of odds and ends. To make it more cosy, particularly in the winter, when the bitter sprout-picking winds found their way through a gap in the hills above the village, Father had nailed an old army blanket over the inside of the door and Mother, as always concerned about my well-being, would, when frost and icy winds demanded it, bring mugs of hot cocoa, which in addition to attending to my innards I found useful for wrapping my hands around to keep them warm. In later years when grown up I often made my way down the yard to lift the latch of my old sanctuary and enter where, sitting in silence in the darkness, I would try to recapture some of the magic of the hours that I spent there as a child.

One of my earliest treasures was a wild greenfinch with an injured wing that one of the grooms from the stable had found in the lane outside the smithy. Supervised by my mother I lined a cardboard box with cotton wool and placed the bird in it, and in time, after I had found the correct things to feed it on, it became quite tame and would stagger about in its box dragging its injured wing whenever I approached. Seeing that it was determined to survive in spite of its injury Father made it a wooden nest box which for a short while had its home in a corner of the fireplace in the parlour, and each morning as soon as I awoke I would rush downstairs to make sure that my little friend was all right. Thus after a while it came to know and trust me.

As time passed and much to everyone's surprise its injured wing partially righted itself until eventually it was able to fly, albeit only in short bursts, and Father moved the box to a position inside the kitchen window. Thus on sunny days when the window was open it would launch itself out into the yard and hop and fly onto the wood stack where it perched singing its little heart out. One day in the early spring it found itself a mate and after a brief courtship they took up residence in the nest box which by then had been moved and secured to the wall of the wash-house and in due course, proceeded of course by a flurry of nest building, they settled down to raise a family. In the fullness of time four little ones came along, this being followed by a period of frantic feeding with Mother Greenfinch making innumerable trips backwards and forwards while her mate with the injured wing did his best in the yard outside. We never saw the going of the little ones but for the rest of that summer their parents repaid us with their singing; tragically however, it was to be my little friend's last summer.

One morning Mother came down and found him lying dead in the yard outside. We never did get to know how it met its end. Perhaps having done its duty and produced four of its kind to take its place, it had thought it time to go. Sitting on a stool in the kitchen I held the tiny cold body in my cupped hands while the tears coursed down my cheeks. Mother, in her efforts to console me, explained that it had gone to a far happier place where God would give it a new wing, but it was quite a while before I could be consoled. With all due ceremony we buried it at the bottom of the garden and Grandad made a small wooden cross to mark its last resting place. I shall never forget that tragic moment in my life, insignificant though it may have been in the light of others I should experience later in life.

Time passed and the seasons came and went as inevitably they must. On fine summer days with the warmth of the sun on our faces Grandad and I would often sit on the wooden bench that was set against the ivy-covered wall of the smithy where, with legs dangling, I watched fascinated as the smoke from his pipe went curling up into the air. Sometimes by chance or more likely for my amusement, he would produce perfect smoke rings which once launched drifted lazily about in the still air until at last, forces spent, they became just wisps of smoke, and watching their progress I often wondered where they went to. Perhaps the billowing white clouds that drifted over the village on lazy summer afternoons were the result of hundreds of Grandads puffing away at their pipes; no doubt the little folk who lived at the bottom of the garden would know the answer, I thought.

Inevitably there were 'red letter days', one such being the day that Father, having been shopping in Cheltenham, brought home a crystal wireless set which, after a great deal of inspection and discussion, was installed in the parlour. The aerial required to make it work was run from a tall pole set at the bottom of the garden passing through a hole drilled in the kitchen window frame on its way into the parlour, where it was connected to the set. As far as I recall it was the first one in the village and consequently was, for a while, quite a novelty. It only boasted one pair of headphones which meant that family and friends had to take it in turns to listen to the sounds that came from faraway London, thus at first our parlour was very rarely empty, particularly at broadcasting times.

On bath nights when, with the reluctance of all small boys, I was forced to take a bath in the old zinc bath tub, which incidentally, when not in use, hung from a metal hook driven into the outside wall of the kitchen, I would wait and watch while it was filled with hot water brought in from the coal-fired boiler in the wash-house. After climbing in Mother would set about lathering me with carbolic soap and scrubbing me pink, after which, clad in warm nightshirt I was allowed to listen to the wireless set. Not that I understood one half of what I was listening to but it was a good excuse to spend another half hour in front of the fire before Mother called out, 'Quick, upstairs before the nine o'clock horseman comes,' followed by 'up the wooden hill to Bedfordshire'. Safe and warm in my bed I would lie listening to the wind as it moaned its way around the chimney stack and make forms and faces out of the changing shadows cast by the flickering flame of the candle as they danced and cavorted on the ceiling above me, then just before the sandman called Mother would come up and tuck me in, her last words always being, 'Have you said your prayers?'

The time for growing up was upon me before I realized it and to this end I had my first haircut. After a great deal of discussion and tears from my mother it was decided that the time had arrived to be rid of my golden curls, an operation that required the services of Yanto Jones, local sheep-shearer and part-time barber, who over the years had left his mark on most of the heads of the male population of the village. Having seen the poor old sheep standing shivering in the fields after they had been shorn I began to fear the worst, however, seeing that I had very little choice in the matter I resigned myself to it.

When the fateful day came I was taken out into the yard and seated on a high wooden stool after which one of Mother's sheets was draped around me. With head bowed and looking a picture of abject misery I listened while Father and Yanto discussed things, not that there was any question of style or fashion but seemingly certain formalities had to be observed, one of which was the drinking of several glasses of cider by Yanto. At last all was ready and standing behind me with clippers and scissors at the ready Yanto would clear his throat noisily and blow his nose into a large coloured handkerchief which he kept in his coat pocket before commencing operations, the first of which was the disposal of my long curls followed by the feel of the cold clippers on my now unprotected neck. Looking down, which at that moment was the only way I could look, all I could see were the masses of golden curls lying on the ground and it was then that panic struck. Gripping the edges of the stool with both hands I began to holler at the top of my voice and was only consoled when Mother assured me that I was getting what she called 'a big boy's haircut'. Then with the deed done and me shorn and mortified, the sheet was removed and I was lifted down where no sooner had my feet touched the ground than I was off down the yard as fast as my legs would carry me, not stopping until I had found refuge in my lean-to hideaway where Grandma found me later. Opening the door she peered into the gloomy interior and on seeing my new haircut raised her hands in horror saying, 'What in God's name have they done to my little lamb?' The outcome of it all was that we both finished up having a good cry. The first time I saw myself in the mirror I hardly recognized the cropped head with a fringe in front as belonging to me, however being by then convinced that it was all part of growing up I was forced to accept it with as much grace as I could muster.

My first day at school was, as was to be expected, a traumatic experience. There were tears of course when I suddenly realized that for the first time in my life I was being forced to leave the protection of home and loving parents and be delivered into an unknown world where strangers would have charge of me. Led by the hand I dragged my feet up the lane, Grandad Mumford coming with us as far as the top leaving Mother to take me the rest of the way to the school, where I was handed over into the care of a most formidable woman called Mrs Rowan, who was to be my teacher. Mother said her goodbyes and I followed her out into the playground hoping against hope that at the last minute she would change her mind and take me back home. But it was not to be; reaching the top of the school path she turned and waved and then she was gone. Feeling utterly miserable and deserted I wiped away the tears that by then were beginning to course down my cheeks, realizing at the same time that there was nothing to stop me opening the gate and following her, but somehow I knew that I mustn't. Suddenly a hot little hand was placed in mine and turning, I came face to face with a little girl of about my own age whose jet black hair hung in plaited pigtails about her shoulders and whose eyes were as blue as cornflowers in the summer. There we stood, just looking at each other without a single word being spoken, then almost as if by mutual consent we turned and made our way hand in hand into the school, where the formidable Mrs Rowan was waiting. In itself it was a simple enough incident, one which is no doubt experienced by thousands of young children starting school for the first time, however for me it was something special even though at the time I didn't realize just how important a part she was to play in my life in the future.

Except for measles, chicken pox, and an occasional inspection by the 'Nit Nurse' my first years at school were fairly uneventful and Phyllis, that little girl of my first day, shared them with me. Right from the beginning we became firm friends and often as a sign of my friendship I took her small bunches of flowers gathered from our cottage garden. Once when I gave them to her she stood on tiptoe and put her arms around me before kissing me full on the lips, an experience I found most embarrassing seeing that the act was performed in front of my classmates. I allowed her to share my lean-to hideaway and its secrets, even permitting her to keep her dolls in the old carpenter's chest, not that she was overkeen on dolls preferring to tag along with the boys and share our tree-climbing, birds-nesting, cowboys and indians pursuits. And so we grew up without even being aware of it and the time soon came to leave the junior class and take our place in the big boys' and girls' world.

Chapter VII

To mark this important milestone in my life I was taken by train to Cheltenham to be fitted out with all the essential trappings a young lad would have need of in order that he might enter into this new world with the correct amount of dignity. First came strong leather boots with real leather laces followed by a flat cap, two jerseys, one brown, one red, worsted short trousers and knee-length stockings with broad red hoops round their tops. Wandering around the stores wearing my newly-acquired cap I watched fascinated as messages and small change were placed in metal containers and sent winging on their way on overhead wires to the cash desk, where an elderly lady, sitting behind a glass partition, deftly unscrewed the lower half of the containers, and after taking out the contents, sent them speeding back to the counter from where they had started their perilous journey.

With all purchases seen to it was back to the station to catch the train back to Lavington, where on arrival I sauntered up the platform leaving Mother to carry the parcels containing my newly-acquired finery. At the entrance to the ticket office Mr Stringer the Station Master stood eyeing me up and down. 'Hello, young shaver,' he called out, 'hast been shopping in Cheltenham then?' Whereupon being full of my own importance I began to reel off all the things Mother had bought me until, stopping me in my flow, Mr Stringer asked, 'And who gave thee that bobby-dazzler of a haircut then?' a question that immediately deflated me and brought me down to earth, causing me to make a dash for the station exit, head down, not at that moment wanting to discuss the matter.

One of the first lessons that I learnt on donning my newly-acquired finery was that by tradition stockings were always worn down around the ankles, and that the sleeves of jerseys were meant to fulfil the role of handkerchief in the absence of the real thing, which more often than not had been used for other unmentionable purposes before becoming lost or discarded. The trousers held up by real braces reached well below my knees, and in their pockets I soon learned to carry those small items which young boys deem necessary for survival, the most important of which were a penknife, a piece of string, a fishing-hook carefully wrapped in newspaper and one or two sticky sweets which, when required for eating, invariably had to be prised away from the linings and consumed with a liberal coating of fluff adhering to them. Fortunately having by then been introduced to cod liver oil, syrup of figs, and liquid paraffin this created no great problem.

Now that I was able to read and write a whole new world was opened to me, a world inhabited by heroes both imaginary and real, whose daring deeds fuelled the fires of my imagination and enabled me to travel to far distant places. On dark winter evenings, with an open book in front of me, elbows on the table and chin cupped in hands I sat in the mellow lamplight roaming Sherwood Forest with Robin Hood and his merry men and travelled across vast oceans to meet up with Ben Gunn and Long John Silver on Treasure Island. Deeds of daring from the pages of the Boys' Own Annual held me spellbound and on Saturday mornings I would wait eagerly for my Comic Cuts which Father always collected from the village stores with his newspapers, altogether a world of fantasy that shut out the realities of life and held them in obeyance until later, when I was better able to cope with them.

It was about this time that Tommy Whitworth came into my life, a lad who was destined to become my best friend. He and his widowed mother had recently moved into the village from Birmingham, Mrs Whitworth having taken up the position of housekeeper to Percy Slatter of Home Farm whose wife had recently passed away. Being about the same age Tommy and I soon found that we had many things in common including Phyllis who, true to her sex, didn't take long to realize that there was a distinct advantage in having two strings to her bow. Tommy was a cheerful, cheeky lad with an infectious sense of humour whose freckled-faced grin was guaranteed to melt even the hardest of hearts, and right from the start the three of us formed what my Father was fond of referring to as 'The Terrible Trio'; not that there was ever anything malicious in our escapades although I must admit that we did indulge in most of the fairly harmless pastimes such as apple and cherry scrumping and door-knocking. In the long summer days we roamed the countryside spending hours on the banks of the pond behind the cricket pavilion where, lying flat on our stomachs, elbows propped and chins cupped in hands, we watched the antics of the pond skaters and water boatmen as they moved across the surface of the water with quick, jerky movements and followed the flight of the darting dragon flies as they hovered on lace-like wings above the tall reeds.

On other days when all avenues of adventure had been explored we went down to the railway station to watch the trains. Leaning over the parapet of the road bridge above the station we immersed ourselves in the smoke and steam as the engines passed under, then a mad dash to the other side to repeat the performance as it emerged. Taking care not to get in the way we watched and sometimes helped with the activities going on on the platform, marvelling at the way the porters rolled the heavy milk churns up to and into the guards van. However our greatest thrill was to stand well back to watch the express trains as they thundered through in clouds of smoke and steam, their whistles screeching. On rare occasions when time permitted we were allowed to climb the wooden steps up into the signal box to watch Mr Rawlins, the signalman, cloth rag in hand, secure and release the large red-topped levers that sent the red and white signal arms on the gantry at the top of Stebbington incline up and down, and drink tea from the white enamel mug that when not in use hung above the desk on which Mr Rawlins did his writing.

On lazy carefree days when free from school we romped in the hayfields helping, and at times hindering, with the loading of the hay. With horses hitched in the shafts and the load high and swaying on the wain we followed on foot to the rickyard where, sitting on the fence that enclosed it, we watched the workers unload the hay onto the rick. Then it was a mad scamper to the wagon to climb aboard to enjoy the ride back to the field hanging on to the sides as it swayed and pitched in the rutted cart tracks. Sometimes if we were lucky one of us would be hoisted onto the broad back of one of the horses where with legs less than adequate we hung onto the hames for dear life. Back at the field we joined the men as they sat under the trees to share their lunch of cheese and pickle sandwiches and generous slices of home-cured ham, while the unhitched horses, tethered to wagon wheels and with a spray of elder tucked into their headbands to keep away the flies, stood contentedly tossing their heads and flicking their tails as they munched away at the piles of hay at their feet. Even now after the passing of the years I can recall the heady scent of new-mown hay, the smell of sweating horses, the tang of leather harness and the chatter and laughter of children as they chased and played, all under a blue sky with never a cloud in sight.

In late summer, when the fields of rippling corn, studded with blood-red poppies and yellow corn marigolds, stood ready for harvesting and harvest lightning lit the sky at night, we helped in the stacking of the sheaves and chase the many rabbits that came darting out of the uncut wheat, watching fascinated as the flocks of hungry sparrows fluttered and argued as they perched precariously on the waving brown ears. Often when we thought no one was looking we sneaked down to where the men had left their jars of cider, each of us taking a nip. Thus, as the day wore on, tired from chasing the rabbits and drowsy from the cider, we crawled under one of the wagons and settled down to sleep until roused by one of the farm workers.

Late one afternoon, after spending most of the day helping with the harvest below Hulberts Farm the three of us lay on our backs on the side of Oak Hill watching the puffy white clouds drift slowly across the sky. With hands behind our heads we listened to the clear notes of a skylark as it trilled its way higher and higher into the blue void above. Suddenly Tommy broke the silence: 'Why do grown-ups kiss and cuddle and go all daft with each other, then get married like wot my Aunty Flo did?' He asked the question aimed at no one in particular, taking us by surprise. For a while nothing was said, then raising herself into a sitting position Phyllis offered: 'Grown-ups 'as to get married afore they can sleep in the same bed but I ain't ever going to get married. I be going to be an old maid like Miss Parker.' Here she paused for breath. 'On t'uther hand,' she continued, 'I might marry both of you two, but that 'ud mean having to write two names in the big family bible wot my dad keeps in the front parlour and I don't think that he 'ud like that.'

Now Miss Parker, the lady Phyllis had referred to, was a dear old soul of some eighty summers who having neither kith nor kin lived alone in a cottage at the bottom end of the village. Not being too sprightly she rarely ventured out, however the children held her in great awe believing that she was a witch who on moonlit nights flew around the village on her broomstick with her black cat sitting behind her. On the rare occasions that she ventured out into the garden the sight of her in her long black skirt and a floppy black hat hiding a wrinkled old face that had more than its fair share of wrinkles and whiskers was enough to trigger the imagination of any passing youngster who happened to stop and peer through the bars of the gate. Phyllis had apparently not

111

finished on the subject as, getting to her feet she started off again. 'I be going to get my babies from Cheltenham Hospital where my Mam got me from 'cause I heard my Dad say that they do a better job there than they do at Evesham,' after which she sat down and was quiet again. Not to be outdone in the matter I added, 'Don't be daft, babies don't come from Cheltenham nor Evesham, they comes from under gooseberry bushes 'cause that's where my mother said she found me, under the one that grows atop of our pigsty.' Pausing, I waited to be challenged but seeing that neither Phyllis nor Tommy seemed inclined to do so I let the matter drop. It was all so innocent and little did we realize that in the not too distant future the answers to the many questions which our parents had to face at times would be answered under very different circumstances.

Hot summer days were for swimming and where better than down at the stream that fed the Mill Pond? One Saturday afternoon tired and sweaty from romping in the hay the three of us set off across the fields, eventually finding ourselves on the banks of the stream. 'How about a swim?' Tommy asked. The idea, tempting as it was, caused Phyllis and me to halt in our tracks. 'Us ain't got any swimming costumes,' piped up Phyllis. 'Then us 'ul have to go without any, won't us?' replied Tommy. As for me, seeing that the situation had never arisen before, I hesitated to agree, that is until Phyllis, much to our surprise, said, 'I don't care if you two don't.' And that seemed to settle the matter, so off we raced to find a quiet spot well away from the mill where, sitting on the bank under a willow tree we started to take our clothes off. Phyllis, who seemed to be the least embarrassed, was soon parading up and down naked as the day she was born and looking at her I felt strangely disturbed, however it wasn't long before Tommy and me were standing beside her, our clothes neatly piled against the trunk of the tree. Overwhelmed with a natural curiosity I watched Phyllis as she chased about and although as yet I hadn't given the matter a lot of thought I did realize that girls were different to boys in many respects, and here was confirmation. Phyllis clothed and Phyllis naked were two very different things. Laughing and splashing we waded in the shallows, the soft mud squelching between our toes while higher up the stream an otter, disturbed by our presence, slipped quietly into the weeds at the water's edge. On the opposite bank a kingfisher, uncertain what to do, sat on its watch post eyeing us with head perched on one side as, uninhibited, we wrestled and held each other until at last tired and out of breath we clambered back onto the bank where we lay side by side while the sun dried our naked bodies. I have often wished that I might have had a camera to record those innocent moments but alas it was not to be, so as with many things it must remain a beautiful memory of an unforgettable moment that on reflection brings a lump to the throat and a tear to the eye.

Thinking back on those long summer days I recall the many thunderstorms that struck the village, those awesome demonstrations put on by nature to remind us how vulnerable we are. I have always been troubled by them right from an early age but there was one occasion when all alone I had to face the terrors of a particularly nasty one and it happened thus. At the time I would have been about seven years of age and had been sent by Grandad Mumford to deliver a message to some friends of his at the top end of the village beyond the church.

It was late afternoon and the day had been hot and sultry, one of those days that saps the energy out of man and beast as my father was fond of saying, and away to the south, over the Cotswold hills a ribbon of menacing dark cloud had begun to gather and the air, still and humid, seemed to wrap itself around the village causing even the birds to be silent. Having delivered Grandad's message and not being in any hurry I tended to dawdle, finding much of interest to explore along the way.

Later, sitting on the stone steps of the water fountain by the church, I watched the twisting eddies that were beginning to stir the dust at my feet, becoming so immersed in their antics that I failed to hear the rumble of approaching wheels as Jed Whishart led his horse and wagon up to the drinking trough. Jumping down from where he had been sitting on the shafts he came over and stood looking at me. 'Well, young master Mumford,' he said, 'looks as if there be going to be a storm. Best get thee home afore it breaks else thy father 'ul tan thy breeches if thee do go home all skimpt and wet.' Nodding to show that I had heard him I sat watching as the horse buried its velvet muzzle in the clear water to drink, until at last, having had its fill, it raised its head and with water still dripping from its muzzle looked at me with its large, soft brown eyes almost as if it were saying Thank You. After a further word of warning Jed took his seat again and catching up the reins brought them down with a quick slap on the horse's rump. 'Walk on,' he ordered and off they set down the village street.

Meanwhile away beyond my vision dark storm clouds were gathering, tossing and twisting as they began to blot out the sun. Then suddenly from nowhere a chilling wind sprang up rattling the branches of the tall elms that bordered the churchyard, leaving me still deep in thought as I continued to watch the dust spirals at my feet, hardly noticing the occasional raindrop that plopped into the water, to leave a large bubble which floated for a second before bursting and becoming lost. Out in the roadway Turkey Haines's black cat paused on its way back to its home territory beyond the privet hedge, with ears pricked and tail erect it stood for a moment watching and listening, then having reassured itself that I meant it no harm, it continued on its way to shelter and safety. By then it was getting quite dark and looking up and around I could see that a storm was gathering. Suddenly a bolt of brilliant blue light shot from the clouds and went to earth in one of the trees in the park to be immediately followed by an almighty crack of thunder that echoed round the hills before becoming lost way out over the Malvern Hills. Scared out of my wits I got to my feet and raced over to seek shelter under the lych-gate at the bottom of the church walk where, crouching on the seat, I buried my head in my hands and waited for the next crash. In the uncanny silence I heard, faintly at first, an ominous rushing sound, then for the second time a cold wind hit the village, bending and swaying the tall trees and causing unlatched gates to bang against their gate posts as they swung backwards and forwards. Then the rain came driving across in a solid sheet that beat on the roof of the lych-gate with the ferocity of a thousand kettle drums.

Within minutes the road outside became a swirling torrent that swept everything before it as it raced down the gutters and from the steep thatched roof of Turkey Haines's cottage it ran down like a waterfall, hitting the ground below with a force that sent the earth from the flowerbeds splattering halfway up the whitewashed walls. A solitary rook caught by the storm tried desperately to reach the comparative safety of the swaying elms but swept by the wind it was blown in the direction of the woods above the village. Petrified by it all I was convinced that the end of the world had come and that I should never see my parents again. Unable or more likely unwilling to move I continued to crouch as the thunder rolled and the rain lashed down, then, after what seemed an eternity, the storm started to abate and ease its way north on its way to give the Malverns a taste of its fury. Suddenly, as if by magic, all went quiet and from high in the branches of the tall fir tree outside Lil Walker's cottage a lone song thrush started to sing its heart out as if to

114

welcome the first rays of sunshine that by then were beginning to break through the edges of the dark storm clouds.

Venturing out from under the lych-gate I stood for a while watching the raindrops as they dripped from the bushes that overhung the church walk to form bubbles in the muddy pools that lay beneath, while from an old elder nearby drops of rain ran down in a curtain of rainbow-coloured beads that stirred up the rich scent of elderflowers and dog roses as they fell making everything smell fresh and clean again. Slowly the warm sunshine began to flood the vale penetrating even the darkest of corners to drive the wet shadows out in a veil of white misty vapour. Suddenly a voice called out: 'Be you all right, young Mumford?' It was George Walker on his way up to Home Farm for the milking. 'I be that, Mr Walker,' I replied, after which I took one quick look around before taking to my heels down the village street, splashing in and out of the puddles as I went and being mightily glad to be on my way back to Forge Cottage.

Soon it was autumn, the time of the year when the trees stood silent and brown as they waited for the frosts and snow of winter, frosts that would freeze the ground and tempt the chilling winds to stir the dead leaves and send them scurrying this way and that before bringing them to rest in hedgerow bottoms and dark, damp corners. A time when even the most timid of creatures ventured closer to their human neighbours in search of food and shelter and Master Robin, modesty forgotten, would venture into the kitchen if the door be open and take crumbs from Mother's outstretched hand. Wrapped in overcoats and scarves against the chafing winds and with hands warm inside gloves backed with coney fur we bowled our wooden and iron hoops up and down the village street and spun our gaily-coloured tops. Then on fine crisp mornings with our misty breath hanging in the air and jewelled cobwebs swaying in the hedgerows, for all the world like delicate lace necklaces, we followed the hounds and explored the dark, silent woods where the damp decaying smell of autumn still lingered and where the fern-covered banks, having long since lost their green mantle, lay brown and sodden. This was the time of year when old Dan, the willow-cutter, would be busy gathering and stacking his winter fuel against the walls of his little cabin set in the woods above the mill in readiness for the short days and long cold nights of winter. Dan was a strange man and very little was known about him other than that shortly after the war he had appeared, built himself a little hut and taken up basket weaving.

One morning in early December the three of us, that is Tommy, Phyllis and me decided to pay him a visit. Winter was upon us and snow had fallen in the night transforming the countryside into a glistening fairyland as the morning frost twinkled on the untrodden snow. Suitably-gloved and wrapped we met at the fountain at the top of the village before making our way across the silent white wilderness of Two Farthings Fields and down to the mill where, not being in any particular hurry, we lingered to pelt each other with snowballs, watch the wild ducks slipping and skidding on the frozen surface of the mill pond and follow the progress of the strutting moorhens who, with heads hung wandered about searching for food amongst the bare reed stalks that thrust themselves out of the ice. With glowing cheeks we skated small stones across the frozen surface until at last, tired of our play, we left the skidding ducks and the dejected moorhens in peace and started on our way up through the woods where, guided by the unmistakeable smell of woodsmoke we fought our way through the undergrowth until at last we came upon a small clearing.

Making as little noise as possible and seemingly unobserved we crouched to watch the object of our visit as he busied himself filling an old smoke-blackened kettle, which when full he hung over the wood fire. Sitting on an upturned box, with the dark woods behind him as a backcloth, he presented an awesome picture, clad as he was in an old army greatcoat and woolly hat. With his grey-flecked beard and long straggling hair hanging about his shoulders he reminded me of a picture of the Prophet Moses that I had once seen in Grandad's illustrated Bible. Convinced that we were unobserved we crouched and watched until suddenly much to our amazement he called out, 'And what might you three be up to?', the question causing us to panic as for the life of us we could not think of an answer. 'Come on then if you be coming,' he continued, at the same time motioning for us to join him round the fire.

Feeling and looking sheepish we rose and made our way over to him and sitting on a fallen log, for all the world like the three wise monkeys, we waited while he surveyed each of us in turn with steel-blue eyes that looked out from under white, shaggy eyebrows. 'What be your names and where might you be from?' he asked. Galvanized into action we all started to speak at once until raising both hands heavenwards he stopped us in our flow. 'Hold hard there,' he said, 'hold hard. Not all at once. Let the little Missy have her say

116

first as is the way if you be gentlemen.' One by one we introduced ourselves, telling him our names and where we lived, but even as we spoke I had a sneaking feeling that he already knew as, turning to me, he said, 'Your father be the village blacksmith, bain't he? Him and me be old friends.' Sitting fascinated we watched as he spooned helpings of tea from a battered old tea caddy into an equally well-worn enamel teapot after which operation he took the kettle from the fire where it had been steaming and, rattling its lid, he poured some of its contents into the teapot, before setting it back down by the fire. Reaching behind him he produced as if by magic two battered enamel mugs, an empty tin from which the label had been removed, and a white china teacup which came minus its handle. Then, taking up the kettle again, he rinsed them all out and shook them dry before placing them on the ground in front of him. Reaching behind him once more he produced a tin of sweetened condensed milk from which he extracted generous spoonfuls and dripped one into each of the assortment of teacup, mugs and tin then taking up the teapot he topped them all up. Now I doubt if any of us had ever tasted tea made with sweetened condensed milk before, being more used to fresh milk from the dairy, however, strange to relate, after a few sips I came to like it even though at first it tasted strange to the tongue. Warmed by the tea and with hands reaching out to catch the heat from the fire we sat in silence while Dan, obviously glad of our company and having such an attentive audience, told us a little about his life in the woods and about the wild creatures that allowed him to share it with them.

This was the first of many visits that we were to pay to Dan's little kingdom, each visit adding to our knowledge of the countryside around and the wild creatures that inhabited it. Sitting in respectful silence we watched as he wove the willows into baskets, some for potato gathering, others for fruit picking, also sturdy log baskets, neat shopping baskets and two-handled clothes baskets. When the time was right we helped in the gathering and stripping and steaming of the willows and went with him into the woods to help coppice the material from which he made hurdle fencing, thatching pegs, and rake and besom handles. The world he opened up to us was full of fascinating creatures. He taught us the habits of the wily fox and took us to the best vantage points from which to view the vixen and her cubs at play, also to places deep in the woods where the wild deer gathered to choose their mates, and at the right time of the year to rub the velvet from their newly-acquired antlers. He showed

117

us the nesting places of his feathered friends and led us along secret pathways to fern-covered banks where badgers came out at night. Thus it was from him and his teaching that we learned to respect all wild things.

One morning when the three of us were sitting watching him at work he stopped what he was doing and put his finger to his lips to command silence. With eyes wide and ears straining we waited, our attention directed to an opening in the undergrowth on the far side of the clearing and as we watched a young hind stepped out into the open, eyes wide and nostrils twitching, as it tested the air for signs of danger. Slowly and daintily it advanced towards us, neck arched and ears alert, then reaching in his pocket Dan took something out and offered it in the palm of his hand. Step by step the animal approached until it was within reach of the proffered hand, then, sniffing and exploring it took the titbit and began to chew, all the time keeping a wary eye on us. Suddenly it froze, ears swivelling to catch any signs of danger, then with one bound it took off back into the shelter of the woods and was soon lost to sight.

Later that day sitting with my parents we related our adventure and after listening they told us a little more about our friend of the woods. He had apparently come from a fairly well-to-do family who had farmed on the other side of Burford on the Oxfordshire border, and at the outbreak of war had volunteered, seeing service in France where he won the Military Medal for saving the life of an officer under fire. When the war ended he returned home but didn't stay long as, saddened by all the killing and destruction he had seen, he just walked out and wasn't seen again until he reappeared in the woods above the mill. The locals at first were suspicious of him but once they came to realize that he was not just another troublesome tramp, they accepted him and Sir Howard, who owned the woods, gave instructions that he was to be left in peace to enjoy his chosen way of life. Concluding, Father told us that most of the information had been gleaned from Harry Gibbons, the gamekeeper, who had served with him in the same regiment.

It was through knowing Dan that we became friendly with another local character, Shaun Andrews, self-professed poacher and rat-catcher, known locally as 'Jigger'. That he was originally from 'across the water' was evident from his soft Irish brogue and the fact that he referred to everybody as 'yer man'. How he came to be known as 'Jigger' was common knowledge, particularly to those who frequented the Drovers Arms, for it was there that after spending an evening drinking the local cider he was apt to perform an elaborate Irish jig, the steps of which I doubt would ever have been recognized by any true son of the Emerald Isle. Come 'shut tap' friends would guide him out into the yard and point him in the general direction of his cottage which lay across the fields in the lee of Oak Hill, then off he would stagger with his little Jack Russell bitch at his heels. How he ever managed to find his way without the aid of a lantern was a mystery, but as far as was known he never came to any harm.

Being Irish he had the gift of the 'soft talk' and even when caught with a brace of pheasants secreted in the capacious pockets of his old jacket he was always able to talk his way out of it, however, for all his blarney there wasn't another man, with the exception of Dan, who knew the surrounding woods as he did, and many's the time gamekeepers would seek his advice on matters relating to pests and vermin, especially at gamebird rearing time. Again, like Dan, not a lot was known about him before he came and settled down in the district other than that shortly after taking up residence his wife up and left him to live with a market gardener from out Badsey way. Summer and winter he wore the same garb, knee-length moleskin gaiters that covered corduroy-clad legs, an old jacket with deep pockets in which he kept all manner of things including his ferret and last but by no means least a deerstalker hat with earflaps which he always wore hanging down. Consequently, as he strode along, the flaps flapped up and down giving the impression that the hat was about to take off. Seven days of the week he wore round his neck a multi-coloured kerchief which, if you happened to get near enough, smelled of woodsmoke and horse liniment, however his crowning glory were his flowing whiskers which were stained brown from the use of his clay pipe which never seemed to be out of his mouth. Strangely enough he very rarely carried a shotgun, preferring to do his poaching quietly with snares and a catapult, and it was said that without the use of either he could charm pheasants out of the low branches of the young fir trees where they were apt to roost for the night.

However, in spite of his nefarious activities, he was well thought of in the village and many's the brace of pheasants or couple of rabbits that found their way into the back porch of Constable Hodge's cottage. Quite by accident I found out that my father also benefited, as at times a brace of partridges or a plump hare would appear in the smithy in payment for favours Father had done for him, one of which I gathered was the making of gaffing hooks which

Jigger put to good use on his periodical visits to friends in mid-Wales when, in the company of others of his ilk, he poached the fat salmon in the upper reaches of rivers that made their way down from the high mountains. It was from him that we learned how to set snares for rabbits, trap and skin moles, and perfect the art of going through the woods as silently as red indians, merging into the background at the slightest snap of a twig or the alarm call from some startled cock pheasant. All this added to our knowledge of things and I firmly believe that, important as our schooling was, the most valuable part of our education came from the world outside.

Now my father used to say that a lad wasn't a lad until he had broken his first window, got scabs on his knees and had his first fight. Needless to say I passed those requirements with honours quite early in life. My first real fight came about at school and at the time of its happening landed me in hot water, even though it wasn't my fault. As in most schools we had our bully, a hulking great boy called Jessey Talbot, the son of a carrier who lived down at Little Cheltenham, a fair-sized lad who, although not over-intelligent or quick on his feet, managed to rule the roost with the help of his two cronies, and I must admit that most of us were scared of him.

One afternoon during playtime Tommy, Phyllis and me were squatting in a corner minding our own business when up comes Jessey and his two pals and, reaching down, he grabbed hold of Phyllis's pigtails and pulled her to her feet causing her to yell out in pain. Jumping up I aimed a punch in his direction but what happened next I have no clear recollection other than that I finally came to lying on the floor with blood pouring from my nose and Phyllis bending over me. That day, after school, I went into the smithy and told Father what had happened not, I assure you, being too proud in the telling. After listening he took me by the arm and marched me over to the cottage where he handed me over to Mother who, on seeing my bloodstained shirt, got herself into a proper tizzy. Fretting and scolding she cleaned me up and found a clean shirt, at the same time threatening to put on her best bonnet and go down to Little Cheltenham and beard Master Jessey Talbot in his den, however, after a deal of convincing she at last gave up the idea. Sitting in the kitchen, cleaned up and mortified, I listened while Father gave me some good advice. 'John, my lad,' he said, 'as you grow up you will find that there are times to stand up and fight and times to run away, but always remember to stand up and fight for the things that you believe in, whether they be to do

120

with your family, your friends or your country. But most important of all always protect the weakest.' Even to this day I remember those words of advice given me so long ago and I have done my best to live up to them, however at the time there was a more important matter to be dealt with in the shape of Master Jessey Talbot.

During the next few weeks when he could spare the time Father schooled me in the rudiments of self-defence. My pride had been hurt, I was anxious to set the matter straight and as it so happened I hadn't long to wait. One morning Phyllis, Tommy and me were making our way down the school path when we were confronted by Jessey and his two cronies. Sizing up the situation and not wishing to see me spreadeagled on the ground again Phyllis did her best to drag me away, but I was having none of it as I knew that unless the matter be settled there and then he would go on making our lives a misery. Taking off my jacket I handed it to Tommy then, after rolling up my sleeves in a most workmanlike manner I pushed my way through the crowd that had started to gather and strode up to where Jessey was waiting hands on hips and legs apart. 'Be you ready, Jessey Talbot?' I asked, 'because I be.' The look on his face was a treat to see. Stepping forward he grabbed me in a bear-hug and the two of us fell to the ground wrestling, which I found was not the best situation in which to indulge in the finer points of fisticuffs. Backwards and forwards we rolled on the dusty ground until at last, thoroughly out of puff, we stood up and faced each other. Then without a word of warning he aimed a punch at me which I parried just as Father had taught me. Temporarily off balance he swayed and this was my chance to strike so, aiming a blow, I caught him in his midriff just above the belt-line. Down went his head and I finished the job off with an uppercut that caused his mouth to snap shut like a rat trap. Holding his head in his hands he slowly sank to the ground where he crouched spitting blood from his split lip. Suddenly the crowd, which up until then had been cheering us on, went silent, the reason soon becoming obvious as elbowing his way through the now scattering youngsters came the Headmaster followed by the formidable Mrs Rowan who grabbed me by the collar and frogmarched me back into school. There I was stood in a corner to await my fate leaving the Headmaster to administer to Jessey who was still nursing his jaw and split lip.

That morning after prayers I was given four strokes of the cane, two on each hand, a punishment which I considered a small price to pay for teaching

Master Jessey Talbot a lesson. Just as I was leaving school for home Mrs Rowan gave me a note for my father who, after reading it, taxed me for my side of the story, so in my own words I told him about the fight and what had transpired afterwards. Listening intently he waited until I had finished then taking the note he screwed it up and threw it onto the coals of the forge. I never did get to know what was in it but at the time it seemed of little consequence. Before I left Father added these few parting words: 'Don't make a habit of it, lad, remember the advice I gave you,' and with that he reached in his waistcoat pocket and produced a sixpenny bit which he handed to me. 'Well done,' he said, and that was an end to it. I had no more trouble with Master Jessey after that, in fact after a while we became quite good friends which after all is just as it should be.

Chapter VIII

A nd so the seasons came and went. In the spring we combed the woods
and hedgerows for birds nests, fished for newts and tadpoles in the
pond at the bottom of Callow Lane and gathered bunches of daffodils and
bluebells from the woods above the Hall, blissfully unaware that each day
that passed was bringing us nearer to the closing days of our youth.

Christmas, with its usual flurry of preparations came, a time when fact
took a back seat and fantasy reigned, a time of wonderment when children
came into their own. With the exception of the war years there had always
been a Christmas party for the estate workers held in the village hall and
although strictly not eligible somehow I always managed to get included.
Organized under the patronage of Lady Armstrong who contributed most
generously towards the cost of the catering and other incidental expenses it
was one of the highlights of the year, eagerly looked forward to by the younger
generation of the village.

Picture if you will the hall hung with holly and mistletoe and decorated
with paper chains that criss-crossed the room, and from which hung gaily-
coloured paper chinese lanterns and bells. Underneath these festive decorations
youngsters crawled around and across the trestle-tables arranged down the
centre, while harassed parents, leaning over to make last minute adjustments
to the display of good things with which the tables were laden, were kept
busy keeping an eye on the more venturesome who, when they thought that
no one was looking, were won't to reach up and stick a not-too-clean finger
into a tantalizing jelly or wobbly blancmange. From the walls dusty deer heads
with wide-spreading antlers looked down, no doubt thinking of all the many
strange things they had witnessed – hospital beds and wounded soldiers in
wartime, whist drives, dances and wedding receptions in peacetime, and the
comings and goings of generations of villagers. Up on the stage situated at
one end of the hall stood the Christmas tree gaily decorated with coloured

balls and ropes of glistening tinsel, around the base of which were stacked the presents that later in the proceedings would be distributed by Father Christmas.

So the scene was set and at long last, with some sort of order restored, the children were eventually seated at the tables, that is, after several minor squabbles had been sorted out, where one or other of the excited children protested loudly as they expressed a wish to be seated next to a friend or playmate; a trying time when legs were smacked and bottoms plonked unceremoniously down on hard wooden seats. I well remember one Christmas in particular when, not being content with the good things on my plate, I filled the pockets of my jacket with jelly. Why, perhaps I shall never know, but I do remember that my mother wasn't too pleased. With the last bun eaten and the last glass of lemonade drunk the tables were cleared and stacked away, and the children given their freedom leaving their by now harassed parents to organize the rest of the afternoon and evening's entertainment.

Then as if by magic Father Christmas, in the shape of Gadget Sharp, appeared on the stage and took his seat beside the Christmas tree, his appearance causing an unnatural hush to descend. 'Merry Christmas!' he boomed. 'Merry Christmas!' echoed back from the sea of eager faces that were now edging their way forward to the front of the stage. One by one they mounted the steps and approached to receive their presents, the boys adopting an air of bravado as they took their gifts and rapidly got down off the stage, while the little girls, in their frilly party frocks, lingered demurely with heads hung and hands clasped behind their backs as Santa patted them on their heads, enquiring if they had been behaving themselves. Scattered round the hall in small groups parents, equally as excited and curious as their offspring, helped to unwrap the gaily-wrapped parcels, and soon the hall was echoing to Oooh's and Aaah's as the contents were revealed. Then with presents either clutched tightly to young chests or lodged with parents for safety the games began, games which included blind man's buff, charades, and pass the parcel, all of which were enjoyed with the maximum of noise and enthusiasm.

Finally, to finish off the evening, a magician, specially imported from Evesham entertained with feats of magic and dexterity. Wide-eyed and open-mouthed the children watched as he pulled a rabbit out of a top hat and produced a seemingly endless string of flags from an empty box. After such a long and exciting day some of the children began to flag, parents nursed the tired-out younger ones for whom the occasion had been a little too much, leaving the more energetic to chase and slide on the slippery floor boards regardless of the damage to best suits and party frocks which in a very short time became unrecognizable as the immaculate starched and ironed attire that had entered the room a few hours previously. Majestic and awesome in tweeds and feathered hat Mrs Pulley mounted the stage and called for order while Mrs Haines sat at the piano, hands poised above the keyboard, as she waited for the signal to commence playing the National Anthem. Then with this sung there followed a mad dash to the cloakroom to retrieve hats, coats and scarves until at last with all missing offspring gathered and accounted for, they filed out in orderly fashion through the entrance door receiving an apple and an orange before stepping out into the cold, dark night.

In Aunty Tessa's village shop a great transformation had taken place as shelves were cleared of their everyday commodities and stacked with gaily coloured boxes of dates, figs, crystallized orange slices and caddies of tea decorated with pictures of the King and Queen and Buckingham Palace. From the planked ceiling, ropes of glistening tinsel hung down over bottles of port wine that stood in parade order alongside tins of biscuits, boxes of chocolates and Turkish delight, while in the small ante-room adjoining the main shop toys of all description awaited inspection. Lead soldiers, painted and ready, rested in their cardboard boxes; tin metal engines all set for winding and setting on their shiny rails; and dolls with long golden curls and blue eyes shaded by long, dark eyelashes waiting with outstretched arms for some little girl to take them and love them. Pushing and shoving as boys have a habit of doing we stood with our noses pressed against the window panes speculating on what Father Christmas would bring, occasionally having to clear with gloved hands the mist that had gathered on the panes caused by our warm breath. There is no time quite like Christmas when you are young, a happy nostalgic time when families get together round log fires with friends and neighbours who have been invited in to partake of mince pies and drink toasts to absent friends, and when parents, remembering their own youth, enter into the spirit of things.

A week or so before Mother would persuade Father to take us to Cheltenham by train to see the decorations and mingle with the hosts of shoppers who crowded the pavements, crowds that carried us along with them past windows gay with coloured lights and festive decorations. On the broad sidewalk with

125

the mists from their breath rising above them the Salvation Army band played carols as they stood in a circle, coat collars pulled well up and mittened hands fingering their instruments. Lingering for a while we joined in the singing then it was off down the promenade to where the window of a large store demanded attention. Behind its glass front cardboard reindeers stood hitched to a sleigh piled high with gifts and, sitting in the driving seat, an old gentleman resplendent in red robe and white beard and whiskers, the whole tableau set in a winter landscape that glistened with artificial frost and snow. Inside the store we jostled with the crowds of shoppers who, laden with parcels and rolls of festive wrapping paper, wandered about no doubt wondering what to get as presents for distant aunts, uncles, nieces and nephews while above on wires strung between counter and cash desk the metal containers sped backwards and forwards. Then at the end of the day we made our way back to the station to catch the train back to Lavington and the peace and quiet of the countryside.

There are so many things to be remembered about those Christmases of long ago – the cold frosty mornings when the world outside lay silent under a blanket of snow and icicles hung outside the bedroom window; the waking in the early hours to explore the contents of the pillowcases which the night before had been left hanging on the end of the bed for Father Christmas to fill; and breakfast eaten sitting crossed-legged in front of the fire with the smell of damp clothes airing on the fireguard lingering in the background. How wonderful it is that these things stay with us even in the autumn of our lives. Sitting on the hearthrug with toys unwrapped from secretive parcels strewn around, and not being too sure which to admire or play with first, or to turn our attention to, we would survey the net Christmas stockings filled with crayons, books, sweets and chocolate money and the clockwork mice that scurried across the floor when wound and released, an Aladdin's cave that only came just once a year.

With the goose slowly cooking in the oven of the range in the kitchen we went to church to meet up with other villagers who in Sunday best sat rosy-cheeked and ready for action with prayer books clasped in gloved hands that rested on coat-covered laps. With the service over there was the brisk walk back to Forge Cottage, kicking and scuffing through the snow, Mother and Grandma having gone on ahead to examine and baste the goose, the smell of which drifted out to meet us as we opened the door. From the warm parlour

126

the flickering light of the fire reached out in welcome, the sudden draught causing a puff of smoke to curl back down the chimney bringing with it the homely smell of burning logs.

Then Christmas dinner when the fat brown goose, sitting on mother's best willow-pattern serving dish with legs trussed, was brought out and placed in front of Father to be carved, the portions being forked onto eagerly-held out plates. Following all this came the Christmas pudding, always the highlight of the occasion, brown and steaming with a sprig of holly stuck in its top. It was brought in with all due ceremony to be served out to the loved ones sitting around the table whose faces you hope will be with you for ever. Sadly, however, with the passing of the years, they only disappear and become misty images, names to be struck off Christmas card lists as they passed on.

In the late afternoon with the table cleared and the washing up seen to, we settled down to play all the traditional games, snakes and ladders, ludo, happy families and charades being amongst the favourites, after which with oil lamps lit to await the inevitable contribution from Grandma Beasley who, although not being noted for the quality of her singing, would insist, rise and make her way to the piano indicating with discreet cough and eye messages that she was ready to perform. With Mother poised over the keyboard she would stand one hand resting on the polished top, the other holding a sheet of music which everyone knew she couldn't read, being displayed more for effect than anything else. Then after a few introductory notes off she would launch into 'Little Grey Home in the West', 'Come into the Garden, Maud' or 'Bird of Love Divine' and 'Thora', all delivered slightly off-key, much to the amusement of Father and Grandfather who, sitting at the far end of the parlour, cringed visibly each time she attempted a high note. Sometimes in the quiet of the evening I can still see her standing delivering the immortal sentimental words of 'Thora', words guaranteed to bring a tear to the eye, particularly when delivered to a captive audience well primed with home-made wine:

> I stand in the land of Roses but dream of a land of Snow
> Where you and I were happy in the years of long ago
> Nightingales in the branches, stars in the magic skies
> But I only hear you singing, I only see your eyes.

Mr Beasley, not to be outdone then followed with 'The Green Eye of the

Little Yellow God', the fact that he treated us to it every Christmas making very little difference. Then came Father's turn. Rising to his feet with his thumbs hooked under the straps of his braces he gave us 'Ode to a Fieldmouse' and 'The Charge of the Light Brigade', the only two poems he could remember from his schooldays. Just before midnight the Beasleys would take their leave of us and lantern in hand make their way up the lane. Standing at the door with the cold air trying to sneak its way into the warm parlour we waited until the sound of their footsteps disappeared into the darkness, then turning, shut out the night.

In due course and in God's good time I was enrolled at Sunday school, Tommy and Phyllis coming as well. Now whether the arrangement was for our spiritual benefit or for the convenience of our parents was never made clear to us, however it was somewhere to go on winter afternoons when every available space in front of the fire at home had been commandeered by drowsy parents. Sunday school was a completely new experience, full of avenging angels, the two main characters being one called Jesus and the other The Devil. A picture of the former hung on the wall above where we sat, showing a tall gentleman with long golden curls that reached down to His shoulders, and I remember thinking that in Heaven there was a Yanto Jones waiting to cut them off and leave Him with a shorn head like mine. I did once venture to tax Mrs Pollard, our teacher, on the matter but as I remember she quickly changed the subject leaving me wondering that perhaps He and He only knew the secret of eternal shoulder-length curly hair, and if He did I wished with all my heart that He would tell me so that never again would I need the services of Yanto. Laboriously using our forefingers to point out each word we read the good book without understanding one half of what we were reading, in spite of the efforts of the good Mrs Pollard who did her best to guide us through the troubled waters of the New Testament. In retrospect I often wonder if it was the sight of Mavis Travers, who usually sat opposite me, reaching for her handkerchief which she kept tucked up one leg of her bloomers that interested me more. Still it was all done in innocence, all part of the painful process of growing up and as most young people do we managed to grope our way through a maze of seemingly unanswerable problems and situations.

Following the natural progression of things Tommy and I eventually joined the church choir, our parents coming along to see and admire us as we took our first journey from vestry to choir stalls, unfortunately however during that very important occasion Tommy, having eyes only for his mother who was sitting in one of the front pews, turned to the left when the rest had turned right and had to be pulled back into line by Charlie Wilmore who was following behind. During what to us were boring sermons we ogled the girls in the front pews, and flicked wet paper pellets at Phyllis who would persist in sticking out her tongue at us when she thought no one was looking. In spite of those long-suffering sermons there were compensations and each Sunday after the evening service we, the choir boys, were taken over to the parsonage where we were ushered into the study by Parson Collins and given chocolates from a box which he kept in a large roll-topped writing desk. Years later when happening to relate our escapades to other grown-ups I was relieved to learn that the lack of reverence we showed at times was fairly common practice among young boys who were apt to see it as a natural progression to higher things when, with voices broken, they took their places in the back stalls from where they could enjoy the liberty of boxing other young choristers' ears with prayer or hymn book.

There was however one occasion which we treated with great respect, without at the time realizing why, and that was the Armistice Day service when, led by Parson Collins, we walked in procession from the church to the war memorial. With the autumn wind billowing his white surplice and ruffling his thinning grey hair he led us in the singing of 'Oh Valiant Hearts', and sheltering behind Eli Small during the two minutes' silence I watched my mother and father who with solemn faces stood in the front rank of the assembled villagers. With heads bowed they paid silent tribute to those of their friends whose names were carved on the stone cross, and even at that tender age I realized that it must have been particularly harrowing for my father who not only had known those men, but had experienced at first-hand the horrors that finally claimed them. How sad that we, the young ones, who on that day long ago stood paying homage to those of another generation, were blissfully unaware that in the not too distant future we should have the same solemn ritual enacted for some of us, victims of another war, the beginnings of which before long would start to rumble around Europe. With the service over for another year we made our way back to Forge Cottage; there was no gay conversation along the way, no laughter, and walking by my father's side I remember looking up and asking in all innocence: 'Why do men have to have wars and kill each other?' He didn't answer and Mother, sensing that I had chosen the wrong moment to ask such a question, quickly changed the subject.

Time moved on and I was growing up fast. Eli Small, at the grand old age of eighty-four, passed away. It was Fred Newman who found him; neighbours not seeing Eli about had raised the alarm and Fred, who happened to be handy, forced his way in through the kitchen window only to find Eli laying on his bed fully-dressed and dead as a doornail with a jar of cider by his side and a blissful smile on his face. Twitcher Morris, the cricket team's long-standing umpire, didn't have such a peaceful end. One afternoon, while sheltering under an oak tree down Columbine Lane during a particularly violent thunderstorm, he was struck by lightning, and Stodger Millett, his life-long pal and fellow umpire, having lost his wife and not being over capable at looking after himself had gone to live in an old folks' home in Evesham. Constable Hodges, after a lifetime of service, had retired and he and Mrs Hodges had gone to live near to a married sister in Somerset; and so slowly the old pattern was beginning to change and new faces took the place of the old generation of villagers now resting in the churchyard.

Not long after the departure of Constable Hodges a new policeman arrived, a city man, not used to our country ways and for a while the villagers were a little apprehensive, but they need not have worried as all went well and the odd brace of pheasants still continued to appear in the back porch of the police cottage. Down at the railway station things had also changed. After years of faithful service in both peace and war Alby Stringer, the station master, had retired and Herbert Tanner was promoted to take his place. Alby, however, continued to live in the village managing to spend a great deal of his time down at the station 'keeping an eye on things', as he would say. At the smithy life went on much as usual and as I was now coming on thirteen I was able to help my father, making myself useful on Saturdays and during school holidays. Phyllis, now showing signs of developing into a young lady, began to take an interest in more feminine things such as dresses and fancy hats and shoes with high heels, and slowly I came to realize that the days of the Terrible Trio were drawing to a close. However the bond that had held us for so long was still there and we continued to enjoy each other's company, sharing the many pitfalls of growing up along the way.

On my thirteenth birthday Mother laid on a party to which several of the boys and girls from the school were invited, one of whom was my old adversary Jessey Talbot with whom by now I had become good friends. After tea we played all the usual games including the ever popular 'Postman's Knock' and it was during the playing of this that something occurred which, for reasons at the time I didn't understand, greatly disturbed me. Standing in the dark passage I waited for my victim to join me, not knowing of course who it would be, then suddenly the door opened and there stood Phyllis and in the brief glimpse I had of her before she stepped out into the darkness I suddenly realized that she was no longer the harum-scarum little girl who had held my hand on that first day at school and with whom I had swum naked in the mill stream. Closing the door behind her she stood waiting, then almost as if she was determined to make the first move she put her arms around me and kissed me full on the lips, a kiss that seemed to go on for ever. 'John Mumford,' she said at last, 'when be you going to grow up?' I wonder how many of us remember our first kiss, the one that stirred up many strange feelings and created a moment when we realized that innocence was fast fleeing and that suddenly we were on the threshold of manhood. Holding her I pressed myself against her feeling the warmth and shape of her supple body, then just as my head was beginning to swim with the magic of it all she pushed me away, her eyes bright and wide, and in that moment I was certain that from then on things between us would never be quite the same.

Back in the parlour I did my best to avoid her feeling that perhaps I had caused offence. Luckily Tommy caught my eye and motioned for me to join him outside where, putting his fingers to his lips to command silence, he led the way down to my lean-to shed where, after making sure that no one had followed, we entered, closing the door behind us. Producing a packet of cigarettes and a box of matches he took one out and handed it to me and not wishing to appear unsophisticated I took it and held it between my fingers much as I had seen grown-ups do. After several attempts we managed to get the things lit and going and for the next few minutes we crouched against the wall puffing and coughing and trying to figure out what all the attraction was about smoking. Suddenly I began to feel sick and looking at Tommy I could see that he had gone a pale shade of green. Staggering to our feet we were just about to make a dash for the door when it was thrown open and standing there were my father and Phyllis. 'Well, well,' he said, 'what have we here? Two young gentlemen enjoying a smoke, no less.' However by this time neither

Tommy nor I was in a fit state to stop and argue. Pushing past we staggered out into the yard where, leaning against the pigsty, we were both sick. Grandad Mumford, when told about it, thought it was hilarious and topped it off by relating how when he was a lad he and his pals had made cigarettes out of dried ivy leaves rolled in newspaper, a concoction that I imagined was far more lethal than our Woodbines. Mother scolded and for a while would have nothing to do with either of us and Father gave me a lecturing, warning me what to expect if ever he caught me smoking again. Oh yes, I shall long remember my first attempt at smoking but most of all I shall remember my disturbing encounter with Phyllis in the dark passageway outside the parlour.

During my last few months at school I suffered the loss of two very dear people. Grandad Mumford had been ailing for some time and in spite of the doctor's assurance that he could find very little wrong with him other than old age the family were worried. One hot sunny afternoon in late June, having just got home from school, I called in at the smithy as I always did and was surprised not to see Grandad sitting in his usual place by the forge. I taxed Father about it only to be told that he too was worried as he had not seen him for some time particularly as Mother and Grandma were out visiting Aunty Tessa at the shop. Crossing the yard I went into the cottage having a strange feeling that something was wrong. Opening the door to the parlour I saw Grandad apparently asleep in his rocking chair and not wishing to disturb him I tiptoed out closing the door behind me, little realizing that he was beyond waking. Mother found him when she and Grandma returned and I was immediately sent to fetch Doctor Hemmings. I think we all knew what his examination would show so it came as no surprise when he told us that Grandad had passed away. Grandma bore it bravely and at the time didn't shed a single tear but it was plain that she was bottling up her grief.

It was a sad house that night. Father and a neighbour carried Grandad's body upstairs to his bedroom while Mother went to fetch Mrs Lyes, the midwife, who also did 'laying out'. As for me I wandered in and out of the cottage stunned by my loss and trying hard to be grown up about it, all the time remembering the times when Grandad and I had walked the meadows and woods sharing the wonders of nature, and of other times when we had sat together in the garden shed while he recounted tales of his own boyhood. From now on the shed would be empty, no trembling hand would reach up and take down a bottle of his favourite 'medicine' and never again would the air be filled with the aroma of Anstay's Black Shag Tobacco, or smoke rings rise up in the still air on a summer's day. I wanted so desperately to cry but the tears just wouldn't come. All I had was a dull, empty feeling of loss, the same feeling that I had felt on the death of my little greenfinch friend.

That night lying in bed I took to remembering again and this time the tears came. Sobbing my heart out I buried my face in the pillow so that no one should hear, then I felt a hand touch my hair and looking up I saw it was Mother with Father standing beside her. They stayed with me for a while then they left the room and as Father closed the door behind him I heard him say, 'Leave the lad be, dear, he will find his own way back.'

The day before the funeral Grandad was taken down into the smithy. Having spent the greater part of his working life there it was what he would have wanted. When the time came for him to take his last journey they loaded his coffin onto Len Hubbard's wagon and we all walked behind it to the church, where they buried him in a quiet corner under an old yew tree. Standing at the graveside I realized, perhaps for the first time in my young life, the true meaning of loss. In the still air the bees droned lazily and the sun having found its way through the overhanging branches threw dappled patterns on the ground below. Then with the parson having said the final words we filed past the grave to pay our last respects before returning to Forge Cottage. In the crowded parlour, family and friends stood talking in hushed tones while they drank their tea and ate the sandwiches Mother had prepared, and looking across the room to where Grandad's chair stood by the fireplace I half expected to see him sitting there, but it was empty, only his pipe and tobacco jar standing on the table beside it bore testimony to the fact that he had ever been there. Feeling out of place I crept out into the yard and sought refuge in the old garden shed where, sitting in the rickety wicker chair, I felt his presence and now and then caught the unmistakable aroma of Anstay's Tobacco.

The weeks passed and although we did not know it at the time we had another shock to come. Grandma who had never really got over the loss of Grandad gradually began to pine away and try as we may there was little anyone could do about it. One morning just six weeks after Grandad had passed away she died peacefully in her sleep and we laid her to rest with him. They still lie there to this day and on their headstone is carved, in addition to their names and dates of birth, the simple inscription, 'He worked on the anvil of life but now he has laid down his hammer and is at rest.' We wrote to

Beckey giving her the sad news, having to follow it up with another letter telling of Grandma's passing. It was a double shock for her and we all knew how helpless she would have felt being so far away.

In the August of 1934 I celebrated my fourteenth birthday and at the end of that same year I said goodbye to school, as did Phyllis and Tommy, all of us being about the same age. I cannot in all honesty say that I left with any feelings of regret although later in life I did wonder if in fact they were not after all the best years of my life. However like so many of my age I was in a great hurry to rush headlong into the grown-up's world in order that I might sample all the exciting experiences that I had come to believe were waiting there. Having left school it was taken for granted that I should follow my father into the smithy to take up the trade of blacksmith and seeing no reason or having any wish to argue with the arrangement I started work after the Christmas.

Now a lad's first day at work is or should be a memorable occasion. No lying in bed until the last minute, no frenzied dash up the lane to arrive at school just before the assembly bell went. Instead, at seven-thirty, clad in my first pair of long trousers, collarless flannel shirt, and new flat cap it was out into the smithy to open up the shutters and get the forge going. That first memorable day was the beginning of a long apprenticeship during which there was much to learn. Luckily, however, having helped in school holidays and at other times I had a fair idea of what was expected of me. How well I remember how proud I felt sitting, mug of tea in hand, cap pushed to the back of my head and sweat running down my forehead as I took my first working tea break with my father.

But what of my two friends who had shared my schooldays? Phyllis, now on the threshold of womanhood and already a devoted reader of 'Woman's Beauty' and 'Modern Woman' magazines, had been lucky enough to get a job at the post office operating a small manual telephone exchange that had recently been installed in Mr Launchberry's front parlour to serve the few telephones that had been installed in various homes in the village, and in the new public telephone box that had been erected in the street outside Aunty Tessa's shop. Tommy, restless as ever, tried several jobs on the estate, none of which seemed to suit his fancy, so he eventually finished up helping out on the farm where his mother was housekeeper.

We now had mains electricity and water and although several of the older inhabitants bemoaned the passing of the old oil lamps most admitted that the new service had many advantages. However, there were other great changes that had taken place, the estate in its wisdom having decided that most, if not all, of the cottages in the village were in need of modernization. When our turn came we had the workmen in for six weeks while they built an extension to the cottage which provided a bigger kitchen and above it a bathroom with a separate toilet. So after many years of faithful service the old brick privy at the bottom of the garden was finally given over to the spiders and other creatures that we had been forced to share it with.

To celebrate the installation of the telephone Father, who had already written to Beckey to obtain her telephone number, arranged to call her. Gathered round the instrument we waited in eager anticipation for the operator to ring to advise us that the call that Father had booked was coming through. Tessa, who had been fetched over from the shop, sat fidgeting with her dress, while Mother, true to form, was all of a dither as she paced up and down the parlour muttering that she would never get used to the new-fangled gadget. Suddenly the bell rang startling us all out of our wits; Father rose and, grasping the stem of the upright candlestick instrument, he pressed the earpiece against his ear at the same time shouting at the top of his voice, 'Be that you, Beckey?' a question that was followed by a prolonged silence as he realized that he had only got as far as the operator at the other end, who was trying to connect him. Luckily after what seemed an age he eventually got through, however, he still continued to shout at the top of his voice, that is until Mother reminded him that if he shouted a little louder Beckey would be able to hear him without the aid of the telephone. Pressing round we eagerly awaited our turn to speak but time was limited, each conversation having to be restricted to, 'Hello, how are you?' and Beckey's reply. Then when my turn came I pressed the earpiece to my ear, but by then being overcome with it all I could only stand and listen to the faint voice at the other end repeating, 'Hello, who is that?' The incident of the telephone call to Canada remained the main topic of conversation for quite a while afterwards, particularly over the counter in Aunty Tessa's shop where customers were given a blow by blow account of the happening. To the villagers it seemed nothing short of a miracle that we had been able to speak to Aunty Beckey all that way away in Canada.

Slowly and without hardly noticing it the old order of things was beginning to change. Parson Collins at the age of seventy-six, and now almost too feeble

135

to mount the pulpit steps, had called it a day and he and Mrs Collins had gone to live in a church retirement home in Bournemouth. Shortly before they left we held a going-away party for them in the village hall. They were a grand old couple who had seen our little community through good and bad times, many of those present having been baptized and married by the Reverend. As a parting gift we gave them a Westminster chiming clock suitably inscribed, 'Presented by the grateful villagers of Lavington on the occasion of their retirement, July 1935'. It was an emotional moment when they stepped up onto the stage to accept the gift from Master Grahame and his wife and theirs weren't the only eyes that were dimmed with tears that afternoon. Holding the clock the good parson started to make a speech: 'My good and true friends,' he began, 'we are going to miss you after being such an important part of our lives for so long. Having looked upon you as our family we shall always remember you in our prayers,' and it was at this point that his voice wavered and came to an abrupt halt. Seeing how overcome he was Master Grahame stepped forward and gently led him off the stage which was the cue for Mrs Haines at the piano to strike up 'For he's a jolly good fellow', a sentiment that echoed back from the voices in the hall. The following week the new parson arrived, an earnest young man with a gangling wife who was apt to take her responsibilities far too seriously, and it took them some time to settle in the dark vicarage at the top end of the village and get used to our country ways.

Now fifteen, I was at last beginning to adjust to my new life as a worker. I learned quickly and was soon able to take a great deal of the work off Father's shoulders. As for Tommy, after toying with several mad ideas which in spite of the fact that he was too young, included the Army and the Navy, he finally settled for a job as carter handyman to Mr Collins up at Bank Farm. So with Phyllis at the Post Office and Tommy at Bank Farm, the 'Terrible Trio' took their first tentative steps into the grown-up world. Both Tommy and I continued to sing in the choir, although due to the fact that our voices had broken I don't think we contributed an awful lot to the singing, however, in spite of our various commitments we still managed to spend a great deal of our free time together. Although as yet not quite old enough to be considered for the cricket team, both Tommy and I managed to get involved with the village football team who in the winter months played their games in the dairy paddock next to the village hall. As in cricket there was always a certain amount of rivalry between our lads and those of the neighbouring villages and often in the absence of a competent referee or one bold enough to award penalties to either side, the games often degenerated into 'free-for-alls' when old scores would be settled. Most of us, not having the proper kit, played in our working clobber, all that was required being that jackets should be removed and trouser ends tucked into socks. There was however one concession and that was that we were allowed to keep our flat caps on. It was all very basic but it was from those games that we learned quite a lot about the rougher side of life. However, as time passed we sought more refined pastimes, going to dances in the village hall and even venturing further afield to others held in the Co-op hall in Evesham, being conveyed to them in Len Hubbard's newly-acquired 32-seater bus. At harvest times we drank more cider than was good for us, experienced our first hangovers and smoked far too many cigarettes, much to the disgust of Phyllis who had taken it upon herself to keep a motherly eye on us. In the proper season we fished in the pond behind the cricket pavilion, hired ourselves out as beaters when the pheasant shoots were held and went eel stitchering in the pool down at the mill while Danny still lived in the woods above. Unfortunately, having so many demands on our free time, we didn't visit him as often as we should have done, however we consoled ourselves with the thought that he would understand.

One Sunday morning shortly after my fifteenth birthday Father took me rook shooting on Ewart Hopkin's ground down Columbine. Up until then I had never been allowed to touch Grandfather's old double-barrelled shotgun, which for as long as I could remember had rested on horn pegs let into the wall above the fireplace in the parlour, and often as a lad I had stood looking up at it wondering if I should ever be allowed to fire it. That morning before we started out Father took me into the smithy and gave me a brief lesson on gun-handling and the do's and don'ts when firing, but I am ashamed to say that after having watched grown-ups shooting and being at the right age when I knew it all, the advice given went in one ear and out of the other. Mother packed a few sandwiches and gave me another talking to at the same time warning me to behave and do what I was told.

So, primed with good advice, a knapsack, and Grandad's shotgun Father and I set off up the lane. It was a blustery morning and the wind bent the tall trees that stood at the back of Bank Farm. As we walked I kept eyeing the gun which Father was carrying under his arm, being hardly able to contain myself in my eagerness to get on with the firing of it. On reaching the site we were joined by other farmers and farm workers who after being allocated their positions in the field bordering the wood stood to with guns at the ready. Suddenly a dozen or so rooks flew out from the safety of the trees and putting two cartridges into the gun Father snapped it shut and handed it to me. Now remember I had never fired a gun before and in my haste to do so I forgot all the good advice given to me. Lifting it to my shoulder I suddenly realized how heavy it was but by then it was too late. Steadying it as best I could I pointed it skywards in the general direction of the now fast-disappearing birds and let go with both barrels. With a kick like a mule the butt recoiled and banged into my shoulder, and catching me off balance, sent me flying backwards. The next thing that I remembered was lying in a ditch half-filled with muddy water with several grinning faces looking down at me. Wet and mortified I was dragged back to safety where with water dripping out of the bottoms of my trousers I stood listening to the ribald remarks of the others, who I learned much later had been expecting it to happen, and who in fact would have been greatly disappointed if it hadn't.

It was some time before I was allowed to go shooting again and I can assure you that I took better heed of the advice given. As for the rook at which I had aimed, it apparently escaped without injury which is more than I could say for my shoulder which remained sore for some considerable time, my pride taking a little longer to heal. The story of my first rook shoot naturally did the rounds of the village, a fact that didn't do my ego a lot of good and for a long time afterwards several of the older villagers, when passing me in the street would enquire, 'Done any rook shooting lately, lad?'

Now it was about this time that Clare Richardson came into my life, a young lady from Pershore who happened to be staying on holiday in the vicinity. We first met at a dance in the village hall and the fact that she chose me as her partner for the evening went straight to my head. Tommy, as always my guide and confidant, warned me to be careful obviously seeing something in her that I couldn't or just wouldn't, however to be fair I did realize that in addition to being older than me she didn't belong to our class, and Phyllis made no secret of the fact that she thought Clare to be stuck up, observations which for some strange reason only made her more desirable in my eyes. Unfortunately it caused a rift in the 'trio', the first serious one in the whole of our relationship so far, but being the age I was I thought I knew it all and

Clare encouraged me to think that I was a cut above the other lads. If I had stopped to think I should have realized that I was out of my class and riding for a fall.

Clare was a young lady of varying moods, one minute she would make me think I was the most important person in the world and in the next she would ignore me almost as if I didn't exist. Perhaps I should have seen the danger signals right from the start, but being besotted with her, I didn't. Most weekends after she had returned home I cycled the miles between Lavington and Pershore in all weathers to see her and more often than not she would keep me waiting at the gates at the bottom of her parents' driveway before condescending to come down and see me. As to the reason why I was never asked to call at the door it never occurred to me to ask but it should have been obvious that her family, being well off and living in the large house that they did wouldn't have looked too kindly to the son of a blacksmith knocking on the door enquiring after their daughter. Clare apparently had a wide circle of friends of her own class, several of whom I met briefly, and there were occasions when, after having cycled all the way to see her, two or three of them would be in attendance hanging on to her every word and falling over themselves to do her slightest bidding.

During the whole of this brief interlude in my life Phyllis and Tommy stood by and watched as I continued to make a complete fool of myself, but being the good friends that they were they never attempted to interfere. My parents too kept a low profile although I had the feeling that they desperately wanted to warn me that I was swimming in unknown waters and getting way out of my depth.

Fortunately for everyone concerned matters came to a head and it happened this way. Arriving at the gates of Clare's house on one of my Saturday visits I waited for over an hour without the slightest sign of her. Angry and frustrated I decided that enough was enough so parking my bicycle I opened the gates and boldly made my way up to the front door where, after ringing the bell, I waited. Suddenly it was opened by a uniformed maid who informed me that Miss Clare was out and that she didn't know when she would be back. Thanking her I turned and started to make my way back down the drive when I thought I heard the sound of voices coming from a summer house standing in a secluded corner of the garden. Pausing, I listened, then throwing caution to the winds I made my way across the lawn and mounted the stone steps. Peering through the glass panel of the door I saw a sight which made me pull up sharp, for lying on a pile of cushions were two bodies one of which I recognized to be Clare's. Not waiting to knock I burst in and Clare, on seeing me, sprang to her feet and grabbed something from a pile of clothes lying on the floor beside her in an attempt to cover up the fact that she was naked. Her companion, also devoid of clothing, and obviously not being quite sure how to deal with the situation, just lay there making futile attempts to get back into his trousers. Leaning down I grabbed him by the arm and yanked him to his feet whereupon Clare screamed for me to let him go, however I didn't hit him but just shook him like a terrier shakes a rat, and all the time I was doing it he made no attempt to retaliate but just covered his head with his hands and whimpered. At last my anger subsided and letting him go I watched as he slumped to the floor, then looking over to where Clare was crouching in a corner I suddenly saw her for what she was. I wanted to go over and hit her, fortunately common sense prevailed so, turning, I made my way to the door where just before I walked out into the fresh air I turned once again and looked back. 'You bitch,' I said, 'you bloody bitch,' and with that I left.

I don't remember a lot about the ride back that day other than thinking that I should have to face my friends and admit what a fool I had been. I never saw or spoke to Clare again; she just disappeared from my life, no doubt having found some other impressionable young lad to play her games with. Phyllis gradually thawed out but Tommy, determined as always to enjoy his moment of triumph adopted an attitude of 'I told you so'. All in all it was a lesson well and truly learned and I saw to it that I never made the same mistake again realizing only too clearly that the Clare's of this world invariably marry into their own class to become bored conservative housewives with a nanny to look after their children, and a husband who is something in the City.

That same year we lost Herbert Tanner in rather tragic circumstances. He had never married but he did have two loves in his life, his lady friend Doris Weaver and his motor cycle. Which of them came first in his affections no one was ever quite sure, tragically however one Saturday night, when returning from attending a dance in Tewkesbury with Doris on the pillion, they collided with a lorry coming from the direction of Evesham and both were killed instantly. The whole village was shocked by their deaths and it seemed so sad that after courting for so long they had missed their chance of a happy life together.

On the day of their funeral the villagers gathered in our little churchyard to bid them farewell, it was a lovely sunny morning and as I stood there looking around at familiar faces now mirrored with sadness I realized how lucky they were to have so many true friends to mourn them and be present at their going. At the grave's edge Herbert's ageing parents clung to each other as the young parson said the last few words, then both coffins were lowered side by side into the grave. Slowly we filed past and I remember thinking what stroke of fate had saved Herbert from the horrors of the last war only to have his life taken from him in a motor cycling accident; somehow it didn't seem fair. I suppose we can only play, to the best of our ability, the hand that life deals out to us; perhaps it is just as well that we cannot see too far into the future. Looking over to where Albert Stringer stood leaning on his stick I wondered what was going through his mind; was he thinking of that day long ago in a hot summer when Herbert, in his loyalty, had said, 'Reckon I'll go along with Mr Stringer. He 'ul need somebody to look after him with all they loose women about.'

Our little community, having only just begun to settle down after the Great War, the general strike and several other minor upheavals, was suddenly jerked out of its complacency by the death of King George and the abdication of Edward the Eighth, the subject of Mrs Simpson being discussed in guarded conversation at the coffee mornings down at the parsonage and in the privacy of cottages. The old ones of the village were convinced that it was an act of God sent to punish us for our sins, and so what with this shattering news and the Great Depression that was holding the country in its grip, the crowning of King George the Sixth came as a welcome relief.

One by one the old characters of the village were beginning to disappear. Jigger Andrews, now the cemetery side of sixty, and still at his poaching games, had bought himself a pony and trap, his old legs not now relishing the long walk back to his cottage after 'Shut Tap'. Come the end of the evening, drunk or sober he would be helped into his trap and the pony given a sharp slap on its rump, whereupon it would set off at a steady walk not needing the use of reins, as having done the journey so often, it needed no guiding hand to see it safely home and to its stable, where on arrival it would stand patiently waiting until its master had sobered up enough to unharness it and lead it in. One night Tommy and me and several other lads decided to play a trick on Jigger. While he was in the pub we took the pony out of the shafts and led it into the paddock adjoining where, after closing the gate, we passed the shafts of the trap through the bars and re-harnessed the pony into it. Staggering out into the darkness Jigger was guided to the trap and climbing aboard promptly fell asleep relying on his faithful friend to see him safely home as it had always done. Jack Harris the landlord found him the next morning and with the help of Archie Watcott, the postman, who just at that moment happened to be passing put the matter to rights and sent Jigger on his way, no doubt wondering how it was that he was going home in daylight.

All around times and things were on the change. Up at the power house the two large engines, now no longer required owing to the advent of mains electricity, were dismantled, Uncle Ted luckily being retained as estate electrician. Tommy, unpredictable as ever, flirted and fell in and out of love with regular monotony. As for me now, having gotten over my affair with Clare, I had sought solace in the arms of a young lass from Winchcombe by the name of Violet, a wise and worldly young lady who, in spite of her name, was no shrinking flower, and it was she who was destined to guide me through the chicanery of sex. Sitting in the back seats of the cinema we petted and explored gradually finding our way through the maze of exciting things that were on offer. In trembling anticipation I placed my hands on warm suspender-clad thighs and explored the tantalizing curve of young breasts under silk blouses, then ultimately to experience my first full sexual encounter in the back seat of a friend's motor car parked behind the village hall, which I will admit was not the most romantic of places to launch myself into that until then unexplored world, but it sufficed.

In the summer of 1937 Percy Slatter from Home Farm died and the property passed to a brother. Luckily, however, Tommy and his mother were not forgotten, as in addition to a small sum of money he left them a cottage down Leyfield. At the smithy little had changed and life went on much as usual. For five and a half days a week we sweated at the forge, Saturday afternoons in the summer being more or less devoted to cricket. In our cottage every room now had an electric light and Mother, determined to keep abreast of the times, bought herself an electric iron thus making redundant the old cast-iron ones that she had inherited from Grandma Mumford; cold and blackleaded, they were put into service as doorstops, an ignominious end to old friends which had given of their best over so many years. Beckey, at the ripe old age of forty, had got herself married to an officer in the Royal Canadian Air Force and her letter giving us the news also contained photographs of the wedding. How we all wished that Grandma Mumford could have lived to see the day her wayward Beckey had finally settled down.

Chapter IX

I was eighteen now and coming to the end of my apprenticeship, thus I was able to take on more and more of the work at the smithy. Much to my surprise I finally got my place in the second eleven cricket team, an achievement that for some reason greatly pleased my parents. Playing my first game was quite a milestone in my life and I remember feeling ten feet tall as clad in my new flannels I ran down the steps of the pavilion and made my way to the wicket; the fact that I was out first ball in no way detracted from the importance of the occasion and I was just as proud as I walked back.

Following the fashion of the times and influenced in no small degree by our frequent visits to the cinema in Evesham we imitated the American film stars in both dress and mannerisms, firmly of the belief that they all lived in palatial mansions with swimming pools and drove around in large flash motor cars. Imaging ourselves on Humphrey Bogart, we wore black shirts and white ties and in summer paraded around in silver-grey flannels with twelve-inch bottoms and chequered sports jackets. In the winter months we resorted to fifty-shilling tailor suits and belted Cromby overcoats, wore polka dot kerchiefs around our necks and Harry Roy trilby hats, the latter being always worn at a rakish angle. Puffing away at Woodbine, Kensitas and Black Cat cigarettes and downing the odd half pint of beer on a Saturday night we were determined to prove that we were quite capable of taking our places in the new and exciting world that we had inherited from our parents. However in all this the most satisfying thing as far as I was concerned was the fact that at last I was able to escape the attentions of Yanto Jones, preferring to travel to Evesham to have my hair cut by a more stylish barber, not that anything special was required, short back and sides being the fashion at the time. Tommy for some inexplicable reason seemed to have settled down and appeared to have set his cap at Phyllis, a fact that in a way worried me.

On summer days when free to do so the four of us, that is Tommy, Phyllis,

Violet and me often took trips into Evesham where, lazing on the river bank, we filled ourselves with Sharp's sugar bon bons and Imperial Mints, and listened to records of Roy Fox, Carrol Gibbons, and Bing Crosby played on a portable wind-up gramophone. Looking at Phyllis as she lay stretched out in the sunshine, her firm young breasts rising and falling with her breathing, I realized her power to stir me and that I had need of her. As time passed I became conscious of the fact that I was falling in love with her. Perhaps without even being aware of it I had felt that way for a long time, however I never gave her the slightest indication of my feelings although there were times when I was almost certain that she knew. How things would have turned out had they been allowed to follow their natural course we were never to find out as fate and events were already at work shaping our destinies, and before long we were to find ourselves being swept along on a tide of events over which we had very little control.

From across the channel came the first rumblings of trouble as Herr Hitler, drunk with power, flexed his muscles and became more and more arrogant in his demands. Father, who had seen it all before, prayed that this time the world would come to its senses and so avoid another catastrophe like the last one. Mother too was apprehensive and whenever the subject of war was raised she would look at me with the first signs of fear in her eyes. In the world beyond our village events were on the move, an appeal was launched for voluntary air raid wardens and Mr Chamberlain signed the Munich agreement with Herr Hitler over Czechoslovakia, then, almost without warning, Mr and Mrs Beasley passed away, their deaths casting a shadow over the whole family. Nancy took it hard and for a while was inconsolable, however the subsequent marriage of her brother to a widow lady from Broadway helped in no small way to take her mind off her loss, the announcement coming as a great surprise particularly as the lady came complete with a grown-up family. Quite wrongly as it turned out we had always assumed that having left it so late he would remain a bachelor, however we were all pleased for him, and one Saturday afternoon we all travelled to Cheltenham where they were wed at the Register Office, followed by a small reception at Nancy's parents' cottage which, since the death of his parents, Ted had taken over.

As was only to be expected the village was full of talk of war and down at the Drovers Arms the experts were already busy weighing up the pro's and con's as they sat in the newly-furnished lounge bar. Jack Harris the old landlord had retired and a brewery had taken over, and in so doing had brought the Drovers up to date. The taproom had become the 'Lounge Bar' and the small room adjoining it had been completely refurbished and labelled 'The Snug'. The old barrels which for many years had stood behind the counter had gone and the beer was drawn by ornate pump handles that were connected to the cellar where the casks now lived. The new tenants were a young couple from up north who had brought with them a most formidable barmaid called Daphne who at first sight seemed quite an amenable sort of person, however as some of the locals soon found out she had another side to her, a 'no nonsense' side, and it took quite a while for them to get used to her.

In spite of all the upheavals and changes one thing remained undisturbed – old Zetter's chair, which fortunately had been allowed to stay in the same place that it had stood for so many years. Since he had passed away a legend had grown up around it fostered mainly by the locals for their own amusement. Strangers were warned not to sit in it being told that if they did queer things would happen to them and strangely enough very few were prepared to take the risk, that is until one Saturday evening a crowd of university students roared up in their sports cars and took the place over much to the annoyance of the regulars who viewed their intrusion with unconcealed hostility. They were a noisy lot and it wasn't long before one of them, a strapping young chap with great broad shoulders and blond hair, sat himself down in Zetter's chair, pint pot in hand. For a moment there was silence as we all waited to see what would happen but of course nothing did, anyway our blond friend was too deep in his cups to worry and luckily after an hour or so he and his friends left and roared away into the night in their flashy sports cars singing and hooting their horns. Needless to say everyone was glad to see them go. The next morning, having occasion to go up the village, I ran into Constable Fowler our local Bobby. 'Morning, John,' he called out, 'hast heard about the accident up at Gabons crossroads last night?' Assuring him that I hadn't and curious to know more I crossed the road and joined him.

'It appears,' he continued, 'that a motor car driven by one of them young chaps who were in the Drovers last night crashed into the stone wall outside of Floss Hall's cottage. Sergeant from Winchcombe telephoned me fust thing this morning. Apparently the passenger escaped with minor cuts and bruises but the driver, a big blond chap were killed, the column of the steering wheel having gone straight through his chest. Floss were abed when it happened but when her heard the crash her got up and helped pull one young chap out, but there was very little they could do for t'uther. By the way, were it true that the big chap were sitting in Zetter's chair last night?'

'Yes,' I replied, as I turned away, 'come to think of it he did.' Now whether you believe in such things matters not but it was strange that in spite of our warnings that young chap had tempted fate by sitting in the chair.

Christmas came and Ted and his wife and family joined us at Forge Cottage. Mother prepared and cooked the traditional goose and in the morning we all attended church, in fact spending the day much as the family had always done in the old days. With dinner over and cleared away we gathered round the fire to listen to Father's new wireless set and talk, each of us wondering what the coming year would hold in view of the news from across the channel. The Christmas tree with its candles stood in the corner and the parlour was decorated as always with sprigs of holly and mistletoe, however some of the magic seemed to have gone. Perhaps it was because there were no young children playing on the hearthrug in front of the fire, no boxes of toy soldiers, no books, no crayons. Grandad's old rocking chair, now taken over by Father, still occupied its time-honoured place in the far corner of the parlour and on the table standing beside it his tobacco jar, faded and crazed, stood to hand. Sitting in the half light, with the glow of the flickering flames lighting up our faces, we reminisced about old times, of other Christmases when we had listened to Grandma Beasley singing 'Come into the garden, Maud' and 'Bird of Love Divine', and sat in rapt attention while Father, standing with his back to the fire and thumbs hooked under his braces, had recited 'Ode to a Field Mouse' and 'The Charge of the Light Brigade' leaving Grandad Mumford to rock gently backwards and forwards in his rocking chair. Pausing for a moment in my journey into the past I looked down at my hands, now rough and calloused from working in the smithy, and it was then that I realized just how far away those days were.

And so we entered 1939 little realizing what a momentous year it was going to be. Events such as the Flower Show and cricket matches were discussed without the usual enthusiasm, as at the back of all our minds was the thought that in view of the news it wouldn't be wise to plan too far ahead. In the May all 20-year-old young men were required to register under the Military Training Act and in July the first batch was called up, to be followed a short while later by the 21-year-olds. It was about this time that a great parade took place in Hyde Park in London of ATS, WRNS, Ambulance Corps and Women's Land Army, all these activities tending to confirm what we in the village were beginning to dread.

However in spite of the gloom that seemed to have settled over everyone it was decided to go ahead with the annual outing to Weston-Super-Mare. August Bank Holiday Monday arrived and following the tradition of past years it was arranged that we go by specially chartered train, the choirs and villagers of Great Mickleton and Little Easington joining us. In the station yard Mother and Father, Violet and me waited for the arrival of Mrs Whitworth, Tommy, Phyllis and her parents. All around was bustle and excitement as the motor coaches chugged up to deposit their cargos of excited parents and children, and in a quiet corner ponies were being unharnessed from now unfashionable day carts and traps and led into an adjoining paddock, where they were set free to graze and wander in peace until their owners returned at the end of the day. Sandled and cool in their just-below-the-knee length summer dresses the young girls stood fingering the loose strands of their bobbed or shingled hair and flicked the ash off the cigarettes which they held between manicured fingers, much to the disgust of the older women who, making no attempt to hide their disapproval, raised their eyebrows and sniffed. The young men, freshly-shaven and Brylcreamed, clad in sports jackets and flannels and with Woodbines dangling from their lips eyed the girls, all the while conversing in an exaggerated American drawl acquired from long hours spent in the local cinema. On the platform there was the usual noise and confusion as Mr Harris, the station master, and his two porters supervised the loading of the carriage. Meanwhile from high above, free for a while from their commitments in the hereafter the ghosts of Nathan Powell and Herbert Tanner looked down on it all nodding and smiling as they recognized the faces of old friends amongst the milling crowd that were busy getting themselves settled in the carriages. At last with all doors secured the train got under way and slowly eased itself out of the station. With the sun now well over the horizon it got into its stride passing quiet villages where patient plodding horses drew creaking wagons along narrow rutted lanes that were overhung with sweet briar and honeysuckle, and where in thatch-draped cottages housewives, with nothing more urgent to attend to than the midday meal, looked out of kitchen windows onto flower-strewn gardens where all that could be heard was the gentle drone of bees as they searched amongst the roses.

It was the lull before the storm and the nation, blissfully unaware of the horrors soon to be unleashed, went about its business being at the time more concerned with the results of the Test Match than the progress of events taking place across the channel. At a level crossing just outside Weston-Super-Mare a convoy of Army lorries stood waiting our passing, the camouflaged vehicles of which were packed with fresh-faced youngsters clad in khaki who, blissfully unaware where they were bound for or what their ultimate fate might be, leaned out and waved and cheered as we passed. In a corner of the compartment Father sat deep in thought as he gazed out of the window. Perhaps he was thinking of the times when he and Mother had made the same journey in those golden days just before the last war when, young and in love, they had sat holding hands and making plans for the future unaware of the heartache that lay ahead of them. Now it seemed that the whole scenario was about to be enacted again.

Outside the station at Weston the cloaked and bowler-hatted cabbies and their startled horses had long since gone and in their place stood a dozen or so motor cabs, shining, soulless metal monsters which lacked the art of showing the whites of their eyes and flicking their tails. Their drivers, with the inevitable cigarette between their lips, sat in the driving seats, one arm resting on the sill of the open window as they waited for fares, no flicking of whips and raising of bowler hats as potential customers glanced their way; they just sat and waited. On our way to the beach we passed boarded-up shop premises from whose gilded signboards the paint was already beginning to peel and where on the plywood sheets that covered the windows ominous Territorial and ARP notices fluttered in the lazy breeze that was blowing up from the sea.

Down on the sands Mother, with her inevitable knitting, and Father, pipe firmly clenched between his teeth and newspaper spread, sat in their deckchairs enjoying the sun and sea air, so leaving them in peace Violet and me, and Tommy and Phyllis, took off our shoes and stockings and trudged through the warm sand passing on our way other young couples lying full length, the girls with dresses drawn well up above the knee, their young escorts, jackets and ties discarded, lying beside them with trouser legs rolled up as far as possible to display expanses of white leg strapped with colourful sock

149

suspenders. Down at the water's edge the donkeys plodded backwards and forwards carrying a new generation of mothers and fathers while along the seafront the girls in their short summer frocks, hair done in the latest fashion and scarlet lips set in well powdered and rouged faces, paraded up and down inviting admiring looks from the young lads who, pipes in hand and hair firmly in place, called out saucy remarks, all the time weighing up the chances of a brief romance before each went their separate way at the end of the day.

Aunty Tessa with Uncle Albert in tow sat listening to the band, Aunty no doubt remembering the times when she and Beckey had paraded along the same seafront inviting admiring glances from another generation of young men who not long afterwards had laid down their lives on the battlefields of France and Belgium. Up in the bandstand the musicians, smart in their regimentals, wet their lips and turned the pages of their music, then, as the conductor raised his arms and tapped his baton on the music stand in front of him, they set to with a will and before long had the feet of their appreciative audience tapping. The children, busy with buckets and spades, still built their sand castles and clamoured for ice cream much as they had always done while their ever-suffering parents, tightly wedged in deck chairs, their faces covered with their newspapers, dreamed of fish and chips, tea and beer, not necessarily in that order.

With candy floss in hand the four of us toured the amusement arcades laughing and nudging each other as we sorted through the saucy postcards displayed on the sidewalk outside the gift shops, then in the afternoon we went dancing in the Winter Gardens where in the cool sophisticated atmosphere of the ballroom we waltzed and foxtrotted to the music of a reasonably good four-piece band. Changing partners I stole a dance with Phyllis feeling her warm and supple against me as we glided around the floor and it was then that I experienced the same thrill that I had felt on that day when I had held her in the dark passage outside the parlour at home. Luckily she kept her eyes averted otherwise she must have read what was on my mind, then I suddenly had a wild impulse to turn her face up to me and kiss her; perhaps it was the magic of the waltz or more likely the fact that I was in love with her, I don't think I shall ever know as the moment passed, quickly leaving me with the feeling that she had been aware of my intentions. Confused in mind and not knowing quite what to do I silently prayed for the dance to finish and when at last it did I walked her back to where Tommy and Violet were sitting hoping against hope that neither of them would notice my confusion.

That night travelling back to Lavington I sat in the carriage with Violet's head resting against my shoulder secretly wishing that it were Phyllis beside me. The thought, guarded as it was, made me feel guilty and looking across at Tommy and Phyllis sitting opposite I was glad that I hadn't made a fool of myself.

Relentlessly the year raced towards its end. In the closing days of August we bade farewell to two more old friends – Mr Bowman who for so many years had been the estate manager, and Gadget Sharp who died peacefully in his sleep at the ripe old age of seventy-two. September came and we waited for the inevitable blow that all of us knew soon must come, then on the first day of the new month Herr Hitler ordered his troops into the Danzig corridor and the die was cast. For two more days we held our breath sure of what must happen but not knowing when, then on the third of September we and the waiting world got our answer.

It was a lovely sunny morning with just the slightest hint of autumn in the air and gathered round the wireless set in the parlour we waited for the announcement by the Prime Minister, Mr Chamberlain. The atmosphere in the room was tense. Mother sat with hands clasped on her lap and Father stood behind her, his hands resting on her shoulders. As for me, excited but at the same time apprehensive, I paced backwards and forwards between fireplace and window, eyes fixed intently on the fretted front of the wireless speaker. Suddenly it sprang into life and after a few crackles and scratching noises the voice of the Prime Minister came loud and clear,

'This morning the British Ambassador in Berlin handed to the German Government a formal note stating that unless we heard from them by eleven o'clock that they were prepared at once to withdraw their troops from Poland, a state of war would exist between us. I have to tell you now that no such undertaking has been received and consequently this country is at war with Germany.'

Stunned by the announcement we remained silent each of us trying to come to terms with the fact that this would be the last day of peace and the first day of war. Reaching over Father switched the wireless set off and looking across to where Mother was sitting I could see that her eyes were beginning to fill with tears, no doubt just at that moment she was remembering those heartbreaking days when she had seen Father off to war and of the lonely years she had spent waiting for his return. Feeling that I wanted to be alone for a while I left and went down to the bottom of the garden and there sitting on the low wall I tried to get my thoughts into some sort of order. Looking over the fields towards Broadway I half expected to see that it had changed but it still looked the same. A few sheep grazing in Longmeadow raised their heads and looked in my direction then resumed their grazing; after all the great events that were taking place wouldn't affect their little world.

Later that day I decided to take a walk up to Tommy's cottage, his mother answered the door and I could see that there was no need to mention the momentous news that had come over the wireless as she had the same look in her eyes that I had seen in my mother's. Tommy joined me and together we walked up the lane and across the fields to the foot of Oak Hill where, leaning against the gate that gave access to the path that wound its way around the foot of the hill, we stood for a while in silence, the only sounds to be heard being the rustle of the breeze in the branches of a nearby tree and the far-off rattle of a tractor as it lurched its way down the lane above Hulberts Farm. It was Tommy who broke the spell. 'John,' he began, 'you and me have been good mates for a long time and if you have a mind to volunteer so shall I, leastwise that is what I have always understood was agreed on. We could of course wait for our call-up but there again being agricultural workers we might be exempt, but I wouldn't want it that way, neither would you.' Faced with the necessity of replying I had to admit that I hadn't as yet come to any definite decision. 'Let's leave it a while and see how things work out; there's plenty of time,' I replied at last, and so that is where we left it. Although we had been expecting it the Prime Minister's announcement had shaken everyone, however in the best British tradition sleeves were rolled up and preparations made to make the best of things.

Doctor Hemmings, now well past sixty, had decided to retire and he and Mrs Hemmings moved into Rose Cottage at the bottom end of the village, his place being taken by Doctor Robinson, a middle-aged man who came from some place up north complete with a wife and daughter. Jigger Andrews, now long past his best and no longer able to carry on with his poaching, had gone back to Ireland, and Danny, our friend of the woods, his health deteriorating, had finally moved to a rest home in Evesham.

Tommy and I went to visit him just before they took him away from his cabin. It was a sad occasion and I couldn't help but feel that a part of our lives was going away with him, however we realized that he had reached the stage where he could no longer look after himself and going to a home where he would be cared for was for the best. Just before he left he shook hands with both of us. 'I often used to wonder which one of you would marry the little Missy, but now I shall never know,' he said, then turning to me, 'remember, John lad, what happens in a man's life is already written and cannot be altered. Take care, and may God go with you.' Looking at him as he stood there with his few belongings bundled up and laid on the ground beside him we realized how much we had to thank him for. He had taught us so many things and I know that neither of us will ever forget the friendship shown to us by a gentle old man with whom we had shared part of our formative years and who was now in the autumn of his life. On the way home we stopped at the Mill mainly for old time's sake. The ducks and moorhens were still there but the old mill wheel, not having been used for many a long day, was now silent.

Very slowly we were getting used to adapting ourselves to wartime conditions. London had already had its first air raid warning although as yet no serious raids had been experienced, however it did serve one useful purpose: it put the capital on its toes, its citizens going about their daily business with gas masks in cardboard boxes slung over their shoulders and eyes that searched the heavens for the first signs of danger. In the sky above the silver barrage balloons swung gently at anchor, proof indeed if proof were needed that before long the enemy planes would come, and so one way or another we gradually became used to living in a strange new world of ration books, identity cards, and blackout after dark and the fact that the use of motor vehicles was restricted, petrol coupons being issued only to those whose transport was needed for war work, although it soon became evident that there were ways and means of getting hold of a few gallons of this scarce commodity.

Almost as soon as war had been declared the great evacuation of children from London and other threatened areas had begun. By train and motor coach they left clutching their little parcels in one hand and battered and well-worn teddy bears and dolls in the other. Like goods awaiting delivery they stood with labels around their necks, brothers and sisters, their childhood squabbles forgotten, clung to each other as they gazed tearfully out of carriage windows where, on the cold platforms, and near to tears themselves, parents waved and shouted good advice, no doubt wondering if they were doing the right thing in sending their children away.

On the Monday following the declaration of war Lavington received its quota of evacuees. Gathered on the platform down at the station they stood in groups, bewildered and apprehensive as they viewed the unfamiliar surroundings, however, once sorted and organized by the good ladies of the reception committee they seemed to settle down and take an interest in things. In two's and three's they were sorted and allocated to cottages where rosy-cheeked strangers took them inside and plied them with tea and cakes before showing them up to unfamiliar bedrooms under thatched eves whose latticed windows looked out on to what for them was a completely new world.

Mother had put her name forward and in due course two of the evacuees were delivered to the smithy. They were brother and sister, aged nine and ten respectively, who came from the East End of London, a couple of frightened little cockney sparrows who, lost and unsure, clung to each other as they stood on the doorstep. The sight of those two little creatures pulled at Mother's heartstrings. Kneeling down she put her arms around them and drew them to her and the response was immediate as in a matter of seconds they were clinging to her and crying. Much as we expected, they were at first homesick and realizing this we went out of our way to make them feel loved and wanted. The little girl's name was Nellie, Nell for short we were informed, while her brother was called Arthur, although having a surname like Bell it was only natural that he should answer to Tinker, so Tinker it remained. It was amazing how little they knew about the countryside and its ways. We took them up to the dairy to watch the cows being milked where, standing open-mouthed, they came to realize that milk didn't come from bottles but first had to be taken from the strange restless creatures that were delivering it into bright shiny buckets, their only comment being 'Cor blimey,' delivered in that strange cockney language that we were going to have to get used to. I took them into Grinnels Orchard to show them the few remaining apples that clung to the now near-bare branches and when time permitted we went for rambles through the woods and over the fields where I introduced them to all the delights and mysteries of nature that in the past Grandad Mumford had shown me, even

154

letting them share the little folk who I managed to convince them still lived at the bottom of the garden. To satisfy their insatiable curiosity I unlocked the door of the old cycle shed with all its mysteries, and even allowed them to take over my sanctuary which when I was their age had played such an important part in my formative years.

At first, unable to take in all the new and bewildering experiences they kept very much to themselves, however inevitably as time passed they made friends amongst the village children and before long memories of the East End and their upheaval from its familiar surroundings became swamped by the excitement of life in the countryside, the pleasure of which it had to be admitted the village children were apt to take for granted. Fortified with meat and jam sandwiches and a bottle of Tizer to wash them down they picnicked in Long Meadow and sampled the delights of fishing for minnows in the shallow stream that ran down the hill by the side of Bank Farm, where sitting for hours with their jam jars and home-made fishing nets they watched the slow moving water for signs of the elusive fish.

When the snow hung from the branches of the old yew tree behind the cottage and the perky little robin flitted from bough to bough in the hawthorn tree at the bottom of the garden, they explored the pond at the end of the lane, marvelling at the ice that edged it and at the clear water beyond in which the wild ducks paddled and quacked in nervous anticipation of titbits. Wide-eyed they knelt down to wonder at the first snowdrops that hung their delicate white hoods to tell us that spring was on its way and later, with winter gone and the air full of magic they gathered bunches of the wild flowers that were appearing in the warming earth and watched fascinated as the birds, courting done, flew in and out of the ivy-covered walls of the smithy searching for nesting places.

About a month after their arrival their mother came to visit. She was a thin nervous little woman with all the characteristics of an East End Londoner but as we were to find out, she had a heart of gold. As this was her first visit to us we were a little apprehensive, not knowing if it would unsettle the children, but as it turned out we need not have worried as there was so much to show her, so much to be explained, and the hours passed all too quickly. Later standing on the platform at the station we expected the worst but the children coped very well. Leaning out of the carriage window their mother promised to visit again soon and as the train pulled away Tinker and Nellie put on brave faces as they tried to hide their true feelings.

Christmas came and their mother returned to spend a few days with them, bringing presents from various aunts and uncles and letters from their father who was in France serving with the Army. I shall never forget their little faces as they sat cross-legged in front of the fire while their mother read the letters to them or the look in their eyes as they held a photograph of him in his uniform.

On some of the farms around land girls had taken the place of local lads who had either volunteered or been called up for the services. They were a mixed lot, coming as they did from all walks of life, some having been hairdressers, some secretaries, while others had come straight from university. Not having ever walked behind a horse or mucked out a stable or pigsty, they all had to start from scratch, however to their credit they soon knuckled down and learned to accept roughened and chapped hands, and early mornings and late nights when after a hard day they took to their beds in quiet farmhouses, where floorboards creaked and mice scratched behind the wainscots. Soon they would become experts in tractor-driving, thistle-dodging, ditch-digging, sowing and harvesting, and the gathering and clamping of potatoes on cold wet mornings, all for the princely sum of twenty-eight shillings a week.

Up at Bank Farm Tommy was in his element having two of them working with him. Fortunately they were two very streetwise young ladies who certainly knew their way around and the first time he attempted to get fresh with one of them they both ganged up on him and, catching him alone one morning in the barn, they wrestled him to the ground and took off his trousers which, once removed, they nailed to the lintel above the door, much to the amusement of Mr Collins and the embarrassment of Mrs Collins; however it was a lesson well learned and Tommy never made the same mistake again, at least not with either of those girls.

In the village things had now settled themselves down on a wartime footing. Harry Lucas, who had been appointed our air raid warden, made the most of it as he nightly paraded up and down the village street blowing his whistle and shouting 'Put that light out'. With his ego extended to near bursting point he insisted on carrying out an inspection of the pigsty that Jim Larner was intending to turn into an air raid shelter for himself and his family, the inspection having been arranged to take place one Saturday afternoon. News of its happening had spread round the village, so by the time Harry arrived a fair-sized crowd had assembled to watch the proceedings. Dead on time and dressed in his best suit Harry was welcomed with wolf whistles and ribald remarks from the audience, now eager to see some action, and they hadn't long to wait. Adjusting his steel helmet and gathering together what dignity he could, Harry was ushered through the gate of the sty and into the dark recess of the covered portion while outside the silent crowd of onlookers waited for the inevitable to happen. Suddenly all hell was let loose and the most unearthly screams issued from within the pigsty. What Harry had overlooked was the fact that the pig was still in residence and was taking his afternoon nap inside where, fumbling in the dark, Harry had fallen over it. Resenting the intrusion on its privacy the pig charged round and round in the confined space grunting and squealing until at last it burst out into the open with Harry, who by then was convinced that he had met the devil, clinging on to the pig's back hollering for help. Coming to an abrupt halt as if to catch its breath the pig remained stationary for a moment then, having got its bearings, it suddenly kicked out and took to charging round the pen unseating Harry in the process and depositing him in the straw and muck, and Jim, cornering the animal, called for assistance to get Harry to his feet and out of harm's way. Finally rescued, our intrepid air raid warden was helped out into the lane after which, smelling of pig manure and with his ego slightly deflated, he made his way back to his cottage and a change of clothing.

Much to everyone's relief the novelty of his newly-found status wore off, influenced in no small way by the incident with the pig, and the fact that one dark night Shenna Lawson waited on the garden wall of his cottage with a bucket of cold water which as Harry passed on his rounds he leaned out and threw all over him.

Late one afternoon shortly after Christmas I was working alone in the smithy when I became aware that someone had entered and looking up I saw Tommy standing in the doorway. Obviously ill at ease he shifted from one foot to the other almost as if he had something on his mind. Putting down the job I was working on I went over to him. 'What brings you here, Tommy lad?' I asked. At first he didn't reply, then almost as if he was relieved to get it off his chest he blurted out, 'I have made up my mind to volunteer for the Army. I know

157

us alus said that when the time came us would make the decision together.' Here he paused as if expecting me to say something, not that I could have, his announcement having taken me completely by surprise, however, it was his next bit of news that really staggered me. Almost as if he knew the effect it would have on me he half-turned away before coming out with 'Phyllis and me are getting engaged now.' Although the possibility had at times crossed my mind, I couldn't or rather didn't want to believe it. Up until then we had in a way always shared Phyllis, although thinking on it I had to admit that of late they had showed signs of becoming more involved with each other, however, pulling myself together I realized that this was not the time to show my feelings, so shaking his hand I wished them both well, adding that if he was going to volunteer then I would go with him.

Mother, when told of Tommy's engagement to Phyllis, didn't seem at all surprised, but when I added that Tommy had decided to volunteer and that I was going with him she received the news in silence almost as if she had been expecting it. Father on the other hand said very little other than to remind me that he had had to make a similar decision years ago and he knew just how I felt. Fortunately, as it does sometimes in life, fate stepped in and solved the problem.

One morning a message came for me to report to the estate office, so full of curiosity I duly presented myself at the appointed hour to be met by Master Grahame who, after enquiring after the well-being of my family ushered me into his office. Sitting himself down at his desk he spent a few moments shuffling through some papers that lay in front of him, leaving me standing and wondering what it was all about, then leaning back in his chair he began:

'John, your father and I volunteered and served in the last war, however this time things are slightly different. Help will be needed to keep things going on the home front, a task which in its way is equally as important as serving in the armed forces,' here he paused, 'I don't know what you have decided to do,' he continued, 'or even if you have given the matter any thought, but Mr Collins from Bank Farm tells me that your friend Tommy Whitworth is going to volunteer and under the circumstances you may have a notion to do the same,' the latter coming almost in the form of a question, however before I could answer he went on, 'I have in front of me a letter from the Ministry sent in reply to a questionnaire in which they asked for the names and occupations of any estate workers who I could recommend for deferment, it being considered that some of them would be of greater use carrying on with their normal jobs. I know that the blacksmith's shop does not strictly come under the estate however I took the liberty of including your name on the list, feeling that your father will need your help with all the extra work he will be called upon to do. I won't press you for an answer but would advise you to think the matter over carefully and perhaps to talk it over with your father. Then once you have made up your mind you must let me know.'

Slightly bewildered by the sudden turn of events I walked back to the smithy where Father was waiting to learn what it had all been about and how I had got on, although secretly I had the feeling that Master Grahame had already discussed the matter with him. Sitting on the bench under the window, cap in hand, he listened while I told him what had transpired and for a while after I had finished he just sat gazing into space while I waited for him to speak. 'As you know, lad,' he at last began, 'many years ago I had to make a similar decision, and believe me it wasn't easy, however once I had come to one I didn't waver. You must make up your own mind but whatever you decide neither I nor your mother will try to influence you although you know that we would rather you stay.' Then with nothing more to say he got to his feet, put his cap back on his head, and walked over to the forge, grasped the handle of the bellows and began to pump.

That night I lay in bed turning things over and over in my mind, wondering what to do for the best, and knowing that while there was a part of me that wanted to stay there was also a part that kept reminding me of my promise to Tommy.

The next morning Phyllis called. Father was away on some business or other which perhaps was just as well for I had a fair idea why she had come. She wanted to find out how I had taken the news of her engagement. Not willing to broach the subject myself I kept on working in between talking about village gossip, in fact about anything other than her engagement. At last with conversation nearly exhausted she brought the subject up. 'Tommy tells me that you might be going to volunteer for the Army. I shall miss you both.' Here she paused as if gathering strength for the next question. 'Did he tell you that he and I are getting engaged?' Here she stopped, obviously waiting for me to answer. Turning to face her I said how pleased I was at the news of her engagement; as for volunteering I hadn't yet made up my mind. Looking back on it I suppose it was the matter of fact way I had accepted her news that upset her. Somehow I don't think it was what she expected and I could swear that there were tears in her eyes. Then just as the awkward silence that followed was becoming almost unbearable, she left and, pausing at the doorway, said, 'If it were possible I'd marry both of you, you know that,' and then she was gone.

What it was that finally decided me to give up any idea of volunteering I shall never know but that is just what I did. Mother of course was delighted as I knew she would be. Tommy, on the other hand, just shrugged his shoulders and accepted it, but I was grateful that neither he nor Phyllis said anything to make me feel guilty. The night before Tommy was due to leave for Aldershot the three of us met down at the Drovers Arms for a farewell drink. He was in high spirits; for him it was a new challenge, the start of a new adventure. Phyllis on the other hand was very quiet and said very little and all through what turned out to be a fairly noisy evening she sat with her drink in front of her, adding little or nothing to the main topic of conversation, Tommy's departure. Once or twice I caught her eye, but each time she turned away almost as if she was afraid that I might read something there, something which she felt unable to admit to.

The next day the two of them called in at the smithy on their way to the station and after Father had wished Tommy all the best I walked with them to the top of the lane. It was an awkward moment when the time for parting came, we had been pals for a long time and I must admit that I felt guilty, however, shaking his hand I wished him luck adding the usual 'Take care of yourself.' There was very little else I could say really, then just before they disappeared from view, Tommy turned and called out: 'Take care of Phyllis for me, John.' Waving in acknowledgement I watched until they were out of sight, glad that he didn't know just how much I wanted to do that.

Busy at the smithy and helping on the land when possible the time passed quickly and before I knew it Tommy, his training finished, was coming home on leave. Phyllis brought the news to me on what was to turn out a memorable day. I was alone at the time, Father having gone up to the stables. She came in very quietly and it wasn't until she called out my name that I realized that she was there. Turning to face her I could see at a glance that something was troubling her, she didn't look her usual bright self and for one horrible moment I wondered if anything had happened to Tommy. Going over to her I put my hands on her shoulders. 'Whatever is the matter, love?' I asked. Thrusting an opened letter into my hand she said, 'Tommy is coming home on leave and he wants us to get married before he goes back.' Still holding the letter I looked at her, failing to understand why she should be so upset, after all it had been taken for granted that they would marry. She should have been overjoyed and full of plans for the future, however I could see the tears in her eyes and just at that moment I wanted to take her in my arms and comfort her.

Not to this day have I yet come to understand the vagaries of women and have often wondered why Phyllis should have come down to break the news to me even before she had told her parents. However in spite of what I assumed were misgivings on her part, arrangements for the wedding went ahead. They were to be married in church by special licence and I was asked to be best man. Naturally I accepted; under the circumstances I could do no other.

It was the first wartime wedding we had had in the village and one or two of the local lads who happened to be on leave at the time came, their uniforms lending a splash of colour to the occasion. Phyllis looked radiant in her bridal outfit and bearing in mind that material and such were in short supply her mother and helpers had done a good job. As for Tommy, for once he appeared to have lost a little of his usual self-confidence, fidgeting and looking over his shoulder as we waited for the bride. Suddenly the waiting was over and at a signal from the Parson the organist struck up the wedding march and Phyllis, on the arm of her father, started the slow walk down the aisle to where Tommy and I were standing. Then at last she was there and stealing a glance at her I thought I saw a faint smile tremble on her lips.

The thoughts that went through my mind at that moment were and always will be private, but glancing at Mother sitting in the front pew I could see by the look she gave me that she knew what they were. I had often given thought to the day when perhaps I should walk down the aisle with my wife on my arm, my secret being that as far as anyone was aware I had never put a face or name to that unknown woman, but seeing Phyllis standing there in all her glory I had to admit that I wished it were me at her side.

With the service over there followed the usual photographs and congratulations, after which we gathered at the village hall for the reception, speeches were made, toasts were drunk and the cake cut, all amid the usual chatter and laughter as friends and relations gathered in small groups to discuss any subject which the liberal supply of drinks conjured out of loosened tongues.

With flushed face Phyllis mingled with the guests and I watched her as she went from one to the other receiving congratulations and the occasional well-meant kiss. Then she came over to me; it was a moment I had been dreading. 'Remember that day when the three of us sat on Oak Hill and I couldn't make up my mind which one of you to marry?' she said with eyes starting to fill with tears. 'I'm sorry, John, but you will always have a very special place in my heart. But there, you know that, don't you?' Luckily before I could reply a voice behind me called out, 'Go on, John, kiss the bride.' It was Tommy. Putting my hands on her shoulders I drew her to me, the scent of her dulling my senses and making my heart beat faster. Then our lips met and for a brief moment nothing else seemed to matter. Suddenly a hand was placed on my shoulder and a voice said, 'That's enough, John, leave some for us.' And so the magic of the moment was gone. Turning and not daring to look at Phyllis, frightened of what I might see in her eyes, I walked away.

A crowd of us went down to the station to see them off on their honeymoon, which was to be taken in Weston-Super-Mare and walking back up the lane with Mrs Whitworth after the train had gone she suddenly drew me to one side. 'Do you think that they will be happy?' she asked. 'What makes you think they won't be?' I replied. She didn't answer straight away and so we walked on in silence, then 'I wouldn't say this to anyone else but you, John, but I have an awful feeling that their happiness will be short-lived. Don't ask me why because I don't know.' Thinking it best, I didn't attempt to enlarge on the subject but it certainly made me think.

Chapter X

Although now only in the first year of the war the magnitude of the task ahead was beginning to get through to people and we braced ourselves to face the storm that we all knew must soon come. Tommy was now in France and in the village Percy Wood, George Arkell and Bill Walcott had formed the nucleus of our local Observer Corps, their point of observance being a wooden hut that had been erected on the top of Oak Hill where, fortified with flasks of tea and the occasional nip of brandy, they took it in turns to scan the sky for enemy aircraft.

Over the wireless came the call for volunteers for the newly-formed Local Defence Volunteers, jokingly referred to as the Look, Duck and Vanish Brigade and those of us who were able joined up as one man, our headquarters being set up in the old pumping station adjacent to what had been the power house. The main advantage of the location was its proximity to the Drovers Arms which by means of a hole in the fence at the bottom of Harry Gibbons's garden and a short walk round the side of his cottage could be reached quite easily. Our early efforts to look and act as a formidable defence unit were to say the least verging on the comical particularly when we paraded in the dairy paddock wearing our LDV armbands and armed with a motley collection of hastily-improvised weapons. Master Grahame had assumed command and Father, who had retrieved his old steel helmet from the garden shed, was made second in command. Fortunately this state of affairs didn't last long as not long afterwards the LDV became the Home Guard and what with the issue of uniforms, rifles and other bits of essential equipment, plus of course the help given by those who had served in the last war, we were soon able to march and drill with some resemblance of military efficiency. There had been several letters from Tommy and although I saw very little of Phyllis she managed to keep me up to date with all his news.

Things on the war front were now beginning to hot up, Hitler started his blitzkrieg tactics and so, with the surrender of the Belgian Army, the bulk of the British Forces started the long trek back, a journey that was to end on the beaches of Dunkirk. On 30 May it was officially announced that with the help of the Royal Navy, assisted by an armada of small boats manned by civilians, most of the troops had been safely taken off the beaches, however details of this were very scarce and in the village we waited anxiously for any news of local lads who had been in France.

Shortly after the announcement of the evacuation Phyllis received notification that Tommy had been wounded but was now safely in hospital somewhere in England. His had been a short war and it was just his luck to be at the wrong place at the wrong time. Quite naturally both Phyllis and Tommy's mother were frantic with worry not knowing the extent of his wounds or where he was, however fortunately it wasn't long before they were notified that he was in a military hospital in the vicinity of Peterborough. Phyllis came round with the news and after discussing it with her I volunteered to go with her and Tommy's mother to visit him.

After a long and somewhat tedious journey on the train we finally arrived at Peterborough only to find that the hospital was some miles out of town, luckily however with the help of a somewhat infrequent bus service we managed at last to locate it on the edge of a small village. It was a large country house standing in its own grounds and approached by a sweeping drive up and down which a constant stream of ambulances and other military vehicles were making their way. Mounting the flight of grand stone steps we entered to find ourselves in a huge empty hall, empty that is with the exception of a plain desk set just inside the doorway at which a corporal of the RAMC was sitting. Phyllis, worn out by the journey and by then thoroughly apprehensive, gave him particulars and he asked us to wait at the same time indicating a row of chairs opposite.

Fortunately we didn't have long to wait before a nurse came along who informed us that it would be all right to see Tommy, after which she lead us along a maze of corridors eventually coming to a halt before a door which we were to learn led into a small ward of six beds. Before she entered however she stood for a moment with her hand on the door handle. 'Mrs Whitworth,' she said, addressing herself to Phyllis, 'have they given you any indication of the extent of your husband's wounds?' Phyllis shook her head and just at that moment I had the feeling that we were being prepared for some bad news.

'Your husband,' she continued, 'was wounded during the evacuation at Dunkirk. A bullet was lodged in his head, however this has been removed, but I must tell you that at the moment we are not sure if any permanent damage has been done; only time will reveal that. You may find him a little incoherent but this is mainly due to the drugs we have given him.' So saying, she opened the door and ushered us into the room where Tommy was lying in a bed by the window which overlooked the garden. By then Phyllis was near to breaking point but she bore herself bravely as she and Tommy's mother stood by the bed. As for me, realizing that the moment should be private for the two women I quietly withdrew, closing the door behind me.

Outside in the corridor all was hustle and bustle as the staff went about their business. Wandering about I dodged busy nurses who appeared from dark corners laden with armfuls of folded blankets and bed linen, and all around was that unmistakeable hospital smell, a smell of disinfectant and starched cleanliness. Then, just as I was about to start to find my way back a hand tapped me on the shoulder and a voice said, 'The two ladies are leaving now so you can go and see Private Whitworth for a few minutes.' Opening the door of the ward I entered. He looked so small and frail as he lay propped up with pillows, his head swathed in bandages, not the laughing devil-may-care Tommy of old but a face mirrored with pain. Sitting at the bedside I found it difficult to make conversation, finding myself at a loss for the right words, all I could think to say being, 'Well, old mate, how are you feeling?' On reflection a pretty stupid question to ask. Turning his head towards me he tried to reply but seemingly the words wouldn't come so grasping his hand I added, 'I wish I had all these lovely nurses to look after me.' All routine stuff said more to cover my embarrassment than anything else.

God forbid that I should have said what was really going through my mind like, how awful it was to see him lying there as memories of chasing about in the hayfields and swimming in the millstream came flooding back. I thought of his wedding day and how handsome and proud he had looked and I asked myself was it only yesterday, so much seemed to have happened in such a short space of time. Suddenly a voice behind me broke into my thoughts: 'I'm afraid I must ask you to leave now.' It was the nurse, so letting go of his hand I stood up. 'See you soon, old mate,' I said as I turned and made my way back to the door where, halting, I looked back just in time to see him raise his hand perceptibly, but I could see that his eyes were expressionless.

165

The journey home was not a happy one even though I tried my best to assure them that Tommy would be all right in time, but the going was heavy and I must admit that I was glad when finally we reached Lavington. The long walk up to the village seemed interminable. Oh, how I wished that Phyllis would break down and cry but she didn't, however I was sure that she would later, so after seeing Tommy's mother to her cottage I took Phyllis home where, standing with one arm round her, I knocked at the door and waited. Her mother answered and stepping forward put her arms around her daughter and for a moment they just stood saying nothing, then quietly she led her inside. 'I'll see to her now, John,' she said as she closed the door.

The weeks passed and eventually Tommy was moved to a convalescent hospital just outside Cheltenham, which made it a lot easier for visiting. I went with Phyllis several times to see him and as time passed he seemed to get much better and more like his old self again, the good news being that it wouldn't be long before he would be discharged and sent home. It was about this time that there came about another upheaval in our lives. Nellie and Tinker, our two evacuees, had a visit from their mother who, on arrival, informed us that she would be taking them back to London. Mother did her best to dissuade her, pointing out that having just got used to us and settled down it might be unwise to uproot them once again, particularly in view of the risks from air raids in London, however, in spite of our combined protests she remained adamant and so arrangements were made for the children to leave. Reluctantly their few possessions were gathered together and packed and Mother went down to the station with them, Father and I having said our goodbyes at the cottage. As the train drew away they leaned out of the carriage window, tearfully waving, the memory of their tear-stained faces remaining with Mother for ever.

Little did any of us realize then that the span of their young lives was already drawing to a close as in the December of that same year we received a letter from their father telling us that all three of them had been killed in an air raid. I shall always remember Mother's grief the day the news came. I can see her now sitting in the parlour, the opened letter on her lap and a look of utter disbelief on her face. There were no tears, just a sad silence and realizing that just at that moment there was very little that we could say or do to help we left her alone in her grief. The house wasn't the same without them. We

166

missed their cheerful cockney chatter and the innumerable questions that they were apt to fire at us in their search to understand the ways of the country, and there were times when I found myself standing at the door leading into the yard expecting to see them laughing and chasing about as they once did, two little cockney sparrows who, just as they were beginning to find out what life was all about, had suddenly had it taken from them.

And so the first year of the war dragged on. Jessey Talbot, the lad with whom I had had that memorable fight at school, had been killed on the beaches at Dunkirk. I was glad that we had become friends if only for a short while, just another casualty in a seemingly senseless war during which the casualty lists were now getting longer and longer. At the smithy we were kept busy six days a week doing work for the Ministry of Agriculture as well as attending to all our local commitments. Tommy, now more or less recovered, had been discharged and was back home, and he and Phyllis went to live with Mrs Whitworth down at Leyfield Cottage. The estate had found him a job at the timber yard and although I didn't see a lot of them they seemed to be settling down all right. On the odd occasion that we met down at the Drovers Arms he appeared to be his old self, but in spite of it I had a nagging feeling that deep down things were not quite what they appeared to be. Anyway, I argued that time would tell and in the meantime we could only hope.

Hardly had we got over the sad news about our little evacuees than another surprise came along, this time a pleasant one. Sitting having tea one Saturday afternoon we were surprised to hear a knock at the door. Mother being nearest got up and answered it and what a shock she had, for there standing on the doorstep, suitcase by her side, stood Aunty Beckey. The next few minutes were to say the least hectic as we all got up and rushed over to greet her. She looked much the same, a little older perhaps but that was only to be expected and oh, how the tongues did wag, everyone firing questions at her at once, so much so that at last Father was forced to call for silence to allow Beckey to have her say.

Later that night, gathered in the parlour, she told us about her life in Canada and of the events that had brought her back to England, and as she talked I found myself looking up at the photograph of her in her nurse's uniform that stood in its silver frame on the mantelshelf. She looked so young then but so much had happened since those far-off days. She told us that her husband, a wing commander in the Royal Canadian Air Force, had been posted to England with a bomber squadron that was stationed somewhere in Lincolnshire and that she had been allowed to travel over with him, drawing comfort from the fact that although he was a trained pilot his age would prevent him from flying on operations. She had found accommodation in a village near to his station and he had been allowed to live out with her, but unfortunately, due to service commitments he had been unable to accompany her this time, but had promised that on his next leave they would both come to visit and stay for a while. She told us how she had met up with her husband, Stanley. He had been married previously, his wife having died some three years before they met. Luckily there hadn't been any children of the marriage and this had made their association that much easier. For quite a while they had just remained good friends enjoying each other's company and finding out that they had a lot in common, so when the threat of war appeared on the horizon, and realizing that time was passing them by, they decided to get married.

Beckey stayed with us for a week and the day before she left I walked with her up to the churchyard to visit Grandma and Grandad's grave. All was silent as we stood looking down on the last resting place of those two dear people then, sensing that she wanted to be alone, I left and waited for her under the lych-gate from where I could just make out her lonely figure standing under the old yew tree. What thoughts were going through her mind at that moment? I wondered. Was she going back over the years when young and fancy-free she had made such wonderful plans for the future, and perhaps regretting that the two people now lost to her had not lived long enough to see their proud, wayward Beckey happily married? The next day she left, promising to come back soon, and Mother and Aunty Tessa walked her to the station to see her off.

Time passed taking Jack Harris the late landlord of the Drovers Arms with it. He had a grand send-off, most of the villagers turning out to see him laid to rest in the churchyard. He left behind him a nation which, standing alone, waited for Hitler to launch his invasion, and in the village we waited for the dreaded sound of the church bells that would tell us that the Germans had landed. Official notices appeared on the village noticeboard telling us what to do in the case of an invasion – bits of sheer propaganda which if the truth were known very few would remember if the time came to put them into

168

action. Mr Churchill, in a broadcast to the nation, said, 'If the invader comes there will be no lying down as we have seen other countries do. We shall defend every village, town and city.' Stirred by these noble words the nation buckled to the first task of reorganizing and re-equipping the Divisions that had made their escape from Dunkirk. Our village Home Guard, now more or less ready for any eventuality, took its place alongside the Regular Army, standing to at dawn and dusk, ready to deal with any emergency, while in the daytime those working on the land toiled with their rifles never very far away as they scanned the skies for the first sight or sound of trouble in the form of glider or parachute troops.

Following the fall of France, Britain stood alone. Place names were removed from signposts and obliterated from milestones, and in some cases even from war memorials, all this activity being accompanied by an outbreak of spy and fifth-column mania, during which identity cards were checked and re-checked. In the summer and autumn months derelict hay wains and other broken-down farm wagons had been scattered at random across the larger meadows and other places where enemy gliders might attempt to land, and on commons and parkland deep, wide trenches had been dug, the earth from them being piled up in heaps to break up any wide expanse of grassland. Luckily as history will record the invasion never came, instead the enemy intensified his air attacks, a period that was to be known as 'The Battle of Britain'.

One afternoon, with the sun beginning to warm the cold earth, I went up to the churchyard to tend Grandma and Grandad's grave. Kneeling beside it completely immersed in what I was doing, I failed to be aware that someone had approached and was standing behind me, that is until a well-known voice said, 'Hello John, it's only me.' Rising I turned to see Phyllis, and looking at her and knowing her as I did I could see that something was troubling her. 'John,' she continued, 'can we talk?' Nodding, I took her hand and led her over to a seat set under the churchyard wall where, sitting down, I begged her to tell me what was wrong. Suddenly she burst into tears and quite involuntarily I put my arms around her and drew her towards me, holding her until at last she regained her composure and was able to tell me why she had come. It appeared that Tommy, in spite of his outward show of being his old self, had started to have periods of deep depression and, when in one of these moods, was almost impossible to live with. Neither she nor her Mrs Whitworth could handle it. Twice she had gone back to her mother and on

169

these occasions Tommy would beg her to return, promising that he would pull himself together. For a while all would be well and he would go out of his way to be nice to her, however it didn't last and it wouldn't be long before he would once again lapse into one of his sullen moods of silence.

Listening to her I could tell that she was near to breaking point but for the life of me I couldn't at that moment think of any words which I could use to comfort her, knowing only too well that if I had made any move to show her my love and concern in her present state she would have been vulnerable, and would probably have regretted any show of affection when later she had time to think, so I just held her and listened. Sitting in the quiet of the churchyard she poured her heart out to me as she had never done before and when at last she dried her tears she apologized for breaking down like she had. I walked with her as far as the lych-gate where, stopping for a moment, I took her hands in mine and reminded her that I should always be around to help if she should need me. 'I know, John,' she said, 'I know,' and with that she reached up and kissed me; then she was gone.

What with my Home Guard duties and work at the smithy I had very little spare time on my hands, consequently I saw very little of Tommy or Phyllis. September came and autumn began to stretch its long fingers over the woods above the village. Hitler, having changed his tactics, began his blitz on our major cities, and so the long nights of terror started. With the early mists beginning to gather in the hollows at the foot of Bredon Hill, Alby Stringer passed away peacefully in his sleep at the age of seventy-six and so another link with the past had gone. Phyllis was still doing her job at the post office and one Saturday afternoon I bumped into her as she was leaving work. She told me that things between her and Tommy had improved, but even as she spoke I knew that she was covering up for him, her face telling me all I wanted to know. She looked dull and listless, however with that loyal and independent spirit that had always been part of her nature she assured me that she could cope. Watching her as she walked away I made up my mind to have a few words with Tommy to see if I could knock some sense into him, at the same time being aware that I should have to tread with caution and try and arrange things to make it appear that any such meeting was casual.

Fortunately the chance came sooner than I had expected. I was working on my own at the smithy at the time and Tommy came in with a small repair job for the timber yard. We stood talking for a few minutes on things unrelated to what I had in mind, then Father came in, so making my excuses I walked down to the gate leading into Long Meadow, hoping that Tommy would follow. Luckily he did and was soon standing beside me. 'I have a fair idea what it is you want to say to me,' he began, 'but it ain't any of your business. It's between Phyllis and me,' and with that he turned to go. 'Hang on, mate,' I called after him, 'just hear me out. At least you owe me that much.' Almost reluctantly he turned and came back. 'Tommy lad,' I continued, 'you and me have known each other for a long time and naturally I can't help but worry about you and Phyllis. Perhaps if you told me what was wrong I could help.' For a while he didn't reply but just stood with his arms resting on the top rail of the gate gazing into space.

'To be honest I don't know what is happening to me, John,' he began at last. 'There be times when life just don't seem worth living any more. Things and people have changed. It was all so simple when we were kids.' Here he paused and not wanting to interrupt his train of thought I kept quiet. 'Look at Phyllis, sometimes I wonder how she puts up with me, I know she tries her best. It could be that I don't know what I want out of life; it's almost as if I am reaching out for something that isn't there any more. There are times when in the middle of the night I relive those hours on the beach at Dunkirk, hearing again the gunfire and the screams of the wounded and dying. Perhaps it would have been better if I had died with them. It would have made things a lot simpler.'

Almost as if he felt he had said too much he stopped and waited for me to reply. 'Tommy, lad,' I began, 'you and me have shared good and bad times and I only wish that there was something that I could do or say that would help. You have a good wife in Phyllis, one of the best, and it's not fair that you treat her the way that you do. Christ man, can't you see what you are doing to her or is it that you don't care any more?' Then I waited, fully expecting him to blow his top and tell me to mind my own business, but he didn't.

Taking courage, I continued, 'You must try harder, mate, after all you and Phyllis have the rest of your lives in front of you. Just remember and be thankful that you weren't among those hundreds of young men who didn't make it back. I'm damn sure that any one of them would be glad to swap places with you, so count your blessings, and stop feeling so bloody sorry for yourself, otherwise you are going the right way to lose everything including your wife.'

Holding my breath I waited, wondering if I had said too much but apparently I hadn't. Looking me straight in the face, he said, 'Thanks, mate,'

171

then he turned and walked away.

Christmas came and we celebrated it quietly. Following family tradition we went to church on Christmas morning in the company of other solemn-faced villagers, most of whom still had memories of another time in another age when they had come to pray for the safe return of fathers, husbands and sons some of whom were resting in the churchyard outside in the company of old Zetter Parsons, Jack Harris and Alby Stringer, names and faces that belonged to a life now gone for ever. Looking over at Doctor and Mrs Hemmings sitting in the same pew that they had occupied for the best part of forty years, I wondered if they too were reflecting on all the momentous happenings that had taken place since the day that they had arrived in this sleepy corner of Gloucestershire, of all the babies that the good doctor had brought into the world and of the older ones who, when their time had come, he had sat beside and comforted.

On the wall opposite a shaft of sunlight rested on a pale oak board that hung there, a board upon which were recorded in letters of gold the names of Nathan Powell, Harry Fieldman, Walter Richards, Harry Stevens, Nacky Pitt and Charlie Bowers, a roll of honour of those of the village who had laid down their lives in the last war of 1914 to 1918. No doubt visitors in the years ahead would stop to look up and read their names and the words 'lest we forget' that were written under them, wondering what sort of people they were, then after signing the visitors' book, they would walk quietly out into the sunshine closing the door behind them. In the pew in front my parents sat side by side. They had known those lads whose names were recorded for posterity on that simple oak board. The land over which they had fought and died had long since been grassed over to cover the scars of war. Now it was all set to happen again.

As 1941 came rushing in, almost taking us by surprise, we prepared to settle down to face another year of war, realizing at last that it was going to be a long drawn-out job. Searching my conscience, something which of late I had often found myself doing, I had to admit that I didn't feel right about my deferment, so after much soul-searching and after giving the matter a great deal of thought I made up my mind to do something about it. With that in mind I arranged an interview with Master Grahame at the estate office. Sitting in front of him I tried to explain how I felt and after hearing me out he said, 'I think I understand how you feel, John, however the matter seems to have been taken out of our hands as only today I received notification that your deferment has been terminated and that you were now liable for call-up, so I suggest that you wait until you hear officially,' and with that he rose and leaning across his desk held out his hand. 'Good luck, John, we shall miss you in the Home Guard.' Then just as I reached the door, he added, 'Take care of yourself.'

When I gave the news to Mother she accepted it with an air of resignation and Father said very little other than that he had been expecting it for some time, so it was just as well that shortly afterwards I received orders to attend a medical in Cheltenham, followed two weeks later by my call-up papers and railway warrant to Catterick in Yorkshire.

The night before I was due to leave I arranged to meet Tommy and Phyllis down at the Drovers Arms. Tommy of course was full of good advice having gone through it all himself, while Phyllis on the other hand said very little. The following morning I set off alone to catch the early train. Father walked with me to the top of the lane and before turning back shook my hand and bade me take care of myself; and so with those well-meant words of advice I set off for the station. The lane leading down to it was empty and the chill winter wind whistled through the bare branches. There were no foxgloves, no garlands of honeysuckle in the hedgerows. Why couldn't they have let me wait until summer? I thought. It would have made a much more pleasant departure.

During the long journey north I watched the unfamiliar countryside flash by, a tapestry of hills, valleys and sombre industrial cities with their rows of terraced houses, and where in dark satanic mill towns tall brick chimneys reached up into the sky. It was a new and exciting experience which fortunately left little time for me to wonder what was waiting for me at the end of my journey, at Catterick Camp. Arriving at Darlington in the late afternoon I changed trains and took the little branch line to Richmond where two three-ton trucks were waiting to convey the newcomers, who by now numbered some twenty or thirty, up to the camp. By this time it was getting dark and we were glad when at last, checked and allocated barrack rooms, we were taken over to the mess hall where we were given a hot meal.

Two days later we started on the long programme of medical check-ups, the issuing of uniforms and equipment and the first of our many inoculations. Luckily the days seemed to fly by leaving us very little time to worry or feel homesick and it wasn't long before having completed our basic training and drilled and moulded into something resembling soldiers we were ready to be posted out to our various units. My final interview went particularly well as after a question and answer session with the interviewing officer I was posted to the RASC and ordered to report to a depot just outside Hereford, an arrangement that suited me fine seeing that it was only some thirty miles or so from Lavington.

Given seven days leave before reporting I walked up and down the platform of Darlington station feeling a lot better about things than I had on the day of my arrival. Perhaps it was because my conscience was now clear and I was now part of the war effort, and so it was with this feeling of achievement that I alighted on Lavington station where, with a seven days leave pass in my pocket, gas mask with steel helmet strapped to it and forage cap set at a jaunty angle on my head, I set about walking up the lane to the village. On the way I met Harry Gibbons who at first didn't recognize me, but after peering closely said, 'My God, it be John Mumford. Seeing you in that uniform takes me back a piece. I remember your dad when he fust came home on leave and damn me if you don't look just like him from a distance,' then after shaking my hand he went on his way still mumbling to himself. I was glad that I had met someone who knew me. It made me feel accepted and less like an outsider, silly really seeing that I had only been away a couple of months.

On arriving home my first call was at the smithy where from the sounds coming from within I gathered that Father was still working. Standing in the doorway I watched as he heated and pounded a length of iron bar on the anvil, then suddenly without turning he said, 'Welcome home, lad. I sensed you were there. It must be that familiar smell of khaki,' and with that he put down his hammer, turned and came over to me. With his hands on my shoulders he held me at arm's length, looking me up and down. 'Reckon you'll do, lad,' he said, but I knew he was proud of me, and so we stood for a while talking until at last it was time to go over to the cottage.

Opening the door he stood back and let me go in first; Mother was busy in the parlour laying the table for supper and having heard the door open called out, 'It's about time you packed up working so just go and get your hands washed and come and sit by the fire. Supper won't be long.' She was halfway to the kitchen before she realized that I was standing there. Putting her hands to her face all she could say was, 'Oh John, oh John,' then she rushed across the room and flung her arms around me. Later, gathered around talking, she admitted that in that first brief moment when she had seen me standing in the doorway it had rolled back the years reminding her of Father when he had come home on leave before leaving for France.

I asked after Tommy and they told me that as far as they knew things were much about the same and that he was becoming more and more of a recluse. He had been to Cheltenham to see a specialist who apparently, after examining him, had to admit that he could find very little wrong physically, but as for his mind, it was really a question of time. All this information Mother had gleaned from Aunty Tessa who had got it from Mrs Whitworth.

The next morning I met Phyllis in the village and she more or less confirmed what I had been told. Looking at her I could see that she had aged and I began to wonder just how much more she could take. There was so much I wanted to say to her but I knew it wouldn't be wise for both our sakes. I walked with her to the top of the village and before she left to make her way back to Leyfield Cottage she said, 'I think I know what you want to say, John, but don't. I can cope. Just make sure that you take care of yourself. I couldn't bear it if anything happened to you.' With that she left and I watched her go until she passed from sight beyond the lodge gates.

I spent most of my leave helping Father in the smithy and taking long walks alone in the woods above the village and down to the mill where just above it Dan's old hut still stood cold and neglected, with its roof covered by brambles and the foliage of young trees that were now beginning to take over. Standing there I remembered the times when Tommy, Phyllis and me had used to visit, the log on which we used to sit like the three wise monkeys was still there but the clearing seemed to have got smaller, perhaps because of the undergrowth which was slowly encroaching on it, and I wondered how long it would be before it completely disappeared. What a pity it was that we had had to grow up. Why couldn't things have stayed just the way they were in those far-off days? I thought, however I knew the answer even before I had asked the question.

On returning home I found a package waiting for me and on opening it soon realized that it was for Father as in it were the letters and watch that had belonged to his friend Charlie. The letter that accompanied them was from a solicitor stating that Charlie's mother had passed away and that in her will she had requested that the items be forwarded on to Father. I took the parcel and letter out to him in the smithy where he was at work and when I left he was sitting on the seat under the window staring into space with the watch and letters on his lap. Brusquely I wiped away the beginnings of a tear, after all he was entitled to his memories, he had earned them.

On the last evening of my leave I decided to take a walk up onto Oak Hill. The day was drawing to a close and long shadows were beginning to creep down the slopes. For a moment I hesitated, wondering whether to climb to the top or make my way home, then suddenly I became aware of a figure hurrying across the park towards me and as it drew nearer I saw that it was Phyllis. Breathless she finally caught up with me. 'I was on my way to the smithy to see you, John,' she began, 'I didn't want you to go back tomorrow without a word, anyway, there are things I want to talk about, that's if you want to listen.'

Side by side we walked up the hill path. It was the first time for quite a while that I had been alone with her other than on our chance meetings in the village, then on reaching the gate by the keeper's cottage we stopped. Suddenly she began to cry. 'Hold me, John,' she pleaded. I needed no persuasion. Taking her in my arms I raised her tear-stained face and kissed her, feeling her tremble as I did so. Still sobbing she clung to me and so we stood in the gathering darkness while I struggled to get my thoughts in order. Somewhere in the back of my mind alarm bells were ringing. It would have been so easy to have forgotten that she was married and at the moment very vulnerable. Fortunately common sense prevailed and the moment passed, then she began to tell me her story.

Seemingly she had reached the end of her tether and feared for her safety and sanity, as on two occasions Tommy had become violent and attacked her, and once he had even turned on his mother for trying to intervene between them. I did my best to calm her, knowing that there was very little I could do other than to provide a shoulder to cry on. Between sobs she unburdened herself and it took all of my willpower to stop me from doing what I so desperately wanted to do, however after a while she pulled herself together and, breaking free, wiped away her tears.

'I'm sorry, John, I shouldn't have burdened you with my troubles. I know it's not the answer. Please forgive me. Before you go I want you to know that

I love you and although I could never admit it I always have. If only I had listened to my heart, things could have been so different but it's too late now. I made my choice and so shall have to make the best of things. Take care and write when you can.'

With that she left me and I watched her go until she became swallowed up in the gloom. I wanted to call her back but I knew that it would be folly to do so, the moment had passed and fate was to make sure that it would be some time before our paths crossed again. I didn't hurry back to the cottage, there being so much on my mind, however one thing I did realize all too clearly and that was that for both Tommy and Phyllis's sakes there were things that I must forget. The past would have to remain a closed chapter.

The next morning saying my goodbyes to all the family I set off for Hereford and my new posting. As the train pulled out I began to hope that at the last minute Phyllis would come running up the platform but of course she didn't; perhaps I had been watching too many movies. The weeks that followed were to say the least hectic, giving me little time to feel homesick, not that I over indulged in that, having taken to Army life better than I thought I would. There were new friends to be made and new experiences to be met head on. We did our driving instruction and were eventually given our WD licences. For some obscure reason I made more effort to go home when weekend passes were available. Perhaps it was the thought of running into Phyllis again, I don't know, all I did know was that I hoped she and Tommy by some miracle might solve their problems.

We were now well into the second year of the war and it was about this time that one of life's inexplicable chance meetings took place, meetings which when circumstances are right come along when least expected. We had taken a convoy of lorries up to Acton in London to have certain modifications done to the vehicles, a job that was to take the best part of a week. It was a large, busy depot, one of its few advantages being that it carried a cadre of ATS girls and naturally some of the lads soon got themselves fixed up.

One morning while working on my truck, bonnet raised and head well inside the engine, I heard someone say, 'Blast, that's done it,' and pulling myself from under the bonnet I turned to see an ATS girl bending down examining a tear in one of her stockings where she had snagged it on one of the packing cases that stood nearby. Watching her, oily rag in hand, I took stock, my first impressions being more than favourable. She was about my

177

height as near as I could tell but what struck me most was her flawless skin, dark brown eyes and a mouth that was meant for laughing. Straightening herself up she asked, 'Seen enough, have you?' 'Sorry,' I replied as I turned away, then almost as an afterthought, I added, 'Can I help?' 'Not unless you have a spare pair of regulation stockings,' she replied. So coming to the conclusion that that was the end of our brief encounter I got on with what I had been doing, however much to my surprise she came over and stood beside me. 'Are you with that lot from Hereford?' she asked, and on learning that I was she told me that her mother had known someone from there many years ago, the outcome of it being that I invited her out for a drink after duty that evening, and I must say that I was flattered when she agreed.

Sitting in the lounge of the Greyhound pub she told me she was from the other side of London, that she had been married, had a young daughter who she had left in the care of an aunt out in the country and that her husband had walked out on her just before war broke out and she hadn't seen him since. It appeared that she was some four years older than me, not that it made any difference as far as I was concerned. I told her about Lavington and the smithy and for some reason about Tommy and Phyllis, and the more we talked the more I became attracted to her. We seemed to have a lot in common, consequently by the time I had seen her back to her quarters I realized that she had made a great impression on me and that I wanted to see her again.

On the day we left for Hereford she came to see me off. Lowering the window I leaned out of the cab and took her hand. 'I'll write, Mary,' I promised as we moved off. 'You do that,' she replied, then turning, she made her way across the barrack square leaving me with the feeling that somewhere in the future our paths would cross again. Just before she disappeared from sight, she turned and waved.

On my next weekend pass I went home feeling that perhaps I had neglected them for too long. They were of course overjoyed to see me and I had to admit that it was good to be home again to enjoy Mother's cooking and all the other home comforts after living in barracks. Things seemed much about the same. Mother had run into Phyllis outside the village stores and from what she could gather things between her and Tommy hadn't improved a lot. However there was one disturbing development. He had taken to drinking heavily and spent most of his time down at the Drovers Arms. At first Phyllis had taken to going with him but after a while she had been unable to cope, finding it well nigh impossible to deal with his heavy drinking and the hours of sullen silence that usually followed.

That evening, acting on the spur of the moment, I decided to go down to the Drovers and perhaps find an opportunity to have a word with Tommy. He was sitting alone in a corner when I arrived and not wanting to walk straight over to him I first went up to the bar and ordered a drink. Fred Newman was standing there and after shaking my hand we stood talking for a while. 'Shame about young Tommy,' he said, 'all of us can't help but feel sorry for him but it's that Missis of his that we are more concerned about. She has a hell of a life with him,' then he stopped short, almost as if he felt he had said too much. 'Sorry, John lad, I forgot you and him are mates.' 'That's all right, Fred,' I said, 'forget it,' and with that I made my excuses and picking up my drink walked over to where Tommy was sitting and easing out a chair sat down beside him. Rising unsteadily to his feet he shook my hand and slapped me on the back, saying it was great to see me and asking how I liked Army life. I let him ramble on for a while then seizing the opportunity of a lull in the conversation I asked after Phyllis. He didn't reply immediately. It was almost as if he were searching for the right words, then at last he said, 'Oh, she's great. She couldn't come tonight as she has things to do. I'll tell her that you are home. I know she would like to see you,' then he lapsed back into silence. Looking around the room I could see that many of the regulars were watching, almost as if they expected something to happen. 'Tommy,' I ventured to ask, 'don't you think you are hitting the bottle a bit hard? Why not call it a day, drink up and I'll see you home?' For a moment he just stared at me then rising to his feet, glass in hand, he stood swaying backwards and forwards. 'What the hell have it got to do with you?' he demanded at the same time giving me a shove that caused me to overbalance backwards spilling my drink all over the table. Picking myself up I rose and stood looking at him, not quite sure how to react. Luckily at that moment Fred Newman came over and taking me by the arm led me away. 'Leave him be, lad,' he said, 'there's nothing you or anybody else can do to help. Us have all tried.'

The incident I had to admit had shaken me more than I cared to admit; only then did I realize just how far along the road of self-destruction Tommy had gone. We had been such good mates in the past and seeing him like that hurt. Looking over at him slumped in his chair made me aware of what Phyllis was having to put up with and on the spur of the moment I half decided to go

179

down to Leyfield Cottage to make sure that she was all right. Luckily common sense prevailed and after I had thought it through, I knew that if I had have done, it would only have made matters worse. It had put a damper on my short leave. What was happening to us, I began to wonder, was it the war or were we changing that much that we were beginning to forget old friends and old loyalties, friends who in the past had been such an important part of our lives?

That night when I returned home I told my parents what had happened down at the Drovers and they both agreed that I had done the right thing in not retaliating and not going down to see Phyllis. Later I told them of my meeting with Mary the ATS girl in London, impressing on them not to read too much into it as at the moment we were just good friends. Mother listened intently and after I had finished nodded in agreement, however I had the feeling that she didn't believe me, this being born out by the fact that she insisted that when next I wrote I invite Mary down to stay for a few days on her next leave.

During the next few weeks Mary and I kept in touch and being due for seven days leave I wrote to her suggesting that perhaps I might spend a few days of it with her, and if it were possible for her to get leave at the same time for her to return with me to Lavington. Much to my delight her reply, when it came, confirmed that she could arrange leave to coincide with mine and so it was that one Saturday morning I boarded the train at Hereford en route for London. She met me on Paddington Station and we retired to a small cafe just outside where, faced with not too hot cups of tea and not too fresh iced buns, we sat talking, the extent of our conversation being about ordinary things for knowing that we were to spend the next few days together I was careful not to let any hint of intimacy creep into the conversation. Suddenly without warning she asked if I had made any arrangements about where I was going to stay while I was in London, something that in my hurry to see her I hadn't given a lot of thought to, thinking perhaps that if the worst came to the worst I could put up at the YMCA or one of the service clubs. Putting her cup down and looking me straight in the face she asked, 'John, do you want to spend our few nights together?' The inference was plain and for a moment I didn't know quite what to say. 'Sorry,' she continued, 'perhaps I shouldn't have asked but time is so short and who knows what might happen in the future.' Reaching over I took both her hands in mine, the look in my eyes telling her all she wanted to know as she accepted the promise of a few hours of stolen happiness.

We managed to find accommodation in a small guest house in Sussex Gardens close to Marble Arch where, standing on the doorstep I think we both felt a little guilty. The lady who answered our knock looked kindly enough, a woman of the world who realized that we were just two young people who for a few brief hours wanted to forget the war. She made no comment as she ushered us inside but smiled as if to let us know that she understood.

Later that night with only the fitful light from an uncooperative moon to light up the room we sat on the bed talking. 'John,' Mary began, 'I must know, do you really want me and have you forgiven me for being so forward?' Wanting her so much I didn't answer but just took her in my arms, feeling her respond as I did so. She gave herself to me willingly and we made love with all the tenderness and abandon of two young people experiencing it for the first time. All through the night I held her against me feeling the warmth and strength of her, while outside in a world which just at that moment we had very little interest in, the air raid sirens wailed and in the distance could be heard the bark of the AA guns and the dull thud of exploding bombs.

The next day she took me round London, a city that was already beginning to show the scars of war. Down in the dock area I saw for myself the devastation, it was all so different from the peace and quiet of Lavington. Often in the past when a young lad I had listened while Father told us of the rape and devastation inflicted on the cities and countryside of France during the last war, even so I wasn't prepared for London in the Blitz. During the hours of daylight the streets were thronged with people, servicemen and women of our own armed forces rubbing shoulders with others from Canada, New Zealand and South Africa, all jostling with sober-suited civilians with gas masks in cardboard boxes slung over their shoulders and neatly rolled umbrellas in hand. In the main shopping areas girls with scarf-covered heads minced along on high heels, their handbags bulging with ration books, identity cards, clothing coupons and a host of other wartime necessities, while high above the clouds the grey barrage balloons swung this way and that on their mooring cables as the wind took them. On AA sites the guns stood ready with muzzles pointing skywards while their steel-helmeted crews, weary from a night of action, sat around smoking the inevitable cigarette and drinking the inevitable mug of hot, sweet tea.

We walked down streets where blackened timbers and rubble gave stark evidence of where houses and shops had once stood and where in quiet corners the first signs of a new life were appearing, as long-forgotten flowers and weeds struggled through the piles of brickwork and broken slates in an attempt to cover the scars of war. Yet in spite of all that people were doing their best to carry on. On one shop, whose windows had been boarded over, was a notice 'Business as usual', a simple announcement that typified the spirit of the people who night after night had endured the horrors and destruction of the air raids. Christmas was only a few weeks away and many of the larger shops were already starting to decorate their windows in an attempt, defiant in its way, to bring a ray of normality back into things. Hand in hand we walked the streets taking afternoon tea in Lyons Corner House at Marble Arch, where in the warmth and under the subdued lighting we listened to a four-piece orchestra playing a selection of Strauss waltzes. It was all so civilized and had it not been for the scattering of uniforms it could well have been any afternoon in peacetime.

After spending three days there we said goodbye to our understanding landlady and London and left for Lavington. I had the feeling that she was sorry to see us go; in a way she reminded me of my mother and in saying that I couldn't have paid her a greater compliment. Lavington station; it was good to be home again after the hustle and bustle of London and its air raids. It was dark when we arrived and during the walk up to the village we stopped once or twice to enjoy the silence, something that Mary hadn't experienced for a long time. As we walked I told her more about Tommy and Phyllis and a little about the times we had shared in the days before the world had gone mad. Listening in silence she made no comment until just before we turned into Callow Lane she stopped and asked, 'Was there something special between you and Phyllis?' the question taking me by surprise. I couldn't deny that there had been but I hastened to assure her that although I was still fond of Phyllis anything else was buried in the past. Somewhere in the back of my mind I had the feeling that she was hinting that, at least for the time being, there couldn't be any permanent understanding between us and almost as if she was reading my thoughts she took my arm and squeezed it. 'Don't worry, John,' she said, 'I understand, let's make the best of what we have and leave the future to take care of itself.' When we reached Forge Cottage Mother received her warmly and fussed and tended her like a long-lost daughter, the one I firmly believe she would have loved to have had.

That night after supper we sat talking and swapping confidences during which we learned that Mary's real father had never married her mother and that he had been killed in the last war. Her mother had subsequently married and she and her husband had brought Mary up. Unfortunately her mother had died shortly before the outbreak of the present war and her stepfather had left and gone to live with a brother in Sunderland. Alone and seeing no way out she and her boyfriend had decided to get married and there had been a daughter, Alice, who was now in the care of an aunty. The marriage unfortunately didn't work out and twelve months later her husband had up and left her. She hadn't heard from him since and it was then that she had decided to join the ATS.

It must have taken a lot of courage to tell her story and when she had finished the telling of it we all sat in silence, not being quite sure what to say then, reaching down, Mary picked up her travelling bag and from it took an envelope in which was the faded sepia photograph of a young soldier in the uniform of the last war. 'This is the only thing I have of my mother's. I found it amongst her few possessions after she died. It is a photograph of my father, as you will see from the inscription on the back. Why she never showed it to me when she was alive is a mystery, but no doubt she had her reasons.' Here for a moment she paused and just sat staring whistfully at the photograph. 'She never told me much about him,' she continued at last, 'other than to say that she had loved him and would have married him but for the fact that he insisted that they wait until the war was over.' Now what transpired during the next few minutes I found hard to believe, indeed I still do. Mother, after taking the photograph, handed it to Father saying as she did so, 'He was a good-looking chap, don't you think so, Dad?'

Taking it from her he studied it for a moment then, picking up his glasses from the table beside him, he walked over to the window where he stood for a while holding it to the light. I shall never forget the look on his face when at last he turned towards us. Then without saying a word he left the room and we heard him mount the stairs up to his bedroom. By now thoroughly mystified and not knowing what to expect we waited. We could hear him moving about but had no idea what he was up to, then he came back, and going over to Mary handed her a bundle of letters tied with ribbon and a watch and chain.

'Mary, lass,' he began in a choked voice, 'prepare yourself for a shock. These things were your father's. His name was Charlie Bowers, he was a comrade of mine and I took them from his body on the day he was killed in France. After the war ended and not knowing quite what to do I took them to his mother in Hereford where she told me all about her son. When she also passed away her solicitors sent them back to me and I have kept and treasured them hoping against hope that one day I could return them to their rightful owner, you.'

Stunned by what we had just learned we just sat, none of us being able to find the right words to express our feelings. Mother went over to Mary who was sitting with the letters and watch on her lap and put her arms around her; then the tears came and Mary sobbed and sobbed while Mother held her. Looking over at Father I nodded and we both rose and made our way out into the kitchen, feeling that it was better to leave the two women alone for a while. Much later Father told Mary of his friendship with her father and how they had been more like brothers than just friends. As for me, I could only marvel at the twist of fate that had brought Mary and I together that day in Acton and so rescue a simple love story from the mists of time. All in all it turned out to be a memorable leave and when the time came to go nothing was mentioned about my eventual posting overseas, something which I knew would not be long delayed. My parents came to the station to see us off, me to Hereford and Mary back to London. Standing on the platform waiting for the train Father took Mary in his arms. 'Look after yourself, lass,' he said, 'you need have no more worries or regrets about your father; he was a good man and a brave one. Incidentally, he once saved my life but that's another story. All I would say is this, I am proud to have known him and to have been his friend.'

Christmas came but neither Mary nor me managed to get leave; instead we spent the festive season such as it was in barracks. Early in the New Year news came that Aunty Beckey's husband Stanley had been reported missing in a raid over Germany. Mother wrote to tell me, adding that Beckey had returned to Lavington and was for the time being going to live with Aunty Tessa at the shop. Poor Beckey, just when she had found happiness it had been snatched away from her. None of us had ever met Stanley but we mourned his loss just the same. He had made our Beckey happy and that is all we could ask of him. I wrote her a short letter of condolence, not knowing quite what to say under the circumstances. It seemed that of late death was becoming an accepted part of our lives and every day somewhere a wife or mother was receiving that dreaded telegram telling them of the loss of a loved one. As I wrote the letter to Beckey I sat pen in hand searching for the right words. Sorry seemed so inadequate somehow; after all it was only a word.

Back at the depot life went on with monotonous regularity, the days coming and going, some of them unnoticed, lost in the regulated way of Army life. During my short stay in Hereford I had come to know the city and surrounding countryside, one of my favourite places being the cathedral where, when feeling the need to be alone, I often sat. Looking around the vast nave I pondered on the people and events that those grey walls must have seen in their time, the pageantry that must have passed beneath its vast vaulted roof and the death and destruction it had survived over the ages, at the same time wondering what sort of people they were who had planned and built this magnificent monument to a God who had ruled their daily lives with such stern finality. He came from nowhere, a stooping grey-haired figure dressed in a plain black cassock. Halting beside me he placed one hand on my shoulder. 'May you find the peace that you are seeking, my son,' he said, after which he went quietly on his way and was soon swallowed up in the darkness beside the altar. I have often wondered who he was and there are times when I feel that perhaps he was just a figment of my imagination, however of one thing I am sure and that is, fact or fiction, I shall never forget that kindly face that smiled down on me that day in Hereford Cathedral.

Soon our peaceful existence was shattered by the news that we were being posted overseas, where to we had no idea, but the issue of tropical kit gave us a clue. Granted seven days embarkation leave I wrote to Mary asking if she could arrange a few days leave to coincide with mine, and this she was able to do. It was now June and summer had come early, bringing warm days and long sultry nights. I met Mary off the train at Lavington and the first thing I noticed was how tired she looked, but that was only to be expected after the sleepless nights she had spent in air raid shelters, however I was sure that a few nights sound sleep and Mother's cooking would soon bring the roses back to her cheeks. She had brought with her some recent photographs of her daughter Alice, who was now five years old. They showed a round-faced youngster with a mass of golden curls and I gathered that Mary got to see her quite often. We spent most of our leave walking the countryside and visiting Evesham and Cheltenham, and in order to show her a little of the countryside

185

I hired a car from Harry Haines, our local taxi man, and took her up into the Cotswolds visiting Broadway, Snowshill, and Chipping Campden. We didn't question where the petrol came from thinking it best not to ask.

Walking up the village street one morning we ran into Phyllis. It was an awkward moment for all of us, however I introduced Mary as a friend of the family, a white lie, I knew, but one I felt it better to tell just at that moment. I asked after Tommy and was glad to learn that he was a lot better and that things were slowly getting back to normal, however watching her as she spoke I had the feeling that it was all being said more for our benefit than anything else. She left us at the path leading up to the post office and, after wishing us well and shaking Mary's hand, she walked away, then when she was well out of earshot Mary said, 'John, there is no need for you to explain, I could see it in her eyes. Women know about these things.' I didn't argue, there was no point anyway.

That same evening the four of us, that is Mother and Father, and Mary and me, went down to the Drovers Arms. The place was fairly full when we arrived and at first we failed to notice Tommy and Phyllis sitting in a corner of the lounge, that is until a voice called out, 'Over here, John lad,' and looking I saw that Tommy was waving and indicating for us to join them. The fact that he was on his best behaviour was all too clear. Putting his arm around Phyllis he went out of his way to make a fuss of her, all plainly being done for our benefit. At first we found it hard going, the conversation such as it was being centred around old times and some of the things we had got up to in our young days, then Father told them the story about Mary's father and the almost unbelievable coincidence that had brought her to Lavington to meet his old army friend. It was near to closing time when we rose to go. Turning at the doorway I saw that Phyllis was watching me and just at that moment I happened to catch Mother's eye as she looked from one to the other of us. The warning was obvious: be careful, lad, it said.

On the last day of our leave Mary and I decided to take a walk through the woods above the village. What guided our steps up Oak Hill and to the stile leading into the hazel thicket I neither know nor for that matter care. Sufficient to say that there in the stillness of that June afternoon we stood for what seemed an eternity, unaware that in another age two others had lingered on that very spot, unsure and hesitant. They too had been lovers, two people who, captured by the magic of a June night, had given themselves to each

186

other as they listened to the nightingale. Turning to face me Mary called my name. 'John,' she said, 'this is perhaps the last time we shall be alone together for quite a while.' I started to answer but she put her fingers to my lips commanding silence. 'No, John, just listen to me. I dread to think of what might happen in the months ahead and although I have the feeling that you and I can never belong to each other I want you to make love to me.' Her eyes were shady and misty and as I looked at her I sought for the right words but none came. Luckily none were needed. Reaching out I helped her over the stile and hand in hand we forced our way down the overgrown path that lead to the clearing in the hazel thicket where, in the stillness with only nature to cover us, we made love. This time there was no nightingale; perhaps just at that moment he had other things on his mind, however it didn't seem to matter.

How long we lay there would be hard to tell. In my heart I knew that this would be the last time I would hold her for quite a while and, loath to let her go, I pressed her to me. It was in those few precious moments that I realized how much I loved her. Reluctantly at last we rose and made ready to leave. Then hand in hand we walked through the dark woods, each reluctant to say what was in our hearts, each of us aware that any barrier that had existed between us was slowly fading into obscurity.

Early the next morning, after saying our goodbyes all round, we left. My parents came with us to the station and there were tears from Mother as I knew there would be. On the high banks the foxgloves nodded their heads and in the mist-covered hedgerows honeysuckle, wet with morning dew, reached out in welcome. It was an occasion fraught with sadness, but then partings always are, occasions when there are long periods of silence when one or the other is not quite sure what to say in case the wrong words come tumbling out of trembling lips. Just before the train arrived Father put his arm round Mary and kissed her on the cheek. 'Take care, lass, don't forget to write to us and remember that you will always be welcome to come and stay.' Then, turning, he held out his hand to me. 'Good luck, lad, take care of yourself.' Mother hugged us both and I'm sure that it must have stirred up many memories of other times when she had to say goodbye to Father on that very platform. They both stayed waving until the train was lost to sight round the bend by the signal box then, turning to Father, Mother said, 'I wish, oh how I wish,' but he stopped her from saying more.' 'I know what you wish, old girl,' he replied, 'but let's just leave things to work out for themselves as I'm sure they will.' Mary and I parted on Evesham station, her train for London leaving before mine to Hereford. As the train pulled away she leaned out of the carriage window. 'Write to me, John,' she called out, 'write to me.' And then she was gone.

Chapter XI

The next few weeks were filled with preparations for our final move, the long train journey through the night to Glasgow passing like a dream, then almost before we were fully aware of it we found ourselves aboard the troopship that was to take us away and be our home for quite a while. The voyage down the Clyde, the open sea and the long voyage round the Cape to Alexandria in Egypt was a never-to-be-forgotten experience. At Cape Town we changed into tropical kit and 'got our knees brown' as the saying was and it was from there that I managed to post letters to my parents and Mary. Speculation as to our ultimate destination was rife so it was with a feeling of relief that just before we entered the Gulf of Aden it was announced that our destination was Egypt, and after a long hot journey through the Suez Canal we finally arrived there.

It was good to get ashore and feel firm ground under our feet and gradually we began to get acclimatized to our new surroundings. The docks were a hive of activity as cargoes from home were unloaded and transported by road to outlying areas where they were stacked in huge dumps and covered with camouflage netting, and looking across the vast expanse of scrub and desert it was hard to believe that the Germans were only some sixty miles away. Quickly learning to take advantage of any shade we left the heavy work to the locals who as long as there was something to steal at the end of the day worked hard enough, the art of blending into the background coming naturally to them particularly at the first sign of trouble.

Troopships, whose deck rails were lined with fresh-faced youngsters, arrived daily, their occupants being whisked away to outlying districts to become acclimatized and train for the battles that lay ahead. Australians, New Zealanders and Indian troops mingled with lads from Scotland, Ireland and Wales, a motley collection from the four corners of the Empire, many of whom were to find their last resting place in the heat and dust of the desert. How different it all was to a lad like me who before had never been any further than London and Weston-Super-Mare.

Not far away, Rommel and his victory-flushed Africa Corps were almost within sight of the greenery of the Nile Valley and the domes and minarets of Cairo, and throughout August and September battles raged as he tried in vain to break through the line of defence that had been thrown up round the Alamein sector. Plagued by flies and heat we sweated out our guts ferrying essential stores and water almost up to the front-line troops.

In August Lieutenant General Bernard Montgomery, later to be simply known as 'Monty', took over command of the Eighth Army and from then on things began to change rapidly. Officers who had served under General Wavell since 1940 at GHQ in Cairo, only a lorry ride away from the desert, and known to the troops as 'Cairo Canaries' or 'Groppi's Light Horse', enjoyed their last days of siestas after lunch, short working days and long meal breaks, some being returned to the UK as unsuitable, while others less fortunate were posted to forward units out 'in the blue' where they soon learned what soldiering was all about. One of the less popular innovations thought up by 'Monty' was physical training, a torture that had to be endured by officers and all other ranks before breakfast.

However in spite of, or perhaps because of, all his new ideas a new feeling swept through the ranks of the remnants of the Army that had been driven back to El Alamein. Reinforced and re-equipped with tanks and 25-pounders, and with a leader who not only kept everyone in the picture as to his intentions, but more importantly instilled in them the belief that in spite of his reputation Rommel was not invincible, confidence in themselves and their leaders grew apace, and on the nights of 23-4 October, in brilliant moonlight, the British guns, which were set at intervals of twenty-three yards along a front of some six miles, opened up a terrific barrage directed at enemy lines and minefields in front of El Alamein. Then on 1 November the tanks, followed by the infantry, broke through. Not being directly involved we stood by until, with very little warning, we found ourselves taking the long road into the desert.

One morning, busy storing the camouflage net on top of the cabin of my truck, I looked down to see a solitary figure standing staring up at me. It did have a voice, however, and suddenly it asked if I were Driver Mumford. Climbing down, wondering what it was all about, I nodded in confirmation upon which he informed me that his name was Jimmy Greatorex and that he had been assigned to me as my co-driver. My first impression of him nearly convinced me that he would have been better off employed in the cookhouse or the company office, however, as I was to find out later, first impressions can be and often are very wide of the mark. He was a thin, wiry lad with an elfish face, but notwithstanding there was something special about him and after exchanging christian names and shaking hands we strolled back down the line of trucks to where a few of the other drivers had got a brew going. He told me that his home was in Liverpool although I had already guessed as much from his scouse accent. He hadn't been in the Army long and it appeared that it had been fate coupled with the perverseness of an interviewing officer that had landed him in the RASC. Like me he had expressed a wish to become a driver and having been given some sound advice beforehand, when asked for details of his civilian trade, he said he had been a cook, safe in the knowledge that owing to the way the Army worked he would be called upon to do something just the opposite.

Being a scouse he was a born comedian, his attitude to life being that if you looked hard enough there was a funny side to most things, and I well remember one story he told me about his old grandfather back in Liverpool. It appeared that the old gentleman was bedridden and during one of the many raids a landmine exploded close to his terraced house, the blast blowing the windows in and sending Grandad and his bed out through the door onto the landing. The rush of air that came to fill the vacuum caused by the blast propelled him gracefully back into the bedroom, the unbelievable part of his story being that when the rescue people came up to see if he was all right they found on measuring the bed that it was four inches wider than the door opening.

During his training as a driver there had apparently been several mishaps, his way of explaining them being 'I don't know, they just happened.' One day when out driving with an instructor, he attempted to pass under a low railway bridge, the result being that the vehicle became well and truly jammed under it. On another occasion, having parked his truck, unfortunately as it happened on a slight incline, he forgot one of the cardinal rules which was to leave it in gear and fully apply the handbrake. Sitting with the other lads enjoying a cup of tea and a fag he looked through the window to see his truck slowly making its way down the main street, finally to come to rest with its bonnet in the window of a ladies' hairdressers, much to the consternation of two elderly customers who were sitting having their hair seen to.

Listening to his tales of mishaps I had the feeling that the officers and NCOs at the training depot had been glad to see him safely aboard ship bound for foreign parts in the hope that his accident-prone activities might be harnessed to the general war effort. In civvy street he had been a carpenter by trade so naturally he had been nicknamed 'Chippy'. We knew very little about his life prior to the outbreak of war other than that he was single and had a brother serving in the Merchant Navy. On the subject of women I had the feeling that he was scared of them, this perhaps being explained by the fact that he had an Aunty Emily, a most formidable woman, whose withering look he reckoned could stop a tramcar at fifty paces and who whenever she came to stay used to make his life a misery.

Reluctantly we at last said goodbye to Alexandria and moved in convoy up the dusty roads towards El Alamein, some forty miles away, progress being slow as we weaved our way past returning vehicles, often having to pull off the road to allow the passage of tank recovery vehicles and other heavy traffic. During daylight hours the sun beat down making anything metal untouchable and the dust raised by the traffic found its way into everything, hair, clothing, and even into the carburettors of our vehicles resulting in frequent stops to clean them out, a chore that on many occasions resulted in burnt hands where they had touched parts of the overheated engine. Chippy, in spite of his reputation, soon proved himself a good mate and although at the time we did not know it we were to share quite a few hairy moments as we drove backwards and forwards carrying rations, supplies, and jerrycans of water, plus the occasional soldier who, having a few days leave, was hitching his way back down the line. Living mainly on bully beef and hard tack, with a pint of water a day for drinking, washing, and shaving, we somehow survived.

Luckily at times the odd chicken passed our way and there was one occasion when a young pig provided a rare feast for Chippy and me and several lads from the 9th Australian Division. Questioned by an officer as to how they had come by it they explained that the pig had refused to answer when challenged so they had had to shoot it and rather than leave it by the roadside they had decided to eat it. Water as I have said was strictly rationed however, as the campaign progressed, large underground storage tanks were built thus cutting down the need for the number of jerrycans that we were having to ferry up and down the line. Eggs were a welcome addition to our meagre rations and they seemed to be available in fairly large quantities; where they came from and where the hens were that must have laid them we were never quite sure, but no doubt the Arabs, knowing the reputation of the strangers within their midst, kept them well out of sight. Secured on a piece of string we lowered the eggs into the radiators of our lorries where more often than not the water would be boiling; others we fried on the hot, flat stones at the side of the track. As the road at times ran fairly near to the sea we were able to enjoy a dip, a welcome relief from the heat and dust of the desert. Naked as the day we were born we plunged into the water, brown all over except for the portion round our lower regions where our shorts had been, officers, NCOs and other ranks all splashing about, truly a democratic army.

Somehow the fact that I had been a blacksmith in civvy street leaked out and before long I found myself lumbered with all manner of minor repairs, mainly to the lorries, repairs that were carried out under the most primitive of conditions, but I enjoyed doing them and if I needed anything I only had to ask Chippy who would disappear only to return later with the required item and a look on his face which said 'Don't ask'. The desert or 'Blue' as it was fondly known, might well have been a paradise for tacticians and tank battles but to us it was a foretaste of hell, blistering hot by day and ice cold by night, the only protection from either being underneath our trucks. Swiftly after the sun had gone down the flies came crawling over our bodies and faces, congregating in the corners of our eyes and mouths in search of what little moisture was there, then as the temperature dropped we huddled for warmth wrapped in our greatcoats, praying for morning when the whole pantomime would start all over again.

Our mail caught up with us at irregular intervals which was only to be expected seeing that we were continually on the move, however when it came it was welcomed. Mine from home usually contained all the village gossip with a special mention from Mother who said that they were all praying for my safe return, adding that Aunty Tessa had a map of North Africa in her shop and a note in capital letters saying 'this is where our John is'. Father, as any old soldier should, boasted of his son's exploits in the desert. Where he was getting all his information from God only knows but apparently it earned him a few drinks down at the Drovers. Chippy, whose mail to say the least was rather sparse, enjoyed me reading parts of mine to him so much so that after a while he was far more interested in the goings on in Lavington than he was in the events taking place in his home town of Liverpool. I received two letters from Mary, both of which to my surprise and secret delight she signed 'All my love, yours, Mary'. She was still at Acton and had kept in touch with my parents. At least the flame was still burning, I thought, and so the days passed and apart from the occasional visit from enemy aircraft, life wasn't too bad.

Each time we stopped for any length of time the local Arabs, accompanied by their many children, appeared from nowhere offering baskets of eggs in exchange for cigarettes or parcels of used dried tea leaves. Like little elves the children stood in their pathetic ragged garments, their brown eyes melting even the hardest of hearts, but it didn't do to leave anything portable lying about as they were as good if not better than their elders at thieving. Additional hazards came in the form of scorpions and snakes, not that we saw a lot of either fortunately. However there were times when just to add to our discomfort enemy bombers would pay us a visit, resulting in having to spend time in ditches by the roadside where, with heads down, we watched as hardy souls with bren guns tried to bag themselves a jerry plane as the ammunition trucks went up in smoke. All in all the desert, a term which should be applied very loosely, was a most inhospitable place consisting as it did in the main not of golden sand but a mixture of small stones and gray volcanic grit, the desolation of it all only being relieved by patches of scrub and infrequent wadis in which tanks were apt to park themselves hull down.

By 3 November the Germans were in full flight, the only resistance coming from isolated pockets of Italians who they had left behind to cover their retreat. Driving conditions were appalling and following another vehicle meant navigating through clouds of gritty dust that penetrated everything, eyes, ears, mouths and noses. Advance supply dumps had been set up wherever two 'trighs' or trails crossed, and as our lads advanced we were kept busy stocking these up.

Then, as if heaven-sent, and quite out of the blue, Chippy and I were given orders to transport several large packing cases and two captured Italian officers back to Cairo. At night we slept under our trucks at the side of the road protected from the cold by our greatcoats or anything else we could use, while in the daytime, pestered by the usual flies, we were forced to make frequent trips to the wayside 'Desert Roses', which were basic latrines set well back from the roadway. Throughout our journey our two travelling companions were quite content to stick with us, not that they had much choice seeing that even if they had decided to 'scarper' there was nowhere to go, their general attitude seeming to be a feeling of relief now that their war was over. The journey back took us the best part of six days and on reaching Cairo we handed them over to the Military Police. In a way we were sorry to see them go; they had been good company on the journey and although their command of the English language had been limited and ours of Italian non-existent, somehow we managed to communicate with them even if it was mainly by sign language.

The three days leave we had been given before having to return enabled us to see a little of the city and after searching around we found accommodation in an Army leave centre where for the first time in months we were able to enjoy the luxury of hot baths, a change of clothing and beds with clean linen sheets. Cairo was a fascinating place and as everything was new to us it took quite a while to get used to its sights and smells. It was a city where poverty and affluence walked side by side, where elegant ladies sat at tables set under the trees on the sidewalk, their over-bejewelled hands and ample bosoms making us suspicious of their true calling. Contrary to common belief our first thoughts were not of women and the delights they had to offer, the threat of venereal diseases and other unmentionable consequences keeping our minds off such things, particularly when we were told that Monty had placed the brothel area of the 'Birka', a place well-known to soldiers both in peace and war, out of bounds.

Cairo abounded with canteens and all in all the food on offer was fairly good, making a change from the sand-coated desert grub we had been having. However I must admit that even though there was a fairly wide choice we invariably came down on the side of egg and chips, or for that matter anything as long as it came with chips. There were cinemas where English films were shown with Arabic sub-titles, or conversely Arab films with English sub-titles. One of them, I clearly remember, had a roof which was slid back at night to let in the cool air of the evening, and incidentally more flies to join up with others already inside. In addition there were various 'clubs' for other ranks where Coptic christian ladies relieved unsuspecting squaddies of their meagre pay, plying them with 'Cherry Brandy', a concoction that except for its colour bore little resemblance to the real thing, consisting as it did mainly of coloured water. However a certain amount of alcohol was available, the most popular being 'Stecca Beer'. What its origin was we never found out but after being brought up on the brew at home it was nigh impossible to get drunk on it or

195

even get merry.

All too soon our few days leave came to an end and so loaded up with stores, water and fuel we set off back along the dusty road towards Tunis, leaving others to enjoy the facilities and delights of 'Groppi's Ice Cream Parlour' and the Victoria and Kiwi Clubs. Ahead of us stretched the long desert road, a road littered with Divisional and route signs that stood in silent watch over the discarded refuse of war. On the way we passed ambulances bound for field hospitals down the line, a grim reminder of the price that was being paid, while to either side, half buried in the sand, abandoned vehicles and burnt-out tanks stood silent and forgotten, silhouetted against the cloudless blue sky. Near to them looking for all the world like scattered molehills were the hastily-dug graves of both friend and foe, some with markers others without, showing the last resting place of young lads who, still in the fullness of life and primed with a spirit of adventure and patriotism, had started out on what was to be their last journey.

November and down came the rain accompanied by heavy dust storms causing new hazards when vehicles, which had become bogged down in the mud, either had to be manhandled out or shifted with the aid of another vehicle. Soaked to the skin one minute and blinded by heat and dust the next we pressed on, our only glimpse of sanity being the letters from home which provided a somewhat tentative link with the real world. What I wouldn't have given for just one brief hour walking the fields and lanes of Lavington, to smell freshly cut grass and hear the distant sound of familiar voices on warm summer evenings.

Sitting one day in the shade of the truck with Chippy, an open letter on my lap and pipe well primed and lit, I let my mind travel the miles between the mud and dust of Africa back to the quiet of the countryside and the smithy at the bottom of Callow Lane, seeing my father as he worked at the forge and hearing the ticking of the grandfather clock in the parlour of Forge Cottage. Chippy, who up until then had remained silent as he read the contents of a rather tattered paperback novel he had picked up at the roadside, suddenly put it down and staring at his outstretched feet said 'Hammer', this being the nickname he had given me ever since he had found out that I was a blacksmith. 'Hammer, have you ever thought what funny things feet are? If they were turned round the other way just think how much nearer to things we could

196

stand.' Now I hadn't given a lot of thought to the problem but looking at my own feet encased in muddy army boots I could see that he had a point.

'Another thing,' he continued, 'that sun up there is ninety million miles away and yet the warmth of it still reaches us.' By then I was all ears wondering just what pearl of wisdom would follow. 'Yet,' he continued, 'when I used to fetch the fish and chips from the chippy round the corner at home they were always cold by the time I got them home.' Seeing that there was no answer to his logic, at least not one that I cared to get involved in, we both sat for a while contemplating the ungainly feet that stared at us from the ends of our sunburnt legs.

In one of the letters from home I learned that Billy Turnbull from Fox Farm, Toddington had been killed in the desert campaign and the thought struck me that perhaps by some quirk of fate he had been the occupant of one of those hastily-dug graves I had seen along the way. Still, if he were, I reasoned, I knew he would forgive me for passing without paying my respects, after all I didn't know him all that well. Phyllis wrote me a short letter taking great care not to make it too personal but just wishing me well and sending best wishes from herself and Tommy. Mother in her letter said she had heard from Mary who had asked for my address having apparently mislaid it, and so Christmas came and went, passing without any undue interruption in our daily routine; one day was apt to follow another with regular monotony and at times it was hard to remember what day of the week it was, that is unless the visit of a passing padre, who called in to conduct a service, reminded us that it was Sunday. In an effort to at least observe tradition a few of us got together on Christmas Day to read our mail and drink a few cans of warm Canadian beer, mindful of the fact that we weren't so very far from where the birth of Jesus had started it all.

The war at least for us was going well. The enemy, now in full retreat, was taking little or no steps to hinder our advance. In our rare off-duty moments we scrounged and read books that one or the other of us had come by or had been sent from home. Passed from one to the other they were finally discarded, dog-eared and dirty, and left lying in the desert, their few remaining pages flipping backwards and forwards stirred by a breeze that would soon bury them in the shifting sand.

February found us in the area around Gabes. There had been no rain for five days, even so it was as well to keep to the roadway as the dirt tracks leading up into the hills were only just about passable. One morning, en route to a stores dump in the vicinity of Tebessa, we were travelling in an empty truck, a fact that although at the time we didn't realize it was to prove our salvation. Things seemed fairly quiet as we made our way cautiously up a track that led away from the main highway, then as we rounded a bend we were confronted by a large tank transporter which had shed its load, blocking the trackway. With a steep bank on one side and the way ahead blocked I had no alternative but to make a wide detour to the left, not realizing that we were travelling over ground that hadn't been checked for mines, although the fact should have been obvious owing to the absence of white tapes.

What happened next neither Chippy nor I remembered until much later. Suddenly the truck shuddered, there was a blinding flash, then it lurched on for another few yards when there was another explosion. In the minutes that followed I seemed to be struggling along a dark tunnel at the end of which was a tiny pinpoint of light. From a distance indistinguishable sounds echoed as if they were being bounced around a large empty tiled room, then it all died away and the next thing I remember was a voice.

When I came to there were blurred faces peering down at me and someone said, 'Lie still while we have a look at you.' It was the voice of a RAMC doctor who luckily had been passing and heard the explosions. My whole body felt as if it were on fire; I didn't seem able to move either arms or legs. The only thing I remember was that my shirt and shorts were warm and sticky with blood. Between spasms of pain I managed to ask after Chippy and was relieved to learn that he had survived after which I remember very little until I came to in a field hospital lying in a bed with clean white sheets and a nurse bending over me. 'Well,' she said, 'we thought we had lost you but it seems that you are determined to stay with us. Lie quietly and I'll fetch the doctor to have a look at you,' and with that she left to be shortly followed by a young lieutenant who, sitting on the side of the bed, began:

'Well, old chap, we have had to carry out two operations to take out fragments of metal from your hip and leg and from a wound in your shoulder. You have lost a lot of blood but as far as we can see there doesn't appear to be any permanent damage, however I know you will be pleased to learn that Driver Greatorex is here in hospital with you. Unfortunately his injuries are a little more serious and I'm afraid he has lost the lower part of his left arm but don't worry, he is making a good recovery. Now for the good news: we shall shortly be sending you both down the line to a hospital in Cairo so all you have to do in the meantime is to get as much rest as you can.'

After he had gone I lay thinking about Chippy, wondering how he would cope, however knowing him as I did, I knew that he would, the important thing being that we had both survived to tell the tale. I didn't get a chance to speak to him until we were both safely installed in the hospital at Cairo, by which time I was fairly mobile and therefore able to make the short trip down the corridor to the ward he was in. Searching along the rows of beds I finally located him sitting up reading and I remember thinking that even from a distance he looked better than I expected him to look. Seeing me approaching he leaned over and nudged the chap in the next bed. 'See this bloke coming towards us, you want to watch him, he's the one that drove our truck into that bloody minefield.' By that time I had reached his bedside. 'Sorry, Hammer,' he said, 'I couldn't help getting a dig in. Let's face it, you always were a lousy driver.' We sat talking for a while then a nurse came along to change his dressings, so making myself scarce, I crossed over the ward and chatted to a chap in the bed opposite.

After a while the nurse emerged and pulled back the curtains around Chippy's bed space at the same time calling over that it was all right for me to return, adding that she didn't want me to stay too long. Sitting down in the chair by the bedside I waited for him to speak. 'Hammer,' he said at last, 'what do you remember about hitting that bloody minefield?' The question, abrupt and straight to the point as it was, caused me to pause before answering. 'It's OK,' said Chippy, 'I shall have to get used to this.' So saying he held up his damaged arm. 'Let's face it, it could have been a hell of a sight worse.' Hesitatingly I began:

'I don't know if you will believe what I am going to tell you, mate. I can hardly do so myself, however here goes. The explosion was like a brilliant white light that sent spasms of pain shooting right through me. Vaguely I remember trying to crawl away but it felt as if I were getting nowhere, then suddenly I was in a long tunnel at the end of which was a bright light behind which shadowy figures seemed to be moving about. I couldn't see who they were; to me they were just vague shapes, then finally I heard a voice that seemed to be coming from one of the figures which said, "Come on, Jacko, don't give up now," then two strong arms lifted me up, but even then I couldn't see anyone. Suddenly everything went black and like you I don't remember any more until I came to with a couple of the lads from the tank transporter bending over me. Later, although dazed and still in shock I do remember one of them saying that some idiot had gone into the minefield and dragged both of us out, but at the time, being more concerned about our plight, they had paid little attention to our rescuer, only to find later that he had disappeared, and that's about it.'

For a while neither of us said a word then Chippy asked, 'What's make of it all, mate?' 'Don't rightly know,' I answered, 'however there is one thing that puzzles me, and I feel that somehow I should know the answer – why should whoever it was have called me "Jacko"?'

We spent a further two months in hospital and slowly we began to recover and find our way back to something approaching normal. Then one day I learned that Chippy was being shipped back to the UK for further treatment. Just before he left I walked with him around the grounds and we talked, wondering if we should ever meet up in civvy street after the war. Ours had been a brief friendship but nonetheless a sincere and deep one, and I knew I was going to miss him. Halting and holding out my hand I reminded him to keep in touch, then just before we parted he said, 'Hammer, it's a fact of life that each time you say hello to something new you have to say goodbye to something old. I have a feeling that we shall meet up again, mate,' then turning he walked away and I watched as he boarded the ambulance that was taking him to the docks. Just before it pulled away I could just see him waving through the window and that for the moment was the end of a comradeship that had been forged in the heat and dust of the desert.

As yet I hadn't written to my parents to tell them that I had been in hospital, thinking it better to leave it until I was fit again, after all, what they didn't know they wouldn't have to worry about. I hadn't had any letters from home for some time but that was only to be expected, bearing in mind how I had been shifted about during the last few months. Then a whole batch of letters caught up with me and although some of the news in them was by now out of date I read and re-read them. Mother told me that Mary had written to her asking if she thought it would be all right to write to me. What made her ask that I couldn't imagine seeing that I had already had several letters from her; women, they say, do the strangest things. Tommy and Phyllis seemed to be making out and Phyllis had asked Mother to include their best wishes when next she wrote to me.

Just as I was resigning myself to a long stay in hospital I was told that I was being shipped back home and almost before I had got used to the idea I found myself aboard a hospital ship that had called in at Alexandria on its way back from India. The voyage home was pleasant enough and luckily trouble-free, however I wasn't sorry to see the skyline of Southampton where we docked and from where we were transported to a military hospital near Dorchester.

My first task after settling in was to write home, being fully aware what a shock it would be when they received my letter telling them that I was back in England. One afternoon I was sitting alone in the grounds when I heard someone call my name; it was one of the nurses who told me that I had some visitors. Curiosity now thoroughly aroused I sat and waited, wondering who it could be, thinking perhaps it was one of my old Army mates, or possibly Chippy, then just as I was running out of possibilities a voice behind me said just one word, 'John,' then I knew. Turning I saw Mother standing there with Father and Aunty Beckey. Hugging and scolding me for not having told them before they all tried to talk at once and in between I somehow managed to explain, however they insisted that I tell them all about my encounter with the minefield and the subsequent happenings. Father, when he was able to get a word in edgeways, shook my hand. 'Good to have you back, lad,' he said, and I knew by the emotion in his voice that he really meant it. Mother of course dealt with the matter in her usual way, chattering away nineteen to the dozen to hide her true feelings, bless her. One of the nurses brought tea out and we sat, for what seemed hours, just talking. I told them about Chippy and of our adventures in the desert, concluding with the fact that I was now on the mend and if all went well I should be home really soon.

When the time came for them to go I walked with them as far as the driveway where Harry Haines was waiting with his taxi and after more hugs and handshakes they finally climbed aboard, promising to come again before long. I watched them go until they disappeared out of sight through the entrance gates then, feeling utterly homesick I made my way back into the hospital; the sun had gone in and just at that moment I didn't want to be alone.

Two weeks later I had my final operation, only a minor one as it turned out, this being followed by a few weeks of convalescence and before long it was Christmas. Now there are plenty of worse places to spend Christmas than in a military hospital. The wards were decorated and hung with holly and mistletoe, the latter being in great demand especially when the nurses were about. We had the traditional Christmas dinner with all the trimmings after which a choir from the local church came in and entertained us with carols.

There were cards and parcels of course from my parents and Aunty Tessa and Aunty Beckey but the one I was most surprised to receive was one from Mary which had been forwarded on. It was signed, 'with all my love' and across it, written in bold capitals, were the words 'I still miss you, damn you'. Sitting looking at it I suddenly realized that in all the upheaval of the last year or two I hadn't given a lot of thought to my future or who I wanted to share it with, that is of course providing that there was anyone that would want to. All through my teenage years I had romantically assumed that Phyllis and I would eventually get together but her marriage to Tommy had knocked the bottom out of that. Then Mary had appeared on the scene turning everything upside down. I knew that she had only to give me the slightest encouragement and I would have asked her to marry me, but I had the feeling that she had assumed that there could never be any permanent understanding between us as long as the ghost of Phyllis hovered around.

Early in the New Year I left hospital and the Army and was sent home on discharge leave. I can't say that I was sorry, feeling no regrets when I handed in my hospital 'blues' and received a civilian suit and overcoat in exchange, after which they took me to Dorchester station and saw me safely aboard the train. So ended my short but fairly eventful Army career.

There were only two of us in the compartment, myself and a middle-aged gentleman who, after a while, struck up a conversation. I think he felt lonely and just wanted someone to talk to. He told me that his only son had been killed at El Alamein and was quite pleased and surprised when I told him that I too had been there. 'Well,' he said, 'thank God that at least you survived. I hope you find all is well when you reach home. You see, a week after receiving the news about my boy, my wife was killed in an air raid.'

We parted company in London where I had to change trains. I couldn't help but feel sorry for him; the war had taken his son and his wife and now there was nothing but memories for him to go home to. Then just as he was

202

about to leave me he turned and said, 'Take care and be grateful for what you have, lad, because you never know when it will be taken from you.' With that he walked away and was soon swallowed up by the crowd.

For the greater part of the journey home I kept thinking about that poor old man and as I watched the countryside slip by I wondered what other tragedies were being enacted in the rows and rows of houses that edged the railway track. No doubt each would have a story to tell in the years to come when all that would be left would be memories and faded photographs of sons and husbands to remind them of happier days. At one of the stations a large overdressed woman accompanied by an equally large companion, both dressed in country tweeds and loaded down with parcels, got into the compartment. Ignoring me they continued to talk in those loud affected voices their sort adopt when they seek to impress their importance on others. Listening to them I gathered that the war was proving most inconvenient, they couldn't get this and that was virtually unobtainable and they didn't know how they were going to get by. Then the one that was doing the most complaining remarked most pointedly, 'I don't know how some men manage to stay out of uniform. I hope they can live with themselves.' I didn't rise to the bait but decided that it was better to just sit and try and ignore them. Luckily a few stations on they departed, still complaining and quite frankly I was glad to see the back of them.

At last I found myself on familiar territory and soon the wooded heights above Lavington and the broad flank of Oak Hill came into view. For the best of reasons I hadn't written to tell my folks that I was coming home, preferring it to be a surprise and feeling that for the time being I didn't want to meet anyone as I wanted to re-enter my old world at my leisure. Alighting on the platform I stood for a while looking about almost as if I needed assurance that everything was just as I left it. Someone came out of the porters' room and as he passed he bade me the time of day but I didn't recognize him. He was a stranger to me as was the young lad who took my ticket at the exit.

Shouldering my small pack which contained my few belongings I started slowly up the lane towards the main road, a truck passed me on its way down to the station and on its side was painted the White Star of the American forces. Mother had mentioned in one of her letters that they were stationed in the vicinity, even so visual confirmation came as a bit of a shock. Outside the village store a jeep was parked and sitting in it were two American GIs chatting and chewing gum, who looked up as I passed. 'Hey there, Buddy,' one of them called out and not wishing to appear unfriendly I raised my hand in acknowledgement. On reaching the top of Callow Lane I halted for a moment to get my bearings. Up until then I hadn't seen a familiar face, a fact that in a way disturbed me, making me feel like a stranger. Looking about it seemed that everything had got smaller than I had remembered it. Grinnels Orchard looked much about the same and as I rounded the bend at the bottom of the lane I saw that the pond was still there and that the area in front of the smithy was still littered with various bits and pieces of discarded farm machinery through which the nettles and last year's bindweed had grown. Searching for some tangible sign of my past I was relieved to see the old Titian tractor lying rusting and discarded under the overhanging blackthorn hedge that bordered Grinnels Orchard, the sight of it bringing back memories of many happy hours playing on it when I was a lad.

Gathering myself together I made my way up to the smithy and sat myself down on the seat outside, the same seat that Grandad and I had used to sit on as he made the smoke rings hover and curl. Suddenly a voice broke through my reverie, 'Welcome home, lad,' it said and turning, I saw Father standing in the doorway of the smithy, cap pushed to the back of his head. Wiping his hands on his leather apron he came towards me arms extended. 'It's been a long time, lad, far too long. Thank God you have returned safely. Come on, let's get you over to the cottage,' and with that he took my small pack off me and with one arm around my shoulder walked with me across the yard to the door of the cottage.

Stepping over the threshold was an emotional experience which I shall long remember. I felt as if I had been away for years when in fact it was only just over a year since Mary and I had left to go our separate ways. It was amazing how much had happened in such a short space of time. Leaving me standing in the parlour Father went out to the back from where the sounds of Mother's busying came. Looking about me I saw that nothing had changed; the old grandfather clock was still ticking away in the corner and on the high mantelpiece above the fireplace the photograph of Aunty Beckey still looked down from its silver frame as it had always done. In the corner by the fireplace Father's rocking chair stood invitingly beside the table on which stood Grandad's tobacco jar, and looking down at the rug laid out in front of the fireplace, I could just make out the tiny bare patch which many years ago as a

204

small boy I had, when having nothing better to do, found a loose thread and pulled and pulled until it unravelled. On the hob the kettle stood gently simmering, the steam from its blackened spout rising to mingle with the smoke from the smouldering logs before both made their way up the dark chimney, and embracing it all, that special aroma that made it home, the lingering scent of Father's tobacco and the smell of damp clothes drying on the airing rack above the range in the kitchen. Yes, I thought, it was good to be back.

She came into the parlour holding the china bowl in which she had mixed the chicken's feed and so busy was she scolding Father for not having filled the log basket that at first she failed to notice me. Suddenly she stopped dead in her tracks and the bowl crashed to the floor scattering its contents, then rushing towards me she flung her arms around me at the same time scolding me for not letting her know that I was coming home.

Later sitting in the parlour I had just started to recount some of my adventures when the door burst open and in came Aunty Tessa and Aunty Beckey whereupon I was subjected to another session of hugs and endless questions. Then with all that seen to they settled down to bring me up to date with all the village news. The Americans I gathered were billeted in Nissen huts down at the old brick yard and apparently at first the villagers were slightly overwhelmed by them, not knowing quite what to expect, but they soon came to realize that most of them were just ordinary lads, who had been uprooted from their folks and homes, and transported across the sea to a strange country with whose inhabitants they only had one thing in common and that was that they more or less spoke the same language. Never so far in the war had the youngsters seen so much candy and chewing gum, or the girls so many pairs of nylon stockings, the latter I was told more often than not being given for services rendered. Very quickly however friendships had been made and generally the village had settled down to living cheek by jowel with their cousins from across the water.

That night, lying in bed in my old bedroom which Mother had made ready for me, I pondered on the many questions that my return home had raised. I wondered how Tommy and Phyllis were making out, hoping against hope that at last they had sorted out their difficulties. I thought of Mary and those few precious hours we had spent together before I had been posted overseas, wondering if perhaps by now she had found someone else. I hoped not, for secretly I had to admit that she meant more to me than I cared to say. My feelings for Phyllis had over the past few months begun to change; perhaps at last I was beginning to admit that she was lost to me, and for that matter had been for some time, however I knew that I should never be able to forget her seeing that she had been a part of my life.

The next morning I rose early and after breakfast joined Father in the smithy where, sitting watching him at work, it suddenly dawned on me that it would soon be time for me to join him even though he had insisted that I take my time before doing so. Sitting there I thought of the many times in the past when I had pictured him working in the glow of the forge in the peace and quiet of Lavington. Now all that was reality and here I was back home ready to take up life where I had left it on that morning when I had taken the train to Catterick Camp.

Feeling the need to be alone for a while I took a walk up onto Oak Hill. I was now twenty-four although there were times when I felt older. My wounds had healed and gave me no trouble except for the odd twinge when the weather turned cold and damp. All things considered I had been lucky, now it was time to get my life sorted out. One thing was for certain and that was that eventually I should take over the smithy from my father just as he had done from his, the only difference being that when his turn had come he had had a wife to share it with him. Looking down at the village lying below somehow made me think of the day that Mary and I had made love in the hazel thicket, recalling her words to me. 'John,' she had said, 'this is perhaps the last time we shall be together. I dread to think what might happen to us in the future and although I know that you cannot completely belong to me I want you to make love to me, perhaps for the last time.' Thinking of her lying in my arms and remembering all the tender words she spoke while we made love made me realize just how much I was missing her.

Although we had kept in touch Phyllis had stood like a barrier between us. Rightly or wrongly she had assumed that there could never be anyone else. Now I knew how wrong she had been and that all these years I had been clinging on to a dream that had been born in the uncomplicated days of our youth. Perhaps it was just as well that at the time I couldn't see into the future. Who would have thought that Tommy and Phyllis would have ended up the way they had or that we should find ourselves involved in a war that was to alter all our lives?

I thought of Violet, my first girlfriend, who had taught me so much about life, wondering how things had turned out for her, and of Clare with her posh boyfriends who had made me realize that all that glistens is not gold. Strangely enough I had long forgiven her and secretly I hoped that perhaps in quieter moments she would remember that callous youth, the blacksmith's son, whose affections she had played with. Away in the distance a curlew called, a haunting sound, a sound that stirs the memory and sends shivers down the spine so, shaking off the fit of nostalgia that was beginning to make me feel sad, I rose and after taking a last look at the hazel thicket made my way back down the hill towards the village.

Three weeks later I started work alongside my father in the smithy. I hadn't seen either Tommy or Phyllis since my return but promised myself that at the first opportunity I would rectify the omission. I didn't want to go down to the Drovers Arms, at least not at the moment, somehow the thought of mingling with our American cousins didn't appeal to me. One evening after work I washed and changed and without telling anyone where I was going made my way down to Leyfield Cottage. Phyllis answered the door and the look of astonishment on her face told me that she had no idea I was home. Ushering me into the parlour she introduced me to an American GI who had risen from the chair where he had been sitting. 'John,' she said, 'this is a friend of mine, Abe Sherman, who is stationed with the Americans down at the brickyard Mother has gone visiting Mrs Walker up in the village and Tommy is down at the Drovers.' Watching her as she spoke I sensed a hint of guilt in her voice. It was almost as if she was making excuses, however not wanting to get involved I shook hands with Abe and for a while the three of us just sat talking, although I must admit that I found the situation very awkward seeing that the sole purpose of my visit was to find out how things were between her and Tommy. Abe seemed a decent enough chap and when he learned that I had been out in North Africa with the Eighth Army he plied me with questions leaving Phyllis sitting to one side saying very little. Fortunately after about an hour Mrs Whitworth returned so I was able to make my excuses and leave.

Phyllis came to the door with me and before I could even say goodnight she volunteered the information that Abe was only a friend and nothing more. 'If only you knew how lonely I have been, John,' she said, 'I know you of all people would understand. Tommy is no different and every day sees us draw further and further apart,' and with that she leaned forward and kissed me lightly on the cheek. 'Goodnight and take care,' she added before closing the door. Walking home in the dark I wondered if Phyllis realized that she was playing with fire; Tommy must surely know of Abe's visits, his mother must have told him.

Over supper I raised the subject with my parents; Father was as always non-committal, Mother on the other hand was a little more forthcoming and she told me that Phyllis's friendship with the American was the talk of the village, although seeing that Tommy spent most of his time down at the Drovers Arms and knowing the way he treated her, very few blamed her.

The next morning I received a letter from Mary which started off by saying that in the absence of any other address she was sending it to Forge Cottage knowing that it would be forwarded to me. Eagerly I read and re-read it but what I was looking for wasn't there which I had to admit wasn't surprising seeing that it had been some time since we had last met. Perhaps by now she had put it down to just another wartime romance, however the fact that she had bothered to keep in touch gave me some hope. Reading it I gathered that she had left Acton, was now stationed at a depot near Market Drayton and that her daughter was still with her Aunty out in the country. Obviously she didn't know that I had returned to England and was now out of the Army, as in the concluding part of the letter she said that she hoped I would soon be home and that in the meantime I was to take care of myself.

On thinking the matter over I made up my mind to write to her to ask if we could meet and much to my surprise and delight her reply came almost by return. She said that she had been bowled over by the news that I was now back in civvy street and couldn't wait to hear all my news, the outcome of further letters between us being that we arranged to meet on Shrewsbury Station, an arrangement that would be easier for both of us.

On the journey up one question kept going through my mind: was I meeting Mary in the hope that we could take up where we had left off or was I just trying to catch up on the past? However not being able to decide I left it be to see how things worked out. As the train made its way through the countryside, I could see where in disused sidings and branch lines, that ran between high banks, wagons loaded with tanks and trucks waited in grey camouflaged lines, all marked with the white star of the USA, and on many of the platforms of the stations at which we stopped troops were lined up waiting for special troop trains to take them who knows where. For some time there had been talk of a second front and I felt sure that all these preparations had something to do with it.

Feeling for some reason vaguely uncomfortable in my demob suit I sat watching all the activity taking place, then a sergeant in the artillery, who was sitting opposite, leaned forward and said very quietly, 'I bet you are glad to be out of it all, mate. I see by your badge that you are a discharged serviceman.' Warming to him and seeing in him a way to relieve my conscience I found myself telling him about my brief war in the desert, and when I had finished he said, 'I haven't been overseas yet but by the look of things it won't be long. I'm off on seven days leave to see the Missus and kids,' and with that he took a well-worn wallet from his battledress pocket and from it a photograph which he handed to me. 'That's us on holiday in Blackpool the summer before war broke out,' he said, and taking it from him I sat looking at it wondering how his family were coping. Anyway he was lucky to have a wife and family waiting for him and I couldn't help but hope that when it was all over he would return safely and once again take holidays in Blackpool.

Slowly the train pulled into Shrewsbury station and in a flurry of steam ground to a halt. Half way out of the carriage I stopped and held out my hand. 'Good luck, Sarge,' I said, 'I hope all goes well with you, enjoy your leave.' For a fleeting moment he held on to my hand. 'Take care, lad, you've done your bit,' and with that we parted. I often wonder what happened to him and if he survived to take his wife and kids on another holiday. Elbowing my way through the crowds of service people that thronged the platform I finally managed to reach the station exit; she was waiting for me and I could see at a glance that she hadn't altered. Running towards me she flung her arms around me and it was at that moment that the answer to the question I had been asking myself for most of the journey came.

Sitting in the canteen just outside the station she told me all that had happened to her since our last meeting and about her daughter who she had visited the previous week, while I brought her up to date with all my news. And so we talked and talked, then just as we were about to leave she asked after Phyllis. It was almost as if she had left the question until last, however I think I knew the reason; she wanted to sound me out, so I told her as much as I knew including the fact that apparently she now had an American boyfriend, a piece of news that seemed to surprise her although I had the feeling that she wasn't exactly shocked.

We spent the rest of the day exploring Shrewsbury finishing up at an old coaching inn, whose name I have long since forgotten, where we managed to get a seat by the window overlooking the street. Choosing what I thought to be the right moment I took her hands in mine. 'Mary,' I began, 'there is something I want you to know. The ghost of Phyllis was laid a long time ago.' Then just as I was about to tell her how much I had missed her and how I hoped that our relationship could come to mean more than friendship, the spell was broken by the appearance of the waitress with the menu.

I didn't get another chance to bring the subject up although I had the feeling that she was waiting for me to do just that, and so the afternoon wore on until at last it was time for her to go. I walked with her to the bus station to catch her bus back to camp and just before she climbed aboard I managed to ask, 'Mary, tell me, is there anyone else?' For a moment she hesitated then leaning forward she kissed me full on the lips. 'No, John Mumford, there isn't,' and with that she was gone. I stood watching until the bus had passed out of sight after which I made my way back to catch the train to Lavington.

All next day while working in the smithy my thoughts were of Mary, wondering if she could ever be interested in a blacksmith's son. Perhaps she couldn't see herself settled down to a life in the country. Then of course there was little Alice to be considered: how would she fit into the scheme of things?

Two days later I had a letter from Mary saying how good it was to see me again, nothing more. However, there and then, I made up my mind that I wouldn't let matters rest until I had an answer from her one way or another. My parents naturally wanted to know how things were between us but in all truth there was very little to tell them other than she was fit and well and that she had sent her love. I know that in a way they were disappointed as it had been plain to me for some time that they would have loved to have Mary as a daughter-in-law, however they didn't press me further on the matter and so for the time being it was let bide.

Chapter XII

It was now the middle of May, there were signs of unusual activity down at the brickyard and putting two and two together we guessed there was something big in the offing. By now I had settled back into civilian life and much to everyone's surprise had rejoined the Home Guard, feeling that under the circumstances it was the least I could do.

The week before they finally pulled out the Americans organized a farewell dance in the village hall and more out of curiosity than anything else I went along being, like my father, not any great shakes at dancing, although watching the jitterbugging that the Americans were so fond of made me wonder. The hall was crowded and looking around I was surprised to see Phyllis and Tommy there so making my way over to where they were sitting I grabbed a vacant chair and sat with them for a while.

Phyllis seemed pleased to see me and for once Tommy was just like his old self again. Naturally they both demanded to know where I had been hiding myself and without telling the real truth I was able to think up some good excuses with which they seemed satisfied. Looking at Phyllis I thought she had aged but there, I thought, I suppose we all had. It wasn't only that the care lines under her eyes were deep, she seemed to have lost a lot of the lustre and vitality that had been so much a part of her. Once or twice I caught her looking at me almost as if she wanted to talk and her chance soon came when the band struck up a ladies' 'excuse me' waltz and almost before the first note had been played she stood up, and taking my hand, said, 'This is my dance, I think.' Somehow I managed to keep in time with the music without treading on her toes, but it was plain that as far as Phyllis was concerned dancing wasn't the object of the exercise. For a while we danced in silence, then gripping my arm she said, 'Why haven't you been down to see me again, John?' Reading the danger signals I chose my words carefully. 'You are a married woman now, Phyllis, and shouldn't be dating old boyfriends. By the way, how is

Tommy behaving himself these days, is he treating you all right?' Luckily, before she could answer, someone tapped me on the shoulder and a voice said, 'Excuse me, pal.' It was her friend Abe Sherman, so gratefully I handed her over to him. Crossing the hall I joined my mates from the Home Guard.

I didn't get the chance to talk to Phyllis again but perhaps that was just as well as I had the feeling that she was looking for a way of escape from an unhappy marriage and I didn't want to get involved. Then just as I had made up my mind to leave I heard voices raised in a heated argument, and on going over to where a small crowd had gathered, I saw in a flash what the trouble was. Tommy was laying into an American GI. Pushing my way through I grabbed hold of his arm and twisted it behind his back. Red of face and seemingly having lost all control he took some holding, however I managed to gasp, 'What the hell is this all about?' at the same time guiding him away from the crowd.

'It's that bloody Yank,' he shouted, 'he's been carrying on with my wife; I'll kill the bastard if I get my hands on him.' By this time a couple of the Home Guard had come to my assistance and between us we got Tommy into a side room where after a while we managed to calm him down. Then just as we had almost got it sorted an American officer came in to apologize even though it hadn't been the GI's fault. Taking him to one side I explained about Tommy, fortunately he seemed to understand and hands were shaken all round. Then it was back into the hall where the dance was once again in full swing. After making enquiries I learned that Phyllis had already left so thinking that perhaps it would be wise to walk Tommy home I offered to go with him seeing that by this time he was his old self again.

'What the hell did you think you were up to back at the village hall?' I at last ventured to ask. 'How could you humiliate Phyllis like that in front of all her friends?' He didn't answer but just shuffled along beside me. Determined to have one last go at him, I asked, 'What's wrong, mate, what in God's name did you think you would achieve by starting a fight?' Here he stopped me. 'John, my friend,' he said, 'I'm not the same old Tommy you used to know. I left him on the beaches at Dunkirk. Sometimes I think that there is little point in going on. Phyllis despises me, I know she does. Perhaps it's all my fault but somehow I can't help myself; she should have married you, John.'

'Don't talk so daft,' I managed to reply, 'Phyllis still loves you in spite of everything and I am sure that if only you would meet her half way things

212

would work out between you. Why not give it a try? At least you owe her that much.' By this time we had reached Leyfield Cottage. 'Goodnight, mate,' he said as he closed the gate behind him. 'Thanks for trying to straighten me out but you're wasting your time,' and with that he turned and made his way up to the cottage door. Waiting, I lingered until he was safe inside before making my way home in the darkness wondering what those two would have to say to each other in the morning.

During the closing days of May a great change came over the village. Down at the brickyard the Americans were all packed up and ready to move and all through the night trucks rumbled down to the railway station where two special trains were waiting in the sidings. No one was allowed on the platform, normal trains had been cancelled but specials went through, their carriage windows blacked out. Then one morning they were all gone except for the few that had stayed behind to clear up the camp, after which we of the Home Guard were ordered to do a twenty-four hour guard on the station premises and patrol the line for three miles either way. For nearly a week all communication with the village had been virtually non-existent, no outgoing post was allowed and all calls through the village telephone exchange were monitored. By then it was plain that something big was about to take place and naturally all thoughts turned towards the second front, so it came as no surprise when on the morning of 6 June we learned that the Allies had landed on the French coast.

I received several letters from Mary and much to my surprise one from my old pal Chippy Greatorex who seemingly had settled down well to civilian life and had been down to Roehampton several times for the fitting of his artificial arm. As yet he hadn't managed to get a job but he expressed the hope that once his treatment was finished he would be able to take up his old trade of carpentry, the specialist at Roehampton having confirmed that this might be possible. So when I replied to his letter I invited him to come and visit when he got himself settled, feeling that a few hours in his cheerful company would do me the world of good. Now that the Americans had gone the village was strangely silent and the villagers were honest enough to admit that they missed the extra goodies such as maple syrup, tomato ketchup, Coca Cola, peanut butter and many other extras that would now be unobtainable, plus of course the fact that the girls would miss their nylon stockings and the children their candy.

During this great upheaval dear old Doctor Hemmings passed away; he had had a good life but had been ailing for some time, nevertheless we all missed him, missed his pony and trap going up and down the village street, and not being able to go over and chat with him on sunny summer afternoons up at the cricket field. It didn't seem possible after all the years he had shared with us that he had finally gone. There was a good turnout at his funeral, members of the Home Guard providing the bearers for his coffin which, in recognition of the service he had rendered his country in the Great War, was draped with the Union Jack. He was laid to rest alongside old Zetter Parsons; they would be good company for each other those two.

Gradually the village settled down to seeing the rest of the war through. Things were going well in France and slowly but nevertheless surely the light from the lamp of victory was beginning to pierce the gloom that had hung over Europe for so long. The Americans had suffered severe casualties during the landing on Omaha Beach and we wondered if any of our late friends had been amongst them.

The year passed and great battles were fought, battles that now belong in the memories of old men and to history, then just before Christmas news came that the brickyard had been taken over again and was to become a prisoner-of-war camp which was to be guarded mainly by the local Home Guard. The first batch of prisoners arrived by train shortly after Christmas, it was a bitter January day and the poor devils looked frozen as they marched through the village on their way to the brickyard. Most of them were young lads and even though they were Germans we couldn't help but feel sorry for them. At first they were viewed with a certain amount of hostility, particularly by some of the old soldiers who had fought against their fathers in the last war, however as time went by they relented, and some of them were even allowed out to work on the farms. On occasions one of them would bring a horse to the smithy to be shod and Mother, soft and kind-hearted as always, would insist that he be given a cup of tea and a slice of home-made cake; somehow I don't think that Father was too keen but he never showed it. I suppose it was only natural for him to resent them when he thought of all the good pals he had lost in his war, in particular his friend Charlie.

* * *

Almost before we realized it, 1945 was upon us. Mary continued to write and although I had spoken to her several times on the telephone she hadn't as yet given any intimation that she might take up my offer and come and visit. Relaxing in the parlour one evening just after supper I heard the telephone ring. Father answered it and I could see by the look on his face that something was wrong. 'It's for you, lad,' he said, handing me the receiver, and as I took it I had an awful feeling that I wouldn't want to hear what I was going to. It was Harry Gibbons on the phone. 'John,' he began, 'best get over to Tommy Whitworth's place, I reckon there's been an accident.'

Dropping the receiver I grabbed my coat from the hanger in the hall and dashed out without even a word of explanation. Stumbling through Grinnels Orchard and somehow managing to avoid the trees in the dark I finally arrived at the keeper's lodge where Harry was waiting for me and he told me what had happened. Apparently he had been out in the yard seeing to his dogs when he heard voices raised in anger coming from the direction of Leyfield Cottage, after which had come two distinct shots followed by an awful silence. Realizing that something was wrong and knowing of my friendship with Tommy and Phyllis he had rung me before ringing the constable who he said was on his way. Torches in hand we hurried up the lane towards where shafts of light were streaming out into the darkness from the windows of the Whitworth's cottage. Fumbling with the latch of the gate I was just about to open it when the voice of the constable called out, 'Hold on, lad, let me go in first,' and so saying he pushed past me and made his way up the path towards the front door which was standing open.

We waited for a while and then just as we were about to follow him in he came out, his face ashen white. 'I shouldn't go in there, lads,' he said. 'Harry, you dash back to the keeper's cottage and call the doctor, then ring the police at Cheltenham and tell them we shall need an ambulance.' By this time I had an awful sick feeling in the pit of my stomach. Pushing past the constable I stumbled into the parlour and even though the light was on at first I didn't see anything, then my attention was drawn to something lying half under the table, partly covered with the tablecloth that had apparently been pulled off. Bending down I lifted the cloth aside and to my horror I saw that it was Phyllis lying in a pool of blood, a look of sheer terror on her face. I knew that it was useless to check for any signs of life so gently I pulled the lids of her eyes down and covered her face. I had seen gunshot wounds before and

215

judging by her injuries death must have been instantaneous. Looking around my attention was drawn to something lying underneath the window. I hadn't seen it before owing to it being in the shadow. Drawing back the full-length curtains I think I knew what I would see. It was Mrs Whitworth and like Phyllis I could see that she was beyond help.

By this time the doctor had arrived so leaving him to carry out his examinations I went upstairs where entering the first bedroom I came to I stripped the sheets off the bed and took them back downstairs into the parlour where the doctor, having finished his examination, was talking in low tones to the constable. Gently I covered both bodies after which I went out into the kitchen where I was violently sick.

By this time the ambulance had arrived and after the police had completed their investigations the bodies were taken away to the mortuary in Cheltenham. When it had gone preliminary statements were taken from those immediately concerned and it was while this was taking place that I suddenly realized that in all the confusion no one had given a thought to Tommy. It was fairly obvious that he wasn't in the cottage so after mentioning it to the police I volunteered to go with Harry and our local constable to look for him. Perhaps if I had been thinking a little more clearly I should have realized that wherever he was he was carrying a gun, and having done what we, by now, had assumed he had done he wouldn't be in a very balanced state of mind. First we combed the outhouses and buildings in the immediate vicinity but found nothing. Then, just as we were about to widen our area of search, one of the Cheltenham police came over with the information that Sid Arrowsmith, the signalman down at the station had phoned Harry's father to say that he had seen someone climbing down the bank by his signal box.

Lanterns and torches in hand we set off for the station where on arrival we were met by the station master who advised us not to walk the line until the mail train, due in a few minutes, had passed, adding that after it had gone we should be alright as the next train was the eleven forty-five from Cheltenham. Standing on the platform with a cold wind blowing I suddenly realized how ill-prepared I was to undertake a long search in the countryside, having only my working jacket to keep me warm. Fortunately there was a fire still burning in the waiting room so we all went in to take advantage of it while we waited. The mail train was dead on time, we heard its whistle as it thundered down the long straight beyond Broadway and within minutes it went roaring through the station enveloping everything in a cloud of smoke and steam, causing doors to slam and sending the paper debris that had collected between the lines soaring up into the night sky after it had passed. We waited until the noise of the engine and the rattle of the carriages over the points by the signal box had died away then, lanterns in hand, we set off down the track where we were met by Sid Arrowsmith.

'He went that way,' he called out, at the same time pointing down the line. Warning him to keep his eyes open we moved on and after carefully searching for a few hundred yards found a double-barrelled shotgun lying halfway up the banking at the side of the track, and it was then that I began to fear the worst. Slowly we pressed on then came a shout from the constable who was some way ahead of us.

'Over here, lads,' he called and rushing to join him we found him staring down at the mangled body of Tommy. It was plain what had happened: he had been hit by the train. Grabbing a lantern off Harry I made my way back to the signal box and borrowed an old piece of tarpaulin which I took back to the scene and covered Tommy's body with it. Standing looking down at all that was left of him I wondered what his thoughts must have been in those last few minutes, wondering if it had been an accident or had he done it deliberately. Perhaps I shall never know the answer, however, whichever way it was he wouldn't have known much about it and I suppose that that in itself was a mercy.

I don't remember a lot about the walk home; all I could think of was Phyllis and Mrs Whitworth lying on the floor of their parlour and Tommy mangled and lifeless underneath that dirty tarpaulin sheet. They were both gone now, those two people who for such a long time had been an important part of my life, somehow I felt unable to come to terms with the finality of it; at that moment it all seemed like a terrible nightmare. My parents were waiting for me when I got back to Forge Cottage. Father took one look at me and after sitting me down by the fireside poured me out a stiff whisky. Bit by bit I was at last able to tell him about the night's happenings as Mother, her face ashen, sat listening and occasionally calling out, 'Oh my God, oh my God.'

Still in a state of shock I at last managed to find my way upstairs to my bedroom leaving my parents sitting in the parlour. I didn't undress but just lay on the bed reliving the horrors of the last few hours and it must have been near to daybreak before I fell into a fitful sleep, remembering nothing until I heard Father moving about in the yard below. Just after we had finished breakfast the constable called to tell us that formalities had now been completed but that he would require a more detailed statement from me later, then he rode away on his bicycle up to the keeper's lodge to see Harry. By this time the news of the tragedy had spread round the village, some spoke of it in whispers while others stated quite openly that they weren't surprised seeing how unstable Tommy had been of late.

Later at the inquest they recorded a verdict of murder in the cases of Phyllis and Mrs Whitworth, and suicide whilst of unsound mind in Tommy's case. Naturally there was the usual morbid interest by the press who sifted and sifted until they had bared all the gruesome details, luckily however, after a few weeks, they lost interest and the village was left in peace.

On the day of the funerals the whole village was in mourning, curtains were drawn as a sign of respect and even the Drovers Arms closed for the day. Sombre and silent I walked with my parents and Aunty Tessa and Aunty Beckey up to the church. As we entered the lych-gate we could hear the organ playing and from up in the grey tower came the tolling of a single muffled bell. The church was near full when we entered and owing to the lack of seating we were ushered to the back to sit in the pews normally occupied by the Armstrongs and their visitors. Master Grahame and his lady had already arrived and as I went to sit down he leaned forward and tapped me on the shoulder. 'Sorry it had to turn out like this, John.' 'Thank you, sir,' I managed to reply. One by one the coffins were carried into the church, followed by Phyllis's parents and several relations of Mrs Whitworth's, Tommy's being draped with the Union Jack and born by members of the Home Guard. They had asked me if I wanted to be one of the bearers but somehow I just couldn't bring myself to do it. Looking at the coffins as they lay on the trestles in front of the altar I realized that two of them contained all that remained of two very dear friends who had been such a great part of my life, knowing that, unless at some time in the future I put pen to paper, no one would ever know how great a part that was. Phyllis and Tommy were buried together in the same grave with Mrs Whitworth close by and as they lowered the coffins into the ground the tears came and my Mother, who was standing by me, squeezed my arm tightly to show that she understood; I hadn't cried in a long time but I felt no shame in doing so.

After the service was over I left and walked through the park and up on to

Oak Hill where, sitting alone, I tried to get the emotions that were sweeping over me under control. They were no more now, those two dear people; if only I could put the clock back and relive those carefree days of playing in the hayfields and swimming in the mill stream. I thought of the day when the three of us had sat on the side of the hill and Phyllis had said, 'I ain't ever going to get married. I be going to be an old maid like Miss Parker; on t'uther hand I might marry both of you.' Memories, that was all that was left now.

Slowly the war dragged on and up in the churchyard the grass grew to cover the newly-dug mounds, then quite unexpectedly I received a letter from Mary in which she asked if she might take up our offer to come and stay. Delighted, I replied by return, arranging to meet her on Lavington station. As she stepped out of the carriage onto the platform she hesitated for a moment before coming forward to meet me and in those first few moments I knew that my feelings for her hadn't altered. I remember thinking how much better she looked, more relaxed, more like the old Mary I had first met in Acton. Walking up the lane I told her in more detail about the death of Phyllis, Tommy and Mrs Whitworth and when I had finished recounting the horrors of that night she stopped and turning, took my hands in hers.

'I'm so sorry, John,' she said, 'I know just how great a part of your life they were and even though you would never admit it, Phyllis was in love with you right up to the end. There were times when I found myself being jealous of her but knowing that I had no right to be I never told you or wanted you to know. She was always there between us, John, and in the end I gave up hoping.'

Taking her in my arms I kissed her. 'It's all over now,' I said and with that she seemed to be content.

She only had a few days leave and we spent it walking the countryside leaving Father to carry on alone at the smithy, an arrangement he readily agreed to as both he and Mother had made it obviously plain that they were glad to see Mary again. On the last day we walked up to the churchyard to pay our respects to those of my family and friends that were buried there. It was a sad moment. Over the trees in the park the sun had just thrust its way through the scurrying rain clouds, lighting up the grey, squat tower of the church as it did so and sending shadows down the village street. Hand in hand we wandered amongst the graves of those who in their lifetime had added so much to the rich tapestry of the life of the village: my grandparents,

219

Phyllis and Tommy, Alby Stringer the station master, Herbert Tanner, Doris Weaver and Zetter Parsons, the list was endless.

Treading carefully we made our way amongst the graves and out into the park beyond, neither of us wanting to linger, the place being too full of memories. Onwards and upwards we went through the fresh wet grass with no clear idea of where we were going until, with the wind stinging our faces, we suddenly realized that we were high on the slopes of Oak Hill. Down below us the village, sleepy and unconcerned as always, was going about its business. In the tall elm trees beside the churchyard the rooks protested and circled and in the distance came the rattle of a train as it approached Lavington station. Standing there I wondered what was going through Mary's mind. Turning, I placed my hands on her shoulders and as I did so she turned to face me. I think she knew what I was going to say.

'Mary,' I began, 'although at times I found it hard to admit even to myself, I have loved you ever since that first meeting in Acton but somehow I could never summon up enough courage to tell you; perhaps I was afraid that you would have been offended seeing that you were married, or maybe it was that I wasn't seeing things too clearly, I don't know.'

She started to say something but I stopped her. 'Just hear me out, please,' I asked. 'Perhaps there were a thousand reasons why you didn't want to get involved, your husband, your daughter for instance but believe me all those things could have been sorted out,' here I stopped, feeling that perhaps I had already said too much. Releasing herself she walked a few paces away, then turning to face me she began:

'I think that the time has come to be honest with each other, John. I believe you when you say that you love me but that's not enough. It would be so simple for me to say that I loved you in return, that would be the easy way, but ever since we met, Phyllis was between us and in the end I gave up hoping that perhaps in spite of your loyalty she was lost to you. Then there are other considerations, our difference in ages, and Alice my daughter whom you have never met. Are you prepared to take on the responsibility of another man's child? Oh John, it hurts me to have to say all these things but they must be said, whatever else we must at least be honest with one another.'

Here she paused and I started to say something but she stopped me. 'There is something else you must know,' she continued, 'my husband died in the early part of the war, apparently he had joined the Merchant Navy and was

220

lost at sea. I never told you the truth when we first met, having a husband in the background was a shield against anyone getting too close emotionally and I wasn't ready for that, however you were different and by the time I had made up my mind to tell you Phyllis appeared on the scene. The thing is, John, where do we go from here? One thing I must know and be absolutely certain about and that is how you will get along with Alice and she with you. I hope you understand why I ask this. It isn't that I don't love you, I do, but after the break-up of my first marriage I have to be quite sure that the next time, if there is to be one, will be for ever, so let's just leave things to work out for themselves,' and with that she took my arm and we started back down the hill.

Later when thinking on what she had said I had to admit that it made sense although if I were to be honest it was not quite what I had expected; perhaps I had been guilty of taking too much for granted. Mother was waiting when we got back to the cottage and I had the feeling that what she was looking for and had hoped for wasn't there. The next morning I walked Mary to the station to catch her train hoping that she would give me further words of encouragement but she didn't. Leaning out of the carriage window as the train pulled away she bent forward and kissed me. 'Patience, John,' she said, and with that she was gone.

Chapter XIII

The year turned and although she kept in touch both by letter and telephone we didn't meet. In a way it was an unnatural relationship and although I had told my parents how things were between us I know they were concerned for me. They were longing to see me settled down but as I explained to them it wasn't that easy there being so many things to be taken into consideration. Quite unexpectedly Sir Howard passed away at his London home and they brought him back to Lavington to be buried. He was laid to rest beside his ancestors in the family plot hard by the gate leading out into the bottom lodge, just another sad day for the village; but somehow like all the other occasions that for some strange reason had become almost commonplace we accepted the finality of it, the only good thing that came out of it as far as the village was concerned was that Lady Armstrong, no doubt wanting to be near her son, whose wife was now with child, had come to stay.

Father, always a bit set in his ways, was gradually dragging himself into the second half of the century and there was even talk of him taking driving lessons with a view to getting a small motor car, then quite out of the blue he was offered a job on the estate in charge of general repairs. Knowing how he felt about the smithy and its family tradition we doubted whether he would accept, however much to our surprise he did, after all, he said, it had always been understood that one day he would hand over the blacksmith's shop to me and now was as good a time as ever, and so it was arranged that I would take over at the end of May when he started his new job.

The war in Europe was drawing to a close and Germany and her allies, now on the verge of defeat, prepared to surrender. News filtered through of the liberation of the concentration camps at Buchenwald and Belsen where thousands of prisoners were found dead and dying, the horror of it shocking us all. Feelings against the German prisoners down at the brickyard ran high

222

and sad to relate there were several instances of retaliation against them when they were working out on the fields.

On 8 May Winston Churchill broadcast to the nation telling us that the war in Europe was over and that the Germans had surrendered unconditionally on Luneburg Heath, the news being received with wild delight in the village. From the grey, squat tower of the church the bells rang out once again. Neighbours came in and with all work at a standstill they crowded into our parlour to toast the victory with Father's home-made wines. Needing a breath of fresh air I left them to their celebrating and went out into the yard where I was surprised to see one of the German POWs standing holding the reins of a horse he had brought to be shod. Going over to him I took the reins out of his hands and tied them to a ring set in the wall after which, by means of sign language, I indicated that I wished him to follow me into the cottage. His appearance in the parlour caused a sudden hush to descend and for a moment I began to wonder if my bringing him in had been a wise move, however having gone thus far I could do no other than sit him down in a chair and pour him a drink. Looking around me at the enquiring faces I thought it best that I say something so, glass in hand, I stood up and began:

'Friends, the war is over for both us and our friend here. You can't blame him for all the evils done by a few of his countrymen. Have you thought that perhaps he too has a family waiting for his safe return? My father and I have served our country in two world wars, he in the first, me in the second and yet we bear no malice, so raise your glasses and drink not only to victory but also to peace and a new understanding.'

For a while there was a deadly silence except for a few muffled mutterings from the back of the parlour then Father rose to his feet. 'John's right,' he said, 'there's been enough hate in the world of late.' That seemed to break the ice and so avoided what could have been an ugly situation. It was the longest speech I had made for quite some time but I felt that it was right to make it.

All through May, June and July news came of the liberation of people and countries and the long climb back to sanity began. At home the swallows and swifts returned to take up their old nesting places under the eaves of the smithy and our friendly robin, who in the early spring had nested on the shelf where Great Grandad's mug stood, having seen his early brood safely launched into the world outside, took to watching us from his lofty perch, sometimes venturing down to take a crumb from the titbits laid out on the side of the forge. Out in the countryside the bees supped and droned amongst the May blossom that lined the lanes and up in the woods above the village the first flush of blue showed where bluebells were getting themselves ready to lay a carpet amongst the white of the wood anemones. On the farms there was very little let-up as rationing was still in force, trace and cart harnesses were patched and mended and the single- and double-furrowed ploughs overhauled and put aside so as to be ready for the autumn plowing. What with guard duties down at the brickyard and long hours in the smithy there was little time to dwell on my personal problems, then in August the final episode in what had been a long and weary war was enacted when the Americans dropped the atom bombs on Hiroshima and Nagasaki, followed by the Japanese surrender. And so the war ended and as 1945 drew to a close we entered 1946 with renewed hope.

Down at the brickyard arrangements were being made to repatriate the German prisoners and within a month they were all gone, leaving the camp silent and deserted, then just as I was getting used to the idea of spending my days as a lonely old bachelor fate stepped in and altered the whole course of my life. One evening the telephone rang. It was Mary who told me that she had left the forces and was now living with her Aunty and Alice down in Wiltshire and she asked if I could meet her as there were things that she wanted to talk over with me. Without hesitation I arranged to meet her on Devizes station and for the rest of that week I felt on top of the world. Mother, who I think knew me better than I knew myself, said, 'I told you so,' almost as if she already knew what the outcome of our meeting would be.

On the Saturday I caught the train out of Lavington and after a reasonably short journey arrived at Devizes where alighting onto the platform I looked around for the first sight of her, then just as I was about to panic in case something had gone wrong, I saw her running towards me. It was the first time I had seen her out of uniform, however to me she was still the same Mary, so taking her in my arms I did what I had been longing to do for such a long time. She made no effort to stop me and it was then that I knew for certain the reason she had asked me to come. Her aunt lived in a little village called Bishops Canning a short bus ride away from Devizes and during the journey I tried hard to steer the conversation around to the reason why she had wanted to meet me, but all she would say was wait and see, so with that

I had to be content.

When we finally reached the gate of the cottage my nerve began to fail me. Mary sensed it and squeezing my arm told me not to worry, adding that her Aunty wouldn't bite me. Opening the door she led me into the parlour and sat me down, after which she left saying that she wouldn't be long. Sitting there I took stock and waited, then I heard someone calling in the garden beyond the latticed window, followed by the sound of footsteps coming along the passageway. Bracing myself, I waited, then they came into the room, a short, plump, rosy-cheeked woman with bright eyes and snow-white hair and a little girl with dark shoulder-length hair.

'Alice,' Mary began, 'this is Uncle John, Mummy's friend. Come and say hello.' Looking at me with her wide blue eyes she made no attempt to move so going over I knelt and took her hand, 'I'm glad to meet you, Alice. Your mother has told me such a lot about you, I hope we can be friends.'

All this time Mary's Aunt had stood to one side watching so, rising to my feet, I held out my hand. 'So you must be the famous Aunty Floss I have heard so much about,' I said, then I waited, fully conscious of the fact that this was the moment of acceptance or rejection, however I need not have worried for holding out her hand she replied, 'You are very welcome, John, I hope you will stay to lunch.'

Thanking her I turned to Mary who had been watching events not knowing quite how to further the conversation which up until then had been so formal, however sensing my embarrassment, she took me by the arm and led me out into the garden. 'Well,' she said, 'that wasn't that bad was it?' Putting my hand under her chin I tilted her face upwards, with eyes closed she waited, then I kissed her, a long, lingering kiss that caused her to press hard against me, then breaking free, she looked away for a moment. 'Damn you, John Mumford,' she said at last.

After lunch the four of us sat in the garden enjoying the sunshine. Alice, by then beginning to thaw out, invited me to go with her to see her pet rabbit in its hutch down the garden and soon she was chattering away almost as if she had known me all her life. Suddenly she stopped short and looking straight at me asked, 'Are you going to be my Daddy?' a question asked with all the innocence of youth, and having been taken unawares all I could find to say was, 'We'll see, Alice, we'll see.'

Coming over to where we were admiring the rabbit chewing away at some dandelion leaves we had pushed through the netting of its hutch, Mary's Aunt took Alice's hand. 'Let's go and make a pot of tea,' she said, 'I think Mummy and Uncle John have things to talk about,' and with that they left. Slipping her arm through mine, Mary walked me down the garden path to the gate that led out into the fields beyond. The sun now high in the heavens beat down from a clear blue sky and somewhere in the depths of the woods that bordered the fields a song thrush was proclaiming its territorial rights to anyone who cared to stop and listen. At the stile leading into the woods we stopped and I knew that this was to be the moment of truth for us both, seeing that the last hour or so had quite obviously been a testing time. Mounting the stile, Mary turned and sat on the top rail while I stood and held her round the waist.

'John,' she began, 'I think you know now why I asked you down here. Thank you for being so patient with me but as I told you there were things that I had to be certain about before coming to a decision. I know that by making you wait I could have lost you but that was a chance I had to take. I had to be sure this time so, If you still want me and still feel the same about me I will marry you.'

Just at that moment never had a song thrush sung so sweetly; lifting her to the ground I held her, lost for words. 'Well,' she said at last, 'say something.'

'Mary,' I began at last, 'you know that I have loved you right from the start but as you know there were things that stopped me from telling you. Perhaps it was my misguided loyalty to Phyllis that was the reason, but now I realize that the world that she and I lived in no longer exists. It's time to make a new start. The day that she walked up the aisle with Tommy I should have known, but that's all in the past now and the only thing that matters is that you are going to share the rest of your life with Alice and me.'

That was the second longest speech I could ever remember making and when I had finished we just stood there holding each other and saying all those things that are so private between two people who after what seemed a lifetime had finally come together.

Back at the cottage Mary broke the good news to her Aunty who on receiving it came over and gave me a hug. 'I'm so glad, John,' she said, 'I know you will make her happy and I have no fears about Alice now.'

Sitting drinking tea and planning I felt as if a great load had been lifted off my mind. It had all happened so suddenly and I was only just beginning to realize that at long last Mary and I were to be married. Regretfully the time came to leave but before I left I made them promise that the three of them would come and visit at Forge Cottage and this they promised to do. Mary walked me back to where I was to catch the bus for Devizes and clinging to my arm she kept asking if I thought I had made the right decision and did I want to change my mind as it wasn't too late. Too late, I thought, my mind had been made up a long time ago.

Journeying back in the train I hardly noticed the miles slip by, there being so much to think about, so much to plan. As soon as I opened the door of Forge Cottage Mother must have guessed as, dashing across the yard, she fetched Father from the smithy, and of course following family tradition out came the bottle of his home-made wine. I think Mother was more excited, if that is the word, than I was and she couldn't wait to get her hat and coat on and tear up the lane to the stores to break the news to Tessa and Beckey.

Two weeks later Mary, Alice and Aunty Floss came to stay. It was strange having a youngster about the place again; she was a lovely child and the whole family took to her straight away which was just as well because if they hadn't it could have caused problems. Being just the right age she wanted to know the in's and out's of everything, so to keep her occupied I introduced her to my old lean-to shed and all the other places that had played such an important part in my own young days. Sitting on the wall at the bottom of the garden I showed her where I had buried my little friend the greenfinch and told her about the little people that lived there. Gradually she forgot her shyness and it wasn't long before she began to follow me everywhere I went, spending hours in the smithy watching me at work and wanting to know the this and that of everything. I was aware that Mary was watching us but there was no need for her to worry as by then I was captivated by Alice and was already beginning to look on her as family.

After much discussion it was agreed that we should be married in the village church, so with this in view we went up to see the parson just to make sure that there would be no objection. The date for the wedding was arranged for early June, both Mary and I stating that we wanted it to be a quiet family affair with the reception at Forge Cottage, and much to our relief this was agreed. Then to add to all the excitement Father announced that the estate had given him the chance of the cottage at the top of the lane, no doubt Master Grahame having got to know about my forthcoming marriage had deliberately arranged this, and although both Mary and I would be sad to see them go, the

227

move would solve quite a few problems. The cottage they were moving to was small but as Mother said it would be quite big enough for the two of them and after all they would only be at the top of the lane.

There was, however, one problem to be solved and that was the question of what to do about Aunty Floss, after all she had more or less brought Alice up and it would be a terrible wrench for her to be parted from the child now. Mary and I discussed the problem at great length, finally coming up with the idea that we suggest that she came and lived with us at Forge Cottage; we had plenty of room now that my parents were moving out. Not being on the spot I don't rightly know what persuading took place, but one evening Mary rang to say that Aunty Floss had agreed with one proviso, that she bring all her furniture with her as she was aware that to start off with we should be pretty stretched in that department, and so to everyone's satisfaction the arrangement was agreed upon. The next move was to put her cottage in Bishops Canning on the market, and in this she was lucky, finding a young couple who, once having decided to purchase, agreed to let her stay on until she could move in with us.

The next month was filled with preparations for the wedding, Father agreed to give Mary away and Uncle Ted volunteered to act as best man. I can't say that I was sorry when the great day dawned. Aunty Floss and Alice had moved in the previous week and as is usual on such occasions the cottage was in an uproar as people charged about making final preparations.

Following tradition, Uncle Ted and I walked to the church through Grinnels Orchard along a path that in its time had seen quite a few family processions. This time the bride didn't take the leisurely way round in Percy Slatter's dog cart, nor did we have need of Len Hubbard's wagon, but all went in style in Harry Haines's taxi, specially cleaned and polished for the occasion with white ribbons stretching from bonnet to windscreen. The church was full when Uncle Ted and I arrived, which was no more than we expected, seeing that our village needed no excuse to take a few hours off work and get into their Sunday best. Up in the belfry the bell ringers were doing their stuff, probably with the same old stone jars of cider stashed away in a corner but sadly there was no Ted Walker this time, he having passed away the previous Christmas.

Sitting waiting for Mary to arrive I thought back on all the memorable occasions the old church must have witnessed in its time – the young entering in the arms of their parents and later to be joined in marriage, then the last sad visit when once again they were carried in, but this time to be laid to rest in the little churchyard outside. I thought back to my parents' wedding day in those far off days of the Great War when with the threat of parting, or even worse, hanging over them they had taken their vows, and Phyllis and Tommy, young and in love, who had stood before the same altar little knowing what tragedy would befall them before they had taken the first few faltering steps along the road of life that they had set out on together. I wondered if Grandma and Grandad Mumford were looking down, and Nathan Powell, Nacky Pitt, Alby Stringer, Jack Harris and so many others who in their time had sat in the old oak pews or in the elevated ones of the choir stalls.

Suddenly a dig in the ribs brought me back to earth and turning I was just in time to see Mary start her walk down the aisle on the arm of my father, and behind her all posh in her new dress, Alice bearing a bouquet of flowers. Walking over to the steps in front of the altar, Ted and I waited, and soon she was by my side. Reaching down I took her hand and gently squeezed it just to reassure her. Then the service began.

'We are gathered here in the sight of God and this congregation to join together this man and woman.' I had heard it so many times before, when as a choirboy I had sat and listened. In fact I knew the service almost off by heart, nevertheless when the time came to put the ring on Mary's finger, the words 'I now pronounce you man and wife' took on a whole new meaning. We had the usual photographs taken outside the church, then it was back to Forge Cottage for the reception, Mrs Lyes and two other village ladies having volunteered to stay behind and get things ready. How we managed to get all the guests into our parlour I shall never know, but somehow we did. Mary looked wonderful in her going-away powder blue costume but as I looked at her I could still see her in her ATS uniform. Alice seemed to take it all in her stride, not being at all put out by the fact that she now had another parent in her young life.

We spent our first night at the cottage, Alice sharing with Aunty Floss, then the next day we set off for London where we had decided to spend a short honeymoon. Walking its streets we could see very few reminders of those terrible war years other than the occasional bomb-site. There was still a smattering of khaki to be seen but in the main the pavements were thronged with sober-suited civilians, many of whom no doubt had been in uniform not too long ago. Finding ourselves in the vicinity of Marble Arch we decided on impulse to try to get accommodation in Sussex Gardens at the same place that we had stayed during the war. It didn't take much finding and ringing the bell we waited, not being sure if it would be the same landlady that would answer, but it was, so after enquiring whether she had any accommodation for three nights I added, 'I don't know if you remember us, we stayed with you in the early part of the war. Of course we were both in uniform then.'

Looking from one to the other of us she suddenly smiled and held out her hand. 'Welcome back,' she said, 'I have often wondered what happened to you both.' Then ushering us inside she took us into her private sitting room where over a cup of tea we told her about most of the things that had happened to us both in the ensuing years, and how at last we had met up again and were now married and on our honeymoon. She couldn't have been more enthralled if it had been her own son or daughter and both Mary and I were grateful that she had made us so welcome, after all we had only been two strangers who had happened to pass her way. Whether by chance or intent she gave us the same room. This time there were no searchlights, no sirens, no dull thud of exploding bombs. Remembering that first night I could almost visualize the khaki uniforms carelessly thrown over the back of the wicker chair, which incidentally still stood in the corner of the room, and Mary's ATS skirt draped over the open door of the single wardrobe. Lying in bed, each of us absorbed in our own thoughts, Mary suddenly leaned over and put her arms around me. 'Hold me, John,' she whispered, 'hold me and make love to me. It's been a long time, far too long.'

The next few days were spent making nostalgic trips around London. We had tea in Lyons Corner House at Marble Arch and took a trip over to Acton to visit the place where it had all begun. Everything looked much the same, there were still troops there and as we stood looking through the gates a young couple came through having eyes only for each other. Soon it was time to return to Lavington and reluctantly we said goodbye to our friendly landlady, promising to visit her if ever we were in London again.

Two days later we helped my parents move into their new cottage. It was in a way a sad moment as both Mary and I realized how much Father would miss the smithy seeing that it had been his home for so many years. The place must have been full of memories for both of them but, as we reminded them, they would only be at the top of the lane and could come and visit whenever they wished. A week later Aunty Floss moved in to Forge Cottage bringing her furniture with her and soon she and Mary had everything sorted out and in its place. It was strange at first not to see so many of the old familiar things around, the grandfather clock had gone as had Father's rocking chair and table, however they had left us the piano, not that any of us could play it, but Mother argued that having no room for it in her new cottage, and as it had stood in our parlour for so long, it would be a pity to have to get rid of it.

No sooner had we settled in than we received a visit from an old friend. Hard at work in the forge one morning I heard a voice behind me say, 'I hope you're a better blacksmith than you were a truck driver.' The voice sounded familiar but for a moment I couldn't put a face to it, then turning I saw to my surprise and delight the grinning face of my old mate Chippy Greatorex, and standing with him a woman and two small children. Alice, who as usual was with me in the smithy, just stood wide-eyed not understanding what all the handshaking and hugging was all about until, realizing that she must have felt out of things, I took her hand and introduced her to them. Shepherding them across the yard I took them into the parlour and sat them down. Mary was out, and then I remembered that she had said that there were a few things she needed from the shop, so thinking that perhaps it would be wise to warn her about visitors, I gave Aunty Tessa a ring and asked her to pass on a message. Calling Alice who was busy showing her new friends round the house, I sent her to meet her mother, suggesting that her two companions might like to go with her, so off they went. In the meantime I made Chippy and his wife Doris comfortable, then it was out to the kitchen to put the kettle on, the time-honoured thing to do when visitors arrived. Flushed with hurrying, Mary came into the parlour and putting the shopping bags down, went over and introduced herself, then she came into the kitchen to supervise the tea-making and the opening of the biscuit tin. With thirsts quenched and the children busy playing out in the yard it was time to catch up on all the news and brief accounts of all that had happened since that day we had parted in hospital.

Chippy, it appeared, had managed to take up his old trade again and was now self-employed. His wife was an ex-nurse and he had met her at the rehabilitation centre, a quiet and sensible person, from what I could see, and undoubtedly the right person to have had at his side during the early days of readjustment. They had settled in Kirkby, not far from his native Liverpool, and by all accounts were managing quite well in spite of his handicap, but what pleased me most was that he hadn't lost that impish sense of humour that had proved so invaluable during our brief stay together in the North African desert.

Mary took to them both right from the start and insisted that they at least stay the night with us even though they insisted that they must be on their way, and had only called to say hello, but naturally she got her way as always. Sleeping proved a bit of a problem, but after jiggling things about a bit we managed. After supper with the children tucked up in bed and supervised by Aunty Floss we sat talking into the early hours, going over old times and bringing each other up to date on more recent events. It was so good to see him and to know that things had turned out alright.

The next morning they left, not I may add before we had been called out to see his motor car of which he was justifiably proud, and which with a few adjustments and adaptions he was able to drive. I think Alice was sorry to see them go as she thought it great having two other playmates in the house, however there was one thing both Mary and I were thankful for and that was that she seemed to have settled down and had already made friends with some of the village children.

One Sunday afternoon in late spring, Mary, me and Aunty Floss took a walk through the woods and onto the slopes of Oak Hill. It was a glorious day, fresh and invigorating, and sitting looking across the valley towards the rise of Bredon Hill, Mary and I soon became lost in thought. In the village that spread itself below nothing seemed to stir; wrapped in its cloak of everlasting time it had already taken another generation under its wing. Just to the left of the grey church tower, Long Meadow stood out fresh and green with its scatterings of buttercups and ragged robin and just above the treeline of Grinnels Orchard could be seen the slate roofs of Forge Cottage and the smithy, just two buildings amongst all the others that had played such an important part in our lives. As my gaze wandered it came to rest on the lane below by the keeper's cottage where I could just make out the red brick walls of Leyfield Cottage. It had new tenants now, but looking at it brought back memories of Tommy and Phyllis and their tragic end. High above us a solitary hawk soared and hovered and from the bank above where we were sitting came the chatter and laughter of Alice and Aunty Floss as they went in search of wild flowers. Down in the hazel thicket all was silent, almost as if it was waiting for two other young lovers to come and seek to find the secret of its secluded dell. Turning to look at Mary I began to wonder if she knew what was going through my mind, then leaning over she whispered in my ear, 'To hear a nightingale, my love, to hear a nightingale.' Drawing her close I kissed her lightly on the forehead. 'Thank you,' I said, 'thank you.' With eyes that deliberately taunted me and the ghost of a smile hovering around her lips she asked, 'What was that for?' 'It was just for being you,' I answered.

And so the years passed, Alice grew up into a lovely young lady and eventually went to the grammar school in Evesham, however there was more sorrow to come. Mother, at the age of fifty-seven, passed away. It was a terrible shock to us all as we had never known her to be ill for more than a day, but it was her heart they said. Father took it rather badly and for a while couldn't be consoled. They had loved each other so much those two, and without her he just gave up and drifted. We laid her to rest just inside the churchyard by the lych-gate where she and Father had met on their first date and where they had done so much of their courting. The same year saw the passing of Shenna Lawson, Len Hubbard, and Harry Gibbons and slowly the village began to change as outsiders came in and bought up the old cottages that one by one were becoming available as the older inhabitants came to the end of their days. At the smithy Mary and I got on with our lives and each day that passed I came to love her more and more, then, much to our surprise, Aunty Floss up and left us having made up her mind to end her days with a sister in Bristol. We were sorry to see her go; she had been so good to us in the early days of our marriage, however in spite of our entreaties she seemed to have made up her mind, so in the end we gave in.

In the little bedroom under the roof that had seen my birth, and which had been mine for so many years, books with faded bindings, their pages frayed and torn, still occupy the shelf above the old iron-framed bed, and in one corner sits an old tin trunk almost as if it is waiting for someone to lift its lid and explore the memories that lie within. In it are dresses packed away by hands now still and lifeless, faded photographs of people and family groups now scattered by time and bundles of letters tied with ribbon. There is an old straw Panama hat that had once belonged to Grandfather and the cherished bowler that he had worn to church on high days and holidays, a pair of Aunty Beckey's gloves that once covered hands that gathered the summer rose and held down the scented boughs of lilac, all precious memories of days long gone. In the bottom drawer of the old dresser, buried beneath the clean and starched linen that was scented with lavender bags, lie the watch and bundle of letters that had once belonged to Mary's father; they are safe there, no one will disturb them, that is until the time comes to hand them over to Alice.

There was, however, one more link with the past that came to light. One Saturday afternoon when returning from our usual walk in the woods above the village, we had just reached the fountain at the top end of the street when on looking down towards the village shop we were surprised to see a large motor car parked in front and Aunty Tessa talking to a lady and gentleman. Seeing us approaching, she came forward to meet us. 'John, there is someone here who has been asking after you. He and his wife have come all the way from America.'

Full of curiosity as to who they might be I went over to the car, at first not recognizing its occupants, then the man got out and stepping forward held out his hand 'Hello, John,' he said, 'remember me?' It was then that I suddenly realized who he was. It was Abe Sherman, Phyllis's friend who had been stationed down at the brickyard during the war. Aunty Tessa, by now thoroughly intrigued, invited us all into her front parlour where, with introductions and explanations duly dealt with, we sat and talked of the war days and what had happened to us since. Listening to Abe as he talked I had the feeling that there was one person from those days he wanted to know about, Phyllis, however realizing how difficult it would be for him to raise the subject, I took advantage of a lull in the conversation to ask, 'Do you remember Tommy Whitworth and his wife Phyllis?' Hesitating for a moment, as if searching his mind, he at last said, 'Oh yes, Tommy and Phyllis, they were friends of yours, weren't they? Wasn't Tommy the lad who was wounded at Dunkirk and invalided out of the Army? How are they both, and do they still live in the village?' Eagerly he waited for an answer, and thinking it best, I told him about the terrible tragedy that had overtaken them on that never-to-be-forgotten night. When I had finished the telling we sat in silence and looking at Abe I could see that it had all been a terrible shock to him. Then his wife spoke up, 'What an awful end for two young people,' she said, after that nothing, just a blank silence. I have often wondered if she knew or suspected about her husband's wartime affair with Phyllis; maybe we shall never know, however on reflection perhaps there are some things best left buried in the past.

They stayed a little while longer but before they left we walked with them through the churchyard and on to Leyfield Cottage; myself, I wouldn't have suggested it, but Abe had insisted. He stood for a while, just looking at the cottage; what was going through his mind no one will ever know, as for me I was not and for that matter am still not certain exactly what the relationship between Phyllis and he had been, but I had the feeling that it had been deeper than anyone realized. There was one more visit Abe insisted be made and that was to Tommy and Phyllis's grave and after pointing it out Mary and I waited at a distance while Abe and his wife made the pilgrimage alone. With heads bowed they stood, then after reading the inscriptions on the headstone they turned and rejoined us. Before long they would return to America, perhaps never to pass this way again, but I was sure that Abe could not and would not ever forget the girl who was buried in that quiet country churchyard. Just before they left for Cheltenham where they were staying for a few days Abe managed to get me alone for a few minutes.

'John,' he began, 'I don't need to tell you how truly I loved Phyllis; had things been otherwise I would have married her but it was not to be. Now there is something I want you to do for me when we have gone,' and so saying, he pressed a twenty pound note into my hand 'I want you to put some flowers on her grave. I'll leave you to decide what to put on the card,' and before I could argue he rejoined his wife and they both got into the car and drove off. I did what he had asked and on the card I wrote, 'In memory of a love that had no happy ending, Abe.' The flowers soon faded but the sentiment I was sure would live on.

In the summer of 1963, on the orders of Dr Beeching, they came and took away our railway thus severing one more link with the past. The whole village turned out to see the last train depart; it was a sad occasion and long after it had gone Mary and I stood on the deserted platform thinking back over the years and remembering the great part it had played in our lives. On the way back Father expressed a wish to visit the churchyard and Mother's grave. He was now seventy-one and although slow in his walking his memory was crystal clear and no doubt the closing of the railway had stirred up many old memories. We walked with him as far as the grave then just as we were about to turn and leave him alone he stopped us.

235

'John,' he said, taking a folded and creased piece of newspaper from his pocket, 'I want that you should read this out for me, the light is bad and the old eyes ain't what they used to be,' so saying he handed it to me and in the fading light I began to read.

> 'The wind sighs and in it I hear your voice
> and yet I cannot see you.
>
> Clearly I hear you and yet I cannot touch
> you. Still I must not grieve for you are not
> gone but live on in the soft winds that caress
> your last resting place, a mound of soft grass
> upon which the dappled sunshine dances.'

And so my story ends. Perhaps there will be some who will say that I have taken too long in the telling of it, even so there is a lot that I have had to leave out. As someone said, 'I have a thousand tales to tell but not a thousand years in which to tell them.'

Lavington is still there with all its memories. Aunty Beckey and Aunty Tessa have long since gone and now lie at peace in the little churchyard alongside their parents. Alice is married and lives not far away; she has two children and we are able to visit them quite often. The smithy no longer resounds to the sound of the blacksmith's hammer; now empty and cold, it is at times used for storage. After the war its services were needed less and less and when Father retired the estate offered me his job which I was pleased to take on. Mary and I still live in Forge Cottage; we couldn't leave it as there are too many happy memories trapped within its old walls. Sometimes, in the still of a summer's evening, I hear as from a distance the laughter and chatter of little Tinker and Nellie, the two wartime evacuees and hear my mother calling them from the kitchen, her voice being so real that at times I find myself wanting to answer. I often wonder who will remember us in the years to come and think of the times we lived in. All our lives are spent in creating the past and long may it be so.

CONCLUSION

The car made its way slowly down the lane, its occupants searching the houses on either side as if looking for one in particular. There were two occupants, a young man and a young woman; she was a pretty young thing with long golden brown hair and smiling grey eyes.

'It must be down here somewhere,' she said, taking another look at the estate agent's literature that lay on her lap, 'perhaps we had better stop and enquire.' Just as she spoke she caught sight of an old man working in his garden. Bidding her husband to stop she lowered the window and called out, 'Excuse me, but can you direct us to Forge Cottage?'

'That I can, missus,' came the reply and so saying he stuck his fork into the ground and came over to the gate. 'It 'ul be Forge Cottage you'll be wanting,' he repeated, 'well it be straight down the lane to the bottom where the old pond used to be, then follow round the bend and you'll see it in front of thee.'

Thanking him, the young lady began to wind up the car window then having second thoughts she lowered it again and asked the old man if he knew anything about the property. Pushing up his cap to the back of his head he stood for a while gazing into the distance, a faraway look in his eyes.

'Used to belong to a family called Mumford,' he began at last, 'several generations of 'em lived in the old cottage at one time or another; they were the village blacksmiths and the last of 'em died some years ago. After the war, that's the last 'un, there were little use for the smithy and it closed, and John, he were the last of the Mumfords, went and worked on the estate although he still lived at the cottage. They died there, him and his missus Mary, a lovely couple they were; had a daughter named Alice but she got married and left the village, I don't know where her be now, in some foreign part of the country I reckon.'

Here he paused again, as if trying to get his memories in order. 'They be all buried up in the churchyard,' he continued, then almost as if wanting to change

237

the subject he offered, 'Us used to have a railway station but that be long since gone. Forge Cottage have been empty for quite a while now, estate workers and their families used it for a while but then the estate were sold off and the workers sacked.' Again that faraway dreamy look came into his old eyes and, pulling his cap forward onto his forehead, he sighed deeply before turning and making his way back up the garden where taking his fork he began to dig. Turning to her husband the young girl was surprised to see a look of incredulity on his face.

'He's gone,' he said, and turning to look she saw that the garden was now empty except for a solitary digging fork standing thrust into the ground. Slightly shaken, they continued on their way down the lane and at last drew up in front of a red-bricked creeper-clad cottage where on the wall, in rusting ironwork were the words 'Forge Cottage'. Taking the key from his pocket the young man thrust it into the lock and turning it entered. The door opened into a long passageway and standing for a moment in the half darkness surrounded by a cloak of near velvet silence they waited almost as if they were expecting someone to call out and challenge their entry, but nothing stirred and when at last they dared to speak, their voices echoed round the empty rooms disturbing faded memories of long-gone people, who by reason of their having lived their lives within its walls had left their marks. Entering what the estate agents literature described as 'the parlour', they walked across the room to the stone inglenook fireplace, almost as if they had been drawn to it by some invisible force. Reaching up, the woman ran her hand along the old oak beam that served as a mantlepiece as if searching for something but, failing to find what she was looking for, she turned to her husband.

'I have the strangest feeling that there should have been a photograph standing there,' she said, 'a faded photograph of a young girl in an old-fashioned nurse's uniform.'

Putting an arm around her the man drew her away. 'You must be dreaming, darling,' he said, as he led her back across the room, 'let's explore upstairs,' and with that they climbed the narrow winding staircase. Opening the first door they came to they entered. The sun shining through the latticed window threw a shaft of light across the dusty floorboards to finish up in a far corner where it lit up the faded wallpaper. Leaving her husband's side the woman crossed over to the window and for a while stood looking down at the yard below. She shivered slightly and on seeing this the man joined her, and placing a hand on her shoulder said, 'Nancy, my dear, don't you think you are letting your imagination run away with you?'

For a moment the question remained unanswered, then turning she reached up and put her arms around him.

'I don't think so, John, I don't think so,' she replied.

Slowly the ripple of the incoming tide, laced with
a collar of white foam, spread itself over the two
footprints in the sands of time, then having done so it
continued on its way until at the end of its momentum
it halted for a second before making its way back
from whence it had come. When it had passed the
footprints had gone and the sand was smooth and even.